PARIS BOHEMIAN

MICHELLE FOGLE

Enjoy other great books by Michelle Fogle

City of Liars

Book One in the Lost Tales of Sepharad Series

Heirs of the Tide

Book Two in the Lost Tales of Sepharad Series

Paris Bohemian

This is a work of fiction. Names, characters, organizations, places, and events are either products of the author's imagination or are used fictionally. Any resemblance to actual persons, living or dead, or actual events are coincidental.

Published by Legacy Imprints
ISBN (e-book) 978-1-7379534-5-6
ISBN (paperback) 978-1-7379534-2-5
Cover design by Damonza
First edition

This book is dedicated to the memory of my hippie first love, with whom I hitch-hiked to San Francisco's bohemian haven, Haight-Ashbury – Paul Wade

Prologue

Summer 1878

THERE IS A pattern to my life, one that repeats the way a refrain comes again and again after each verse of a song. This is the third time in my 13 years of life. Everything familiar and loved gets torn away when I least expect it, and then I'm sent off in a state of confusion and sorrow to start all over again, with new surroundings and faces, even though the pain from the last time has barely mended. So, here I am once again on another journey by train. The hum of the engine, the rush of the air outside the passenger compartment window, and the steam whistle moaning a slightly off-key G major sixth chord; blend together in a kind of elegy or requiem that accompanies my journeys. The wheels keep rhythm against the rails in a cadence like the beating of a human heart asking why. Why?

I stare out the window at the Normandy landscape, which spreads out in brilliant green, alive with the full bloom of summer. Brown and white splotched cows graze in the rolling hills dotted with shady apple trees. I glance across the compartment at my teary-eyed nine-year-old brother Conrad, sitting next to our father. This man, who we only see once or twice a year and barely know, is taking us back to Paris to live with him. My only recollections of that place are not pleasant ones.

I should have sensed we would be uprooted again; recognized it like a well-practiced prelude, when my beloved piano teacher Gustave Vinot left Honfleur.

He tried to explain. "It's hard to support a family on the wages of a parish organist." Vinot was offered a prestigious position as a conductor of the orchestra in Lyon. "You're a very talented pianist, Erik. I'm certain your grandmother will locate a fine teacher to continue your training." But his praise was little consolation. He had been a witness to my grief after my mother's death when I was only five, and was a safe harbor from life at the boys' academy. I found a voice for my loss and anger as he taught me to play the piano and organ. He helped me conquer my despair. One of the main pillars in my life had toppled out from under me. And now this.

My father stares at the newspaper across his lap and tugs at the mutton-chop fringe on his jaw. "Merde! Will you look at that? Your uncle Seabird was right. Over in America, that Kentucky bay horse Tenbrook took Churchill Downs beating that California mare, Mollie. I owe him ten francs."

I shake my head and turn my gaze back to the world outside. Who cares? How stupid. Doesn't my father understand the full scale of what we've been through? Isn't he even sad? Grand-mère was his mother. And after Maman died, she's been like my mother, too.

On the day of the accident, a soft breeze drifted off the water of the estuary, the wide course of the Seine where the tide flowed in, causing fresh and salt water to mix. Just before midday, beneath a hazy sky, my grandparents set up camp beneath a huge umbrella pitched in the sand. Grand-père stretched out in the striped canvas folding chair. Over-heated in her heavy dress and petticoats, Grand-mère went into one of the small wooden huts to change into her bathing costume, black bloomers and a puff-sleeve tunic. She then headed into the water to cool off. I knelt in the sand wearing for the first time a one-piece knit bathing suit adult men wore.

Conrad and I spent the entire afternoon using spades and a pail to construct a huge chateau from sand, complete with mote and battlements. Other children playing nearby watched with envy and even drew me to their projects to show them how to make castles of their own. With the incoming of the tide, I returned to safeguard my own construction, piling up a retaining wall to preserve the castle a little longer.

The sun was descending behind us toward the horizon when Grand-père finally roused from his nap and sat up.

"Where is your grandmother?" he asked.

"Didn't she go for a swim?" I replied, looking up from my creation.

Grand-père pulled out his pocket watch to check the time. "That was hours ago. She hasn't come back?"

No, she hadn't. My grandfather stood up and surveyed the shoreline, dread clouding his face. I dropped the hand tools and started to search for her. An hour rolled past as we combed the beach and waterfront, questioned other bathers and passersby. No one recalled seeing her. When it finally started to grow dark, Grand-père brought us home, asking a neighbor to look in on us, while he returned to the beach to continue the search.

But I knew she was gone, even before we left the seaside. I felt it deep inside; the same feeling I experienced the day I found my mother's body sprawled out on the bed. I slipped into my grandmother's bedroom, hunted through her wardrobe until I found her black woolen shawl. Wrapping myself in it, and smelling her smell, I curled up on the bed with Conrad and waited, finally drifting into sleep.

In the early hours of the dawn, I heard the door open. We vaulted from the room, meeting Grand-père downstairs at the newel posts. I needed only to look into his eyes to confirm what I already sensed.

Conrad started to whimper. Tears welled in my eyes but I blinked them away. No. This was not fair. My body became hot all over and my chest heaved with fury. I turned to my brother. "Don't say it. Don't say anything!" My voice cracked.

"Grand-mère."

I grabbed Conrad, clamping my hand over his mouth to stifle his sad sounds. Conrad struggled to free himself. We became a knot of flailing arms, snarling in turmoil. Then, I felt my grandfather's hand firm and gentle on my shoulder.

"Erik Alfred Leslie." He called my name with a burning whisper.

I froze.

The squeal of the brakes jar me back to the present as the train slows. The conductor calls out the name of Rouen station, and other passengers shuffle with their luggage along the narrow corridor outside our compartment. I glance over at my father, again. Maybe he means well and is just trying to take our minds off the sadness. Our family handles these things in very odd ways. I can still recall how Uncle Seabird and my father acted when my mother died, the strange funeral with incense and marigolds, and the festive wake. But now he acts as if nothing happened, blocking it out, trying to get above it all. Perhaps it's safer not to need anything from anyone; not care or attach, not let myself feel or allow anything to matter, if it always comes to this. Maybe that is why my father is dealing with Grand-mère's death in such a devil-may-care way. He saw so many friends die in the war; then losing my baby sister and then my mother. He's found a way not to let it hurt so much. I wish I could be more like him.

My chest aches again, raw and hollow. I had just started to trust enough to find joy and be content. I miss the way I used to feel during Monsieur Vinot's music lessons. But I still have the music to soothe me. Music will always be part of my life. That seems to be the one thing that lasts, that no one can take away.

Paris is nothing like the haunting images that linger in my memory of tumbled-down masonry, impassable streets, and monuments defaced by the war with the Prussians. And because of the new pair of pince nez trimmed with satin ribbon my father bought for me, I can see everything clearer now, too. My father turns to me, taking notice of my gaping wonder.

"Paris has changed a great deal since you last lived here, thanks to Haussmann's genius of modern engineering," he says.

"A genius?" I ask.

"Indeed." My father drums with his fingertips on the crown of my new silk top hat.

I am starting to like this place. The new buildings are dazzling with corbels and plaster scrollwork. They look like stacked cakes with piped on cream. Balconies with black lacy metalwork and louvered shutters in pastel greens and blues trim the windows. Stylish carriages with chestnut and ebony horses line the street alongside omnibuses and taxis, like the one in which we're riding. The people all dress as if going to a wedding.

The news kiosks with cupolas on top remind me of castle turrets. Colorful poster art is pasted all around, advertising everything from crackers and soap to the shows at the café concerts. It's all so inviting and exciting.

"I don't know the first thing about caring for children," father admits. "I'd always left that up to your mother and grandmother, you see."

But I'm not a child anymore. My freckles have faded and I look like a smart young man with fine whiskers on my upper lip; dressed in a stiff collar, cravat and dress jacket. My hair has darkened from copper to mahogany, and I comb it straight back, the way Maestro Vinot did.

"It's best to think of our little family as three young bachelors on the town," my father tells us. That suits me, just fine. My father leads an exciting life and the more I'm around him, the more I want to take part in it. I don't mind that my father never learned to cook, or that his flat doesn't even have a kitchen. I thoroughly enjoy eating many of our meals in cafés and restaurants, when there's no dinner invitation by the numerous friends in my father's social circle. At least he has an old fortepiano, dilapidated though it may be. I can keep up with my practice, even if it makes me cringe because it's so out of tune.

The taxi pulls up in front of the lobby of The Grand Hotel near the St. Lazare Station where we are meeting several acquaintances. Beneath an elegant fringed awning, uniformed doormen open the gleaming beveled glass entry doors. Shiny marble floors peak out from the edges of plush jewel-tone carpets. I feel like I've entered a royal palace.

My father orders us chilled seltzer water with cherry juice and a slice of lime. We nibble on canapés and olives while the adults chat and laugh in a huddle, sipping aperitifs and slurping oysters. Tonight is a special occasion. For the first time, father is taking us to one of the many café-concerts, the Ambassadors. After having a few drinks, the group piles into a large carriage together and we cross town to the Boulevard de Strasbourg.

Columns and carved statues line the front of the Ambassadors like a Greek or Roman temple. Café tables and wrought iron chairs packed with customers overflow onto the sidewalk. On the upper level, carved masks of Olympian gods look down with a welcoming smile. An enticing glow radiates from inside accompanied by the sound of merry song.

It costs nothing to enter the concert hall, although my father is expected to buy us drinks or a light meal with each round of performances. Each row of chairs has trays attached to the backs to set glasses and plates for the seats behind them. It's a noisy and smoke-filled place with brilliant posters adorning the walls. Shopkeepers sit next to well-dressed clerks and lower-class porters and laborers. My father finds us seats together in a row behind his friends, and they readily turn around to converse. I've never experienced anything like this before.

"The program is a tour de chant," my father explains. "It doesn't have a formal beginning like a recital or concert. People just come and go as they please."

The stage has an ornate set and backdrop and a small orchestra provides accompaniment. A beautiful singer dressed in evening clothes sashays across the stage with an elaborate feather hat so large I'm not sure how she keeps it on. She poses and sways while singing a love song. The people in the audience are so familiar with her song, they start to sway right along with her and join in the chorus. When she finishes, they shout bravo and throw flowers.

Next, the tuxedoed conductor waves his baton as a troupe of dancers gallivants out on stage. Each is clad in a low-cut harlequin print dress, trimmed with white ostrich feathers. They swish their skirts and kick their legs in a lively dance, making dainty yips and whoops. But then they separate, fall back into a semicircle, and do cartwheels across the center, revealing petticoats, matching garters and stockings. My eyes widen. I don't quite know what to think, but I'm starting to feel warm all over. I look around, noticing the men leering like salivating dogs at the kitchen door. Women patrons lower their eyes, or hide behind quivering fans. I realize my own jaw is hanging open.

The dancers toss up the backs of their skirts and bend over. The collective jiggle of ruffle-covered derrières sends a quiver through my middle. Then just as quickly, each dancer hides herself in a flutter of Chantilly, and flees the dance floor. The room erupts in lusty cheers. I look at my father. He smiles at me, gesturing enthusiastically for me to clap. I glance at Conrad, who has buried his face in his hands.

An odd-looking gentleman wearing plaid pants, a vest, and cap several sizes too small appears in the limelight. He tells several jokes that seem naughty, but funny all the same. And he sings a shocking song having to do with nasty things, like passing gas, bad breath, and other body functions. By Conrad's bulging eyes and giggles, I wonder if he should be listening to such things. My grandparents would never approve. But our father just laughs and seems nonchalant.

Finally, another unusual female singer comes out onto the stage.

"She is what we call a gommeuse," my father whispers.

A gumdrop? Her costume is a little unsettling to me. She wears black stockings with the garters showing because her skirt is so short, draped with swags of sheer fabric and silk roses. She carries a staff with long fluttering ribbons and a pink rose on top. She reminds me of some of the naughty pictures I'd been shown by older boys at the academy. To make matters worse, her song talks about tasting her cream filled bonbons and licking a peppermint stick. While the words are about candy, by the way she moves around displaying her derrière, and shaking her almost naked bosom; I easily grasp what she's really talking about. Conrad looks confused. But I find myself with an unexpected bulge in my trousers, and I shift my coat to mask it. Warm tingling comes over my body and my heart races. And—I like it, a lot.

When the performance is finished, the whole group moves onto a restaurant for dinner. The hour is late and Conrad is yawning. We're not accustomed to staying up this late. But I am so captured by this spectacle, I never want to give my father a reason to leave me at home with a cold slice of cheese and a baguette.

Chapter 1

November 1880, Paris

I SIT IN the parlor, hunched over on my forearms, clasping my hands together. My mouth is dry as chalk. Over the top of my pince-nez, my eyes follow my father, aimlessly pacing across the carpet. Father tugs at his mutton chops with his eyes pinned to the report from the Paris Conservatoire bearing my first-year jury exam results. I fidget in my chair and glance toward the hearth, where my stepmother Eugenie now stands. My younger brother Conrad steals glimpses from the doorway to the hall where he's eavesdropping.

The look on Father's face alters like passing cloud shadow over the ground. His brow furrows and his mouth purses, as if he tastes something bitter, then brightens to a smile again. Eugenie taps her foot, but the nap of the rug muffles the sound. She holds her arms stiffly folded across the bodice of her heliotrope beaded dress. If she frowns any harder, her face will crack. And she better loosen her corset or she'll explode. That would be rich. A snicker tries to escape my nostrils, but I quickly stifle it with my hand. Finally, father pauses, runs his hand back through his long wavy hair, and turns toward me. I meet his soft stare.

"Very beautiful hands, beautiful sonority," he reads, twisting his whiskers with a strained smile. "No lack of grace or natural talent."

"Yes, but you fail to mention he doesn't work to expected standards," Eugenie blurts out, and marches over to Father. She mashes her finger onto the page. "You see. All four evaluators said the same thing. An ordinary performance. Ordinary. Rather feeble. Flabby technique." The loose skin under her chin jiggles like a turkey as she shakes her head. I glance at Conrad, who is mimicking her. I shift my stare to the carpet to hold back a guffaw.

Father lowers the report to his side, holding me in his gaze. "Ambroise Thomas wrote, 'he should do very well'."

Eugenie clenches her fists. "Don't you realize the gravity of this, Alfred? 'Gifted but lazy', they wrote in January. Now this. He absolutely has to work harder."

Father tugs at his vest. "I think Erik knows what he needs to do, Eugenie."

His vote of confidence warms me. I used to get stomach flutters over the privilege of studying at the Conservatoire. Now, a year later, it's not only lost its glitter, but I shudder every time I walk in the building. They scorn any creative expression. It's nothing but painfully boring German Romantic concertos, day after day. It's strangling me.

"No disrespect intended," I say. "You know from experience how demanding the program is. It doesn't help to be hounded."

Eugenie juts out her chin and beads of sweat glisten on her upper lip. "Hounded? Don't you understand? Article 60 is strictly enforced by the Ministry of Fine Arts. If a student doesn't gain some prize or at least an honorable mention in three successive exams, it's an automatic dismissal. How humiliating, how embarrassing!"

"For whom?" Father asks, raising one brow.

I stand up, my face growing hot. "You act as if it's your reputation on the line. Doesn't anybody care about how this is affecting me?"

Her mouth twists into a snarl. "Hubris! I'll not be addressed that way." She points to the door. "Leave my presence. Alfred, your son is incorrigible."

My chest feels like it's caving in. But I ball my fists and bluster.

"As Madame wishes." I give my waistcoat a sharp jerk and stalk out of the parlor.

Tears start to blur my sight. Why can't she understand? I live for piano. Music is what I was meant to do. She knows that. I want more than anything to create my own original art. But I can't even enroll in a composition class unless I complete this program, and with honors. I'm trying. But her bossy criticism only makes things worse. Now Maestro Descombes has assigned two additional hours of practice per day, of Mendelssohn. Can't he at least assign something enjoyable like Chopin or Liszt? These tired methods and rote repetition of stodgy old music is draining my soul.

❧

June 1882, Paris

Piano students pack the front row in the salon. It's been years of grueling rigor to finish this gauntlet. All of us await our turn to face the panel of critics. Posture straight, heads erect, our polished black shoes gleam, side by side in a neat line. Spectators, including my father, brother, and step-mother are in the rows behind us. It's Judgement Day before the Conservatoire gods, who sit perpendicular to the audience. One by one, they call us up alphabetically. As the examiners work their way through the alphabet toward "S", my gut feels hollow and my heart is a kettle drum. I've worked hard and improved my craft with endless practice. But what if I make a mistake, fall short? I clutch my sheet music so tight it drains my knuckles of color.

The audience hushes. But the salon has a way of amplifying sound: the rustle of paper, a cough, the shifting of a foot against the wooden floor. Even the soft flutter of a woman's fan sends vibrations into the air that resonate with the tremor in my body. A rivulet of sweat trickles down my temple and I quickly rub it away before it adds to my already sticky collar.

"Monsieur Erik Alfred Leslie Satie, come forward," announces my teacher, Emile Descombes. My third-year jury exam begins with sight reading an unfamiliar piece. My hand trembles when I receive the music. "Take your place, please, and good luck," says Descombes. His face is as congenial as a catfish.

This kind of exercise has sometimes been a struggle for me. I set the music on the piano and sit down on the bench. Staring at the keyboard, I draw a deep breath, waiting for the thunder in my chest to soften. Then, I raise my eyes and study the music for a long moment. Schubert's Serenade. I blink. What a relief. At least I'm familiar with how it sounds. The piece is simple because most of the action is in the right hand. No enormous leaps or difficult fingering.

I adjust my pince-nez, place my hands on the keyboard and play. The keys are cool and slippery, but the action is like velvet. Never once do I hesitate, but keep perfect time, slow and somber. It might earn merit if my delivery is unique. I add my own emphasis in place of andante con moto, and scherzo. Without a mistake, I finger each note through to the end. Blood is surging through every part of me and I draw a halting breath. While the examiners make their notes, I massage my hands.

Descombes directs me to proceed to the performance piece. I chose Beethoven's Sonata in A flat major Op 26, because it breaks the strict rules of sonata form. I learned he wrote it as variations of a funeral march. The piece opens with stately formality like a minuet, and I rock myself to the cadence. Then the tempo grows more frantic, like I'm clawing my way up a slippery hill. But in the third movement, the notes rumble like gathering clouds. Every time I play this, the minor keys draw on a heaviness that clutches my heart, and even makes me tear-up. I blink several times to see the music. Finally, the last variation rolls into a waltz with arpeggios, to which I add a playful and carefree emphasis. I have to believe things can still turn out alright in the end.

There, I did it. I conclude my performance without a single mistake. I release a weighty sigh and press my palm against the ache at my breastbone. The room is silent. Applause isn't permitted.

After an excruciating wait, my teacher Emile Descombes stands, shifting his bushy moustache back and forth as he calculates his words.

"Monsieur Satie," he begins. "This was your final opportunity to demonstrate your skill and talent as a pianist." Regret tinges his soft voice as he paces behind me. "While you have worked harder this year, and your technique has vastly progressed, it's clear to me you're not invested in the program."

My stomach drops. I grit my teeth and my neck prickles. How could he say that? Descombes knows how earnestly I tried.

Ambroise Thomas leans forward and strokes his salt and pepper beard, his stern brow creases with disapproval. "A passable performance, average; except for your feeble attempt to improve on Schubert's work."

Then Louis Diémer rises. He's the youngest of the jurists, with a halo of wavy red hair. He's distinguished himself by winning prizes in both piano and organ at an unheard-of young age. "I believe the entire performance was lackluster. Shabby and pathetic. You haven't earned the right to embellish the work of great composers, Satie."

The room remains silent with conspicuous dread. Ladies stop fanning themselves and all eyes turn toward Emile Descombes.

"Lamentably, you've not earned a single honor during your tenure here. I'm afraid the Ministry of Fine Arts excludes you from further studies at this institution."

There's a gasp from the audience. My heart melts like wax. How did I go from "no lack of grace or natural talent", to "lackluster and pathetic"? This program, this place ruined me.

Eugenie stands with an exasperated huff, tosses her fan to the floor and storms out of the salon. My brother Conrad has one hand over his mouth and a plaintive twist on his brow. My father covers his face with his hands. It's a punch to the gut. I've failed him. But I hold my head erect, gather my music, slowly rise, and shamble toward the door.

"Of course, you may choose to continue your training with a private tutor and re-apply again in a year," Descombes says. Small consolation.

I grasp the handles and push through the frosted glass doors. Down the stairs I scramble to ground level and burst out of the entry doors onto the sidewalk. Then, I pitch my sheet music as hard as I can into the street. "Merde, merde!" I rake my face, groan, and turn toward the building façade. "You petrified old farts." I wave my fist. "You think you're some kind of genius, Diémer? With your orange clown hair, you belong on a unicycle in the circus! Stupid sons of bitches!"

Passersby gawk at me and swerve in a wide margin around me. Then I notice my stepmother glaring at me out of the carriage window.

"I can't believe you did this to your father," she says. "After all he invested in you."

My eyes narrow and hot breath pulses from my nostrils. Father never should have married you. You bitch.

"You've ruined everything; let your teachers down, not to mention the strain you put on our marriage. What do you have to say for yourself? Nothing, of course."

"Me? I did everything they demanded, everything you pressured me to do. You all failed me! Betrayed me!" I turn and walk away. I no longer care what my evaluators think; least of all Eugenie. She pushed the Conservatoire on me. I never wanted to perform dreary sauerkraut to their standards of mechanical perfection, anyway. I've been released from a torture chamber. I rub my forehead. But my father, the way he dropped his head in despair is a crushing boulder. How will I ever make it up to him? I don't know how, yet. But whatever it takes, I will restore his faith in me. And this decaying institution, one day they'll beg me to come back and perform. I'll show them.

Chapter 2

February 1890, Paris, Opera District

DESPITE THE SLIPPERY dusting of snow, my pace along this side street quickens as the bookshop comes into view. It's ironic Edmond Bailly's newest enterprise, tucked away off Boulevard Haussmann in the Opera district. Its mystical contents and bohemian clientele are the antithesis of anything promoted or produced at the megalith of music two blocks away. Since the first day it opened, the bookstore has become a hive of creativity for writers, artists, and musicians. The place is absolutely synergetic. They come for the same reason I do; to drink from the well of inspiration. Sooner or later, I'll find that special alchemy to give me an edge. Some unique ingredient will make me standout and rattle the constipated music establishment.

Faux paint resembling green malachite embellishes the shop's paneled façade, with exotic gold lettering like sinewy vines spelling out the name on the display window: Librairie de l'Art Indépendant. I get butterflies just wandering the narrow aisles and perusing the assortment of esoteric religious writings, rare volumes on occult sciences, and all manner of tomes on the fine arts. It's like discovering lost treasure.

Shop owner Edmond Bailly looks up from his roost beside the cash register as I grasp the brass door handle and push my way inside.

His auburn widow's peak and menacing brows project the image of an illusionist; the mesmerizing dark glare emblazoned on posters pasted to newspaper carousels and billboards.

"Bonjour!" I say, removing my secondhand top hat, woolen scarf, and frock coat; hanging them on the hall stand.

Bailly calls out like a ringmaster, "Madames et Messieurs, the Congress of Conservatoire Renegades can now begin. The Chairman has arrived."

I tip my head and feign a puzzled look. Cupping my mouth as if delivering a theatrical aside, I say, "I thought you were the Chairman."

Bailly straightens his waistcoat. "True." He raises his voice again. "Correction, the Chief Attaché has arrived."

I grin and exaggerate a bow to the scattered, amused audience.

"Listen. We're holding a séance tonight," Bailly says. "We're going to summon the soul of Edgar Allan Poe. Can you come?"

I shake my head. "Sorry, I have to play tonight."

"Ahh, what a shame. Go on then, study the necromancy manuals." Bailly shoos me away with the wave of his hand.

Bailly is a wizard of sorts. As an entrepreneur, he's made a niche for himself promoting new young talent. He studied at the Conservatoire a decade before I did, and holds the same contempt for the instructors and their teaching methods. Bailly once told me, "Music and the arts must change with time as each generation finds new things to say". He helped me publish two of my waltzes and a poem I set to music for my best friend Patrice. That's the magic of Bailly's journal, Musique de la Familles.

I saunter down an aisle to my favorite section, sliding volume "D" of Le Grand Larousse Illustrée from the shelf, opening it to Dance, the day's topic of research. From the worn leather cover and the dog-eared pages, many others have consulted it too.

"So, you attended the Paris Conservatoire," a soft voice says.

I lift my face and push my pince-nez higher on the bridge of my nose. The speaker appears to be close to my age. Pudgy, he wears a tan overcoat with a black shearling collar. Dark and wiry waves lay across his forehead from a side part. The fire in his dark eyes, along with a thick beard and moustache, reminds me of an ancient Mesopotamian king. With a disarming smile, he extends his hand. "Claude Debussy."

"Enchanté, Claude. Erik Satie." We shake hands. "And yes, I confess I was an inmate at the penitentiary of creative torture." I hear the snickers of nearby eavesdroppers.

A grin spreads over Claude's face and he chuckles. "So was I. When were you there? Did we know one another?"

I like him, friendly and eager; obviously bright. "I could swear we've met," I say. "I was there from 1879 through 82. Luckily, they released me on my own recognizance. And you?"

"I was gone by 1879, teaching music in Russia, and then in Rome. Paris has changed a lot while I was gone. I can't get over these new buildings, the Exposition Universelle, and that tower."

"Oh that. Some people think it's a shameful eye-sore," I say. "I'm completely stunned by the engineering that must have gone into the thing. Architecture is one of my interests."

"Then, you would love Rome."

"Undoubtedly. Rome, Russia. You've travelled a lot."

"Well, I was there on an academic scholarship at the Villa Medici."

I jerk my head back, wide-eyed. I'd taken Claude for any other struggling bohemian roaming the Paris clubs and cafés. But he must be a Prix de Rome recipient, the Conservatoire's highest honor. Claude has jumped through all the flaming hoops of technical virtuosity. He's the epitome of everything the institution seeks to produce; and everything I wanted to avoid. I tip my head with a wry smile. "Should I offer my condolences? That had to cost blood and tears."

Claude drops his head. "Truthfully, the atmosphere was restrictive. The food wasn't fit for dogs and the monastic quarters were lice filled. I felt so strangled and depressed, I couldn't compose anything worthwhile. I needed to submit something in the end. And after all the grueling effort, they said my work was bizarre. They disapproved of me courting the unusual." He cocks his head to one side and rolls his eyes.

"Courting the unusual," I say. "At least they didn't completely stifle all originality. You sound like the kind of composer I'd like to know."

"I met Franz Liszt, however, and found his talent heart-stopping. What about you?"

"I play piano and harmonium at Le Chat Noir cabaret, and give lessons. I must keep food on the table somehow. But I've also been composing music based on historic dance. I recently had my composition, the Trois Gymnopédies published."

"Really? I'd like to hear a sample," Claude replies.

"Of course," I say. I return the volume to the shelf. Claude follows me to the back room, where Bailly has an upright baby grand tucked away. As soon as I touch the keyboard, a small audience gathers. They stand in the doorway and then turn shipping crates on end as chairs. The tiny room becomes packed for the impromptu recital. Claude leans against the upright.

I begin a slow sensuous waltz, undulating and languorous in an ostinato. Then I add to this accompaniment the restive bittersweet melody that still summons reminders of the lost love who inspired it. Firelight glows iridescent on the folds of a taffeta skirt, whispering with every move. The caress of a shoulder through a crisp sleeve. Lips on the downy skin beneath an earring. Inhaling the jasmine and spice of her black cherry curls. The music's cadence matches the subtle rise and fall of a lover's breath, luxuriating in the moment and relishing every sensation. Ah yes, I can still feel her, Jeanne.

The small audience gives a hushed ovation when I finish. Claude looks at me with wild delight. "I'd certainly like to know what you eat for breakfast."

I stare at him deadpan. "Ambrosia, brought from Mt. Olympus by doves."

Claude bursts into laughter.

"So, you like the piece?" I ask.

"That is a remarkable work. Such simplicity, pared down and pure.

Those unresolved sevenths and the dissonance against the harmony. How did you ever think of this?" Claude squirms with enthusiasm.

I'm delighted and surprised someone of Claude's caliber would be so complimentary. "I was reading Plato, where he talked about the naked warrior dances of ancient Sparta and experimented with a Greek modal scale."

Claude shakes his head, wide-eyed.

"Tell me about your work," I say, "the unusual your professors claim you've been courting."

Claude takes a deep breath. "I composed an exotic piece, called 'Danse bohemienne'. I even sent it to Tchaikovsky." He drops his gaze. "But he called it shriveled."

"Why? Because it's pared down and simplified? That probably means it's fantastic. Let's hear this shriveled bohemian dance."

Claude takes his turn at the keyboard. His hands send a flurry of notes into the air, seasoned with an eastern European flavor. But the little mazurka sounds a bit too Romantic to be modern. It's overwritten and weighed down, and not what I expected to hear. But it's beautiful, in its way. Without question, Claude's keyboard mastery is flawless. I smile and keep time, picturing Slavic peasants in boots and embroidered tunics cavorting in a circle. A short piece, Debussy finishes up with a toss of the head as he strikes the last chord. Bystanders applaud.

I lean in with a grin. "You are one lapin chaud."

"What? Hot rabbit?"

"Musician extraordinaire."

"Merci. I guess I really have been away too long." Claude stands up. "I'm certainly glad to have met you, Erik. I'd like to hear more of your work, but I'm afraid I must get going." He starts toward the door.

I step into the doorframe. "Let's have a drink sometime." I take out one of my calling cards from my breast pocket and hand it to Claude.

Claude pats his pockets. "Actually, I don't have a card to give you at the moment."

I pull out my small music notebook and pencil and hand them to Claude. "Give me your address."

Claude scribbles on the inside cover and hands them back. "Why not come for Sunday luncheon? Noon?"

"Alright, fantastic," I smile. I accompany Claude as far as the hall-stand and watch as he places a wide brim hat on his head.

"À bientôt," Claude says, flashing a mesmeric smile as he leaves the bookstore.

I stand there several moments finding myself so drawn to Claude, it embarrasses me. This is the first time I've connected with someone who implicitly understands my work and seems to share my aesthetic, without explanation. Claude might prove to be a good sounding board and learned ear to test my evolving ideas. And he surely must know people who might give me a chance, and open some doors. But the fact he walked into this bohemian establishment says he's struggling to break free from the rigid forms and traditional style that stifle his unique voice. Perhaps I can help him as much as he could me. I could point him in new directions to go beyond the years of mechanical mastery of dead art.

I wander back to the rows of books to resume my research. But memories I've tried hard to forget come flooding back. Recalling the insults and censure at the Conservatoire still makes my stomach twinge. I don't envy Claude, but I once aspired to the honor he's earned. In retrospect, I'm thankful I've been so free to create. But a part of me still yearns to transcend the shame and disgrace I brought to my beloved father. And I know he still yearns to see me move beyond the café and cabaret scene. What could it mean to become friends with a Prix de Rome? Can we challenge the gods and inspire each other to new creative heights? I yearn for that right down to my bones. And what's really at stake here? Obscurity. A slow and painful death.

Chapter 3

March 1890, 18th Arrondissement

"Six francs?" I square my shoulders. "There must be some mistake. It's supposed to be twelve. I played nearly every night for the past two weeks."

Rodolphe Salis cocks his head to one side and blows out a puff of smoke from the curved ceramic pipe that resembles a miniature saxophone. Beside him sits Emile Goudeau, pen in hand, noting the transaction in a ledger atop the café table. Salis runs his palm forward over his vermillion hair, cut like Napoleon or Caesar, and he squints. "I deducted the cost of your bar tab," he says.

I shift my weight. "What bar tab?"

Salis shoves aside a breakfast plate, the remnants of runny egg yolk and crumbs catching my eye and alerting my rumbling stomach as it clatters across the table, knocking into a coffee cup. "You've been throwing back drinks at the rate of seven or eight a night."

"I thought it was gratis, employee privilege."

Salis twists his moustache. "What gave you that idea?"

"You never docked my pay before, in over a year, but just keep pouring."

Salis sticks out his bearded chin. "Well, it's time to ante up."

I clench my fist, breathing fast and shallow. "That's not fair. How am I supposed to live on six francs?"

"Not my concern. Don't like it? There's the door. The Café of the Incoherents is down the street."

I adjust my pince-nez. "You know I want this job."

"Then sober up and pay your way."

Emile Goudeau sets down his pen and stares at the tabletop, tugging at his handlebar moustache. Salis takes another puff on his pipe. I gather my money, folding the bills and tucking them into my pocket. "Are you going to charge for supper now, too?"

Without looking up, Salis grunts. "No, meals are included for all staff."

At least I won't starve. And Salis didn't fire me. I recall the evening Victor Fumet walked out, and more recently; the songwriter Maurice Mac Nab. I wonder if this is the reason they left. I clench my jaw and turn to go.

Alphonse Allais, the editor of Le Chat Noir Journal, is sitting at the other end of the café and overheard the exchange. He meets my glowering stare as I head for the door. I'm outside on the sidewalk, about to depart, when I hear him.

"Satie."

I turn. Alphonse gestures me back, and I retrace my steps.

Clad in a vest and shirtsleeves, Allais rocks back and forth with his hands in his trouser pockets. With a center part, his hair slopes like two wings to his jaw, where his beard flares out in ragged glory. He brushes his hair out of his eyes. "He's shortchanged everyone at one time or another." He squints against the monocle he wears on one eye. "He's terrible with the books. When he can't make payroll, somebody gets shorted. It was just your turn. It's not personal."

"Surely seemed that way."

Allais pulls out several bills from his pocket. Peeling off three, he hands them to me.

"Thank you, thank you, Alphonse. I'll pay you back. You don't know how bad I need it."

"No, you won't, and yes, I do. I've been there, my friend. I was a founding member of the Incoherents."

"And you lived to tell the tale."

"And so can you." Alphonse takes out a cigarette and offers me another, which I eagerly take. He strikes a match and puffs his cigarette aflame.

I've always looked up to Alphonse, since rediscovering him at the Chat Noir. Not only did he come from my hometown, Honfleur, but the Allais family lived on Rue Haute near my grandparents. He even attended the Boys Academy. But he's 12 years older and was gone by the time I attended.

"But are you in this for the gaiety and decadence, or for the art? I mean, you can drink yourself into an early grave but…"

"No, no!" I wave my hands. "I'm in it for the art."

"Then you have to curtail your personal bacchanalia. D'accord?"

"I'll try."

Alphonse adjusts his monocle and tucks his hair behind one ear. "And don't piss off Salis. He's got a violent temper, as I'm sure you've heard. He accidentally killed a server when he threw a bar stool."

"I've heard a lot of stories. About you, too. Is it true what they say about the Salon des Incoherents? Did you really hang a piece of blank canvas?"

"Not exactly." Allais bounces, grinning sheepishly. "We held it the same time as the Academy of Fine Arts Salon. We wanted to challenge their holy canon defining art; render their whole concept of masterpiece ridiculous. So, we hung a painting titled Apoplectic Cardinals Harvesting Tomatoes at the Red Sea."

I chuckle, shaking my head.

Allais grins and wrinkles his nose. "It was just a framed piece of red mat board. And next to it, we hung the Naked Albino Virgins Playing in Snow."

This strikes me as so funny; my eyes tear up. "A real slap in the face to those priggish art dealers and newspaper critics."

"But just like the Incoherents and the Hydropaths, we're still doing that, Erik. And so are you. I mean, what kind of word is Gymnopedies? It's great! And the music is an exotic trance. You have talent. Don't waste it."

"Thanks, mon vieux."

He slaps me on the shoulder. "You're welcome. See you later?"

I nod with enthusiasm. "You will." I tip my hat and turn to go.

This is what I love most about Le Chat Noir. The writers, artists, and musicians have a tongue-in-cheek approach, use relentless irony and hyperbole for artistic confrontation. Rodolphe Salis might be a capricious asshole. But I can't walk away from this atmosphere of intellectuals and artists, the air thick with tobacco smoke and satire. The most important thing is the welcoming appreciation they offer me for my own art, and the space to cut a unique profile. I don't want to lose that. If only I could make real money.

April 1890- 9th Arrondissement

Sharp pounding on the door startles me. I open the door of my atelier a narrow crack and peek out cautiously.

"It's just me," says Patrice, pushing through the doorway.

"Bonjour to you, too," I mutter, mildly irritated that Patrice interrupted my concentration at the keyboard. "I was worried you were one of my creditors coming with a Gendarme to collect." I close and lock the door behind me.

"Let me borrow your trousers," Patrice says.

"What?"

"Your nice trousers. Let me borrow them, mon vieux. I just got a job and I can't wear these." He tugs at his pant leg, revealing a gaping frayed hole from the crotch to mid-thigh on the inner seam. Then he turns his head both ways, surveying the room. "Hey, what happened to your chairs?"

I drop my head. "I had to pawn them; and the clock, too." I gesture to the mantle.

"What a shame. You need a day job, Erik. Now, let me borrow those." He points to the trousers I'm wearing.

"What am I going to wear?" I ask.

"You don't have to leave the flat until tonight, right?"

"True."

"So, I'll wear them during the day and bring them back so you can wear them at night."

I give a scoffing laugh. "Oh I see. What do I get out of it?

"Uh. My sister will bake you an apple tart?"

"Doesn't seem quite fair."

"Oh, come on, mon vieux." He scrunches his brows. "Please? I'm desperate."

Voices travel up from the vestibule. A quick peek verifies what I feared. It's the owner of the brasserie on the corner and a police officer talking to the Concierge.

"Merde, merde! Tell them I'm not here. Say you came to collect, but I was gone." I bolt out the door and close it behind me. I race up half a flight to the latrine and lock myself inside. Footsteps draw closer, and then there's pounding on my atelier door.

"Open up Monsieur. Don't make it worse than it is. I've brought the police."

There is a lull, and I picture Patrice opening the door. "Monsieur Satie?"

"He's not here." Patrice's voice sounds resolute. "He owes me money, and he said this was his payday. I'm waiting for him."

"Step out of the way, Monsieur." I assume the alternate voice is the Gendarme. The stench of the latrine is beginning to nauseate me, and I cover my mouth and nose with my shirt. There's silence and I strain to hear, as minutes click away. Then the brasserie owner's voice echoes in the stairwell again. "Tell him he better settle up, or else."

"Or else what?" I hear Patrice, his words laced with bravado. I picture him, fists balled and chest puffed up.

"Now, now, Monsieur. There's no call for violence."

"I'll come back," says the creditor. "He better have the money."

I listen for the footsteps, tracing the sound down the stairwell. I'm fairly sure they've left the building and peer out. Then I descend to my atelier.

Patrice waves his hand. "Phew! What a stink."

"Sorry."

"He was looking under your bed and in your trunk. This is awful."

"I know, I know. There's no way I can pay him, either."

"You need to leave before they lock you up."

"Where can I go? I'm certainly not going to crawl back to my father's. Eugenie wouldn't allow it, anyway. Maybe my brother can help."

"Can I still borrow your pants?"

I release a huff of disgust. "You better be back on time." I unfasten the fly and slough the trousers to my ankles. Stepping out of them, I hand them to Patrice.

"I will. I promise." He removes his threadbare pants and gives them to me. I slide one leg into the pants, and then the other. "How am I supposed to compose a masterpiece when I can't keep a roof over my head? I don't know where my next meal is coming from."

Patrice sits on the piano bench and fits his feet into the pant legs. "That's why I took this day job. I can always write at night." He stands and fastens the fly. "Fits well."

"But a day job would mean leaving the Chat Noir. I can't do that. The best creative masterminds in Paris congregate there."

"I know," he says. "So, finding a cheaper place to live is your only other option."

"But giving up my atelier here is like surrendering my dream, failing."

"It is not the apocalypse, Erik. It's just moving. Try different things until you find the right combination."

"You may be right." My hands go limp and I lower my chin. I so much want to resolve this problem quickly, but I'm trapped. Everything is spinning out of control.

Chapter 4

April 1890- 18th Arrondissement

"YOUR NOTE SOUNDED pretty desperate," my brother Conrad says. He wraps his arms around me, giving me a peck on each cheek. He steps back, eyeing me up and down. "You're looking rather lean these days, and if you don't mind me saying so, rather un-kept."

"I know." I blow a resigned puff of air from the corner of my mouth.

Conrad is in his second year at the Sorbonne. He'll be starting an internship at a pharmacy in St. Germaine, and he moved into an apartment with two other students in the Latin Quarter. "What's wrong, mon frère?"

"How do I begin to tell you?" I pace. "Everything was planned out, done right, but it's all falling apart." Facing the window, I steel myself against an unexpected flood of pain. My little brother shouldn't see me weep. This is the first time I'm being honest with myself or anyone else; actually, saying it out loud.

"Falling apart?"

I swallow hard and turn to face my brother. "Promise me you won't tell Father. Swear."

Alarm widens Conrad's eyes. He moves his hands as if smoothing out wrinkles. "Alright. Now tell me what's happened."

"The inheritance money he gave me from Grand-père's estate is gone, all gone. Every centime went into this endeavor. I'm about to lose everything. This studio, my students." I shudder. "I don't even know where I'm going to live."

"How did this happen?" Conrad loosens his green patterned bourgeois ascot and tugs at the bottom of his waistcoat.

"I'm not sure why it's come to this. I probably was in over my head."

Conrad takes a step back, runs his hand through his hair with a sigh. "But you got your music published, and..."

"It hasn't earned enough to pay for the paper it's printed on."

"You're still earning income at Le Chat Noir, aren't you?"

"Yeah, when Salis decides to pay me. And I give lessons, too. But it's still not enough."

Conrad covers his mouth, his eyes searching aimlessly for a reply.

"I've been living a lie, one big illusion, putting on a mask of gaiety and humor," I say. "No one really knows the mess I'm in. But the truth is I'm ruined. Creditors are hounding me. I'll be on the street in a matter of days."

He sinks onto the piano bench, the last of my furniture I haven't pawned besides my bed.

"I walk home alone at night feeling like a complete..." My voice catches and I close my eyes, trying to collect myself. I take a deep breath, staring out the window again. Inky clouds lay against a pale horizon. "My mind has been in a state of panic. The only moment's peace is when I'm drinking or drunk. I'm at the very brink of..."

"Stop talking like that. We will not let that happen. Absolutely not. There has to be a solution. First, we're going to get you something to eat. I'm paying. And then we'll make a plan, d'accord?"

I groan. "D'accord. We must go some blocks away. I owe everyone around here."

"You lead the way."

Wearing my black frock coat, I carry my umbrella for insurance against a likely shower. I can open it to avoid being recognized if I need to. We move swiftly up Rue des Martyrs to boulevard Clichy. Hundreds of windows look down on me from Baron Haussmann's six-story buildings flanking both sides. Patrons cast scornful glances at us from café tables beneath elegant plaster facades with ornate entablature. Conrad and I cross the boulevard.

A corner shop hosts a tobacconist on the ground floor. Conrad stops to buy a pouch of loose tobacco for me and I quickly roll a cigarette. This side of the street hosts a newly erected permanent home of the Cirque Fernando. The structure resembles a spice decanter or Chinese lantern. Workers and porters traverse the narrow strip of sidewalk. Stray dogs and school children scamper from one side to the other. A small horse-drawn cart slows to a crawl against the grade. We trudge along the narrow lane with blue-grey paving stones, climbing the face of the hill.

"There's a marvelous new esoteric bookstore that just opened near the opera," I tell my brother. "I've been reading about the Gnostics."

"Mystery cults of the ancient world," says Conrad, gasping from exertion.

I take a drag from my cigarette. "I suppose I'm curious because they were a heresy against the established order."

"Ah, rebels, like someone else I know and the Conservatoire," he huffs.

I can't help breaking into a smile. "They held heterodox ideas about the universe and the mind. I'm fascinated by the concept of gnosis. There is another reality beyond the realm of senses. Wouldn't it be fascinating to probe that reality?"

"Pishah! You know me, Erik. I'm a non-believer and a scientist. Sounds like a lot of Neo-Platonist hoo-hah being spouted these days. I'll tell you what's interesting. I attended a lecture with that neurologist, Dr. Charcot, on hypnosis. The subconscious mind is the source of urges and impulses, which make us do things. Now that's interesting."

I raise an eyebrow. "Sounds like we're talking about the same thing."

Conrad pauses and looks at me, panting for air. "Maybe."

"Socrates talks about divine insight and divine madness."

Conrad grins. "Along with drunkenness, eroticism, and dreaming."

I snicker. "Oui."

My legs burn by the time we reach the upper end of the street, where the lane ends at Rue des Abbesses. I suggest the Brasserie Carillion, because I've never eaten there. The restaurant occupies a central place at the intersection beneath a small hotel. The host seats us at the windows with a telling view of the neighborhood we'd just traversed and the changing one ahead. This also marks the boundary of the Paris city limits.

I order a mazagran to accompany my meal; the cold coffee and seltzer remedy for a hangover served in a footed porcelain tumbler. Conrad asks for café crème.

"Everyone seems to be exploring states of mind, these days," Conrad says. "Some of the chemistry students study the effects of compounds or plants on the brain."

I lean onto my forearm. "And indulging in them, I assume.

Conrad straightens in his chair.

"Come on, you've tried it, haven't you?" I ask.

He hesitates. "You won't tell Father."

"Of course not."

"Alright. Vin Coca Mariana, a mixture of wine infused with the leaves of the coca plant, and Coupe-Jacques a l'ether, strawberries soaked in ether."

"Ether? Wouldn't touch it."

"And there are some stupid students giving themselves small doses of chloroform."

"You mean kill specimens' chloroform? That's poison." I grit my teeth. "You didn't do it, did you?"

"It scares me. But as a lover of bohemian exotica, I'm surprised you haven't tried it."

I shake my head. "Keep opium and hashish. Just give me Absinthe or brandy. That's all the mind-altering I need." I gaze out at the road, arching up toward Montmartre. With each ascending block, the buildings change in character; becoming an unrelated collection from previous centuries, patch-worked together.

After wolfing down an omelet and sausages, we linger over another cup of coffee. Each of us scours the classified section of several newspapers.

"I'm very grateful for you coming all the way over here and taking me to breakfast."

"It's nothing," he replies.

I have a full stomach for the first time in weeks. It's good to have someone I can truly rely on and confide in. My brother is the best.

"There are a few listings for reasonably priced rooms on the summit of Montmartre. How much have you been paying for the atelier?" asks Conrad.

"105 francs a quarter."

"Well, no wonder you have no money. We're paying 90 split three ways. The 9th is a fine neighborhood, but not economical. But this says 35." He circles one ad with his fountain pen.

"Is that so? Must be a hovel," I say.

"Only one way to find out."

"Montmartre can't be all that bad. Hector Berlioz lived there. They say, in spring he would invite people to stay with him, like Franz Liszt, Chopin and others."

We exit the café and head northwest until we reach the blue paving stones spreading across the face of the butte of Montmartre. The gentle incline widens enough for carriages and a team-drawn omnibus. But the drivers end their transit at Rue Lepic. Beyond this point, the climb becomes arduous. The lanes narrow, becoming steeper, and the surface of the pavement is hazardous with tree roots and pot holes. Conrad and I stop to catch our breath and gape at the panorama of Paris from atop a walled embankment. I notice there are no lampposts, and try to imagine this climb in the early hours of the morning after playing at Le Chat Noir.

The buildings in this quarter are smaller and older; 17th century, I guess. They're separated by weed-tufted garden plots enclosed by low stone fences. According to the flower dealer we pass, this is still not the summit. But she points us toward a shortcut. We hike up a sweet little passageway, bordered by ivy-covered manors with cracked plaster faces and faded green shutters hanging askew. Narrow portals open into patios or porches, where matrons sit on the stoops peeling vegetables or sewing. A group of women go by with baskets of laundry.

The crest of Montmartre looms directly ahead. Atop a craggy knoll, an enormous windmill lifts its black motionless arms against the dapple-gray sky. As we come out onto a tree studded lane, the landscape opens into an undulating plateau. This is a rustic paradise, with windmills, arbors, quiet lanes bordered with cottages, and bushy gardens. But there are very few people. Goats frolic and graze on the thistles, and a handful of chickens peck in the dirt. Seated right there, a slender, starved-looking young man daubs paint on a canvas. He has one brush in his mouth and a paint-stained fist full of others. His mustache looks too large for his face and his cheeks are blue with stubble. He studies the high arching green gate on the other side of the sandy lane. We both stare.

"So, this must be the famed Bal de Moulin de la Galette," says Conrad.

"The summer dance garden Father used to talk about."

A tall wooden fence, layered with peeling posters of seasons past surrounds the enormous park. Adjoining the grounds on the corner sits a bakery café. The overpowering aroma of hot apple galette wafts from its open door.

"Pardon, Monsieur," I say. "Are you a resident here?"

Grabbing the brush from between his teeth, the painter replies. "Bon dia."

"Oh, are you Catalan?" I ask. "My friend Patrice is from Tarragona."

Standing, he gathers the brushes into one hand and offers me his other color-smeared one. "Santiago Rusiñol, from Barcelona. I stay in the artist colony, right here." He gestures with the paint brushes toward the fenced park.

"Which way to Rue Cortot?"

"Oh, very close. Go down this road, Rue Girardon. Then, go left, oui?" He makes a sweeping arch with one hand. "You turn onto Rue des Saules and then, voila Rue Cortot."

I beam, repeating his movement. "Like so?"

Santiago grins and nods, "Ci."

"Thank you." We tip our hats and follow the road down an incline dotted with cottages ending at a stone retaining wall which holds in place a feral field. When we veer toward the Rue Cortot, there's an old buttressed rampart surmounting a similar retaining wall.

"This must have been some sort of fortress or citadel," Conrad says.

The street also lies in the construction's shadow of a new basilica. Peeking above the roofline, the most incandescent white stone campanile and pinnacles loom. Massive scaffolding encloses a central dome in progress. Blue paving stones reappear, dressing up the thoroughfare in front of two elongated buildings with mullioned windows, a mansard roof and dormers. The plaster was once the color of apricots with blue shutters, now faded gray. A tunnel porte-cochere in the center opens onto a small courtyard.

"You think this could be it?" I ask Conrad.

"Let's ask the concierge."

"I wonder if this was once a military barracks. The concierge apartment looks like some kind of guard station."

Through the paned glass doors, I see a spiral staircase. Conrad raps at the door. I gaze across to the far side of the courtyard through a row of trees. There is a third building with the same once glorious 17th century style.

"Good day, gentlemen. Can I help you?"

"Is this the location of the apartment listed here?" Conrad asks, pointing to the circled ad in the newspaper.

"Yes, Monsieur. It is next door, number six. I shall get the key and show it to you." He disappears for a moment, returning with a key ring.

We follow the balding, middle-aged man out to a staircase and elevated walkway along the front of the building. He opens the door and gestures for us to enter. The concierge leads us up a flight of stairs to the second floor. Two apartments flank the landing. He unlocks the door to the apartment. The bare room is a third the size of my atelier. But there's a cozy fireplace in the corner and a window from which I can see the basilica.

"It's small, but clean. Nice, really," Conrad says. "What do you think?"

"What about Grand-mère's piano? It won't fit, if we could even get it up here." I lower my face to hide my growing disenchantment.

Conrad tilts his head, studying my expression. "I can move it to my place; keep it there until you have space for it. I'm sure this is only a temporary setback."

I release a pained sigh; rubbing my forehead, trying to maintain my composure. "But how will I compose? How can I give lessons? Do I have to give up everything?" The strain in my voice is louder than I intended.

"Calm down. Take one thing at a time. You must be practical. You need a place, right?"

"What alternative do I have right now?"

"We can still look at the other listings."

The concierge shuffles his feet and clears his throat. "There's a garden in back with a fountain fed by a natural spring. Would you like to see it?"

"Certainly," says Conrad.

We descend to the street and pass back through the porte-cochere. Across the courtyard stands an inviting rose arbor and lattice fence.

The concierge leads us through the arch to an untamed expanse of wild flowers which seems to drop off sharply. When we approach the edge, I discover a vineyard cascading down the slope of the hill. The panorama of the north captivates me. In the center of the grounds, a concrete fountain dribbles a gentle melody into a small pool. Up here, away from the bustling city, it's so quiet. All I can hear is falling water and birdsong.

Conrad places a hand on my shoulder. "So? You can give the concierge a deposit or we can keep looking. Whatever you want; I'll help you. The dividend from my share of the inheritance money is coming soon. I usually just reinvest it, but you can give it to your new landlord." He gestures to the arbor where the concierge waits.

"It's terribly generous of you mon frère. I'd be homeless without your help." But as I say this, my chest tightens and there's a sinking sensation in my middle. My eyes search the scattered clouds as I draw in a halting breath. I look around at the pastoral Eden; my eyes tracing the butterflies flitting around a honeysuckle draped fence. Small green apples stud the branches of the tree a few steps away. The smell of loamy soil conjures a memory of playing in our grandparents' garden in Honfleur. I get a twinge in my middle.

"It is beautiful here," says Conrad. "Peaceful. Great place for writing and composing."

Gripping my umbrella, I stroke my beard with the other hand. A crisp breeze rifles through my hair, carrying the fragrance of lilac. My brother might be right. It's just temporary. Maybe I can handle living here. But only long enough to make some money and get a bigger place again. I can't compose under all the pressure. I'm getting nowhere. This is a serene place with an artist colony. Conrad is offering to help, financially. I shouldn't be so fussy.

"I guess it will have to do, but just temporarily until I'm back on my feet."

Chapter 5

June 1890, 10th Arrondissement

A WARM GLOW reflects off the embossed copper ceiling inside the billiard hall. Men in shirt sleeves hover over the tables puffing on cigars and pipes. The whorls of smoke drift inside pyramids of light cast onto the emerald felt from fluted glass lampshades. Although our music circles are largely disparate; Claude and I have become near inseparable. Increasingly, he seems to enjoy inhabiting my bohemian cabaret sphere. But I've yet to cross the threshold into his grand musique realm.

"One thing I like about this place is the gasoliers," I say, "rather than using those harsh electric lights." I lean my umbrella against the wall and peel my frock coat from my shoulders.

"Me, too," says Claude. "These wide shades eliminate flicker, which is a real distraction when you're playing." He hangs his jacket by its collar on the hooks above the gleaming mahogany wainscoting. I pull down two cue sticks from the hardwood rack. A white aproned server sidles past me. He carries a tray with two amber Belgian beers we ordered and arranges them on coasters atop the small pedestal tables at the perimeter.

Claude gathers the balls from the underside gullies of the carved legged table. "I just learned this morning Bailly will sell the sheet music of my 'Cinq Poèmes de Baudelaire'."

"Congratulations. I wish you every success. My sales have been disappointing." I retrieve balls from my side of the table and roll them to Claude.

"You know, that private performance my mentor Ernest Chausson organized in March probably gave me the exposure I needed." Claude jars the triangular frame to align the balls and carefully removes it. "I hope it will open other new doors, too. The guest list included several important newspaper music critics."

An invisible hand clenches my gut. "What a great opportunity. Although music critics can turn out to be vipers." I hand Claude a cue stick and he chalks the tip. Why can't I find such a mentor who can open doors and promote my work? "I hope you'll send me a copy."

"I will."

The sharp click of balls in collision and resulting cheers and groans erupt from the table beside us. We both glance over.

Claude gestures to the felt. "You want to break?"

"Go ahead," I reply, and light a cigarette. I stand silently as Claude studies all the angles. Some players throw their power into a break. But I believe that doesn't maintain control of the cue ball. I'm curious to see how Claude tackles things.

"I've set other poems, too," Claude says. "Rossetti's, 'La Demoiselle élue'."

"Rossetti? I love the Pre-Raphaelite Brotherhood."

"You know it, then?"

"Her eyes were deeper than the depth of waters stilled at even," I say. "She had three lilies in her hand, and the stars in her hair were seven."

"One more thing we have in common," Claude says, and leans his face close to the cue. He gives a firm jab and scatters the balls. None roll into a pocket. Claude is not forceful, which suggests his game will be more calculated than aggressive. "Open table, my friend. You're up." Claude walks over to the pedestal table and takes a drink of his beer. "The Pre-Raphaelite Brotherhood's paintings were so unusual they knocked the English Royal Academy on their derrieres."

I step to the rail. "I embrace that aesthetic of reinterpreting music from a previous era, like they did with paintings and poetry."

"The Brotherhood supported one another in the face of such nasty opposition," Claude says. "They kept each other going."

"Indeed." I take a drag from my cigarette and study the spread. Some striped balls came to rest in a cluster, making for a tough shot. But at least the solids are clear. I calculate the angle to ricochet the cue ball off the rail. Pinning my cigarette between my lips, I take my first turn with a clean bank of the orange five into a side pocket.

"Nice." Claude approaches the opposite rail. His eyes trace my next potential angles and trajectories. "When I applied for membership in the Société Nationale de Musique, I thought I'd find such a brotherhood," he says. "But so far, it hasn't lived up to expectations. Last month, I had to withdraw my Fantasie from the concert schedule because they thought it was too long."

"Oh, we wouldn't dare break their silly rules, or do anything different," I say. My next shot doesn't sink a single ball. I walk several steps to my dewy glass and take a few swallows. "Wouldn't it be great if there was an alliance of artists today?"

Claude edges his way around the table, eyeing his options. Then, he launches a defensive maneuver; hits a striped ball to make it difficult for me to get at the cue ball on my next turn.

"You dog! You're good," I say. I snub out my cigarette. Claude is not only skilled, but tactical. I like a joust now and then. I might not get one in the pocket, but at least I can free the cue ball using a reverse spin off the cushion. I make the shot.

"Ho! You're better than I thought," says Claude. "Where did you get that move?"

"My father taught me." I reflect for a moment how he used to sneak us into the billiard hall, bribing us with sarsaparillas if we behaved.

While chalking the cue, Claude examines the table. He sets up an angle shot, sending the green stripe into a side pocket. He steps back and bites the corner of his mouth. Then, with narrowed eyes, he searches my face. "What if I told you there is such a brotherhood?"

I straighten, staring with a mix of skepticism and curiosity. "What do you mean?"

Claude picks up the triangular billiard rack, holding it vertically under the light. "I'd venture a guess this has particular significance to you."

I hesitate and shift my gaze from the billiard frame to Claude and back again. "Are you referring to the Golden Ratio?"

Claude nods. "I knew it. You're already a sincere seeker. Knock and the door shall be opened." He then attempts a combination shot, but doesn't pocket either ball.

"Why so mysterious? Just come out with it," I say. My bank shot sends the nine ball into a pocket and the cue ball in a position for another clean shot at number 15.

Claude leans on his cue. "There are some people I want you to meet."

I pull back, skepticism seeping into my mind. "What kind of people?"

"Come, sit down. Let's talk."

"Don't you want to finish the game?" I ask.

"Why? You're just going to run the table. Isn't it obvious?"

I analyze the scatter and bob my head with a smirk. "Not necessarily. You could easily get the seven with a 60-degree reflection. You really want to forfeit?"

"We can start a new game in a few minutes." Claude starts gathering the balls.

I'm willing to abandon my likely victory, just this once. I return the cue sticks to the rack and then settle into a chair at the small table, taking a sip of my beer. Claude planks down in the seat across from me, lights a cigarette and leans on his forearm.

"Two years ago, I traveled to Germany for the Wagner festival in Bayreuth. It was amazing. While there, I met two men who have devoted a decade to assembling a library of ancient sacred texts and wisdom literature."

I tap one foot. "Sounds intriguing. To what end?"

Claude leans back, crossing his ankle over his knee. He runs his hand through his wavy hair. "Their aim is to restore esoteric learning to better society through the arts."

"You've got me curious. Who are these people?"

Claude leans forward again and speaks in a velvet tone. "Mostly writers, painters, but also doctors and scientists."

"Scientists?"

Claude strokes his beard, his dark eyes burning with conviction. "The list of members includes some of the greatest thinkers in history."

"It sounds too good. This isn't just some kind of side show illusion? Or one of those clandestine sects; the Illuminati or the Freemasons, is it?"

"No. As near as I can tell, they're sincere. They never proselytize. Nor are they interested in the merely curious or the occult parlor hobbyist. They consider themselves guardians of centuries old teachings, from the Pharaohs to the Greeks, down through the Enlightenment."

"Are you part of this Brotherhood?

"I've attended a couple of their gatherings."

"Why not share this teaching with the world?" I ask.

"There are many ways in which this knowledge could be trivialized, corrupted, or manipulated. The Brotherhood protects and preserves it. They're like a loyal order of knights. They move quietly through society for mutual support and the good of others."

"Knights?"

Claude leans closer and whispers. "The Ancient and Mystic Brotherhood of the Rose+Croix. What you need to decide is, do you want in?"

Without him knowing it, Claude has struck a chord that resonates deeply in me. My penchant for all things medieval seems as much a part of me as the red in my hair, and the Norman blood of Vikings running through my veins. I'm suddenly giddy and can't find words. As far back as I can remember, I've loved castles, knights, and Gothic architecture, making me an eager apprentice. I've been earnestly searching for a way forward, musically. Can this be genuine or is it some kind of ploy? But if I say no, this opportunity may never come again. I could lose my best chance for success. The back of my neck tingles. "What do I need to do?"

Chapter 6

June 1890, Paris, 9th Arrondissement

PACING AIMLESSLY ON the sidewalk, my eyes search into the distance for Claude. Golden lights awaken in the honeycomb of chic apartment windows overlooking Avenue Trudaine. A lavender haze settles over the city. My former studio stands only a block and a half away. When I first moved there, I underestimated just how difficult starting a business would be. I was grievously unprepared. At least I'm surviving now. But my musical career has not progressed as I'd envisioned. I've written numerous pieces, and even had a few published. But despite paying for advertisements and garnering a few positive reviews in the cabaret journals, my royalties barely break even.

On the other hand, Claude has multiplied his sales. I'm hopeful Claude's invitation to this gathering will translate into advantages for us both. We both believe there is a mysterious, untapped wellspring of material from which composers, artists, and writers may draw. If only we can find the channel to tap into it. Perhaps an esoteric brotherhood of artists could have the answer.

Certainly, I was skeptical about the Brotherhood of the Rose+Croix at first. But, my curious appetite for the arcane rather out-weighs my doubt. I followed-up at the Bibliothéque Nationale and Bailly's bookstore to learn more about them. Renaissance physician Paracelsus described them as a hermetic order of mystic philosopher doctors. Forerunners and geniuses of the Western world were among their ranks; Isaac Newton, Rene Descartes, Dante, and Blaise Pascal. And to think they've invited ME into such rarefied company.

I spot Claude, sauntering toward me from the direction of Rue Condorcet. He's quite the flâner in his wide-brimmed hat, flowing scarf, and blue lacquer cane.

"Beautiful evening," Claude says. He grasps me by the shoulder and we exchange kisses on the cheek. "This is it." He gestures upward toward the arching windows and a full balcony supported by large brackets shaped like sound holes on a violin. There are no shops on the ground floor of this exclusive residence. "Are you excited?" Claude asks.

"I haven't been able to stop thinking about it," I reply.

"Allons-y!" With the gleaming brass doorknocker, Claude raps on the heavy oak doors. A uniformed doorman ushers us inside. After surrendering our wraps, we ascend a short staircase to a second set of entry doors, standing open. The pungent, woody fragrance of incense transports me across a threshold of time and space. A handful of well-dressed attendees wander the expansive trapezoidal studio, examining the volumes lining bookcases to the height of the picture rail. What a feast for the mind. Some shelves display archeological treasures such as an Egyptian falcon-headed canopic jar, ceremonial masks, or a piece of Byzantine mosaic. I must have a closer look.

"This is the library of the Marquis, Stanislaus de Guaïta," Claude says softly. "He's a poet and expert in metaphysics. He's published two volumes of verse, The Dark Muse and The Mystic Rose."

We make a brief tour around the perimeter, eyeing the books and relics. Tufted Cordovan sofas frame the edge of a huge Persian carpet in the center of the room. Three high-back velvet chairs dominate the far edge, with their backs to a marble mantle and gilded mirror. The only sounds are the ticking mahogany clock and the purr of quiet conversation. We finally settle on a couch.

"Where's the music?" I whisper. "They need some music. A harp or cello."

Claude nods with a smile.

I survey the mahogany table in the middle of the rug. Candles glow from a massive candelabrum. A freestanding brass cross overlaid with an inverted triangle gleams from atop a pedestal. They wove a garland of red roses through the center. Wisps of sandalwood smoke trail from a perforated brazier beside the cross. The wall clock tolls the eight-o'clock hour. A well-dressed young man comes through the entry doors.

"That's the Marquis," whispers Claude.

"All rise," he says in a deep and solemn voice. A score of fraternity members and guests stands. Two other men enter the room and de Guaïta seals the doors. In single file, the three begin a slow procession around the perimeter. The young man following the Marquis has collar-length blond hair. Both dress conservatively in well-made black three-piece sack suits. There is nothing bohemian about their cravats and neatly trimmed full moustaches. Each wears a V-shaped white satin band down their chests bearing curiously embroidered symbols in red, black, and gold. As they march, I can't help thinking it would add to the pageantry if there were a processional or plainchant anthem to accompany them.

The third man has a tempest of dark hair and a long, forked beard. He surveys the attendees with great interest. His dark eyes meet mine with a fervent, penetrating stare. His full-length heliotrope robe whispers with each step. When they reach the regal chairs near the fireplace, de Guaïta remains on his feet while the other two men sit.

"You may now be seated," he announces. "On behalf of Joséphin Péladan; Count Antoine de La Rochefoucauld, and myself, Stanislas de Guaïta, I welcome you."

Joséphin Péladan? He's that novelist who earned an outstanding critical review of his series, The Decadence Latine.

"As you saw when you arrived, our doors are open to seekers of the truth," de Guaïta continues. "You owe a debt of thanks to the person who invited you because he saw something exceptional in you. You bear the mark of genius in your endeavors, and that person believes you are right for the brotherhood."

I glance at Claude edge-wise and we exchange smiles.

"However, the brotherhood may not be right for you. In order to decide, you may attend our gatherings three times. Afterward, you must either choose the path of initiation or find another path. Should you become a member, you advance through the degrees of the order largely through individualized study and preparation. This requires long periods of quiet meditation and practice. Weekly lectures supplement this, like this one tonight. Again, on behalf of the grand officers, I welcome you to the assembly of the Ancient and Mystic Order of the Rose+Croix."

The Count de La Rochefoucauld rises from his chair. His blond hair falls forward over one eye and he tucks it behind his ear. "I would like to introduce the guest lecturer for the evening, Dr. Gérard Encausse. He began advanced medical studies four years ago under the psychiatrist Jules-Bernard Luys, who studied with the famous neurologist and hypnotist, Charcot. This year he became editor-in-chief of the Revue d'hypnologie, and is also co-founder of the journal L'Initiation. He is head of the laboratoire d'hypnologie at the Hospital de La Charité. Please welcome Dr. Gérard Encausse."

The speaker rises from the sofa across from us. He appears only a few years older than me, and I wonder if my science-minded brother Conrad knows of him or his work. The Count and Dr. Encausse position several easels where we can see them readily. They arrange mounted illustrations and a cross-section diagram of the human head.

"My topic this evening will focus on the nature of consciousness," says Dr. Encausse. "Members of the Ancient and Mystic Order of the

Rose+Croix are on a quest for illumination. Understanding the three-fold structure of consciousness, the head, the heart, and the viscera is required. I'd like to begin by having you examine the pieces of art I've displayed." He points to the easel with a small baton. "DaVinci's Vitruvian Man, from 15th Century Italy."

Then, walking to another easel, he points to an intricate drawing with geometric shapes in prismatic colors. "This is a Tibetan sacred image used for trance and meditation." He takes the illustration down, leaning it against the easel legs, revealing an assortment of multihued images. "This is a Mandala from ancient Punjab. You recognize, of course, the Great Pyramid of Giza, with its geometrical parameters traced out. Except for Da Vinci, there is no direct link between any of these cultures and Pythagoras. There was no exchange of learning across time or space. Yet, they are so very similar. So, what is the origin of these sophisticated forms in human civilizations? If not by exchange between cultures, how do we account for the uncanny similarities of these patterns in sacred art? I ask you gentlemen to consider within yourselves. Could these arise through spontaneous development, or is there another explanation?"

These concepts were familiar to me. I'd brushed the surface in my studies of architecture, the use of the Golden Ratio and its application to music. The rest of the room has become quiet. I can hear the whistle of perplexed breathing, the rustle of clothing against squeaky leather.

"As a Rosicrucian, you can discover the answer to this puzzle. We might explain it simply as Sacred Geometry. The human mind may access this information, if only you know how."

Dr. Encausse displays the diagram of the human brain. He explains how the minds of human kind receive the laws governing the universe through the Third Eye. "This place is located inside the skull directly behind the eyes, according to Hindu sages and Buddhist monks." He points out on the chart to the pineal and pituitary glands. "Scientists at the Sorbonne are researching the space between, as a conduit to higher consciousness," Dr. Encausse tells us.

I've known or sensed this place inside my mind. The Muse sends me insights there. But I've never heard anyone discuss it as anything more than an illusion. My nose starts to tingle and I feel light-headed. When I've sat in the great cathedrals, it serves as a lens through which my music flows, Ogives, Sarabandes, and Trois Gymnopedies. What if the Brotherhood of the Rose+Croix holds a special key?

As the lecture comes to a close, my mind is brimming. We leave the studio and descend the stairs. I can't stop smiling. It's as if they had spread a mantle of bliss over my weary, tangled brain. I've finally found confirmation of things I've come to believe on my own. But I've also gained many new thrilling ideas.

I gather my coat, hat, and umbrella. Claude is a few steps behind me. I'm dizzy yet entirely sober. The world outside on the street appears soft and beautiful, outlined with a dusting of silver moonlight. My friend Claude seems to take on a more than human aspect; angelic or spectral. A kind of glow radiates from his face, and his eyes hold an infectious joy.

"So, what did you think?" Claude asks with a giddy smile.

"Utterly supernatural. I want to be in the company of people who think as I do. And they offer guidance."

"That was my experience, too," Claude replies. "To find kindred spirits, brothers… And that is also why I recommended you."

Claude leans close, his eyes tracing the features of my face. For a frozen moment, I have the impression Claude is about to kiss me. My pulse thunders in my throat. I shuffle one foot awkwardly, adjusting my pince-nez. The next moment, I'm baffled by my own urge. A part of me might actually want his kiss. I've never felt this way about a man. What if Claude is falling in love with me? No, that would be weird. It could overturn the turnip cart entirely. Besides, I enjoy grazing the watercress far too much to become a cigar smoker. I throw one arm around Claude's shoulder, and blurt, "Thank you so much for bringing me here."

"You're very welcome," says Claude, looping his arm around my shoulder, and the two of us march down the sidewalk together. "What do you say to some supper?"

"I'm famished," I reply. "But I don't have a sou."

"No matter. One of my favorite spots is just down the street. I've got enough for soup and bread. It's your kind of place."

"Lead the way."

We head down Avenue Trudaine, and I drop my arm and we edge apart.

"I've just met the most gorgeous demoiselle," Claude says. "Gabrielle Dupont. She has the liveliest blue-green eyes and no shortage of other delicious charms." Claude describes their beginnings, meeting at a tailor shop next to a boutique for haute couture where she is a seamstress. He's also making his preference for women plain. But, how do I explain or make sense of what just happened? Did I get it wrong, misread his actions? Or maybe it was just a transient feeling, springing from our shared experience. It probably doesn't mean anything.

At the intersection with Rue des Martyrs, Claude gestures to the café across the street, with its tattered awning slightly askew.

"This is the Auberge de Clou. I know it doesn't look like much on the outside, but I actually favor it over Le Chat Noir," Claude says. "It's a frequent rendezvous place for the Brotherhood. Songwriters and musicians can share their work without feeling exploited, unlike your place over on Rue Laval."

"I've seen this cabaret many times, but never been inside. Several of my friends speak well of the place," I reply.

We reach the entrance, and Claude opens the door. I discover the café has a Norman theme. Rich blue and white tiles cover the floor and similar hued plates display above the picture rail near the open beam ceiling. I scan the sea of diners for a vacant place as lively music emanates from another room. The maître'd shows us to a table.

"You ought to talk to the owner, Monsieur Thomachet," says Claude. "He likely has work as a tapeur à gages. They probably pay as well as Salis does, but without the heartburn."

"Le Chat Noir has been my solitary mainstay for three years," I say.

"Maybe so. But with the Brotherhood of the Rose+Croix we could both find new inspiration and new possibilities."

"It's like we're right on the threshold of something fantastic happening. This deserves a toast." My belly flutters and I feel like I'm floating.

The euphoria of the night carries me through the week that follows. I can't stop smiling. Finally, the evening arrives for the next meeting. Claude and I rendezvous again at the de Guaïta townhouse. The doorman lets us enter the building, and we scale the stairs. But when we reach the entrance, we find the door closed. Claude tries the handle, but it's locked. A notice has been tacked to the wall beside the door which says: All meetings of the Brotherhood of the Rose+Croix have been suspended until further notice.

My limbs soften to jelly. I turn to Claude.

"What? It can't be," he says. His brows pull together and he splays one hand against his chest. "Something must have happened."

"I don't believe this. Did somebody die? I mean..." We both stare at the notice, not knowing what to say or do next. Finally, Debussy turns toward the stairs.

"Let's go over to the Auberge. Someone must know something."

We slink away and trudge down Avenue Trudaine in silence, faces downcast. My mind swarms with defeatist thoughts and echoes of the conversation I had with my brother and father just two nights ago over dinner at Café Véry. When I started to talk about the Order of the Rose+Croix, Father balked.

"Rosicrucianism? Why would you even consider getting involved in anything so specious?"

"It's a brotherhood dedicated to the arts," I explained. I turned to my brother. "Dr. Gerard Encausse from the Sorbonne gave a fascinating lecture. Have you heard of him?"

Conrad grinned at me. "A doctor of neurology, isn't he? Everyone's talking about his study on contemporary occultism."

My father tapped his cigar against the edge of the spent dinner plate. "You're a rational man, Erik, who questions everything in established society. I'm just surprised you'd let yourself be hoodwinked."

"All this occult business; ouji boards and séances, spiritualism." Conrad wiggled his fingers at his temple. "It's all just a little baseless, for me," he says.

"My dear boy. If you must pursue mysticism, make a pilgrimage to Rishikesh at the foot of the Himalayas and bathe in the Ganges. Don't get roped in by some charlatans."

My belly is now in knots and I can't seem to get a full breath. I reach for the door handle of the Auberge du Clou and Claude and I enter. The café is almost empty; the hour is still early for many revelers. The two of us make our way to the bar and climb onto the stools.

"Bonsoir. What will you have?" asks the bartender.

"Beer for me," says Debussy.

"I need something stronger," I say. "Calvados, s'il vous plaît."

The bartender turns to the rows of bottles lining the glass shelves behind him. He returns within moments to deliver the drinks.

Claude addresses him. "Listen, mon vieux. You probably hear everyone's news in the course of your evenings and the many customers. I wonder, have you heard any news about Péladan and the Order of the Rose+Croix? They gather here sometimes, right?"

"They do, or should I say, used to. Did you read Péledan's latest review of the annual salon?"

"Not yet," says Claude.

"Seems he's causing quite a stir, naming himself after some prince. It kindled an uproar with the other fellow, de Guaïta. I don't know exactly what it's about, but the press is dubbing it 'The War of the Two Roses'."

He sighs and looks at me. "Well, that's the end of that," Claude mutters and takes a long draft of his beer.

While the bartender's explanation clarifies why meetings have been suspended, it leaves me with a few unanswered questions. I take a gulp of fiery brandy and stare over my pince-nez at the blurry gleam of bottles behind the bar. My body sinks heavy into the bar stool and I slouch with my elbow propped up on the counter. I can't shake my disappointment. Were they really a bunch of charlatans as Father believes? Could Claude be right, and that's the end of it all? But what about the announcement? It said, until further notice.

Chapter 7

September 1890- Montmartre

GIANT PILLOWY CLOUDS gather in heaps against the horizon and the air is dense with rumblings of an oncoming thunderstorm. The only other rumblings have come from the announcement in the journal, L'Initiation. Joséphin Péladan has been elected Grand Master of the Rose+Croix order under a new rubric, but no other details were given. I don't know what to think about that, but I'll wait and see if anything comes of it.

I step outside my apartment building and descend to the cobbled lane. It's early in the evening. Though my employer's unpredictable tirades are becoming increasingly difficult to tolerate, I'm heading to Le Chat Noir a few hours early. That gives me time to work on some compositional ideas before the first show. I'm learning to adapt without my own piano, but it's taken months. I continue giving lessons to my handful of students, but now in their homes. Living in Montmartre is restoring my creativity. New themes and motifs are visiting me daily, alighting like sparrows at the window sill each morning. But none has taken roost as yet, and therein lies the conundrum.

Much of my creative energy gets channeled into the musical inventions of Le Chat Noir's troupe of entertainers. I haven't yet built a large enough personal repertoire for a solo performance. The only time my father came to Le Chat Noir and discovered I'm part of an ensemble that accompanies other performers, I could tell he was disappointed. I faked a smile and tried to laugh it off. But I'm sure he thinks I'm short-changing myself, and maybe I am. Ironically, he's always relished café concerts and cabaret entertainment. He's the one who introduced me to it when I was only 13, along with my brother. That risqué show he took us to at Les Ambassadeurs is etched into memory. Even so, he believes I'm destined for something greater. His hope prods me like an itch I can't quite reach. But in the meantime, I have to make a living somehow.

I open my umbrella and notice a sharp patter against the black silk as I pass along the stone curtain wall opposite my apartment building. At the intersection, I turn southward, following the gentle curve of Rue des Saules until it divides in three directions. I veer off, about to descend the hill through a grove of trees, when I hear a groan of pain and callous voices. Feet scuffle and there's a crash of some object smashing against the ground. My heart races. I slow my pace and peer into the shadowy pathway ahead. I edge my way nearer, close my umbrella, invert it, and change my grasp to swing it like a club.

It's difficult to make out the details. Two shadowy figures stand over a third man on the ground, fists and feet flailing despite his pleas. I know what this is. They rarely come up this far. Two street apaches are mugging some innocent fellow. I don't hesitate. I let loose with a battle cry, like I learned at age 18 during my year of compulsory service in the infantry. I'd lost my student deferment after I was expelled from the Conservatoire. I charge toward the assailants swinging. They pause in their assault and stand upright. I catch one man on the side of the head. The whites of his eyes flash for a moment before he falls to the ground. The other tries to lunge at me, cursing. But my second swing cracks him across the teeth with the curved hardwood handle. He shrieks and retreats, covering his mouth. A torrent of dark blood runs between his fingers. The first attacker rouses. But as he wavers to get to his feet, I race over and kick him in the balls. The man howls and keels over again.

"Get the hell out of here, you fuckers, or I'll give you some more."

The two seem to have had enough. They stumble off into the darkness, groaning and muttering obscenities. The thought now occurs to me that they could have had a knife or a pistol. I took an enormous risk. I hurry to their target, curled up on his side on the ground.

"Say, mon vieux, are you alright?"

"I'm not sure. It hurts like the devil to even move."

"Let me help you," I say.

He takes my hand and pulls himself to a sitting position with an unsettling moan. I realize when he lifts his face, it's Santiago. He's the artist I met the first day I arrived on the butte. I see him often, painting en Plein air on the byways of Montmartre. Typically, I'll pause for a brief, friendly exchange. A new volley of rain begins to fall.

"My paint box and easel," he says. He clambers to his feet, and together we gather his art and supplies before the downpour spoils his work.

I find Santiago's sketchbook, and tuck it under my coat; bracing it against my chest. Then, I locate a canvas on the ground, and protect it under cover of my umbrella. Santiago picks up his easel, but finds they have shattered it beyond use, so he leaves it. He locates his paint box, gathers as many of the spilled items as he can find in the dwindling light.

"Where's your place?" I ask.

"Not far." He hobbles back in the direction I just came.

I follow him to the end of a cul-de-sac near Rue Lepic. Entering a wrought-iron gate, we scurry past a ramshackle chicken coop, riddled with cobwebs and moss. Patchy weeds and the leaves of shade trees quiver with falling droplets. We speed across the yard. An old greenhouse is attached to the side of a three-storey building. Pale light glows from inside. The glass sides and sloping roof resemble one enormous faceted topaz.

"This is our painters' lair," says Santiago as we approach the entrance. "We call it El Patio. Natural light is ideal for artists."

The greenhouse spans the length of the building, anchored between two arched buttresses of brick and mortar. A climbing rosebush encircles the entrance, with spent blossoms the color of Bordeaux still clinging to the masonry. As we step through the doorway and down into the subterranean cottage of glass, a fusion of linseed, turpentine, pipe tobacco, and red wine seasons the air. Canvases lean askew in every corner with the most exquisite renderings. I set down the painting and sketchbook, and close my umbrella, leaning it by the door.

"Deu meu!" says a black-bearded young man in a grey, wool flatcap. He stands up from his seat beside a small coal stove at the other end of the greenhouse, next to a second young man wearing a red stocking hat. "What happened?"

In the lantern's glow, three fresh bruises are clearly visible on Santiago's face.

"Apaches," I say.

"Thank God, you came along when you did," says Santiago, setting his paint box on shelving constructed from crates stacked on their sides.

I remove my hat. "They accosted me just a few months ago, but farther down on a side street off Rochechouart. I lost my Grand-père's pocket watch in the melee."

"That's terrible," says the young man in the grey cap.

"This is mi amigo, Sadi," Santiago says.

He offers his hand. "Ramón Casas y Carbo,"

I clasp his hand. "Erik Satie."

Santiago gestures openhanded to a third young man coming over from the coal stove. "And this bonhomme in the barretina is Enrique Clarassó. He's a sculptor," Santiago says.

"Enchanté," I reply.

In the center of the greenhouse stands a makeshift table constructed of wooden slats nailed to an old barrel. I hungrily eye the large crusty loaf of bread, a slab of white hard cheese and a sausage in crinkled butcher paper, beside a wine bottle.

Santiago takes off his wet and muddy cape. "Please, sit down. Would you like a drink?"

"I can't stay long, but yes. I was on my way to work when I discovered your misfortune."

Ramón gestures to several stools under the crude table. He uncorks the bottle and pours some wine into an earthenware cup for me. He points to the sausage. "This is butifarra from Vic. Have some." Ramón pours wine for himself and the others.

I sit at the table. Using the knife, I cut off a slice of sausage and try not to show how ravenous I really am.

Santiago takes the cup and raises it. "To our new friend Sadi, who rescued me from the street thugs. Eat well, shit strongly, and don't be afraid of death."

I break into a laugh. Here is another reason I don't seem to make much headway. It's far too easy to get waylaid by the fascinating artists and poets who dwell on this hill and the offer of a free drink.

"Salut," the others cheer and clink together their odd assortment of drink ware.

"So, you're all artists," I say.

Ramón nods. "Santiago and I study at the Société de la Palette, with Puvis de Chavannes."

"I'm also a correspondent for La Vanguardia, the daily newspaper in Barcelona," Santiago adds.

"A writer and an artist. The Société de la Palette is quite a reputable school." Despite their bohemian appearance, I realize they must come from wealthy Spanish families who can afford to support them while attending the academy.

Santiago tears off a hunk of bread, sliding the loaf toward me. "Puvis de Chavannes is an amazing artist and teacher. I'm sure you've seen his murals at the Sorbonne."

"Actually, no. I'll have to cross the Seine and have a look. My brother is a chemistry student there." I break off a piece of bread to nibble and take a gulp of wine.

"So, are you an artist too?" asks Enrique.

"I'm a musician and composer," I say. "I play piano and harmonium at Le Chat Noir."

"Ahh, the cabaret on Rue Laval. We usually go to Auberge du Clou. Our friend Miguel will be starting-up a shadow theatre there soon. But we'll come hear you play sometime."

"I've been experimenting with the ancient Greek modal scale." I lean forward. "Antiquity and the medieval period are of great curiosity to me."

"Interesting you say that. One thing I admire about de Chavannes' work is the way he uses art of the past as a channel to a revolutionary modern art," says Santiago. "He uses subdued colors and forms, flattened to look like an ancient fresco."

"Now you've really stirred my interest." I take another swig from my cup.

"He takes these classical ideals, but simplifies them." Santiago shaves off several thin slices of sausage, eating them from the blade of the knife. "He distills the features down to the most essential elements."

"In Barcelona, we call this style Modernismo," says Ramón.

"I embrace those same ideals of simplification and purity, but in music."

Ramón strokes his beard. "Well, the philosophy behind Modernismo rejects the bourgeois esthetic. The very idea of producing what will sell commercially is the antithesis of true art."

"Not entirely," interjects Santiago. "The artist has two choices. Either he must remain outside of society so as not to betray his art, remain independent. Or, if he remains within society, he must boldly use his art to transform it."

"Transform society from within?" I say. "How lofty."

Clarassó slaps his hand on the table. "You are either the splinter in the finger of the bourgeoisie, or the cockerel outside the window waking them up."

"I wish I could hear more. This has all been so thought-provoking," I say, standing. "But, I'm suddenly reminded of the time and must get going." I finish off the last of my wine.

Santiago rises and we embrace. "You're a lifesaver, mi amigo. Be careful out there."

I thank my hosts for their hospitality, depart El Patio, and walk out into the evening showers. How similar this hive of artists is to the Pre-Raphaelite Brotherhood; Rosetti, Millais, and Hunt. The Muse must have intended for me to happen upon their lair. What a fresh perspective. My gait grows lighter. I lift my chin and whistle in the rain.

❧

Stirred by my conversation with Santiago and Ramon several days ago, I trek to the Sorbonne in the 5th Arrondissement to see the mural they spoke about. I position myself at the edge of the new hemispherical Grande Amphithéâtre. A secular Madonna, the Virgin of Science, sits at the center of the mural, the Sacred Wood. I gasp as I behold the wonderous panorama. Warmth expands through my chest and a thickness grows in my throat.

I open my music notebook to a clean page, and rest it across my thighs. I move the pencil to the staff and touch the lead to the paper. No thinking. Just write. A melody slowly drifts like smoky wisps of incense rising from a copper brazier where vermillion coals pulsate. Then I pause. Another swelling phrase flutters like a restive breeze rifling a diaphanous veil, and vanishes in the ether. Now fingertips outlined in firelight delicately stroke an Aeolian harp. Its silhouette is outlined against an amethyst horizon. The musical architecture then folds back around itself, returning in mirror image to the start as a palindrome. Sensuous tones descend in a final undulation to the last chord.

My gaze now drifts across the colossal mural. A smile spreads across my lips with tingling warmth in my face. I'm so grateful. Finally, the gifts of the Muse are starting to flow again. What shall I call it? Lowering the pencil to the top margin of the paper, I spell it out; G-n-o-s-s-i-s…e-n-n-e. Gnossienne. A new word; a name like Gymnopedies.

Chapter 8

October 1890, Paris, Opera District

Barely five months after settling into my new space in Montmartre, Claude sends a note begging for help to vacate his parents' apartment. Eager to support our developing friendship, I launch a reply, offering my assistance. At the designated time, I arrive in front of the humble building on Rue de Berlin. Claude paces out front, smoking. He wears a three-piece suit and tie and his hat tilts at an angle.

Claude grumbles. "The sooner I leave here, the better. I can't take it one more day." There are no furnishings to transport. An oversized steamer trunk sits on the sidewalk beside a suitcase and a bundle of books tied with twine.

"What happened?" I ask. I had been to supper with the Debussy family on several occasions. Claude's parents were polite but reserved. I sensed no undercurrent or discord, so Claude's hostility comes as a surprise.

"Happened? The same thing that always happens. I'm not wanted. Why do you think I became such a traveler?" Claude snatches the handle of the suitcase and gestures toward the stack of books. I curl my fingers around the twine, and together we heft the steamer trunk.

We totter through the gritty working-class neighborhood along the back side of Saint Lazare station.

"It's my mother," Claude says. "She didn't want any of us. We were always a burden to her. Hell, she sent my two sisters to an aunt when we were young."

I slowly shake my head. What an unsettling revelation. Claude must trust me a lot to be so candid. It makes me think of my sister, Olga, who was sent to live with relatives after our mother died suddenly. But in her case, the life of a bachelor father and two boys wasn't suitable for a girl.

"I'm supposed to be the favored one," Claude continues. "But at twenty-eight, she thinks she can still slap me around like I was eight."

I still hold resentment for the abuse I suffered at the hands of my stepmother. One more common thread ties us like brothers. "I know how you feel."

We reach the intersection of Place de L'Europe, panting and starting to sweat. Ahead, six bustling streets converge. It might be difficult to navigate without a rest. Claude directs me to set our burdens down. My hand burns where the twine bit into it.

"I think the reason my father started me at the Conservatoire was to get me out of the house," says Claude. "He was trying to protect me from my mother's temper."

"Does your father want you out, too?" I ask.

He contorts his mouth. "I'm a useless freeloader to him. He doesn't understand the music world. Since I'm not rich yet, he thinks I should join the navy or merchant marine."

I roll my eyes. "That'll keep you far away. It's so much like my experience. That's one of the reasons I joined the army before I could get drafted, and only had to serve a year."

He again grabs hold of the suitcase. "You ready to move on?"

I take out a handkerchief, using it as a buffer against the cutting twine. We resume our haul, dodging carriages and omnibuses traversing the plaza.

Claude raises his voice over the clatter. "My father has no say, anyway. She's holding something against him, always has, as long as I can remember."

I think of my father and how Eugenie manipulated him, too, at every turn. "What do you think it is? An affair?"

"No, nothing like that," Debussy huffs. "During the uprising of the Paris Commune, my father joined the Communards, actually became a captain. I was very young at the time. After the fall, he went to prison. We had to be taken in by relatives in Cannes."

In this we are very different. "A Communard? My father was on the other side; the Republican Garde that put down the revolt."

"Few people know. It's something we don't talk about in my family. Maybe it's because a threat still hangs over our heads or the shame of dishonor. But I believe she's never forgiven him. It's like he can't redeem himself."

"I see. But why take it out on you?"

Claude drops his head. "I don't know. Sometimes I feel like it's my job to make up for the disgrace, to restore the family name."

"I well know the unspoken obligations of the family ledger book. Who owes a debt, and who earns a dividend? Who determines the cost of belonging? What a terribly bourgeois way to think about family. But if I'd known you were so pressed to move out, we might have shared the cost of a nice atelier. I gave up mine on Rue Condorcet a few months ago."

"I'd have been no help, mon vieux," Claude says. "I'm broke. I'm throwing myself on the good graces of a lonely patron who loves music."

"And you're going to serenade him every night?"

Claude finally breaks a smile. "He's letting me stay in an unused room in his flat until I can save enough to get my own place. I hope to move-in with Gaby."

"Oh, I see. You're getting serious. When are you going to introduce her?"

"I'll bring her by Le Chat Noir, soon."

What a marvel Claude managed to find so generous a patron. However, it makes me wonder why someone with his credentials doesn't find a choirmaster or organist post; or a teaching position at a lycée or collège. But it's hard to imagine Claude ever playing the cabaret scene, as I do. We slog further along a treeless narrow lane.

"I'm sure you know how vital surroundings are to nurture unique compositions," he says.

"Of course, and the right company who inspires rather than discourages you."

"Indeed. And our disenchantment with the Rose+Croix. Although, I did have a turn of good luck in all this upheaval," he tells me.

"Well, I'm glad to hear it."

"Ferdinand Hérold invited me to join a weekly gathering held by poet Stéphane Mallarmé. I tell you Erik, it's almost a brotherhood, though mostly writers. I dare say, the only other musician I've seen there is Vincent d'Indy. But Mallarmé had heard my Cinq poems de Baudelaire. He was so impressed, he's asked me to collaborate on a theatrical production."

"A theatrical production? Sounds promising." A twinge of envy flares in my middle. But then I remind myself that my brotherhood of Spanish artists has helped me tap into the well of rich inspiration, too.

The narrow Rue de Lisbon meets the broad and elegant boulevard Malesherbes. Claude directs our course toward an expansive apartment structure with luminous ivory stone, chic awnings, and ornate grillwork on the balconies. We lodge the baggage on the stoop of number 76. Claude rings the bell beside enormous double doors. One door swings inward and a uniformed doorman surveys the inventory on the doorstep.

"Bonjour. You must be Monsieur Debussy," the man says, tipping his hat. "We were expecting you." He opens both entry doors wide and helps me drag the trunk into the vestibule. He goes to the reception counter and tugs on a bell cord. The sound of footsteps echoes from high in the spiral stairwell. A gentleman in formal attire descends.

"Welcome, I am Monsieur Dupin's valet. He's away, but he said you'd be arriving today. I have your room ready, if you'll come with me."

"Let me help you, sir," says the valet, and he takes the suitcase from Claude. I wrestle the steamer trunk with the doorman up four flights. We pass into an entry hall with burled maple wainscoting and a crystal chandelier. We deposit the trunk beside the armoire in a bedroom and the doorman promptly leaves the room. I notice the writing desk at the window and place the stack of books on top. It feels good to stretch my cramping hand. I meet Claude's gaping stare and shake my head.

The valet draws out a wallet from his breast pocket, sliding several bills from inside, and offers them to me. Everyone freezes, realizing the valet has mistaken me for a porter.

Claude chuckles uncomfortably. "Pardon, Monsieur. This is my dear friend Erik Satie, who was kind enough to help me drag all this across town."

A mortified look spreads over the valet's face. "I'm terribly sorry. Forgive my dreadful presumptions," he says.

My cheeks grow warm. Threadbare trousers and my wrinkled, collarless shirt render me a rag-tag day laborer. But then I dressed expecting hard work.

"When Monsieur has settled in, I'll have coffee and pastry for you in the parlor. Again, I do apologize." He turns with the roll of his eyes and leaves the room.

Claude and I burst into laughter.

"You should have let him tip me," I say. "I really could have used the money."

"I was too stunned."

"When were you going to mention your lonely sponsor is exceedingly wealthy?"

"I knew he had means, but I never expected this." Claude opens his hands and swivels. "Can you imagine composing in these surroundings?"

"Well, you're set for now." We leave the bedroom and move on to the parlor.

"Let's hope it provides my mind the conduit into the reservoir," Claude says.

I don't say so, but this place will only inspire stodgy old sonatas and concertos. The elegance of Etienne Dupin's parlor makes the bohemian in me want to run away. The puff and pomp I've tried to escape, Claude seems to be chasing after. But given his humble origins, I know why. I think it will cost him creatively, and hope it won't divide us. Still, how can I pass up the offer of free food. I serve myself two pastries on a small plate. Who knows when I'll have the chance to enjoy such a treat again? I settle into a velvet Queen Anne chair beside a tea table with a steaming silver coffee pot.

"Recently, I happened to fall in with a warren of artists from Barcelona," I tell him. "They live near me on the butte. They were debating about a trend in art, something they call Modernismo."

"Hmm, sounds intriguing." He takes a confectionary delight and joins me at the tea table. "Making music modern is what we're about." Claude takes the pot and pours coffee for us both.

"According to them, modernization in the arts either comes about by infiltrating institutions and subverting them from within," I tell him. "Or by raising an independent voice from outside that is so bold, it compels them to look in new directions." I set my coffee on the tea table and nearly swoon as the bite of Frangipane cream pastry dissolves on my tongue.

Claude smiles. "Well, I like the idea of being a subversive on the inside. One can use the familiar, traditional forms, but in a revolutionary way," Claude says with a mouthful of his Gâteau St. Honoré, not even trying to maintain etiquette. "The change will be more easily accepted. But I suspect we differ on that."

I smack my lips and take another sip of coffee. "Indeed. When you're on the inside, it's hard not to be tainted by it. It takes a free and independent voice from outside to truly bring innovation."

"Sure, if anyone will listen and not laugh." Claude finishes his treat in one bite. "But wouldn't it be an interesting experiment? Why don't we test that theory?"

"Are you serious?" I ask.

"Why not? Prove me wrong. A friendly wager, a challenge. Shall we?"

I toggle my head in contemplation a moment, and then meet his gaze. "You're on!"

Chapter 9

November 1890, 9th Arrondissement

THE LATE MORNING sun warms my shoulders as I open the door of the Auberge de Clou. The café is frequently empty at this hour, since most patrons prefer their coffee street-side, even on a chilly day. I prefer to try out my compositions without a distracting audience. The owner, Monsieur Thomachet thinks my playing adds to the ambience and it earns me a few tips. But as I enter the darkened dining area, a meeting is underway. Disappointed, I creep around the perimeter to the piano, trying to remain unobtrusive. I silently lean my umbrella against the side of the upright piano and slide onto the bench. I'll have to wait until the proceedings are finished to play. As my eyes adjust to the dim light, I take out my composition book and set it on the piano.

A deep voice, soothing as black velvet emanates from the other side of the room. "For obvious reasons gentlemen, we will have to find a new permanent meeting location. The owner was kind enough to let us gather here today. Be sure to extend your appreciation."

I try to ignore the dealings, adjusting the pages on the piano and lighting the candles flanking the small music shelf. Then, I light a cigarette.

The speaker continues. "In spite of the circus spawned by the journalistic jackals, I want you to know the real reason for severing ties with the Marquis de Guaïta."

Stanislaus de Guaïta? They are talking about the Rose+Croix. I pivot around halfway, piqued between curiosity and alarm. Joséphin Péladan sits in front of the fireplace in a fine suit. His previously wild hair and bifurcated beard are now neatly trimmed. Several other men have gathered around a handful of café tables pushed together. From their manner of dress, the attendees are all moneyed.

"For some time, I've had misgivings about the degree the Kabbalah has been emphasized and the Christian mystic traditions downplayed," Péladan continues.

I recognize the fair-haired Count de la Rochefoucauld as he raises his hand. "Jewish influence is a significant obstacle, particularly for those with title. It discourages their involvement in the brotherhood, and we need their financial backing."

"I'm aware of that," replies Péladan.

That the aristocracy are Jew-haters is a well-known but shameful foible.

"But for me, it was learning the extent of de Guaïta's opium habit," says Péladan. A wave of disparaging groans follows. "There is no place in the brotherhood for such activities, despite its alleged potency to awaken deeper levels of consciousness."

"You decried this vice in your novels for years, as we know well," adds another man I don't recognize.

"The order has but one purpose, to promote a spiritual aesthetic through art, and escape the vulgar and mundane tripe encouraged by institutions like Academie des Beaux-Arts."

I'm relieved to hear Péladan endorse the main reason I was attracted to the Order in the first place.

"As we re-affirm the mission of the Order of the Rose+Croix Catholique, I'd like to propose we launch our own art exhibition, the Salon de la Rose+Croix."

"Marvelous idea," says Rochefoucauld. The others murmur their support for the idea.

I grow even more attentive. The very idea of going up against established institutions and providing a venue for passed-over art and artists strikes a harmonious chord.

"We will put out a call for submissions, but make clear we are not interested in works featuring aspects of modern life, landscapes, or realism. No machines, or horse races. The work must focus on the symbolic, mythical themes of the Ideal. I propose our target date for the first salon be set in Spring. That gives us five months' time to get things organized."

The group begins naming various artists who best exemplify the values of the Rose+Croix; general estimates of costs for such an undertaking, and possible venues. Clearly these are men of means, ready to fund the event.

"I would like you gentlemen to consider another idea, as a way of promoting our aesthetic and inviting greater interest. What if we feature a series of music soirées, showcasing only contemporary composers; those whose work translates the secret and mystical ideas into music?"

I nearly bolt off the bench. I am so thrilled by this possibility I can hardly contain myself. Such a salon could champion my work; give me the exposure I've yearned for, and guarantee a major performance before wealthy patrons. One thing Péladan is definitely good at, is grabbing public attention.

On the other hand, Conrad will think I'm out of my mind. Father will say I've fallen under the spell of a con-man. And the traditional press invariably will attack us. But what happens when Salis finds out? Will it jeopardize my position at Le Chat Noir? Everything could collapse like a house of cards. Or, if I just sit here and say nothing, I could be throwing away the chance of a lifetime. It's definitely outside the mainstream and Claude challenged me to prove him wrong.

As soon as the meeting shows signs of breaking-up, I'm on my feet, approaching the charismatic leader.

"Master Péladan," I say, extending my hand. "I'm not sure if you will remember me. I am Erik Satie. I had just attended my first meeting of the brotherhood back in May."

Péledan's eyes widen and there's a hint of a smile. "What can I do for you, Monsieur Satie."

"Actually, it's what I can do for you, sir. I couldn't help overhear your plans for musical soirées in connection with the amazing salon you are launching. I would like to offer my services. I am a composer. And if you would indulge me with a few moments of your time, I'd like to play a sample of my work for you." This is far more brazen, far more self-assured than I ever thought myself to be. But if Péladan takes brotherhood seriously, he almost has to listen.

"Very well." Péladan gestures to Count Rochefoucauld to join him and the two of them follow me to the piano.

I'm quaking inside, and my heart is hurtling like a scared rabbit, rather than a hot one. Taking several deep breaths, I focus my consciousness through the third eye, quieting the tremor when I place my hands to the keys. After a few beats of silence, I look over at Péladan, who nods his head slowly with a quizzical slant in one brow.

"This piece is called the Ogives, based on medieval plainchant inspired by the stained glass in the Sainte-Chapelle."

"Sounds most intriguing. Let's hear it."

"I'll just play the first movement." I turn back to the keyboard. The melody begins to rise like a soft voice intoning a simple plaintive phrase. Then a grander reply resounds, as if the Sainte-Chapelle itself is answering. A humble hand presses against the cool stone block walls in awe, touching something old and deeply treasured. Vast ogival windows with trefoil tracery draw the eyes skyward where spears of kaleidoscopic color rise toward the vaulted-rib ceiling. Light pouring through a massive rosette window splays glowing colors in every direction. The walls glitter, inset with glass and gilded outlines resembling Limoges enamels of saints and martyrs. The penitent mill around the sanctuary devoid of pews. Their whispered prayers and the scuffing of their footsteps echo through the void.

After I play the last chord, I turn to face my appraisers. Péladan strokes his beard and slowly shakes his head. I'm afraid at first, he doesn't like it. But then he speaks.

"I'm impressed, Satie. You've done something extraordinary here. You've got me thinking about a whole range of possibilities."

I briefly describe my education, cabaret work, and published compositions. Péladan listens with great interest nodding his head. He turns to Rochefoucauld.

"We could offer Monsieur Satie a role, could we not, hire him for a variety of compositions and functions within the Order?"

Rochefoucauld smiles. "Of course. Are you thinking- choir master?"

"Perfect title, yes! What do you say, Satie? Maître de Chapelle de la Rose+Croix."

I'm dumbfounded. "I'm quite amenable. Thank you both for this opportunity."

They each offer their calling cards and I provide mine. After a round of Rémy Martin shots, the two enterprising cult barons take their leave. Only then do I stop to take stock of what I've just done. How will I manage to juggle two jobs, when I'm already too busy with one?

Chapter 10

March 1891- Montmartre

I SIT HUNCHED over a cup of coffee in the empty cabaret. Leaning on my forearm, I gaze up at the ethereal images on the huge painting behind the bar. I shake my head to throw off my gloom. Adolphe Willette painted this macabre fantasy for Salis when Le Chat Noir moved to this location. I've always admired the glossy oil because each time I study it, I see something new.

The images that resonate most today are the bewildered faces of the numerous Pierrots. Each face displays an aspect of lovers, poets, and musicians drifting in a cavalcade of hedonistic revelry and disillusionment. Floating headlong toward death, a quartet of ghostly pallbearer nuns ferries them to heaven. Clouds in the shape of a deaths-head contrast against a backdrop of gaslight gold and emerald sky. The silhouette of the Moulin de Galette lifts its blades, rendered as musical staves. They're annotated with the melody to Au Claire de la Lune and the Lent benediction "Spare Us, O' Lord", in Latin, Parce Domine, the painting's title.

That is how I picture myself, the little guy. I'm Pierrot in a precarious balance between mystical yearnings, the desperation of a starving cabaret pianist, and the artist with lofty aspirations. But I'm now facing a sort of Rubicon.

Besides offering riotous entertainment, Le Chat Noir also publishes a journal. People view the magazine as a source of all things new and notorious. The editorial team regularly singles out some public figure who has distinguished himself through scandal, poor taste, or sheer idiocy. They run the person's name on the masthead. He's listed as the editorial secretary, with some àpropos insulting designation. Readers can't wait to see who they'll lampoon next.

Unfortunately, Rodolphe Salis has gotten himself in hot water. Grand Master Péladan just announced the reorganization of the Rose+Croix under his new rubric. Salis and company view him as a grandstanding charlatan and listed him on the masthead as a "proven ass". And now Péladan has sued. That places me in the middle of a tug-of-war.

A kindly voice interrupts my reverie. "May I join you?"

I look up. My mentor, Alphonse Allais, stands beside me. "Of course. Please, sit."

Alphonse sets his brimming cup and saucer on the table at my right hand, and sidles onto a cane chair. Lighting a match, he reignites his pipe with several aromatic puffs. "Morose, or hung-over?" he asks.

"Probably both," I reply.

"Some seamstress or dancer, I hope."

I snicker. "No." I take a sip of my coffee and weigh whether Alphonse's advice is worth the cost of revealing my dilemma. "If you were caught between two friends who were quarreling, what would you do? You're not in agreement with either side."

Alphonse turns up his hands. "I'd have to declare myself neutral." He plucks a lump of sugar from the cut glass dish, drops it into his coffee, and stirs.

"Let's say, you can't. Suppose your mere association with one is viewed as a betrayal by the other, and vice versa."

Allais twists the end of his moustache. "That is a conundrum."

"To raise the ante a little; imagine your livelihood is at stake."

Allais drums his fingers on the tabletop, studying my face. I've probably said too much.

"This has greater importance to you than an intellectual exercise. You're not involved in that little Rose+Croix adventure, are you?"

I take a deep breath. "What if I am?"

Alphonse rears back, the usual levity draining from his face. "My dear young friend, that is unwise for a whole host of reasons. Because, if Salis finds out, he'll fire you. Péladan just announced he is suing Salis for slander, for Christ's sake."

"I know." I swirl the coffee and frothy head of cream in my cup. "I've been fretting about it. I never expected this to happen." I slurp the bitter foam off the top.

"You are an innocent bystander caught in the crossfire." Allais rubs his forehead. "Péladan is enormously popular and respected by many."

"I rank his work right up there with Flaubert's Salambo or even Zola's writing," I say.

"I confess, I love his novels, too: The Vice Supreme and The Fallen Heart. With a big name like his, anyone could be seduced into believing it could help your career. But his latest stunt is a pitiful, self-aggrandizing charade. Do you know what kind of man you're dealing with?"

"Salis can be an ass, too. Don't tell him I said that."

"Of course not. But Salis is a known quantity. If you're going to align with Péladan, it's best for you to resign gracefully rather than get fired. I'd hate to see you go, but I'd understand."

"I appreciate your advice." I drain my cup, stand, and offer my hand to Allais.

"Be careful, Erik."

Le Chat Noir has no dearth of defectors. Albert Tinchant, Vincent Hyspa, and even Emile Godeau got fed up with Salis and moved on to greener pastures. The clock is ticking and my job security is becoming more tenuous by the hour. If I get fired, I won't be able to survive. I've learned and grown immeasurably as an artist in this place. My political savvy and sense of humor were forged here. But I've been slaving away for Péladan and Count Rochefoucauld for months, composing scores for two plays, not to mention the music for the upcoming Salon of the Rose+Croix. I've yet to see the promised compensation. Obviously, I can't pursue both opportunities without reprisals. There's always the Auberge de Clou. Maybe it's time I hedge my bets, and talk to the owner.

❧

March 1891 – Marais District

As Claude and I exit the ancient landmark, I lift my eyes to the stained-glass windows and ribbed vaults inside the nave of the Church of Saint Gervais. The Sunday choral recital featuring the most amazing Gregorian Chants just finished. It made me lose all sense of time and filled me with a buoyant lightness. These weekly feasts for the ears are becoming ever more popular and some of the parishioners have started to complain about young people taking up too many pews. Imagine that. You'd think they'd want us in church.

"This was an unexpected pleasure, Claude. Thanks for inviting me," I say.

"It's great to see you so happy again, mon vieux," says Claude. "You've not been yourself for some time."

"I'm all nerves, really. If only I can get through these next two weeks. My life is beginning to feel like one of those damnable carnival rides, jerking you up in the air and then dropping you repeatedly, until you retch."

We cross the street and walk along the perimeter of the plaza in front of the Hotel de Ville and then make our way to the promenade along the Seine. The early Spring air is fresh from overnight showers.

"I'd probably feel the same way, in your position. You've poured sweat and tears into this Rose+Croix project."

"A part of me is thrilled to have my music performed for the first time in a major public venue. But another part of me can't wait until it's over," I say.

Looming ahead stands a colonne Morris capped with an onion finial, and plastered with advertisements. There in plain view is the poster for The Salon of the Rose+Croix. In ethereal shades of green, the panneau features two slender women draped in gossamer, ascending a stairway overgrown with lilies and roses, and framed in a border of rose bramble.

"Will you look at that," says Claude. "From the day they first started pasting those posters around the city, it's become the talk of all Paris."

"Yes, but in less than a week, someone set out to sabotage us. We had to order a second run, because during the night, scavengers took matting knives and removed many of them."

"Someone could just be collecting them for resale," says Claude. "Their Art Nouveau style is unparalleled, Erik."

"That's possible," I say. "But unlikely. I'm more worried Péladan has made enemies. Someone is trying to stop us."

"There's no shortage of controversy. I read the interview he gave Le Figaro."

"Yes, and that was a first," I say, "seeing my name on the front page of a major newspaper. What if the Salon is a disaster, a colossal failure? I'm mortified and proud at the same time."

"It's definitely drawing public attention. Says Claude. "I envy you. Did the Grand Officers decide which selections they want performed at the soirée?"

"You'll be surprised." I grin. "They chose the "Sonneries of the Rose+Croix", the processional I composed for the initiation rite."

Claude bounces. "Really? You mean the one where you used the Golden Ratio?"

"Yes. Péladan also wants it to play when the doors open on the first night."

Claude brushes his forehead. "Ouah! That will create quite the atmosphere."

"And it's being published."

"Paris has never heard anything like that." He shakes his head with wonder. "Do you understand what this means?"

"Everything. Over a thousand tickets have sold in advance. 228 unconventional works of art will be on display. Legends, myths, dreams, and allegory, all of which will be viewed accompanied by my music."

"Marvelous." Claude closes his eyes a moment and then leans toward me. "The revolution has begun. And so far, the outlier is inching ahead."

I smirk. "A warning shot across the bow."

We reach the metal suspension bridge that crosses the Seine to Ile de la Cite, the Pont d'Arcole and stand elbow to elbow staring into the rushing waters.

"Things are moving in the right direction for us both," Claude says. "I'm considering a commission to score the incidental music for a new production."

"Great news. Whose production."

"Jules Bois."

I stiffen and turn to face him. "Wait. Not his project Satanic Nights, is it?"

Claude turns and leans his back against the balustrade. "What better opportunity?" He juts out both palms and waves them like a conductor. "Huysmans' final installment of The Damned was just published in the newspaper. It's outrageously popular. And with the new Heaven and Hell cabaret opening, I just thought, here's my chance."

I rub my forehead and waver about offering my opinion. "I'm the first to support freedom of expression and experimentation. You know I'm a free thinker. I don't mean to offend. But from everything I've heard, his work goes too far. Child-sacrifice. Do you want that to be your claim to fame? Especially as your first major work before all Paris?" My heart is thundering.

Claude grows silent and drops his gaze. He folds his arms. I realize my assessment must be hard to hear, since Claude had already abandoned another theatrical project, Rodrique et Chimène. And he'd written to the playwright Maeterlinck requesting to score La Princesse Maleine, but was turned down in favor of Vincent d'Indy.

"I just don't seem to be getting anywhere." He turns back to the surging river, and hunches over the balustrade. "I composed a dozen piano pieces and recently scored three poems by Verlaine. But do you think any of the academic circles and music societies show the slightest interest? What good was a Prix de Rome? I may as well pitch my music into the Seine and dive in afterward."

"Dive in afterward? Don't say those things," I say and put my hand on his shoulder. "I have numerous pieces that have neither been published, nor performed in public, and may never. But these things don't happen overnight. It takes time and a little luck. You're an immensely talented composer, Claude. You're just getting started. We both are."

"It's a good thing we have each other," Claude says.

"What became of the project with Mallarmé? The Afternoon of a Faun."

"I've drawn a blank. I don't know where to go with it."

"Yet," I say, and pat him on the back. "It will come to you when you least expect it."

Chapter 11

March 1892, 8th Arrondissement

THE COUNT DE la Rochefoucauld sent me a blue pneumatic, urgently summoning me to a meeting this morning at the Gallerie Durand-Ruel. The gallery has not yet opened for viewers, when I pace across the hardwood floor toward the anteroom where the ensemble has set up for rehearsal. I can hear a heated exchange, even as I pass the tufted leather couches and clusters of Louis XIV arm chairs in the foyer.

Péledan's voice booms. "You wouldn't dare dismiss him. What gives you the authority to make program changes without consulting me?"

"You might know about art, Joséphin, but you know next to nothing about music."

I recognize the other voice as the Count's. I hope they aren't talking about me. My heart leaps into my throat.

"How dare you try to foist a pitiful amateur onto the public under false pretenses. I told you, I vehemently oppose his participation in the premiere," says the Count.

I hesitate at the arching threshold to the music chamber, quaking from top hat to boot strap. "Pardon, Messieurs, bonjour."

The two combatants turn, their infuriated glare locking on me.

"Oh good, our Maître de Chapelle is here," says the Count. "Satie, you weigh in on this matter, will you?"

I adjust my pince-nez. "Sir?" My stomach roils.

"Péladan believes Louis Benedictus is a suitable conductor for the concert series, and is even trying to insert one of his supposed compositions. As far as I'm concerned, he's a fake, a hobbyist. He can't conduct an orchestra any better than the newsboy on the corner. Don't you agree?"

Still shaking, I measure my words. "Well, he has no professional experience."

"There, you see, you see," hisses the Count. "I've hired Lamoureux."

I gasp. "The eminent conductor Charles Lamoureux?"

"Wouldn't he be far better to conduct your music?"

"Of course. It would be an honor. He's probably one of the biggest promoters of Wagner, whose work you so admire, Master Péladan."

"Regardless, the program has already been printed. We can't change it now even if I agree; which I don't. I insist on Benedictus."

"See here," says the Count. "I have invested far too much into this undertaking to allow you to make me a laughing stock and turn this into a circus. Satie agrees with me. Benedictus is out."

Péladan stomps his foot, the resulting thunder echoing through the gallery. "I won't stand for this. I'm the director of the Salon. I make the final decision."

The two men glare at each other for an excruciating moment.

The Count huffs and runs his hand back across his scalp. "I was hoping it would never come to this, Joséphin. But you give me no alternative. The Gallerie Durand-Ruel is leased in my name and mine alone. Legally you haven't a leg to stand on. I'm legally the director."

"You reprobate. What hubris! If you so much as try to go forward against my wishes, I'll get a restraining order and close the whole thing down."

I wilt with a sinking ache in my chest. My one opportunity to get my music before a huge Paris audience is going up in smoke.

"You just try," shouts the Count.

Péladan snorts and flails his fists in the air, baring his teeth. "I excommunicate you from the Order." He turns and storms out of the salon.

I rub the front of my thighs to soothe my spongy knees. It seems at this moment, all my hard work and dreams have just been snatched from my grasp and pitched down the pissoir. I hang my head to one side with a groan. "Merde, merde."

The Count blows out a flustered breath and straightens his tie. "First de Guaïta, then me. The man is impossible to work with. But we're not sunk yet. You'll see. It may be a setback, but he can't stop us. I'll bring all my forces, financial and legal to bear. We'll have our concert series, I promise you, by the Eye of Ra."

The Eye of Ra? I didn't want to be in this loyalty bind. I hate having to take sides. All I wanted was to perform my music for people who appreciate it. Right now, from where I stand, that dream is an illusion. Everything is in jeopardy.

Nothing in the past six months has gone the way I imagined. After a two-week delay, the Count de la Rochefoucauld prevailed, and the concert series is finally going forward without Joséphin Péladan. The cool air of evening streams through the glass entry doors at the elegant Gallerie Durand-Ruel. Arriving patrons are awash in so many perfumes, the blend is an intoxicating brew. Fans, pearls, and elbow length gloves of every hue imaginable hold the playbill, covered with ogival arches and Chaldean winged seraphim. Despite the traditional art critics' indifference to the painters Böcklin, Khnopff, and Schwabe; the popular press and the public have flocked to the exhibit. They marvel at the hauntingly beautiful images of the Angel of Death, Arthurian legends, mermaids, centaurs, and more. The Salon de la Rose+Croix is underway.

Standing at the perimeter beside a beautiful harp and ensemble, I greet attendees with the Count de La Rochefoucauld, the Salon's underwriter. I'm enjoying the gaping stares, gasps and moans. There's an occasional tip of the head and attentive ear inclined toward the harps and flutes. This brings me a wry smile. Visitors seem to keep time with the heartbeat rhythm of my chivalric music, as they sidle from painting to painting, entranced by the numinous strains.

I catch a glimpse of my father and brother studying the artwork. I'd sent a copy of the program and three tickets to the event as soon as they came off the press. But I see my stepmother chose not to attend. No matter. It may not be the Opera Garnier or Theatre du Chatelet, but I hope my father will be impressed, nonetheless. I easily fall back on the etiquette he taught me as a boy, for our many visits to his one-time employer, Albert Sorel and his diplomatic circle. I hail them with a well-mannered wave. Father's face brightens and they head our direction. We greet each other with a peck on the cheek, and I introduce the Count La Rochefoucauld. Father shuffles back a step and makes a polite bow.

"No need for that, Monsieur Satie," says the Count, offering his hand. "Please enjoy the exhibit and the concert."

Father beams a satisfied smile as I guide them to their seats. I return to Rochefoucauld's side as patrons file into the rows of seating. The Gallerie Durand-Ruel hums with polite conversation, soft laughter and rustling taffeta. I continue doing my share of bowing and hand kissing, leaving the Count to fill in the gaps with aristocratic gossip and horse racing trivia.

This seems like a miracle. I want to dazzle their ears with music unlike anything they've ever heard; the watershed of hard work and self-directed study. I catch a glimpse of my reflection in the window glass against the indigo star-filled sky. My long dark coat sets off my nearly shoulder length auburn hair and smooth copper beard. I stand a little taller and smile to myself.

The ringing of chimes announces it's time for the ensemble to begin the concert. After a few minutes the audience quiets and Charles Lamoreaux raises his baton. The first notes of my Sonneries de la

Rose+Croix fill the salon. A clarion fanfare brings forth a musical vision, a procession of medieval knights marching through the gates of the imagination. Their mail shimmers. Multi-hued gonfalons flutter in the breeze. Once inside the castle walls, the clerics and chanting mystics bestow honor on those gathered. The faces of the listeners are filled with awe. Lips part in wonder and eyes search the ether for understanding. When the ensemble finishes, it brings a stirring applause.

Next, Prelude to the Sons of the Stars sweeps the audience away into a trance. Listeners slowly climb a spiral to gaze into a darkened expanse. Drifting and tumbling, they trace a comet's course through the glittering vastness, past gaseous giants and concentric rings, and finally wandering off into the limitless darkness. When the last strains of music bathed in starlight slowly fade, a stunned hush lingers over the audience. It seems like they have been hypnotized. Count de La Rochefoucauld leads the ovation. The audience rises to their feet.

"Bravo, bravo!"

"They love it," says the Count, patting me on the shoulder. I step forward and bow. My eyes search the seats for my family. They stand clapping. Conrad is shaking his head with a wild congratulatory grin. But my father has a mystified expression. He doesn't know what to think of it. But as he looks around, taking in the overwhelming approval, he shakes his head with the hint of a smile. This brings a twinge to my gut, and I smile, too. My eyes water.

I thought I'd be relieved when the Salon was all over. But as the latest editions of newspapers and journals hit the newsstands, I've been on pins and needles. My intention today is to pour over the critiques of the soirée together with Claude, hoping to learn something useful. I collect a few of the popular periodicals, and Claude is bringing newspapers. I wander down from the butte with a stack of journals under my arm.

Claude's fascination with all things from across the channel brings us to an English tea room today. Although I expect I'll need something a little stronger when we're through. After entering through the leaded glass door, the modest tea room is awash in floral chintz and creamy woodwork. Afternoon sun pours through the open mullion windows with flower boxes overflowing with red geraniums. Claude sits waiting in the corner, porcelain teacup in hand, with a tiered pastry stand and China tea service centered on the table.

"Who'd imagine this kind of place would be to your taste," I say, as we embrace.

"Why, it's a great place to meet women; the right kind, anyway."

I survey the attractive clientele with momentary longing, and nod. "True." I set the journals on an empty chair, remove my hat, and take a seat at the petite table. I drop a chunk of sugar in my cup. A pungent steam rises as Claude pours the tea and I stir to dissolve the sugar.

"Even though you heard the music numerous times; I appreciate you and Gaby attending the dress rehearsal."

"Well, I thoroughly enjoyed it," says Claude. "So did Gaby. Here, try one of these." Claude slides a small basket of currant scones in my direction.

I bring a scone to my lips, smelling the distinct oat and soda flavor. I haven't eaten one of these since I was little, slathered with sweet butter and strawberry preserves the way my Scottish mother served them.

"Joséphin Péladan is far more interested in promoting himself than any ancient revealed truths or inspired social change," I say. "It took me a few months to figure out his real agenda; which was to take credit for my music. But the experience wasn't a complete waste of energy."

"I'm glad things finished on a high note. But I presume that ends your affiliation."

"Péladan, yes. But Count Antoine will be a valuable patron and ally in the future. Had it not been for him, the Salon might never have happened at all. I stepped down as the Maître de Chapelle, however."

Holding the teapot, Claude refills his own cup and quietly stirs in some lemon and sugar.

"I was looking toward the poor house before the exposure brought new work," I tell him. "I've just been offered a commission composing the incidental music for a play, The Nazarene."

"Great! Your name is out there, now. Did you read the article by your friend Allais? I loved his little parody in Le Chat Noir Journal. I hope you're not too terribly angry with him," says Claude, leaning forward, "calling you Esoterik Satie."

I chuckle. "No, not at all," I say. "I loved his play on words describing Péladan, too. Quite hilarious, juxtaposing the faux Mage of Livarot and the malodorous cheese from Normandy, Fromage Livarot."

"Indeed." Claude laughs. He then draws out the latest editions of two newspapers, neatly folded to the article. "Le Figaro said nothing about the music, only the art. But the reporter at Le Temps wrote it afforded him 'a slumber of angels.'"

"Does he mean it was heavenly, or bored him to sleep?"

"I suspect the latter," Claude says, eyeing me as if to assess my reaction. "But Willy's review is the most unflattering."

"I expect as much, from him. Let me see."

Claude hands me the neatly folded copy of Echo de Paris. Rigid as a tombstone, I scour the article with my eyes. "Godly pillars of harmony... he's being facetious." The knot in my stomach twists tighter. "My "Sons of the stars"... 'three neurasthenic preludes'." I close my eyes, shaking my head and then continue down the column. The article finishes with 'tap merchant music from the ex-pianist of Le Chat Noir' which brought me only mediocre satisfaction'."

"Don't take anything he says to heart," says Claude. "The whole point of his column is only to show-off his malicious puns and gratuitous diatribes."

"He's made me a laughing stock." I take a small metal flask with brandy from my breast pocket and drizzle a little into my tea. I offer some to Claude, but he shakes his head.

"That's his job. If he's not cutting someone into ribbons, he wouldn't be Willy."

"He goes way beyond a Pince-Sans-Rire or Fumisme, to the extreme." I have the urge to vomit. I must find a way to issue a rejoinder, get back at him, somehow.

"I really believe you might be the bellwether of a whole new trend. And I'm not alone in that estimation, if the opinions of those in Mallarmé's cabal are any indication. Don't dwell on one or two bad reviews. I'd venture these weeklies are far more complimentary." He brushes a finger down the stack of journals I'd set on the empty seat. "The praise just hasn't caught up with you yet." He pats my upper arm.

"You really think so? I want to believe that. I feel extremely alone much of the time."

Claude slowly shakes his head. "How else would it feel if you're out ahead of the pack? Have faith and keep going, outsider. So far, you're winning the bet. You caught Willy's attention. Make it work for you."

"Our crusade is just beginning." I smile at his vote of confidence. "Your turn is next." But inside I'm still fuming. I slurp my brandy infused tea. "The ridicule still stings. How do I endure and get past it?"

"Erik, it always will, regardless of how great you or I become," says Claude. "I think you have to trust the Muse. Remind yourself she doesn't lie, even if others can't see it."

"I think newspaper critics are would-be writers who can't write, so they take it out on everyone else." I fold my arms.

"Maybe," says Claude. "But with a battle ahead of us, it will get far worse before it gets better. We both need to grow thicker skin, and we need each other. Just wait, you'll see."

Chapter 12

January 1893, Montmartre

COMPOSING THEATRICAL SCORES is becoming a new mainstay for me, keeping coal on the fire, beans in the pot, and my hinges well oiled. My part-time stint playing piano at the Auberge de Clou has graduated into a fulltime engagement with the Théâtre d'ombres, under the direction of Miguel Utrillo. Vincent Hyspa, another Le Chat Noir expatriate, recruited me to work on the holiday production about the Magi called Noël. Together, he and I transformed a traditional Christmas pageant into social and political commentary, cabaret style. The season has finally reached its finale and I welcome a short respite. After these many months of hard work, I'm celebrating tonight with the performers and crew. The director is holding a Fête des Rois at his Montmartre home.

Miguel's apartment borders the grounds of the Moulin de Galette. Opalescent glass sconces cast a warm glow onto rich anaglypta wall covering above the wainscoting. It's rather posh for a professed bohemian. A local songstress, Arlette Dorgère, has arrived just ahead of me. Her well-dressed male companion hangs her fur trimmed cape on the hallstand. How alluring she looks with her tiny cinched waist in a peacock green evening dress. It must be nice to have the company of a lovely lady.

How long has it been since I've known the charms of a woman? Jeanne ended our relationship three years ago. I've intentionally avoided getting involved with anyone, except the occasional tryst at the cabaret. Certain women make a habit of throwing themselves at performers. But these mean nothing and feel empty. However, Patrice has settled into a serious relationship, and Claude has moved in together with his girlfriend Gabrielle. So, I've started to get the itch again. Here I am at a New Year's party, solo.

I stow my wraps. Lingering at the archway, I size up an abundance of feather boas, beaded gowns, and half-exposed bosoms. The air is a mélange of pipe tobacco, ladies' cologne, and alcohol. Guests decorate an evergreen Sapin de Noël with apples, ribbons, and paper flowers. An aproned attendant carries around a lacquer tray with hors d'oeuvres. This is nothing like the raucous bacchanalia last year with these same Catalan friends at their humble dwelling. Much has changed.

Clean-shaven Miguel comes to greet me, an elegant host in a midnight blue dinner jacket. "Happy New Year, Satie," he says, and grasps my hand.

"This is quite an event."

"For all your hard work," replies Miguel and offers me a glass of champagne from a silver tray on a mahogany credenza. "Enjoy, mon vieux."

Santiago comes up behind me, draped in his long black cloak and holding his sketch pad under his arm. "Bon any nou!" he says in Catalan, patting me on the shoulder. "Now that you're here, we can really get this celebration started."

Ramón and Ignacio sit in an adjoining room, where someone plays a simplified version of Au Flambeau on the piano. I saunter into the parlor with Santiago and peer toward the keyboard. Seated at the polished upright is an arresting young woman. Her hair gleams like polished rosewood, coiled against the nape of her neck. Several renegade strands spiral free. Her scarlet moiré gown has mutton-leg sleeves. A handful of guests gathers in a semi-circle behind her, joining in song.

Santiago and I settle into the tufted divan beside our friends. I lean sideways toward Ramón. "Who's the stunner?"

Ramón is already sketching on a tablet of paper. "Don't ask. She is not the one for you, my dear Sadi." he says. His eyes shift back and forth from the subjects to the page.

But I can't help staring at her. Something seems familiar, her hair color or her dainty size. A peculiar pang flickers deep in my gut; haunting and melancholy.

"You don't already know her?" asks Santiago. "I thought you knew everyone on the butte. She moved into the greenhouse atelier right after we moved out."

I scrunch my face, confused. "No. If I'd met her, I'd most certainly remember."

"Mademoiselle Valadon," says Santiago.

Ramón turns to speak directly in my ear. "She used to be Miguel's lover," he says softly, and then glances around as if he'd said something he shouldn't.

"Oh," I groan, straightening. "Used to be? Or, are they still…"

"Who can say," chimes Santiago. "A migratory bird, that one."

"She modeled for Toulouse-Lautrec, Puvis de Chavannes, and even Renoir."

The implications of his comment are not lost on me. I deduce they don't hold her in very high regard. There is likely a whole story they can't share in this setting. But I can wait for the details. At the moment, I don't care.

With a saucy tilt of her head and free-spirited savvy, she laughs. The group negotiates which song to sing next, that she knows how to play; La Marche des Rois Mages.

An overwhelming urge comes over me, like a massive wave thrusting a piece of flimsy driftwood onto the shore.

I stand up. "I think I'll join the singing," I say, handing my drink to Ramón.

Ramón shakes his head. "It's a sad day, my friend."

Santiago rolls his eyes. "Go with god."

Now my core is fluttering like leaves in the wind and my heartbeat dances a rondo allegro. To merge into the group, I wedge between singers and break through to the side of the piano. Propping one elbow on the top, I lean into my hand, watching her and adding my deep bass voice to the song. What a charming heart-shaped face, and pouty sensuous mouth. She glances up with a skeptical slant in one brow, over eyes the color of azure twilight.

"Bonsoir," she says, doing a double-take, as she plays the interlude to the song.

"Bonne année," I beam. The music comes to the verse and I harmonize with the others. I also notice Santiago is sketching me. I smile and Santiago grins back, shaking his head. As the song continues, more people gather around the piano. The entire room fills with voices. When the song finishes, some raise their glasses and a spontaneous applause breaks out.

"You should be the one sitting here." Her alto voice only adds to the mystery of Mademoiselle Valadon.

"You seem to be playing just fine. And anyway, how do you know I play?"

"I've seen you perform; several times. Satie, isn't it? Erik Satie?"

"Yes."

"Call me Suzanne." She offers her hand, searching my eyes. "Will you play? I'd love to hear your music again."

"For you? With pleasure."

One of the servers rings a small bell from the dining room next to the parlor, announcing it is time to slice the Galette des Rois.

"But it appears we have to eat galette first," I say.

Suzanne stands up and sidles away from the piano bench. I sense a sweet quality about her, like a young lamb, feisty but fragile. We file behind the others toward the dining room.

The housekeeper hands out porcelain plates heaped with the frangipane pastry. Chatter mounts as people speculate who will find the féve, the small china figurine, baked into the cake.

"I've been working on a new piece," I tell her, "incidental music for a play, The Legend of Eginhard."

"Who is that?"

"He was a courtier to Charlemagne, who fell in love with the king's daughter, Emma."

"Ahh. Star-crossed lovers."

"They thought so when they eloped and feared they were doomed when Charlemagne caught up with them. But he merely wanted to give his blessing."

"A legend, you say."

I nod. "And what do you do, Mademoiselle?"

"Suzanne. The New Year also brings new ventures for me. Three of my paintings have sold."

"You're an artist?"

"Oil and pastel." She tips her head at an angle with a wry little smile, popping a bite of pastry into her mouth. Her eyes widen. She switches her mouth around and then plucks the féve out onto her plate. "I found the féve," she calls with excitement. "I found it."

Cheers break out in the assembly. Fresh bottles of champagne are opened with much fanfare to toast the queen. A cardboard crown with paste jewels is placed on her head. After toasts for the New Year, the time comes for the queen to choose a dance partner.

All the bachelors draw to the inside of the circle. Suzanne looks all around, amidst sighs and whispers. Her eyes fix on Miguel Utrillo for a moment. He tips his head, his expression shifting from indifference to sad resignation. I can tell he still has strong feelings for her by the unspoken message passing between them. Then she turns to me.

"I choose Erik!" The crowd cheers and laughs. I swallow hard. My boss's former lover holds out her hand. Am I going to regret this? I glance toward Miguel, who stares beneath somber brows. He lowers his face, and gestures openhandedly like he's releasing a dove.

Someone steps to the piano and begins to play a slow waltz. I take her hand and place my other palm on the small of her back. She draws closer to me. My mouth goes dry and my heart trots into a scherzo. I wonder if she can feel the tremor in my touch. Gazing into her blissful face, we begin to dance, slowly revolving, lights scintillating like sparks. The other guests choose partners and join in. I focus on her violet eyes and the softness of her breasts in taffeta pressing into me. Her sweet lilac fragrance is intoxicating. Where will this path take me? The music finally comes to an end, but I don't want our interaction to, and prolong holding her hand a measure longer.

"You mentioned you'd sold some of your own paintings," I say.

She smiles, looking up into my face. "Yes. My dream is to be able to paint full time and never model again."

"What you need is to find a wealthy patron, a countess or duchess."

She glances away. "I wish it were so simple. If only motives were clear and uncomplicated."

I can only guess what she is alluding to. Artists always expect sexual favors from their models. I sense she's had more than her share of debasing self-compromise. And I presume the unspoken rules of patronage are not much different. She strays over to a credenza and takes a glass of champagne, and offers one to me.

I take a sip and give her a soft smile. "I imagine you've been exploited far too many times with few rewards. Reprehensible rakes. No sense of honor and dignity."

Suzanne straightens, and slowly backs away. She has a stunned expression on her face. Have I offended her?

"If I've said something too bold, I certainly didn't mean to upset you. Please forgive me."

"No, you're right. Absolutely right." She blinks hard. "I'm just not used to a man seeing the truth; let alone expressing it with such frankness."

Despite her sassy independent façade, Suzanne conveys a neediness she tries to disguise. It seems compelling and frightening at the same time. She arouses the heroic in me. I'm not sure if that's good or bad. But I want to restore her smile, and shift the conversation away from the personal, sharing some of the fascinating content of obscure books I'm reading. I tell her about my terrible experience at the Paris Conservatoire, and even voice my aspiration to break away from stale music traditions.

"So, have you always been a composer?" she asks.

"Well, I worked in my father's stationery store briefly, did a short tour of duty in the army. Other than that, I guess you could say I'm a Gymnopédiste."

She makes a funny face. "Not a gymnast. A Gymnopédiste? What is that?"

I speak with an affectation like some university scholar. "In ancient Sparta, they held an annual festival in honor of Apollo called Carneian. The youth would display their athletic and military prowess by dancing in the nude."

She laughs. "Naked?"

"Yes. You can see images of them on pottery in the Louvre. The Greeks worshipped the beauty of the human form."

"As an artist model, I'm all too aware of that. So, you're a naked dancer."

I shift my stance and grin. "In a manner of speaking."

"You're also quite the comedian. I should like to see this naked dance."

"That could be arranged," I say in a sultry tone.

She returns a sultry smile, looking me up and down. "Actually, Erik, I'd like to paint you. I want to capture you, just the way you are now, your sensuous smile. Will you sit for me?"

Unable to contain my silly grin, I lower my face. "If you really…" My voice falters.

"Yes, would you? I'd love that." She tilts her head.

"D'accord. Let's see, the cabaret is dark on Mondays and Tuesdays."

"Perfect. Tuesday next?"

I nod. "What time?"

"I finish my art class at 11:00. So, come by my studio in the greenhouse at half-passed."

My heart drums at the thought of being alone with her in her private space. "11:30 it is. I look forward to it."

Chapter 13

January 1893, Montmartre

Crystals frost the windows of El Patio, making the greenhouse studio into a cut glass candy jar. I balance on a stool trying not to move, while Suzanne stands at the easel, brushing paint on the canvas. It's an unhurried late morning, set apart from time in a glass case. The slightest disturbance might break the spell. I'm trying to revel in the moment. But questions and doubts buzz around in my mind like an irritating housefly. How does Suzanne keep her small coal stove so well supplied; while I collect old newspapers to stoke my fire? But I refuse to dwell on that today.

Could there be anything more pleasant than to be with her? Her eyes are all over me, inspecting my features. Clouds of fleeting emotions drift across her face, mixed with dispassionate scrutiny. What am I in her eyes? A friend, a lover, or just a subject. We make conversation at first. Both of us were raised Catholic, but came away from the experience with scars and regrets. Suzanne does not consider herself a religious person. Although, she believes an angel has always protected her.

"I was baptized, Marie-Clementine, a name I've always despised," she says.

"What made you choose the name Suzanne?"

She daubs the palate, then the painting, tipping her head to one side. "Henri Toulouse-Lautrec said it is the name of a popular song from America. It sounds modern."

An unfamiliar feeling washes over me. It scares me. I try to ask with curiosity, "Do you still model for Toulouse-Lautrec?"

A furrow in her brow tells me she doesn't like the inquiry. "Not anymore. He was like an older brother. He encouraged me to paint and showed me how."

I stop talking. Her answer doesn't soothe my insecurity, but I know I have no right to pry. All I know is Toulouse-Lautrec came from an aristocratic family. I'd met the odd little man a few times and admired his artwork. It alarms me to think of her sharing his bed.

Suzanne has drawn out unexpected feelings, surprisingly strong for just having met her. In my gut I know how easily relationships end. Past losses whisper from the corners of my mind; my sister, my mother, my grandmother, Jeanne, and then the silence that followed their inexplicable disappearance. I have to stave off those memories. For now, I want to be possessed by Suzanne, and revel in the moment.

How did she bewitch me so completely? She has dainty hands, so precise and skilled with a brush. Her eyes have a slight downward slant. Her pouty lower lip speaks of a hidden sorrow, even when she smiles. Her often brash and vivacious allure is merely the lacy veil she drapes across it. Meanwhile, she brushes away, stroking gently in the vapors of linseed and turpentine. Her eyes move back and forth from the canvas to me.

"The angle of the light has shifted," she says. "The contrast is poor with the cloud cover. I think I'll let this dry for now. We can work on it another day." She swirls the brush in a small dish of turpentine and then waves it inside a container of soapy water. She covers the canvas with a cloth.

"Don't I get to see it?" I ask.

"Not just yet."

I stand up from my pose, stretch my limbs, and crane my head from side to side to loosen the stiffness. Suzanne walks over to the windows and releases the ties holding back thick drapes. She tugs on the curtains and closes off the outside world of ice. A faint silvery glow descends from the transom and the panes overhead. She saunters over to me, her head tilted, gazing up at me in her sultry way.

"Finally," she whispers. "The dance of the Gymnopédies."

I give a tremulous smile. She reaches up and gently removes my hat, staring intensely into my eyes. Suzanne tosses the hat onto her mauve upholstered armchair. She brings her hands to my face and draws me into a kiss. Suddenly, it is as if smoldering coals inside us both burst into flame. She grasps my frock coat by the lapels and peels it from my shoulders, letting it fall to the floor. My heart races and every vein of my body pulses. I kiss the fine hairs on her neck as I unfasten the tiny buttons down her back. She releases a sensual moan and slides her hands down my thighs.

Garments slough to the floor or drape over furniture. I loosen the strings on the back of her corset, and Suzanne slides it off over her hips. She stands in a sheer, lacy camisole and pantaloons. She lounges back against the fainting couch and beckons to me. I lose myself in a sensual feast. The lilac fragrance melding with her pungent, womanly scent is intoxicating. All awareness of time vanishes as I explore the surface of her skin, savoring her like an exotic greenhouse flower. We entwine our bodies in an opulent pas de deux of sweat and sighs.

Afterward, we lie together in the glow of the coal stove. I can't remember ever feeling this way. My father once told me about proposing marriage to my mother after their first night together. As crazy as it seems, I can picture Suzanne becoming my bride. But who am I? What can I offer her but my undying love? I can barely support myself, let alone take care of her the way she deserves. What could she possibly want from me? I've never made wealth my aim. In fact, I've consciously pursued the opposite, renouncing materialism.

Suzanne takes a deep breath and rolls to her side to face me. "There is something wise about you, Erik. You're like an ancient sage, an old soul in a youthful body. I trust you. I have a secret I should reveal to you, that few others know."

I prop myself up on my forearm and gaze into her face. "A secret?"

"I was a child of the street. At 15, a neighbor took me to Pigalle. I was young and naïve and didn't understand it was the neighborhood of brothels." Her gaze lowers, but floats across a horizontal inner plane as if reading an invisible text. She lowers her voice. "That is where Puvis de Chavannes chose me to be his model, but also to satisfy his less wholesome intentions." She pauses, glancing again at me. "When I became pregnant, he no longer wanted me." Her brow clouds a moment, then she takes a deep breath. "I was still a girl when I gave birth to his child. I kept the baby. Maurice is his name. He stays with my mother, because I can't work and raise him alone." She swallows hard. "Miguel Utrillo felt sorry for me and agreed to give Maurice his name. But he is not the father of my boy, despite what rumors you may have heard."

There's squeezing inside my chest. I tip my head. "You've been through a lot," I say and caress her shoulder. "I didn't even know you had a child. But I wondered if you and Miguel were still together."

"No. That was years ago. Artists can be such despicable men. They're happy to paint me, use me. But when they tire of me, they move on and I am left with nothing."

I'm stirred by her words. I embrace her, cradling her head against my chest.

Suzanne whispers. "Nobody has ever been willing to stay. I'm always abandoned and left behind." She looks up at me. "But I don't feel like an object of passing fancy to you."

A knot tightens in my throat. "I would never do that," I whisper. "You're the kind of woman I want to marry, my little Biqui."

Suzanne sits up. Her eyes shift back and forth, searching mine. A wave of disbelief crosses her face. She nestles back in my arms, clinging tightly.

"Where have you been? All this time, I've been waiting, searching. What took you so long?"

"I got lost along the way. But I'm here now." I kiss her on the forehead and gaze up at the snowflakes falling against the glass panes overhead. A haunting melody streams through my mind.

ᨖ

There is something comforting and primal about watching fire. On the small stool in the corner near the hearth, I warm myself, gazing at the curling and blackened leaves of rolled newspaper. The hot vermillion glow scintillates along the edges of shriveling leaves. It is too cold to go anyplace. I am still reeling and groggy from too much to drink last night. Empty champagne bottles and the pleated wrappers of the chocolate truffles we savored litter the small table. I've been spending money I don't have on things I can't afford, feeding the fiery alchemy to please Suzanne. I'm giddy, but aching and heartsick too. As much as I basked in this paradise at first, gnawing little things make for an imperfect Eden.

"I proposed marriage," I announced to Conrad and my father over a tureen of mussels at Sunday dinner. "I intend to buy an engagement ring, do things right."

I thought they would be happy for me. But my brother nearly choked on an oyster. My father responded first in silence, then with platitudes.

"You're rushing into things. Why don't you bring her to Sunday dinner so we can meet her?" Though subtle, the disparaging furrowed brow and skeptical smirk did not escape my notice. But Suzanne never seems available for Sunday dinner at my father's. I'm forced repeatedly to make flimsy excuses for her.

If only I could pour this mélange of ecstasy and angst into my music. I pick up the pencil and music notation paper preparing to write, but the Muse goes silent. Instead, I sketch Suzanne's image, albeit the most minimal of resemblances. Disarmed like Odysseus by the Siren, I am drunk with the mead of her kisses. I'm gliding sideways, nearing the edge of a cliff and don't know how to turn back.

Suzanne has a tendency to disappear for days, a week, leaving no sign of when she will return. I mutter to myself, and can't sit still. Where does she go? Who is she with and what is she doing? A huge quarrel erupted the first time I asked about it. "Your expectations are suffocating," she insisted. "Your ideas are rigid, old fashioned." She likes things the way they are; on her terms.

On my old stationery, I write a note asking to see her. There listed are three days and times of rendezvous to choose from. When the ink is dry, I leave my apartment to deliver it under her door. Suzanne had just moved from the greenhouse to the apartment building next door, the second-floor studio above the arched porte-cochere. I knock, but there is no one inside. I slide the note under the door and return to my place.

What am I doing, groveling at her feet? I am obsessed. I know it and I don't like the power it holds over me. I dissolve like butter in a skillet whenever she stares at me with her azure gaze. My spirit is becoming as insolvent as my finances. I haven't written music for weeks. My belly growls, so it must be time to find something to eat. Perhaps I can scrape together a few centimes for a bowl of soup at Lapin Agile.

As I come around the curve from her apartment to the front of my building, I hear a familiar voice. Patrice is at my door, pounding as I approach. "Erik, are you in there?"

"No, I'm over here."

My friend spins around. "Mon vieux, how've you been? I haven't seen you for weeks."

I take a deep breath and give a half smile. "I've not been myself."

"Who have you been, then?" He tries to joke.

"Some degenerate creature I don't recognize."

"Pull yourself together, man. I came to invite you to go with me.

I'm meeting Jules Depaquit at the Café on Place du Tertre for aperitifs. I'm writing a satirical piece and I want him to illustrate it."

"I'm broke, mon vieux. How can I go?"

"I've got a few francs. I'll buy you a drink. Maybe you'll feel like your old self again."

I grab my umbrella and off the two of us go, slogging over the slick cobbled street to Rue du Mont-Cenis where the snow has turned to slush. We careen downward to Rue Norvins and the Café de Place du Tertre. The windows are fogged, glowing with welcoming amber light. Patrice opens the door and we go inside.

"Look who it is. It's the long lost Sadi." The voice is my friend Santiago.

"Sadi, Latour, come join the celebration," says Ramón. Seated together at a banquette beside them are Ignacio and Miguel Utrillo. Miguel tips his head back, staring at me through narrowed eyes. There has been an icy distance between us since the party.

Ramón stands up, offering his handshake and a slap on the shoulder. "Sincerely, celebrate with us, my friends."

"What are we celebrating?" I ask.

"I'll get two more glasses, eh?" says Santiago, sliding out of the banquette and returning instantly with two snifters and a bottle of Penedès brandy.

"To my success, and Miguel here," Ramon says. "We're going to America."

My mouth drops open. "America?" I ask.

"My work was juried to display at the World Exposition in Chicago," Ramón says.

"Congratulations! That's wonderful."

"I'll be tagging along to cover the event for several Spanish journals and newspapers," says Miguel. The corner of his mouth turns up on one side. "And we're taking a small troupe to perform a shadow theatre production."

Subtle though it was, I sense spite in Miguel's stare. Miguel delayed new productions at the Auberge. Now I know why. And to think I may have been included in their tour were it not for this failing love affair. America. I shake my head.

"We board a steamer from Calais in a few days," Miguel adds.

"Don't look so disappointed, Monsieur Sadi," says Ramón. He bumps shoulders with me and then raises his glass. "To Art and America!"

The others raise their glasses. "Santé!"

"I wish you all the best, truly," I tell Miguel.

"Sit down, will you?" replies Miguel.

I scoot into the banquette next to him. "It's been an honor to work with you on the Théâtre d'ombres. I shall miss your astonishing showmanship."

"I wish you the best, Erik. I meant to tell you about the show closing at the Auberge. And I expect to return to Barcelona after the exhibition in the United States."

"Had enough of Paris?" I ask.

"Enough, yes. Anyplace is better than here." Miguel looks aimlessly into the middle distance.

No words come. I gulp my brandy and stare at the table. Miguel twists the onyx inlaid ring on his finger with the tension of unspoken sentiments. I take another sip.

Miguel's shoulders heave with a deep inhale. He leans toward me but averts his eyes.

"Be kind to our little friend, eh?"

The hair rises on the back of my neck. "Little friend? I didn't realize you still cared."

"You didn't realize? You do not know what it has been like…" He meets my gaze. "But you will." His words are tinged with regret.

"What do you mean?"

"I'm sorry. Forgive me. I don't mean to sound bitter. I hope things are different for you, sincerely. It's just…" He looks away and then takes a gulp from his glass.

I do the same, emptying mine. My throat burns with the amber liquid. Miguel reaches for the bottle of cognac and pours some into my snifter, and adds a drizzle to his own. I'm beginning to feel the maudlin halo brandy swiftly brings on an empty stomach.

"You should know others have tried to love her, too. No one can tame her. She is like a wild swan. She'll stay for a season and fly away. I would have married her. I supported her financially and artistically. Who do you think paid for that studio of hers? But she keeps one or two other men on the side."

"Always?"

"Always. Before you, there was this young painter, Boissy. He drank himself to death over her. When she set her cross hairs on you, I said, enough. I knew if I stayed, she'd come right back around. First, she starts to disappear. You don't see her for days. Weeks go by. You think she's really gone. Then suddenly, there she is, as if nothing has happened. And when you try to set limits, expect, require something; then, my friend, she makes you bleed. But by then, you can't stop. You're in too deep. You see, I'm going to America to save my life." He takes a gulp from his glass.

"You're a gentleman, Miguel. An honorable man."

"You too, mi amigo." Miguel throws his arm around my shoulders and gives me a hug.

"And put something in your stomach, before you burn a hole in it, eh?" He waves to a waiter. "Yves, bring my friend here your cassolé and some bread." Yves nods and hurries to the kitchen.

Miguel seems to know everything, without me having said a word. I'm shaken to the core by his disclosures. He is telling the truth, because what he described is already happening.

Chapter 14

May 17, 1893, Erik's 27th Birthday

DOORS SHOULD OPEN in a few more minutes. Tapping my foot on the pavement, I lean on my umbrella in the shadow of the Theatre Bouffes-Parisiens. I scan the mass of bobbing fedoras, caps, and bowlers milling along Rue Monsigney in the heart of the business district. Where is that distinct bowler of charcoal grey? Claude's. He's traded his wide brimmed flamboyant style for a more conservative one.

This is not the hour either of us prefers to attend the theater, a midweek matinee. But the hastily printed placard at the entrance explains it all: One performance only. We're here to see the production Pelleas et Melisande, one of the newest creations by Maurice Maeterlinck. It's a rare treat for a Symbolist play to be performed at a small venue that typically hosts operettas. My difficulty finding work, my financial woes, and the uncertainties with Suzanne have taken a toll on me. Claude acquired two tickets as a gift; saving me, body and soul.

I pick out Claude's wiry dark hair and the odd tilt with which he likes to wear his hat. He carries himself as if suspended by strings like a marionette, with the same buoyant gait. I wave, and a grin blooms on Claude's face. We embrace, exchanging a kiss on the cheek. I step back, squinting against the afternoon sun.

"It's terribly generous of you to treat me to the theatre, my good Claude," I smile.

"I'm just glad I could do it," he replies. He glances past me and gestures to the theater-goers surging toward the open doors. "It's been a rough road," Claude continues. "But finally paying off. The performance of 'La Damoiselle élue' at Société Nationale's spring concert made the newspapers, and a little cash."

"Real inside subversive progress, I'd say. The wager swings back your way."

"The critic for Le Figaro said it is likely to cause 'a dangerous revolt in young composers of the future.' The irony is; that's the piece I composed to satisfy the Academy during the Prix de Rome episode."

"Oh, the one the faculty called bizarre?"

"Yes. It just goes to show how things can change. There's hope, brother."

"I have to be reminded. It's so easy to get defeated."

"I made a nice sum on those Wagner concerts I gave earlier this month. too." Debussy reaches in his pocket and draws out the tickets, handing them to the doorman. "If nothing else, there's money to be made playing other people's music."

"I resist that at every opportunity," I reply. "It pollutes a composer's creative brain."

"Maybe, but I just hope the income and exposure continues. I'll be able to move to a better place."

"Move? You just got settled. I thought you liked that apartment in the British district."

"I do. But Gaby is worried about anarchist bombs going off everywhere. She wants to move farther out.

"Yes, I must admit, I'd never attend a performance here, if it hadn't been Maeterlinck," I say. "I worry some anarchist might end it for us all." Now inside, we edge our way to the hat check.

"You'd expect the lawyers and judges prosecuting Ravachol to be targeted. But blowing up a restaurant?" Claude turns over his bowler to the attendant behind the counter.

"They must have served really terrible food," I smirk.

Claude chuckles and slaps me on the shoulder. I surrender my hat and umbrella and take a claim ticket. Debussy leads me to the bar, ordering two glasses of champagne, and we toast my birthday. The house lights flicker, signaling patrons to take their seats. We hurry to the mezzanine, where an usher directs us to ours. Claude takes a paperbound booklet from his coat pocket.

"I bought this a month ago at Flammarion Books. I've been so burdened with this El Cid project; I've only glanced at it. Have a look. It's a copy of Maeterlinck's published script."

"Great. We can follow along," I reply. "I know how disappointed you were when he turned you down for composing the music for Princess Melaine."

"Yes, but I've had several other offers since then."

The house lights grow dim and the roar of the attendees softens to silence. The curtain opens to a darkened proscenium. As the lights come up, the set makes me gasp. They draped the entire stage in a thin gossamer veil and the lighting casts hues of blue and green. It gives the scenery an ethereal ambiance, like a dream. The audience sighs and murmurs.

What unfolds next is a tale of a medieval troubadour. It's a tragic ballad of forbidden love, a secret rendezvous, and jealous torment. It touches a painful chord in me. I'm not sure with whom I identify most, the ill-fated Pelleas or the jealous Prince Golaud.

The characters seem to stumble blindly through what is happening to them. It's as if Maeterlinck has written the play just for me. From its setting in the medieval time, to its many elements of symbolism; it reaches deep inside me and clutches my heart. Tears pour down my cheeks into my beard.

When the final curtain falls, Claude and I rise for a standing ovation, though few others in the bourgeois audience share our enthusiasm.

I absolutely have to set this play to music, either an opera or a ballet; some massive work grander than anything I've ever attempted.

On exiting the theatre, the daylight edges toward twilight. Claude suggests we find a pleasant brasserie for hors-de-oeuvres and aperitifs. We wander several streets, back toward the omnibus station. A lively venue with the aroma of buttery garlic and spirits draws us inside.

"Everything about the play was new. As anti-naturalist as it could be," says Claude, leaning across the red checkered tablecloth.

"I think there is more truth in that dreamlike vision than in any true-to-life drama." I take out a partially smoked cigarette and light it on the café candle.

"Love and death, the never-ending cycle of decay and renewal…"

I stroke my beard. "Did you notice the use of water, the pool, the fountain, befouled waters under the castle?"

"And the symbol of golden spheres," replies Claude, and takes a sip of his beer. "The ring, the crown, the golden ball. Wholeness and order were being lost."

I take a puff from the cigarette and blow the smoke into the air. "It's brilliant, really. It certainly lends itself to musical composition."

"Exactly."

"I'm positively itching to set this play to music. If only I knew how to contact Monsieur Maeterlinck. Do you still have his address?"

The exuberance fades from Claude's face. "I expect so. I'll look when I get home." There is an edge to the way he says this.

I lean in. "Were you also thinking of…"

"No, of course not. Go ahead, by all means. I've got too many projects going already." Claude stares off toward the windows and the darkening street.

I'm certain he really wants to claim it for himself. I take a sip of my beer and glance around the restaurant. The waiter soon returns bringing a plate of appetizers de jour. "I found personal relevance in the play. The love triangle was painful to watch," I tell him.

"Yes. I suppose it would be. Neither man wins," he says.

We pause our conversation to fill our faces with delicious treats. Claude throws back a few oysters and shrimp, washing them down with beer.

I spread pâté on a wad of baguette. "I'm fairly certain Suzanne is seeing another man."

Claude groans and leans his head to one side. "I'm sorry, mon vieux. Merde!"

"Unless she will give him up, I must end this brief love affair."

"This must be a dreadful time. The play must have thrown salt in the wound."

"It gave voice to what I didn't want to admit," I say. "This vexation is seizing hold of me like a fit of Golaud's madness."

"Believe me, I know the sickness. I had to go all the way to Rome to get over mine."

"This will take more than a change of geography, I'm afraid." I toss the rest of my beer down my throat and swallow hard.

"How about another?" asks Claude.

On the way home, the omnibus rattles along Boulevard Poissonnière. When we parted, Claude's scrunched brows and downturned mouth showed his lingering disappointment. Was it wrong to claim Pelleas for myself? Or do I take him at his word, that he has too many projects in the works already. He touts his current successes, while I now flounder. But with my frame of mind, could I even develop Pelleas right now? This turmoil over Suzanne has robbed me of the capacity to compose anything. The last thing I want is for Claude to feel cheated. I love him like blood. I just don't know which is the right path.

The omnibus stops at the intersection with Rue Montmartre. A crowd of patrons clusters near the front of another small theatre. Dressed in an exquisite grey Edgewood town coat, a man catches my eye as he exits the theatre. He beckons with an outstretched hand to a petite woman. At the sight of her hair, a lightning bolt pierces me through the chest. My stomach roils. The omnibus pulls away from the kiosk, but I try to get a better look. How she holds her skirt and tosses her head is undeniable. I'm certain it's Suzanne. She had talked about a stockbroker patron. The Stock Exchange is only two blocks away. My eyes are riveted to the couple until they're no longer in view. I slump into the seat next to a matron with a basket of vegetables. My chest feels like it's been gouged out with a broken bottle.

Chapter 15

June 1893, Montmartre

The vestibule outside my apartment is dark when I arrive home. Once inside, I light the hurricane lamp on a small table. Only after I sit to take my boots off do I see the note slipped under my door. Suzanne must have returned. Not finding me here, she left this message. I snatch the folded page from the floor and read it.

> *I'm sorry I couldn't make a single rendezvous time you requested in your message. But I promise to come see you in the morning after my art session with Degas, around 11:00.*

I lay back on the cot, staring up at the sagging ceiling. Cracks developed during the winter, and it needs repair. It's likely to cave in. Desperation to see her engulfs me. I dread the conversation that has to take place. Is our relationship about to end? Or will Suzanne choose me over the stockbroker? Why would she? My glaring inadequacy twists in my gut. The idea of being alone, of never seeing her again, fills me with panic. The kerosene lamp burns out, leaving me in a fitful trance. But somehow, I fall asleep. It's nearly half past ten in the morning when I awake, with my heart racing. I'm clammy and my mouth is dry.

I splash cold water on my face, comb my hair, and brush my teeth with the last of my washing soda. I pace and I glance out the window. The bed linens need straightening. More pacing. I want to jump out of my skin.

By ten minutes past the hour, I assume she has changed her mind. A porter with a handcart trudges by and two women with baskets of laundry. Then, I notice my dainty Biqui plodding up the hill carrying an enormous canvas under one arm and a wooden handled paint box in the other hand. As she nears the porte-cochere, I can hear the clicking of her high-button shoes against the cobblestones. My heart thunders at my collar and my knees turn to sponge. I hurry out of my apartment to intercept her on the landing.

"Bonjour, my little Biqui," I say. "Let me help you with that." I wrest the paint box from her hand and grab the canvas by its stretcher. We climb the short spiral stairs to her studio. Suzanne doesn't seem to share my enthusiasm. She stares into her drawstring purse, hunting for the key. Fitting it into the lock, she opens the door. Once inside, I close it with my foot. I put her canvas on an easel and place the box of paints on the floor beside it.

Perched aslant on her head, she wears a flat top indigo straw hat adorned with silk flowers. I'd never seen it before, or the voile pin-tucked blouse. She looks like one of those beauties illustrated by the American, Dana Gibson, displayed in journals at the newsstand.

"You look lovely. I've missed you terribly." I put my arms around her, drawing her close. But she is stiff. There's an artificial quality to her embrace and shortened kiss. She doesn't gaze up at me with her usual adoring intimacy.

"So sorry, Erik. I can't stay but a few minutes. I came to leave these things, and I'm off again."

My heart sinks. "But you just got here. I've barely had time to hold you and you're leaving already."

"I know." She pulls away. "We'll find time to be alone together soon."

"But where are you going? What's so very important you have to leave me again?" Panic crawls up my back and rivulets of cool sweat run down my temples. This is it; the moment I dreaded.

"You won't understand, mon cher."

"You must tell me. I'm going mad worrying. I love you and I'm afraid I'm losing you."

Suzanne looks away. "A girl must make her way in this world. What would you have me do? You're destitute."

"Well, I certainly don't want you giving yourself to some man for his money."

A nostril flares and her eyes narrow. "Are you calling me a whore?"

"No. That didn't come out right. I'm saying you've not been honest with me."

"Honest? Well, neither have you. All your big talk about producing an opera or ballet. When is that going to happen? I built my hope on it. It was all a big lie. You're just a cabaret key tapper," she huffs and shakes her head. "No one takes you for a serious composer, Erik. You're a dilettante. There, I've said it. Now, if you don't mind, I need to be on my way." She steps toward the door.

I feel a crushing blow, like a jousting lance has just knocked me off my mount. I'm paralyzed for a moment. I have to make her see. She has entirely the wrong idea about me. She is about to abandon me. I step in front of the door, blocking her way.

"I can't let you just walk out. Let me explain."

"I don't have time for this. There's some place I have to be."

"You're not going anywhere until we talk."

"Erik, let me pass."

"No, not until we resolve this."

"Don't be an ass, Erik." She tries to push me out of the way. "Let me go!" She raises her voice, and her face bunches into a knot. But her size and stature are no contest. I push her back. She stumbles off balance, nearly losing her footing. Her lovely new hat comes loose and falls to the floor and her hair tumbles to her shoulders. I hadn't meant to be so forceful.

"That hurt, you son of a bitch." She cradles her breasts. Then her brows knit and she comes at me with both hands, slapping me on the face repeatedly. "You will not ruin this for me." She knocks my pince-nez from my nose, shooting them across the room. My vision blurs. But I can still see the contempt and fury on her face.

"Stop! Calm down." The volume of my voice surprises me. I grab her upper arm and capture the other flailing one at the wrist.

"Take your hands off me!" She struggles to free herself.

"Not until you calm down. I just want to talk."

"This is how you treat me? There is nothing left to say."

By this point, I'm heated and breathing hard. My eyes fall on the slender shadow where the closet stands ajar. I forcefully back Suzanne toward the narrow space. She struggles to scratch and bite me, and kicks her feet. But I can dodge the hard pointed toes of her shoes. I shove her inside and quickly slam the door, sliding the latch in place.

Suzanne starts screaming and pounding on the door. "Let me out. I can't breathe in here. You asshole."

I stare at the door and fidget with my beard. I take several deep breaths, trying to regain my sensibility.

"Will you just listen?" I say.

"Let me out!"

This is pathetic and horrible. I rub my forehead, bewildered, laughing at my undoing.

"Murder! Murder!"

Things were tenuous before, but they're irretrievable now. Locking my lover in the closet? I am an asshole and an idiot. I look around the room trying to locate where my lenses landed. I spy the black satin ribbon and shuffle over. Footsteps and voices emanate from the hallway outside the studio.

"Mademoiselle, are you alright?"

Merde! It's all over now.

Hearing the neighbor, Suzanne screams even louder. "He's trying to kill me. Help!"

With my pince-nez in place, I look at the closet and then at the door.

The neighbor pounds harder. "What's going on in there?"

"Just a little argument," I shout. "It's none of your affair. Go away."

"No, Monsieur, open up or I'll go for the police." It's the concierge, Monsieur Jacques.

Suzanne continues to plead and pound on the door. The concierge uses his own key to unlock it. Monsieur and his wife burst into the room. The concierge is carrying a hoe and his matronly wife is holding a rolling pin. I rush to the closet, open the latch, and step back. Suzanne speaks only with her eyes, cruel slits; her brows angled in a scornful chevron.

I drop my head. "Forgive me. I'm so sorry. I lost all reason."

Suzanne passes, putting Monsieur Jacques between us.

"Shame, Monsieur. It's not befitting," he says.

The matron brings Suzanne her hat. "Come away now, Mademoiselle. Monsieur will lock up. First, let's get you to safety." Together, they leave the studio.

My head is spinning. I cover my mouth to stifle any sound and stagger toward the door. What have I done?

⁂

I lay on my back; my eyes tracing the widening cracks in the ceiling above my bed. The emptiness I've known since childhood swallows me. People I love always vanish. They abandon me. Will I always be left alone? It's been the perpetual pattern of my whole life. Is there nothing I can do to change it?

Love is just an illusion, a form of temporary insanity. Even friends who have wed their one true love are driven to stray. Mistresses and lovers. I might have become Suzanne's secret lover if I hadn't tried to hang on so tightly. But would being her paramour satisfy me? Claude's tales of his long affair with Marie-Blanche Vanier dissuade me from that folly. Suzanne had also loved me, in her way. Or was that an illusion, too? I turn onto my stomach, burying my face in the pillow.

No matter how I may intellectualize all this, nothing takes away the pain. Her words wound me deeply. I am no longer a hot rabbit, or even a scared one. I am a butchered rabbit; snatched up by the ears; writhing in midair while my entrails are plucked out and my fur hide peeled from my flesh. Every part of me hurts.

She's sold her flesh to a man of means, discarding me like Columbine always does to Pierrot. She chewed up Miguel, Boissy, and now me. Who is next? One day last week, in a fit of exasperation, I took a sheet of my custom stationery and drew a small poster denouncing Suzanne as a two-timing hussy, slid the edge of the paper against the glass pane, anchoring it in the window putty and displaying the scathing pronouncement where everyone walking along Rue Cortot could see it. But vindictiveness doesn't stop the growing agony, either. I took it down.

A short theme of flats and sharps keeps running through my head like a bizarre off-key calliope. It brings to mind Willette's tragic cartoon of Pierrot, straddling the legs of a naked supine Columbina. He's stunned, because he's tickled her to death. Enharmonic bass notes match the ache in my chest that flares each time I breathe too deeply. Non-resolving tritones linger like the swelling in my throat that never goes away. Finally, I give into waves of spasmodic sobbing.

The moonlit room becomes an indigo monochrome still life, a series of Art Nouveau panneau, flat and figurative. Over the repeating discordant tune, I hear voices; one which is coquettish and lilting. There is a flash of red taffeta and the fragrance of lilac.

"I know who you are. Satie isn't it, Erik Satie?" Laughter, champagne. "I love to hear you play." The female voice seems to double and triple like a chorus. "I've been waiting for you my whole life. Where have you been?"

There's a silhouette against the moonlight. Someone approaches through a filmy haze. My heart pounds. I gasp. "Who's there?"

"Bonsoir, my love. I couldn't wait to see you." It's Suzanne's voice. Her naked breasts and hips are outlined in blue. Reaching for her, I lurch forward. She laughs and backs away. Oh god, no more. The specter tumbles backward through the now open window, out into the night sky, arms flailing, copper hair twisting like Medusa. I gape, frozen and powerless. The theme of flats and sharps starts over again. This time tinny chimes of a music box play.

"We shall muster through, my lad. Now tidy up." English words, my mother's words. "Mummie's brave little soldier."

My room alters, as if I'm hovering at the ceiling, watching another version of myself moving around the space. I'm four years old again, wandering to the side of my mother's bed.

"Maman, it's time for tea. I've brought you something. Wake up, s'il vous plaît." I stare into her lifeless face, her eyes unfocused, and her lips pale blue. Everything grows still and grey.

❧

Thundering kettle drums jar me back from oblivion.

"Erik, are you there? It's Conrad." He's hammering on the door.

I drag myself to sitting position, but close my eyes again. My head feels like a thick steel bar has been thrust between my temples. I'm still fully clothed. A yellow stain mars the front of my shirt like a ragged patch over my heart. I stumble to the door and open it just enough to see.

Conrad peers through the crack. "Mon frère, what's happened to you?"

"What are you doing here? I can't believe you came all this way." Conrad had been completing his mandatory service, stationed in Toulon in the Fusiliers Marins branch of the French Navy.

"I'm on leave."

I don't want my brother to see me this way. But I've no energy to explain. I just need to lie down and close out the world again. "I'm just trying to recover." I open the door wider, shielding my eyes against the light.

Conrad enters the shuttered room. He's dressed in his sailor uniform. "What's wrong?" He walks to the window, pushing the shutters outward. Sunlight floods the space. His eyes inspect me and the rash of empty bottles. "You're a wreck, emaciated and pale." He leans on the window sill. "Smells horrible in here." Conrad takes off his cap, fanning the air in front of his face.

I slump back on my cot, yielding for a few moments to the vertigo and inertia. "But I've figured it out."

"Figured what out?"

"This state of lethargy. The second law of thermodynamics confirms it. Entropy is at play." I look over at my brother.

Conrad stares wide-eyed. "Thermodynamics? Are you drunk? When was the last time you ate anything?"

I groan. "No, listen, you're a scientist. It's because energy degrades during the transfer from one body to another. Some of it is rendered unusable. Potential energy would therefore always be less than the initial state."

Conrad shakes his head, contorting his mouth like tasting vinegar. "You're not making any sense."

"It's just physics." I sit up.

"Father sent a telegram and asked me to find you. First you tell us you're getting engaged. Then we don't see you or hear from you. We became worried."

"There's nothing to tell." I stare at my brother's shadow on the hardwood floor.

"Nothing? You cut yourself off from everybody. How can you do that, especially to me? You're not yourself."

I know he's right. I've been drinking most nights until I pass out. When conscious, I can't think clearly. I say things that alarm Patrice and the Catalan artists. Santiago and Ignacio piled me into a cab one night after I gazed for hours at the El Greco paintings Santiago acquired for his new apartment.

I run my hand back through my long hair. Shuffling to the mantle, I locate my pince nez and put them on. "Have I really changed so much?" I stare at my reflection in the mirror over the fireplace. "The body is just the wrapping around the spiritual kernel. But most souls are being strangled by their wrappings. Inside I'm still the same. I still want the same things." I pick up my tobacco pouch and look inside to see if there was enough to roll a cigarette. There isn't.

Conrad crosses the room, takes out his cigarette case, and offers it to me. "What things? What are you trying to do?"

I select a nice firm machine rolled cigarette, tap it on end several times to pack the tobacco and put it in my mouth. My hand trembles when I struggle to open the box of matches. They scatter onto the mantle. "You know; things we've talked about before, the musical revolution. I want to bring new musical forms to the world, challenge what people consider fine music."

Conrad takes a match and lights my cigarette.

"But everything I touch just turns to shit," I huff, gesturing to the spilled matches. My eyes start to well up. This seems to happen all the time now, whenever I open my mouth. I can't stop weeping. I take a long drag, blow out the smoke, and start picking up the mess.

"I've made one wrong move after another. I thought I'd started to find my way. But no. I'm a failure."

"You're not a failure. A bit misguided, perhaps. You're just getting started."

"Even with all these dead ends, I can't see myself getting some meaningless job. Some force still drives me. I have to make music." I clench my fist. "I'm not meant for anything else. I just can't find my way forward." My voice wavers. I swallow hard to strangle off a rising groan.

"You're drinking too much. And all this Gnostic philosophy, that Rosicrucian nonsense… I say it's done you no good. No good at all."

I walk to the open window and gaze out. Taking another puff on the cigarette, I stare at the white dome of Sacre Coeur, taking shape above the roofline against the cobalt sky. "As much as I try to pull myself up, I feel like I'm in a dungeon, shackled by my mind and emotions. I've even considered death as a way out. I always thought

I'd be dead before age 25. I'm overdue by two years. But death doesn't bring about liberation of the soul. Those who haven't achieved Gnosis while embodied are trapped in eternal damnation."

"Eternal damnation? Will you just come down to earth?" Conrad's voice chokes off to a whisper. His eyes are growing glassy, too. "Erik, listen. When we were little boys, I followed you everywhere. If I was scared, you'd put your arm around me and reassure me. If I got lost, you'd always be the one to find me. Now it's my turn to find you; your turn to follow me. Blood is stronger than anything."

"What are you telling me?" I ask.

"We're going to get you some help. Come with me."

"Come with you?"

"Yes, today, right now. Do you trust me?"

I gaze out the window again at the locals going about their day, their lives. I am only sinking farther and farther down. Perhaps Conrad is right. It's time to try something else. "Let me get my coat and umbrella."

Chapter 16

August 22, 1893, Paris

THE WILTING AUGUST afternoon is finally releasing its hold on the breeze, allowing cool relief to settle onto the butte once again. I stand naked at the wash stand, sponging off with cold water, sweetened with a little baking soda. The draft from my open window wafts over my skin. Music from the open-air dance garden at the Moulin de Galette is infectious and impossible to escape regardless of where one lives on the grassy hill.

Claude's carefully penned note sits on the mantle. It is the first invitation I've received all summer. He's been on holiday for months, outside of Paris on the Marne. Back in May, he went all out to acknowledge my birthday, buying tickets to Maeterlinck's play and aperitifs afterward. So, while I lack the means for anything quite as lavish as a play, I have to figure out something appropriate to acknowledge his 31st birthday. I pull on clean drawers and a fresh shirt, fasten my trousers, and then sit on the bed to put on my socks and boots.

The only thing about this fête that gives me pause is the spirits. I have more or less promised Conrad to stop drinking. I'm not sure if I can, entirely. Toasts will be obligatory, whether wine or beer with a meal, or champagne. How can I possibly beg-off Claude's hospitality?

Maybe I can indulge a little, just this once. Other people seem to be able to temper their consumption. Why can't I? But with someone else providing the libations; am I more likely to go full bore? Oui, knowing my record.

I set off on a gradual downhill stroll along Rue Caulaincourt, a road sweeping the hip of Montmartre. Like one of many spokes of a wheel, the avenue converges at Place Clichy where the hum of workaday Parisians harmonizes with clattering hooves and rattling omnibuses. I skirt the edge of the cobbled plaza and jut down Rue Amsterdam. Here, the honey-lit windows of the English style pubs are so inviting. Patrons hoisting their amber filled pint glasses make me groan. What I wouldn't give for a tawny brew right now? I look away.

I spy a tiny shop across the lane selling plaid woolen scarves, and beside it a tea room with dainty cakes and fruit tarts displayed in its cheery windows. I enter the small shop, and purchase a petite Queen Victoria sponge cake, layered with jam and cream. I cradle the pastry box against my chest. Wedged under my other arm is my music notebook, and an issue of Le Coeur to add lively discussion. A limited deluxe edition of my Sonneries of the Rose+Croix is tucked inside.

The bells of Église de la Sainte-Trinité sound the quarter-hour as I arrived in front of the large blue door of a spartan building. I step inside the vestibule and ring the bell. Within moments, footfalls rhythmically trot down the spiral staircase.

"Erik! It's great to see you." Claude's cheekbones are burnished by the summer sun. He holds me in his gaze for a second or two, charged with Claude's unique kind of magnetism. He takes the pastry box and winds the other arm around my neck.

"Welcome back," I reply, returning a one-armed embrace.

He gestures for me to ascend the narrow, winding stairs. At the third floor, he opens a tall narrow door with a transom window. I saunter toward an archway, savoring the cooking aromas of something delicious. Gabrielle offers her greetings from the round drop-leaf table near the window where she is setting out dishes. There are only three place settings, making me the only guest at this soirée. With Gaby's small but steady wages as a seamstress and Claude's feast and famine income from his music, they're likely managing better than I did in my upscale apartment.

Claude edges his way between furniture pieces to reach his grand piano, taking up the entire area near shelving at the far side of the room. "So, what do you think?"

I pantomime my applause. "Bravo! How did you ever get the piano up here?"

Claude points to the tall casement windows. "It was perilous to watch."

"I imagine so."

"Shall we have a drink?"

I blink hard and I draw a deep breath, "Shouldn't we wait for Gaby's wonderful meal?"

"It's just about ready," she says.

Claude walks to the table and deftly wields the corkscrew to open a bottle of red wine. "It's a lovely new Gamay Beaujolais," he says, pouring a little into each of three glasses.

My first impulse is to amble over to the piano. Setting my notebook and music on top, I fold back the keyboard cover and begin playing a few chords. Claude sidles over to join me, holding two mismatched goblets, offering one to me. I stare at the blood red elixir. Where is my resolve? Maybe I should have said something, asked for seltzer. It's too late now. I raise my glass. "To reunions, new apartments, and birthdays."

"À votre santé!" We all chime. Claude and I clink rims.

I lower my glass without taking a drink. "To celebrate the occasion, I brought you this." I draw the sheet music out from between the journal pages.

"What's this?" Claude studies the illustration for a few seconds and a grin of recognition blooms. "Marvelous. To my Rosicrucian brother, on the occasion of his birthday, from his friend Erik Satie."

Claude beams with warm fondness in his eyes. "I have always loved the Rose+Croix music and I'm truly honored to receive it. You'll play for us, won't you?"

"Of course. How about Air du Grand Prieur?" I ask, softly.

"Perfect."

I set my wineglass to the side and pull out the bench, sitting down and arranging the music. Claude edges into the curved recess of the piano, leaning on one elbow. I adjust my pince-nez and bring my hands to the keys. The gentle march pulses, crusading along a country path where slender branches join overhead and sunlight falls through the ogival tracery of leaves. When I glance over, Claude is rocking, trancelike, side-to-side.

Arriving at the first musical shrine, the canticle shifts tempo, raising a plaintive chant toward heaven. A knight-cleric in glittering mail stands before an icon. His polychrome tabard flutters in the breeze. Slowly, my fingers offer the celestial reply in a higher octave. Then the medieval hymn journeys onward to the tender cadence of the human heart in search of deliverance. In the last segment, the melody returns to the first phrase, closing like the elegant back cover of an illuminated manuscript.

I lift my gaze. Claude's glassy-eyed stare makes me uneasy.

"A beautiful dream. Sublime." Claude strains a fragile, one-sided smile. "This piece in particular has a kind of transcendence that soothes the soul."

"I'm glad," I say. Something more is brewing beneath Claude's appreciation of the music. Some levity is clearly in order.

Gaby interrupts, carrying a tray with a soup tureen. "Everything is ready, gentlemen."

We take our places at the table. Gaby lifts the lid on a tureen of lentil and sausage ragout. I've eaten lentils daily for weeks. However, Gaby has made them quite delectable. But this also tells me how impoverished Claude and Gaby actually are, despite the appearance of their well-furnished flat.

"Two new journals hit the newsstands while you were away," I say, sprinkling salt and pepper into my soup. "Have you seen Francois Mainguy's publication, Fin de Siècle?"

"Not yet, but after Guy de Maupassant died, I knew someone would step into the void," Claude replies, tearing a piece of baguette and dipping it into his broth.

"Spare us, oh Lord," says Gaby. "I read that filthy thing. What an outrageous column, 'The Perverse Chronicles'…" She rolls her eyes. "It claims La Gouloue, the famed dancer of the Moulin Rouge keeps a goat for a lover."

Claude and I leer at each other. Claude covers his lips to keep from losing his mouthful, in a burst of laughter.

"I read that article, too," I say. "It gets worse. They quote some lawyer's wife saying, all remarkable ladies do it. But it's tricky. One must take lessons."

"Do you actually believe any of that is real?" Claude asks, turning to Gabrielle.

"Of course not." She brandishes her wine glass. "All the haute couture ladies in the dress shop believe it, poor things. But I don't need a goat." She flashes Claude a sultry smile. He brushes the back of her hand with his fingertips and winks.

"And you also missed the publicity stunt Mainguy staged to publicize the journal," I continue. "A ball mimicking the Bal des Quatre z'Arts."

Claude squints. "You mean, where art students dress up like paintings in the Louvre?"

"Yes, but this featured naked women lazing beneath gossamer and silk. Of course, the police raided it for indecency. Naturally, circulation soared."

"Naturally," says Claude, contorting his face in feigned disgust. He clicks his tongue. "See what I missed. That's what I get for going on holiday." He takes a gulp of wine.

"Maybe you should take advantage of this carnal trend," I suggest. "What do you think? Set some erotic poems, like Sappho, or Astarte."

Claude stares with a deadpan expression. "As long as it doesn't have a goat."

"Goats, fauns. What's the difference?" I flick my beard and bleat.

Gaby and Claude howl. The conversation gives way to appetites, savory ragout and crusty bread. To finish, Gabrielle brings out tea and the sponge cake, oozing jam from between the layers.

"So, what have you been doing all summer, Erik?" Claude asks.

"One of my newer compositions, the 'Gnossienne No. 6', is being published in this new journal, Le Coeur. Our friends Count Antoine and Jules Bois started it. I draw out the periodical. They've asked me to write an article for the October issue."

"What a great way to get our revolutionary message out there."

"And this may surprise you. I've started dabbling with a Mass or Requiem on the organ at the Church of Saint-Pierre."

"Not a Black Mass," says Claude.

"No, a modern one."

"That's certainly au current," says Gabrielle. "Religion has become chic. Women at the dress shop are looking for neophyte or martyr gowns in Liberty silk. Store windows are filled with advertising graphics, jewelry, fashion, even lamp shades that look like sacred objects."

"See. Your mystic-liturgical music started a trend. You're a prophet, Erik," says Claude.

I shake my head. "Prophet? I'd say it's the profiteers. And I don't relish the idea of becoming a cliché."

"All that aside, whatever happened with your plans for Pelleas and Melisande? Did you ever get started on the project?" Claude takes a slurp of tea.

The mention of it immediately stirs up a pang of memory, of Suzanne. That alone is enough to make me want to pick up my wine glass and empty it right there. I shake my head. "It reminds me too much of that bad tooth I recently had pulled. Painful thing."

"Because, if you're not going to pursue it…" A tinge of desperation colors Claude's remark. He breaks off eye contact and begins drawing figures on the tablecloth with a finger.

My friend wants to lay claim to a project I still aspire to compose. Yes, wants it very much. Do I surrender it now? I might have been serious about it in spring, but Pelleas would only tear open the wound. "I can't honestly see myself doing anything with it, Claude. Not soon, anyway. You may as well." I reach over and grasp the wineglass.

"That's big of you, mon vieux. Truly." Claude slides his finished plate away and pushes back from the table, thanking Gaby.

I tuck my napkin beside my dish and rise from the table. "So, my good Claude, show me what you've been working on all summer?"

"Very well." He walks over to the piano and slides onto the bench. I settle into the overstuffed armchair, clutching my goblet as if it were a ball grenade, and then finally put it on the occasional table at my knees; folding my hands in my lap. Claude puts his fingers to the keys.

A solemn, even ominous melody in a minor key fills the room. What austere and exotic tones, with an air of tragedy. Gradually building, the sonorities rumble like an impending storm. I stroke my beard. This is very different for Claude; certainly not his usual style. Maybe he's playing someone else's work; Russian or Hungarian, perhaps.

Claude starts tearing at the keys in a harsh frenzy; his lips grim, ferocity burning in his eyes. The deep bass reverberates in my chest. I draw a breath, turning my head toward Gabrielle, clearing dishes. She meets my gaze with a confirming grimace, shaking her head, as the crescendo of doom rumbles on. Her eyes seem to confirm all is not well.

Perhaps I've been too self-absorbed to see beyond Claude's exuberant smile. I wonder if the same dark torment he once spoke of before lies beneath his cheery façade. There was that time he threatened to throw his music and himself off a bridge. This composition says it all. Such wretchedness is something I understand all too well. Everything about a musician's heart and soul is evident in his music. What he is drawn to listen to, what he plays, and is compelled to compose reveal everything. It's no accident that I've been moved to write a Mass; the cry for redemption and restoration. His playing exposes a maelstrom inside Claude. The anguish pulls at my gut, tethering me with a new affinity to the fleet-fisted maestro hunched over the keyboard.

The melody hurtles into a dazzling collision of chords, and after a rest sign, the piece finishes with a tender succession of high notes, like the solitary call of a meadowlark.

Claude looks up with a wicked smirk, sweat dribbling down his temples. Leaving the bench, he planks himself down onto the settee, across from me.

I purse my lips, twisting the end of my moustache. "Russian five?"

"Good guess. Mussorgsky, a piece from Boris Godunov."

I narrow my eyes, peering intensely into Claude's. "Rather dark."

"Chausson and Bonheur were mesmerized. But with Chausson's guidance, I also reworked my string quartet."

"String quartet." Just as I feared. The older Chausson's work is dreary and boring; and he could only teach others how to be equally dull. "He's certainly expert in that traditional genre."

"Yes, but this one isn't the traditional string quartet you're thinking of." Claude replies. He combs his hand back through his waves. "Infiltrating and subverting, remember? More importantly, with Chausson's help, I managed to get it on the playbill for Société Nationale's upcoming concert."

"Société Nationale? Fantastic." I smile, but tap my foot beneath the occasional table. Pain flares in my jaw from clenching my teeth. This will be Claude's second concert at a major venue. Maybe I'm just envious. I pick up my wineglass, vacillating. Just a sip? I swirl the wine and nose the fragrance. Spun sugar rose petal and cherry. Why am I torturing myself? Put it down.

Claude leans forward with his forearms on his knees. "I must confess something, mon vieux," he says, just above a whisper. "I'm really struggling."

"With two major events in six months, I don't understand why." I angle my head to hear.

"Those are both older works. I'm at a standstill; especially with my setting of Afternoon of a Faun, which I promised to Mallarmé. I'm still unsure of my direction or whether my musical approach is even right."

Now the truth is seeping out. Claude is in a creative no-man's-land. "Ah-ha, I know the feeling well, when nothing you put down on the page seems to work."

"If I can put anything down at all. Merde."

"Quite so." I nod, tugging at my whiskers. "When that happens to me, I have always found visiting a gallery gets the juices flowing again. Art inspires me."

"A gallery?" Claude seems to mirror me, stroking his beard and bobbing his head.

"Well, what if your music could capture a simple idea the way Impressionist paintings do? What if your Afternoon of a Fawn could do with music what Renoir or Monet do with light; keeping the colors fresh, pure, by never adding even one more detail than is absolutely necessary to convey the essence of a thing? The hazy outlines, sensations, textures. You know?"

"Hmm. That would be a radical departure."

"The Salon of the Independents has some great pointillist pieces this summer. You should go see them. Signac, Pissarro."

"I will. Yes. An enormously helpful idea." The mirth fades from Claude's eyes and he hangs his head. "I don't know how to keep going, at times. If it weren't for you, Erik, and people like Chausson…"

"Isn't the reason we get together, to support each other in our work?"

Claude nods, taking a labored breath. He wrings his hands. "It's more than that. Lately, I've reached some moments so dark, I've literally considered taking my life."

Mon Dieu. He's suicidal again, like that time he talked about jumping off the Pont d'Arcole. The sudden ring of silverware dropped against porcelain makes me turn my head to Gaby clearing the table. She rushes over and sits beside Claude. My insides are churning. I can't imagine losing my friend, especially by his own hand. I lean closer.

"You mustn't do that. I love you like a brother."

Gaby can barely find her voice. "So many people care for you. It would destroy me."

"For all its faults, Chausson's music pulled me back from the edge. You don't know how close I came to throwing myself into the Marne. And you, Erik, have given me a reason to keep going. A new direction. Maeterlinck's work and your suggestions about Impressionism have inspired me."

I draw a wavering breath, studying Claude's face. Seems we have both reached a lethal nadir this summer. "I have to admit, I'm no stranger to the torment you describe. I'm glad I could help."

"I didn't want to put more weight on you, knowing you were still getting over Suzanne."

"While you were gone; I was drowning in melancholy."

Claude's brow knots. "But you're such a serious artist of immense talent. You always have a boundless supply of unique ideas."

"Boundless? You make it sound like it comes easy. I struggle, too. You are a Prix de Rome and an invited member of the Société Nationale."

Claude grimaces, shaking his head. "And just how do I continue to live up to that? I feel like a damned imposter."

"I know exactly how you feel. Expelled by the Conservatoire. No diploma. I've been called an incompetent hack." There, I've said it. All the cards are out on the table face up.

"We're so much alike." A bittersweet smirk spreads across Claude's face and he slaps me on the thigh. "What a sad pair."

I laugh. "Pathetic."

"Who else could understand what it's like, what we go through? You're my spiritual advisor. Erik Satie, high priest of the Muse."

"Merde. I am nothing so lofty. We are just brothers in the crucible of Art."

"We've formed our own little esoteric order."

"Yes. And this is our altar." I gesture to the piano.

Claude gets up, threads his way to the table and retrieves the bottle of wine and the remainder of the cake. "So then, this shall be our communion, as we continue our weekly devotional." Claude fills the glasses and raises his. "To the Metropolitan Church of Art."

This is holy wine; a sacrament consecrating our souls in unity to Art; the transubstantiation of the flesh and blood of the Muses.

"To the Metropolitan Church of Art." I bring the glass to my lips and drink.

Chapter 17

September 1893, Montmartre

Summer is at an end, and hordes of Parisians are returning to the city. The Moulin de Galette and the Place du Tertre fill every night with patrons. They hike up the hill to hear music and dance beneath the stars. I, on the other hand, have been making the opposite trek down the hill to Nouvelle Athènes. The simple café on Place Pigalle has always been the haunt of painters. Now that my Catalan friends have returned to Barcelona, I need to find other artists for company.

It's early when I enter the café and take a spot near the windows. Here a table is always reserved for old-timers like Degas and Gauguin. I often run into my friend, artist Marcelin Despoutin here. The host and waiter roll up the shades and opened the windows to let in the night. It's too hot for my jacket, so I peel down to my pinstriped shirt and a vest. After bumming a cigarette, I light it on the candle, and order a cup of coffee. With my music notebook spread open, I'm poised to take down new melodies.

"Bonsoir, Monsieur," says a gravelly voice. I pivot toward it. A middle-aged man, dressed in a finely tailored linen suit, gazes at me with high hopes. Beside him stands a young man, perhaps in his late teens, equally well attired. The elder man seems familiar, someone I'd spoken to a few times. I seem to recall his name, Ravel, an engineer, but ardent music lover.

"Bonsoir, Monsieur Ravel," I say.

"If you please," he says. "I'd like to introduce my son, Maurice. Son, this is Monsieur Erik Satie."

I extend my hand. "Enchanté, Maurice. What brings you to Nouvelle Athènes?"

He has the look of a curious church mouse with oversized ears. Small in stature and bony, his mouth is a tiny hyphen. But a sparkling magic enlivens his brown eyes. The two of them standing here prompts a memory of those occasions as a young Conservatoire student when my father used to bring me out into the Paris cafés and nightlife. "Care to join me?" I ask.

"I'm terribly honored, Monsieur Satie," says Maurice. "I wonder if I might speak to you for a few moments about your work."

"My son is so excited to talk to you."

My belly flutters. "Mai oui, " I say, now quite curious.

The two sit down at the café table. The senior Ravel orders two coffees with cream. I lean back and relax against the banquette.

"I was first introduced to your music several years ago," says Maurice. "My father purchased the sheet music of two compositions, your Trois Gymnopédies and the Sarabandes."

"Is that so?" I'm surprised. "You know, I wrote those pieces when I was not much older than you. What are you, 18?"

"Oui, Monsieur. "

Monsieur Ravel leans forward. "My son wants to be a composer and pianist, too."

"And your work is so remarkable, so new and modern."

For the first time, someone outside my own circle of compatriots is acknowledging they find my work meaningful. I can hardly restrain myself from jumping out of my chair and cheering. "Are you looking for a teacher?"

The elder Ravel shakes his head. "He attends the Conservatoire."

I chuckle. "Oh, the Inquisition of Music!"

Their mouths drop open.

"I was imprisoned and tortured there myself for several years." I look at Maurice edge-wise with a sheepish raise of the eyebrows. "N'est-ce pas?"

The younger Ravel bites his lip to keep from laughing. But his gleeful eyes glisten with a restrained hilarity. His father throws his head back with a loud guffaw. "Your humor is fresh and poignant, Monsieur; in a Pince-sans-Rire sort of manner."

I steeple my hands in priestly gesture. "I want you to know I've since given them absolution, although I myself remain a committed heretic."

Maurice cracks a smile. But I find it hard to read him.

"Actually, Maurice just won the piano competition with the highest honors."

"Pardon, Father, tell Monsieur the truth. My teachers labeled me heedless."

I nod my head with a satyr's grin. "I'm glad to hear that. There is much about technique to be learned there, but never surrender your originality. Stay heedless. Otherwise, they'll stifle everything that could make you a unique artist."

We spend the evening conversing about ancient modes and my experiments with the Greek chromatic scale. I also discover a mutual appreciation we have of folk songs. But in the process, I recognize what is really at stake here. The future of music. What good is it if I produce unique works, if they leave no lasting impact? They simply fade into obscurity. But my published sheet music has gotten into the hands of younger musicians. It is influencing their interests and aesthetics. That is wondrous enough. But I also realize that as Quixotic rebel railing against the windmills of music institutions and art critics, I have little chance of transforming them alone. However, if I get more deliberate, focus on influencing a generation of up-and-coming musicians; they will become the soldiers of change.

Chapter 18

November 1893- Paris, 8th Arrondissement

It's only a beer, I tell myself. Foam spills over the rim of two dimpled pint glasses filled with English stout. I take a long draft and wipe my moustache with my handkerchief. Playing at the far end of the pub, a folk trio makes me rock in time to the music. Sitting beside me, Claude toggles his head with abandon, his eyes closed as if caught in a trance. Other patrons clap in rhythm, broken by an occasional hoot. Accordion, fiddle, and piccolo players have the whole room bobbing like woodpeckers. Their frolicking jig boosts in tempo, galloping faster with each repetition, until the melody reaches a thunderous climax. Voices of the grateful inebriated cheer.

"Those English know how to lay down a folk tune," I say.

"I can't seem to get enough of it." Claude replies with vigorous applause.

Customers in derbies, tweed, and plaid settle into a fugue of laughter and conversation laced with smoke. I pull my small music notebook from my pocket and quickly begin jotting down the melody line while it's fresh in my mind.

"You're taking notes?" Claude asks.

"You never know. I might want to incorporate it in some way."

"Some great works have been crafted using folk music. I'll be interested to see what you do with it." He takes several gulps of his beer and lights a cigarette.

"How was your Belgium trip?" I ask.

"Very fruitful. I played the first sections of Pelleas for Maeterlinck, and it quite impressed him."

"That's encouraging," I say, even though a twinge flares in my gut. "I've had some good fortune, too. I have a new commission to score a play, The Heroic Gate of Heaven."

"Finally, both of us seem headed in the right direction again.

I nod my head with a smile, but Claude becomes quiet, studying his beer glass, running his thumbs over the dewy indentations. Despite our turn of good fortune, something is weighing on him. I finish my notation and tuck the notebook away.

"So, why the long face?"

"I need your opinion, oh benevolent high priest." Claude flashes the hint of a smirk.

I make the now standard steeple with my hands. "Let me guess; you're about to say bless me father for I have sinned."

Claude looks away and takes a drag of his cigarette. "I couldn't talk openly when we were at the apartment with Gaby there. I've become involved with another woman."

I take a sip from my glass, lean back against the banquette, take out my clay pipe and light it with a match. "Who is she?"

"We met last spring at the Salle Érard concert. She's my soloist for La Demoiselle élue."

"Therese Roger?"

Claude nods.

This soprano possesses a delightful voice. However, she is a horse-faced woman with a figure like a gourd. "You had her?"

"Only a few times. She's a proper young lady, well positioned, and well thought of."

I'm not sure whether to laugh or shake my head. Has Claude now fathered a child?

"Chausson has been pressing me to marry and doesn't approve of my beautiful seamstress. He says she's beneath me."

I can't resist a one-liner. I stare at him deadpan. "Seems they both are."

"Stop," Claude says, giving me a gentle shove. "This is serious."

"You set yourself up for that one."

"But who else can I talk to? You're the only person I trust."

"I couldn't possibly pass judgment on you, Claude. I'm no angel," I say.

"You?" Claude gazes at me edge-wise with a raised brow.

"It's true. I once had a tryst. I took advantage of our household maid. When my stepmother discovered the indiscretion, it cost the girl her job, and she banished me from the house."

"Then you can understand. My mentor Chausson has introduced me to a certain echelon of people, even convinced his mother-in-law to underwrite a 10-concert series with me performing Wagner."

"Wagner? What about your music?"

"Wagner is very lucrative. How can I turn it down?"

"So you're considering leaving Gaby for this singer you don't love?"

"Not exactly. Why couldn't I do what many men have done? They marry affluent women for position and then keep a mistress."

I rub my forehead and take several strong puffs of my pipe. Is Claude that calloused, or is he just desperate, exploiting these women for his own gain? He's been living with Gaby for two years, letting her work while he pursues his musical career. The whole thing makes my stomach roil. "And you want my advice?"

"The thing is, they have invited me back to Belgium. They want to put on a whole Debussy Festival. You know how important that is, fielding your work at a major foreign venue before you bring it before a cynical Parisian audience. Therese is coming to Brussels to perform with me. I'm considering announcing our engagement."

I lower my face, shading my eyes. Poor Gabrielle. How can Claude do this? Is he crazy? I take a deep breath and look over at Claude. "All I can say is, I think you're playing with a bundle of dynamite. It will blow up in your face. But it's your life and career, not mine." I don't say it, but what disturbs me about this disclosure far more than Claude's sexual escapades is his backstage duplicity. Is he ever honest with anyone?

December 15, 1894- Montmartre

The air reeks of horse and elephant manure, dulled by a layer of sawdust. I sit elbow to elbow with Claude on the top row of the two-franc gallery seats, watching the center of the ring at the Cirque Fernando. A white-faced clown in yellow, with a flouncy collar and a cone-shaped hat, juggles brass rings. With synchronized drum rolls, he climbs onto an ordinary wooden stool, feigns losing his balance, and fumbles. But he never drops a single ring.

"Good old Boum Boum," I say, smiling. "He has always been my favorite."

Claude stares with clenched jaw and sullen eyes. I don't know quite what to say at a time like this, or whether to say anything at all. I'd hoped an afternoon at the circus might bring consolation.

"I assume you saw the papers," Claude says.

I had. An anonymous letter appeared in Le Matin, denouncing Debussy as an irresponsible debtor and a two-timing philanderer. The seriousness of this scathing diatribe could set us back and doom everything we've tried to accomplish. I can only imagine the cascading effect this is having on Claude's financial backers, not to mention the women named. This calculated embarrassment comes within days of the Société Nationale concert, premiering Debussy's latest composition. It's hard not to conclude the timing is intentional. How mortifying. But I warned him.

"Who'd send such a thing?" I ask.

"I owe many people money who've threatened me with ruin. It could be just about anyone." Claude grips his hands together in a worried knot.

"I certainly know what it is like to be threatened by creditors." But nothing on this scale.

While the circus orchestra plays a lively gavotte, attendees stream into the arena, sidling into alternating rows of red and white. I vacillate between probing for more details, or saying something witty to distract my humiliated friend. Overhead, the gasoliers brighten, turning the dome ceiling the color of lemon and tangerine.

The ringmaster marches center. He introduces Mademoiselle Lala on the high trapeze. Faces turn upward and follow the acrobat's ascent. She leaps from a high platform, swinging from the bar, bending and twisting her body while hurling through the air in glittery nakedness.

Claude gazes upward. "Madame Escudier cancelled the remaining Wagner concerts."

"I'm sure you expected that. At least they lauded your work in Brussels."

"Yes, but now I've lost substantial income."

"I know the words to that song."

The audience gasps as Mademoiselle Lala executes several 360 degree turns around the trapeze bar, emphasized by the blare of trombones.

Claude releases an audible sigh. "And it burned my bridges with Ernest Chausson. I just hope they don't drop me from the Société Nationale program."

"That would be terrible."

With a drum roll and spotlight, Mademoiselle Lala drops and suspends herself from a knotted cord by her teeth. She begins to spin amidst audience gapes and groans. Then a rousing fanfare heralds the finish and the sequined acrobat then descends to the platform.

"Chausson's down dressing really hurt me," Claude says. "I'd intended to dedicate my string quartet to him. But I learned he actually disliked it; said I'd tarnished the nobility of the form."

"Tarnished?" I say. "Wasn't the point to reinvent it? After your landmark composition, the string quartet will never be the same."

"If I'm not blacklisted."

I watch Claude's shoulders heave with a weighty breath, his grave expression unchanged. He continues, "The Paris critics responded to my quartet with virtual silence. I don't know if it's the scandal, or if they decided the work isn't worthy of remark."

"That's not entirely true. Willy did, saying it was filled with originality and charm, but weird and baffling."

"Erik, you've always been more courageous than anyone I know; daring to do what no one else would. I picture you as a high-wire artist, always going out there above the crowd, perilously balanced with your umbrella."

"Or more foolish. I've always had the greatest respect for clowns, because they use humor to show us things we overlook in ourselves."

"True."

"But even better, I fancy myself the clown's dog. He gets to nip at their trousers and expose their asses with impunity. Yes, that's me. But you've met the establishment on its own ground, and driven in a stake, claiming new territory. That's real progress. The wager is in your favor, my friend."

"I feel like I've gone and sabotaged it," Claude admits. "What if everyone in the music establishment now shuns me? All of our efforts will be in vain."

Images of empty concert seats and stacks of cast aside programs flash through my mind. The sour taste of stomach acid erupts at the back of my throat.

"I see myself as a trapeze artist," he says, "risking life and limb, hurling myself through the air, turning somersaults to thrill the audience."

"Yes, until you miss the bar and wind up in the net," I say.

"If there *is* a net," Claude says, shaking his head.

"Well, I see you more as a magician; a little prestidigitation, smoke and mirrors."

"That's a little harsh."

"Making the lady disappear after you wave your magic wand. Sawing a lady in half."

"Not funny, Erik."

"We've got to laugh at ourselves, mon vieux. How else can we get past our own stupidity?"

"That, or shoot myself."

"I know an excellent knife thrower."

Claude rolls his eyes and socks me in the shoulder. "Yes, but then who'd feed you and whose piano would you use?"

His comment knocks the wind out of me. "Touché." I don't talk after that, nor does Claude. We just keep our eyes pinned to the fire jugglers from French Polynesia. They hurl blazing clubs at one another until their bodies eclipse behind twirling spheres of flame.

Chapter 19

December 20, 1894- Paris

Claude paces in front of the Salle d'Harcourt in a tuxedo. "I'm so glad you're here, Erik." He holds out a glossy rose-colored ticket; one of three courtesy admissions for invitees to the Société Nationale de Musique winter concert. The other two are for Claude's parents; although they rarely attend his performances. What a shame to miss an event as important as this one.

"The critics are circling me like a pack of hyenas," Claude says. Tonight is the launch of Claude's Afternoon of a Faun; the first daring sortie anyone has attempted into musical Impressionism.

I square my shoulders and take pride in having given Debussy the idea. "I wouldn't miss it for the world," I say with a smirk, pinching the ticket.

Claude labored for months to bring his composition to life. During our weekly luncheons, we'd sit together at the keyboard and he'd play segments of the piano reduction. But tonight will be the first time I've heard the orchestrated version in its entirety. I can't wait to see how poet Stéphane Mallarmé reacts to hearing his Afternoon of a Faun rendered for orchestra.

Claude and I find our reserved seats, cordoned off by a braided silk cable. Claude rocks at the edge of his seat, wringing his hands; intermittently glancing over his shoulder to survey arrivals.

"Fauré is here," he whispers. "And look; he's with Massenet."

I glance back toward the coterie of Parisian music elite. Far from being shunned after the Therese Roger affair, everyone is acting as if nothing has happened. His mentor Ernest Chausson may have severed personal ties; but as secretary of the Société, he is right there beside the podium with the other officers and founders. Claude's latest compositions have become the locus of great curiosity.

The Salle d'Harcourt fills with a madrigal of soft voices and occasional laughter. White gloved ushers guide attendees to blue velvet seats, matching the cyan ceiling and faux painted clouds resembling a golden dawn.

I reflect on my father's appraisal a few days before when I tried on suits in his apartment. I had described Claude's misdemeanor. But he'd read about the consequent uproar. My father rolled his eyes, reciting the common motto with a sigh of disgust.

"You shouldn't worry yourself. That's the French way. What's your business is yours, and what's my business is mine."

"Live and let live," I replied. Political corruption is presumed and infidelity seems a fundamental right. However, you must never show up at the opera or concert hall without a proper coat and tie. That would be an outrage. Father gave my shoulders a few final sweeps with the lint brush.

"There. You look fine. Unkept, with the long hair." Father set the brush on the dressing table. "I'll say this. All moral indecency aside, take a lesson from your Monsieur Debussy and his Société Nationale concerts. I'd like to see your name on the playbill."

I dropped my gaze, nodding in agreement. "One day you will, I promise."

The five-minute chime signals to the tardy and dawdling to find their places. The salon's polished parquet floor makes a pleasant clatter with so many slippers and fine heeled shoes hurrying across it.

I meet Claude's anxious grimace with a Cheshire cat grin. "Good luck, Claude."

The concertmaster stands up, drawing his bow across the strings, sounding the note for the other musicians to attune their instruments. Next, the young conductor, Gustav Doret, appears from a side door. After the ritual round of applause, bowing, and handshakes, the conductor takes the podium, waits for silence, and then raises his baton.

A solo flute begins with a delicate and languid theme. It floats like the warmed scent of rose and carnation on the summer air, beneath a cloudless sky. Up and down the melody glides, a dragonfly hovering, appraising a stem on which to alight. A harp glissando flutters as a passing wind tickles the leaves; followed by a soft dialogue between harmonizing horns.

A half-human faun rouses heavy-headed from a nap. Still caught in the illusion of his dream, he adds his own pan-pipe melody to the hum and quiver of the woods. As nymphs and naiads pass by him, the faun muses on what sensual pleasures they might enjoy together. Slowly, layer upon layer, muted horns, strings, and harp join in a complex mélange. The hot breath of sighs and lily soft skin undulate in the sacred dance of the earth. Pomegranates burst and blood grapes ripen. Yes, all of Mallarmé's imagery is coming alive.

I imagine all the academics and critics in the audience trying to analyze it. They'll think the music has been improvised. Oh yes, they'll accuse Debussy of having no form. However, Claude has strung together complex musical cells, motifs carefully traded between the instruments of the orchestra. After a few minutes, a hypnotic trance sweeps aside all attempts at rational explanation. I surrender my mind to the pleasure, luxuriating in the spell of a mythic summer afternoon. It no longer matters Claude used a whole-tone scale or whether his transitions move smoothly between different meters. This tone poem is leaving them all dumbfounded. I know this because I am stunned by its splendor.

When Gustave Doret finally lowers his baton and the flautist

Barrère's last note fades, the audience is silent. Then a fugue of applause and cheers build. From the back of the room, a man calls out. "Encore!" This is unheard of, never allowed. A few more rise to their feet, echoing his request. "Encore, encore". Gustave Doret whirls around wild-eyed and grins as the audience stands up, shouting and clapping. I bolt to my feet, yanking Claude along with me.

"My God!" Claude gasps. The color leaves his face, and he totters. I steady him.

The conductor gestures with outstretched arm toward us, acknowledging Claude and causing a new upsurge of cheers and applause. I notice an exchange at the podium between Doret and the Société's officers D'Indy and Chausson. Then the conductor straightens. Facing the audience, he signals with his hands for everyone to take their seats. And when the clamor dies down, he begins the piece again.

The magnitude of this unexpected turn of events takes a few moments to sink in. Claude has shattered a barrier. Not only is The Afternoon of a Faun entirely different and new, but the Conservatoire circle and often cynical Parisian public are in love. Real change is not only possible; it's occurring before my eyes. The august and erotic fantasy fills my ears in this moment of realization. Claude's dream, a dream we share, is coming true.

My eyes grow moist. Right now, I want to be in Claude's seat gloating with pride. And I hate that I want it. I hate my envy for my friend. But I can't deny how desperately I want to be part of this. Claude has earned these accolades. But it's been over two years since anything I've composed received such recognition. I've scored several plays, but I really possess only the most rudimentary skills at writing for orchestra. Claude outstrips me by miles, no, continents. By comparison, I am an amateur. I don't know how to do what Claude has done. There is no way for me to achieve this kind of grandeur.

They perform two other pieces by different composers during the evening. But the Faun eclipses their radiance. When the concert finishes, a swarm of people inundates Claude.

Stéphane Mallarmé rushes over, vigorously shaking Claude's hand. "You truly captured the emotion of the poem and conjured up a scene more vivid than any painting," he says. "You honor me, sir."

The young conductor Doret oozes enthusiasm. "I could just feel it behind me, as conductors can," he says, "an audience totally spellbound. It was a complete triumph. I had no hesitation in breaking the rule forbidding encores."

Newspaper reporters surround Claude, with their writing tablets ready in hand. Young music students wedge in to listen. Gradually I find myself pushed to the periphery, like I don't belong. Claude's Prix de Rome talent has separated us. Right now, this is Claude's moment. My gut is hollow and aching. I drop my head. A cigarette and a stiff drink are what I crave right now. Which way to the door.

Chapter 20

January 1895, Montmartre

My head is throbbing. If I open my eyes more than a narrow stitch, it makes me wince. I overdid it again last night. I didn't intend to get so drunk. I'd told myself I would only have one drink. But then friends and acquaintances bought a second and a third. It tasted so good and went down too easily. Truthfully, drinking to excess has slipped into a routine again. Most nights, I haul myself home in the early hours of the morning. This is not because I've been playing any engagement, either. I'm not performing at all. I'm surviving on the remains of a commission earned last summer. And while I pay lip service to working on a modern Mass, by the time I pull myself out of bed, the day is spent. I'm often feeling too bilious to get much accomplished. I haven't felt inspired to compose anything since that night Faun premiered. I've avoided Debussy, letting him bask in his limelight, even though he keeps inviting me to Sunday Supper. The weeks have become a blur.

I'm nearly broke again. I wrote to Conrad about my plight, hoping he'd be generous one more time. But I'm asking too much of people. I've over-extended my credit, and before long, I'll have to forage cafés for unfinished scraps again.

I put on my overcoat, grab my umbrella and stumble down the

Rue Cortot to the Concierge's apartment to collect the mail. When I arrive at the porte-cochere, I find the Concierge is not home. His wife answers the door. She callously hands me an envelope.

"You're three days late on your rent, Monsieur."

"Yes, thanks for the reminder."

She sneers and closes the door.

At first, I'm relieved to get a letter, hoping my brother has helped me. I stare at the return address and realize it lists a law office. Merde. This has to be something bad. Am I being sued? Is someone trying to collect on unpaid debts? A rush of adrenalin makes my heart gallop and I feel loose in my bowels. My aching head reels. I tuck the letter in my coat and lumber back up the stairs to my room. I slump onto my cot, with the window light over my shoulder illuminating the correspondence. I slide one finger under the flap, pulling the page from inside. Adjusting my pince-nez, I read, my heart thundering in my throat.

Dear Monsieur Satie:

I am the attorney for Fernand and Louise le Monnier, whose father Monsieur Alexandre le Monnier of Honfleur, Normandy, has passed one week ago. In settling the estate, it was discovered the you are named as the recipient of a bequest. Please come to our law office on Thursday, January 10 at 1:00 PM, so I may present you with payment. Be sure to bring legal identification.

Respectfully,

Maître Francois Hagège,

2 Rue Saint-Florentin, Paris 8

Surely this is a hoax. It's too good to be true. But how would pranksters even know the names of my childhood playmates and Grand-Père's most enduring friend? I haven't been in contact with any of those people for years. Could the Le Monniers have known I'm a poor struggling artist? Maybe my father or Conrad wrote to them. It all seems too coincidental.

I've got two days to prepare for this auspicious meeting. Legal identification? I must have the identity card they issued me in the army in my steamer trunk somewhere. I strip off my shirt, but stagger for a moment, still feeling the effects of too much Absinthe. I put the shirt in the wash tub, along with my underwear, and heat some water to soak them in washing soda. If I hang them up overnight, they might actually be dry by morning. And though my shirt will be wrinkled, with a fresh collar and my coat on, no one can tell. At least I won't reek. As destitute as I may be, I haven't forgotten how to make myself presentable.

What if I could stop worrying about making rent, feeding myself, and having to roll cigarettes from others' discards? If I could wear clean underwear and socks without holes, that would be great. I'd pay my friends back for their kind generosity, and all creditors. Then, will the muse speak to me again with a clear mind?

⁂

Maître Hagège purses his lips, switching his moustache back and forth in thought as he scrutinizes my military identification card and then looks at me with narrow eyes. "If this is you, you've changed a lot since this was issued. Don't you have anything more recent?"

"I'm afraid not."

"Alright, then. Here you are, Monsieur Satie." He takes an envelope from his desk and slides it toward me. I retrieve my documents, tuck them inside my breast pocket and rise. Hagège steps around from behind his desk and offers me his hand. "Good luck, and use it well," he says.

"Thank you, Maître." I smile and take my leave. As soon as I exit his office and climb inside the curious wrought iron latticework elevator, I flip open the envelope and slide out the cheque. Seven thousand francs! I shake my head in utter astonishment. My heart flutters and I feel a little drunk. But I haven't had a drop today.

Immediately, I go down the avenue to the Société Générale and open a new account. I also take out a money order to repay Conrad what I owe him, around 250 francs. My tab at Lapin Agile and a few other places I'll pay with cash. But this fund will allow me to reinvent myself.

My next adventure takes me to the huge and bustling department store, La Belle Jardinière. I've never been inside such a place and don't know where to begin. Newspaper advertisements say everything you need is under one roof. The building at the corner of the Pont de Neuf reminds me of a wedding cake. Corbels, intricate moldings, and grillwork ornament the façade. Beige and ivory striped awnings shade the windows. A tingling sensation ignites in my middle. I have money.

The uniformed doorman looks me up and down. I'm a ragged bohemian. It never mattered before, but now I'm a little embarrassed. The man opens the door for me, anyway. Crystal chandeliers with electricity glitter overhead. The upper walls and friezes are painted in muted pastels. Lovely fragrances waft in the air. Sales attendants wearing the same beige and ivory wait on customers from behind glass display cases.

"May I assist you, sir?" asks a gentleman with a black moustache and white gloves.

"Men's clothing, *s'il vous plaît.*"

He gestures with an open hand. "The men's department is up the stairs to your right."

I haven't bought new clothing for nearly a decade. Then, my father had taken me to the tailor for a custom suit. This department store is something altogether different. They call it ready to wear. Clothes in varying sizes line the racks. Suits, jackets, and coats hang ready for purchase on the spot. I've never seen anything like it. Mannequins display the newest fashion with all the accoutrements. Morning coats, vests, and tweed caps. None of these appeal to me.

Then, I notice it. My mouth falls open. The ensemble is unique, strange in fact. Some designer has used the lines and cut of a painter's smock, loose fitting with a few pleats. But the suit is entirely rich corduroy. When I stroke the velvety nap, the color appears like raw umber on an artist's palate. The mannequin displays the suit over the same earthy colored shirt with an attached collar and dark burnt umber silk tie in a floppy bow. A matching hat completes the collection. Maybe it is some kind of sportswear for hunting, or skeet and trap. But the look is not your typical civil servant, the boring grey and dreary black. This is the unique profile I'm looking for. No one on the butte dresses this way. It will make me stand out. It has a poetic and artistic flair that suits me perfectly.

A sales attendant notices me admiring the suit. "May I be of service, Monsieur?"

"How much is it?" I know this question is rather rude.

"50 francs for just the suit. The accessories would be extra, of course."

That is nearly six months' rent. But I can buy ten of them with what I now have in my pocket. I want the whole outfit. For the next half-hour, I try on each piece to find the correct fit; trousers, shirt, coat, and hat. Matching socks, new shoes, with several sets of underwear, complete the buying spree.

Wearing the new outfit and carrying packages and a new umbrella, I walk out of La Belle Jardinière. More suits just like this one will be delivered to my Rue Cortot apartment; one for every day of the week. Not really, but I'm weary to the bone of being destitute. This opportunity will never come again. I want to make sure that when times get tough again, I'll never have to share one pair of trousers with a friend. An elegant but painterly image is the new Erik Satie, my trademark. Whenever I walk out my door, I'll cut a dramatic profile.

Next, I visit the barber shop. He cuts my hair short and trims my beard and moustache in the newest style, the stinger beard. I purchase moustache wax and men's cologne with a woody scent. I happen by a tobacconist and buy two long stemmed ceramic pipes with an ample supply of Black Jack tobacco, an especially delicious import from across the channel.

I treat myself to a fine meal. But in the spirit haze of after dinner liqueurs, I lean back against the tufted leather chair. The sensible part of me is uneasy. I shouldn't waste this money. Reckless indulgence is never a safe thing to do, as fat times never last. I've satisfied my basic needs and even splurged a little. It is high time I think about the best use for this windfall? It wasn't all that long ago Father handed me a cheque for a large sum of money. I frittered away the entire amount of Grand-père's inheritance. I still feel guilty about it. No one has really taught me about investing or multiplying capital, generating a profit. I lost everything. What have I learned since then?

The hotbed of radicals and intellectuals I've been keeping company with at Nouvelle Athènes reject desires for wealth, power, and fame. They affirm living a simple life free from materialism. Don't I believe that anymore? Do I still embrace the philosophy of Socrates and Diogenes of Sinope, who lived in a barrel on the streets of Athens decrying the ills of society? I'm of two minds. Maybe it's too easy for money to corrupt me. Large amounts of it, all at one time, can't be a good thing. Is there no way to keep my ideals and use money for a more noble purpose?

Chapter 21

May 1896- 8th Arrondissement

POWERFUL GATEKEEPERS HAVE refused to take me seriously in the past. With a bit of luck, this evening's casual gathering might bloom into an opportunity. Since conducting Claude's Afternoon for a Faun, Gustave and Claude have become chummy. Gustave also benefitted by the exposure the concert provided. I haven't seen him much in the last year and a half. But Gustave started having gatherings at his flat on Monday evenings. Claude attends regularly and invited me along tonight. He hopes we can convince Gustave to add one of my works to the playbill for the next Société Nationale concerts.

Dressed in one of my corduroy suits, with my hair and beard neatly groomed, I arrive at the apartment on Rue de Courcelles. Hoping for a chance to play them, I've brought the deluxe editions of the Trois Gymnopédies and the Sarabandes.

The first part of the evening we spend enjoying several types of sharp cheese and a chilled Sancerre, in the cool air wafting from the tall open balcony windows. We smoke pipe tobacco and discuss recent offerings at the Concert Colonne and Concert Lamoureux. I'd bought season tickets with my windfall last year. Finally, the time comes to share our compositions, beginning with a preview of Claude's huge work in progress, Images.

Then, it is my turn. My hands shake and my mouth goes dry. I've played these pieces hundreds of times and they're my own compositions. But I haven't performed either in a long time, nor have I played or written music in a year.

"I'm a bit out of practice," I say. I press the pages open against the music rest. With trembling hands at the keyboard, I begin. I strain to play every note accurately. But this slows my delivery and I even hesitate a few times. When I finish, I look over at Claude. He stares with his arms crossed, and his mouth in a twist.

"Come now, Erik. Let me show you how your music really sounds," Claude says. He shifts his eyes for a second toward Doret and then back, as if to convey silently that I'm ruining this chance to impress this young conductor.

"Alright, go ahead," I say, vacating the bench.

I have never heard my piano pieces played by anyone else. Claude's piano style differs dramatically from mine. Claude flutters over the keys with a delicate smooth blending of sound, like a glittering brook or gentle rain shower. My technique is sharper and nuanced, like plucking a flower or picking a piece of fruit from a branch.

With his left hand, Claude begins the bass ostinato of The First Gymnopédie. Gentle as the strokes of a single oar, first on one side, then the other; a varnished oak wherry propels through the still glass of a canal. Each chord is a perfectly spaced platanus tree standing as sentinels along the grass-edged bank, mirrored in the ribbon of water. Dappled light and shadow scatter across the laps of two voyagers locked in a lover's stare, while swallowtails and cabbage whites dance among the hyacinths. I've never conceived of my music this way, but Claude's rendition is dazzling, like a Monet landscape. When his hands finally come to rest, Claude pivots slowly to look at me and Doret.

"Superb, just marvelous," says Doret. "The next thing we need to do is orchestrate the work just like that."

"Orchestrate?" I ask. My stomach drops.

"Absolutely," replies Claude. "I'd be happy to arrange these. That is, if you want me to."

"If it sounds as spectacular as I imagine," says Doret. "I will insure they get scheduled for the Société Nationale winter concert. It will stun them silly."

I gasp. "What an honor. I would be in your debt."

I'm very touched by Claude's offer. I've never known him to arrange any other composer's work as long as we've been friends. He must have sensed how timely and vital this is to me, and he is aware of how creatively paralyzed I've become.

"It's a pleasure, mon vieux." Claude grins. "I'll get started tomorrow."

How terribly big-hearted. Claude is taking his own time to help me. He's ensuring we both have our work performed in front of a large discriminating audience. This could be phenomenal. It's a fresh start, a new chance. If it actually materializes. I swallow hard. Do I dare to hope?

◆

July 15, 1896- Montmartre

"I know the rent is late Monsieur Jacques," I say. My landlord stares me in the face, centered in the frame of my open apartment door. "This is my last twenty francs. You can throw me out and I will just give it to some flophouse nearby. Or you can take it and I'll owe you the rest. Which do you prefer? For nearly ten years, I've been a good tenant here, you know."

The older man's frown softens, and he leans against the doorjamb, gazing upward as he calculates the consequences of eviction. "Erik, you know I don't want to put you on the street. Perhaps this place has become too expensive for you. I have another place downstairs that may be more affordable. Would you like to see it?"

"How much is it?"

"Only twenty francs a quarter."

"Twenty? What a coincidence. Let's have a look." The weight on my chest lightens. The older man is reasonable and not the sang-froid he typically seems to be. I follow him to the ground floor of the apartment building where he unlocks a narrow door painted with blue enamel.

"Voila! What do you think? Cozy, eh?"

I peer into the dark tapered chamber. Who would live here? This is not an apartment. It isn't even a room, but a utility closet. No one expects running water or heat on the butte. But there isn't even enough head-room to stand upright. The only window is the scrollwork vent in the door. Is Monsieur Jacques trying to help me or take advantage of me? But there are no other options. If I go to a hotel, my money will be gone in a few days. If I give my money to Monsieur Jacques, it will keep a roof over my head for a few months. A shiver runs through me.

"It's awfully cramped, for twenty francs," I say.

"I won't charge you arrearages for the other room," says Monsieur Jacques.

I hesitate a moment and then hand my concierge the money. This is just temporary, right?

Later in the day, I move my belongings downstairs into Le Placard with the help of two new acquaintances, Augustin and Henry, both of whom still live with their parents. Henry is a budding songwriter. He wants me to set some of his lyrics to music. I could really use a few francs right about now. My cot fits well enough, and my steamer trunk can go under it. But once everything is inside, the door can't open all the way. I have to squeeze through a narrow gap.

My first night sleeping inside the closet, I lie on my back, staring up into the stifling darkness. Tears trickle down my temples. I clench my jaw to hold them back. Moonlight pierces through the grillwork in the door, taking the shape of a crusader's cross on the wall. It's like I'm in the cell of a medieval cleric, who has taken a vow of poverty. What a fall from grace this has become, and it's my own damn fault. I've been frivolous and cavalier with my money, doing absolutely nothing. What I should have been doing was composing and performing music.

I've watched Debussy's financial and artistic standing rise to a whole new level. He is now respected among the traditional-minded authorities of the old guard and progressive thinkers alike. He has several fresh projects taking shape, eager collaborators, sheet music publications, and a new patron. I envy his success. But if he can do it, why can't I? Hopefully, his orchestration of my Gymnopédies is going well.

August, 1896, Montmartre

Desperation makes men willing to do all kinds of things. I hate to grovel, but I have to generate enough income to put food in my belly. I've run out of alternatives. This unrelenting summer swelter adds to the misery. It's like a Turkish bath in my corduroy suit. Most Parisians of means have boarded a fast train for the coast. It must be nice to spend a month in the country or by the sea. The cafés and sidewalks along Rue Victor-Massé are nearly deserted. Business is slow this time of year. But all I need is a daily meal and a few tips to get by. I've decided to throw myself on the mercy of my former employer Rudolph Salis in hopes he'll be willing to hire me back.

The entrance to Le Chat Noir hasn't changed in the least since the day I walked out of it five years ago. The mail clad doorman gives me an embrace and welcoming smile, and opens the door wide for me.

"How have you been, you wild renegade?"

"You know how it is in the music business," I say. "Is Salis here?"

"Quite certain he is."

They must have heard our voices in the now quiet bar. My mentor, Alfonse Allais, hurries downstairs.

"Well, well. If it isn't my long-lost prodigal son," says Alphonse. "How've you been, you son of a bitch?"

"Surviving."

"I'd heard rumors you'd become a wealthy man."

"You know how that goes. Here today, gone tomorrow."

The now rotund rusty-haired owner comes out from the back office. "What do you want, Satie?" Salis asks with a sardonic grin.

"I hope to have a brief conversation with you, if I may."

Salis eyes me with feigned disdain. But then he does that to everyone. Allais leaves the room and Salis gestures for me to sit at one of the café tables.

"I'm ruined, Rodolphe, my friend. I need to work. I don't suppose you need a pianist?"

"I have someone, but he is not always reliable. The terms haven't changed. I only pay if you cover for the first pianist, or if you are in a production. Food, beverages, and tips."

"Thank you. I'm embarrassed to come to you this way, mon vieux."

"You're always welcome, here."

"Mercie beaucoup. I'll be back this evening." I stand and shake Salis' hand.

"Nice outfit, the corduroy. It's different. You're different. A little more mature, maybe."

"Never," I smile. Have I changed that much in five years? At least I won't starve. I might earn enough in tips to set aside for my next rent, only seven francs a month. Things can only get better from here. Right?

Chapter 22

February 1897- 2nd Arrondissement, Paris

I LOOK ACROSS the cab at Conrad, who sits beside his wife, Irene. Then I turn to meet my father's gaze. I'm glad they are here. My chest expands as I smile. The carriage transporting us comes to a halt in front of the Salle Érard. After many months, Claude's fully orchestrated version of my Gymnopédies will premier tonight. My unique composition is finally going before the Paris music elite in a major concert. The Salon of the Rose+Croix, five years ago, was the only other time my music was performed in a venue of this caliber. The very fact I'm here confirms I'm no crackpot or dilettante. I'm a bona fide composer.

A footman opens the door and I step out onto the blue-gray cobbled courtyard. My uneasy breath crystallizes midair in cold anticipation. I've been here frequently during rehearsals. But tonight, the elegant salon has the radiance of an ancient Greek temple. A row of tall windows framed by white louvered shutters and a bank of beveled glass entry doors gleams like a diamond. The stirring sounds of the orchestra's warm-up drifts across the frosty air. My core flutters like a cellist's tremolando. I hand the concert tickets to Father, while Conrad helps Irene exit the cab.

"I think I'll wait here for Claude, if you don't mind," I say. "We're plenty early. Go on ahead and have a drink."

"We'll see you inside, then," Father says, patting me on the shoulder.

A stream of horse-drawn cabs pulls up to the curb and their passengers disembark. The footmen scurry back and forth, helping the well-heeled patrons in top hats and furs navigate the pyramid of stairs. They've all come to listen and judge. But the Paris bourgeoisie couldn't recognize real art if it sat down beside them and lit a cigarette. Like the Rose+Croix, I believe they will love this performance. Regardless, my alternating major 7th chords are going to dazzle the scholarly establishment. It's a harmony completely unknown, they'll say.

Claude climbs down from an arriving carriage wearing a black derby and double-breasted overcoat with otter collar.

I grin, raising my brows. "Big night, mon vieux!"

"Finally," says Claude, "after seven months' work."

We embrace, kissing on alternate cheeks. Together we scale the stairs, faces lifted, silent and hopeful. The doorman hands me a beautifully decorated playbill. I flip it open, noting what I already know. Still, it is thrilling to see my Gymnopédies scheduled midway through the program. My name is listed next to Claude's, as composer and arranger respectively. I smile. It's really happening.

The usher escorts us across the shiny herringbone wood floor. We sit in the second row of pale blue velvet chairs behind the Société officers. Arching portals separate side rooms swarming with patrons drinking champagne, smoking and chatting. I recognize Father's baritone laugh behind me and look back over my shoulder to where the family sits. Father returns a broad smile, lifting his chin with pride.

Chimes signal the concert-goers to take their seats. Ernest Chausson steps to the podium and voices hush. He gives a brief history of the Société and its purpose. This is the second in the winter series of concerts, focusing on innovative French composers. How exhilarating to be numbered among them. Next, the first violinist, Eugène Ysaÿe, stands and confirms that all the strings are perfectly attuned. The side door opens and Gustave Doret comes out with his baton to applause and takes the dais.

The program opens with a work by one of our friends, Paul Dukas. His Symphony no. 3 in C major is lively and beautiful. Women wave their fans and men tap their feet. I notice Wagnerian influences, but they don't spoil its uniqueness. When the pieces are complete, Gustave Doret turns and gestures to Dukas. The young composer stands and graciously bows to the ovation.

The Trois Gymnopedies are next. My throat tightens. I glance at Claude, who wears a marionette-like smile. I fold my hands, tucking them between my thighs. Claude reaches over and gives my forearm a squeeze. Gustave tosses us a quick glance and turns to the orchestra. I take a deep breath.

Bass violins and cellos begin the low ostinato, pulsing and alternating in delicate rhythm. It's answered by the French horn. The melody rises like a distant sunrise. Ancient lovers linger in a farewell embrace; gazing ruefully at the cruel bronze and crimson sky. Hearts are torn between the call of duty and an aching passion. A solo clarinet voices anticipation and regret, followed by the flute's reply, whispering hope and promises. Claude's orchestration translates my simple piano solo into a vision of antiquity, blending mood and texture with each carefully chosen instrument. When the last strains of the first movement finally fade and Doret lowers his baton, I look back over my shoulder. The audience is dumbfounded. The fans have stopped waving and everyone in the audience is still. Even from a few rows back, I can see Father's eyes glisten, trance-like. Conrad stares slack-jawed, blinking back a swell of emotion.

Doret again raises his baton to begin the next movement. The tempo is much slower than I ordinarily play it, giving the piece an even dreamier, ethereal quality. Opening with plucked harp strings and the tang of the ancient cymbal, tremulous violins carry the melody. The combination creates a vision of sunlight scintillating across a brook-fed emerald pool. It is as if Claude scored my music as a reply to his own "Afternoon of a Faun". The audience is lulled into a trance. The solitary oboe seduces like Zeus gliding among the lilies in the guise of a trumpeter swan. The melody undulates tenderly, sensuously, finally resolving into a melancholy-tinged bliss.

Doret lowers his hands, and the crowd bursts into applause with cheers of bravo. Many rise to their feet.

"They love it," says Claude, pumping his fist. "Stand up." He pulls me to my feet. Gustave gestures toward us and the applause grows. We both bow. My chest swells and I feel like tossing my head back with a bellow. Gustave takes his own bow and leaves the stage for intermission. The ovation ebbs and spectators disperse. Many head into the adjacent rooms to smoke and drink.

"Come on, outsider," says Claude. "Let's meet your public."

I'm trembling all over. "Lead the way. I'm dying for a drink."

We thread a path through the milling crowd to one of the side rooms with a small bar.

"Two champagnes," Claude says, pulling some folded bills from his pocket and peeling off a few. The bar host slides two fluted glasses toward Claude, who hands one to me. "To this victory and more to come," Claude says.

I raise my glass. "To our coup de etat." As I'm about to take a sip, someone bumps into me, nearly spilling my drink.

"Monsieur Debussy," says the man, holding a notepad and pen. "That melody seemed to use an Asian scale, didn't it? And it has a very unusual title. Care to comment?"

I speak up. "It was by design, to capture the spirit of ancient Sparta."

The journalist doesn't respond, but keeps his eyes pinned on Debussy.

"The material is based on the 12-tone system," Claude says with his usual charismatic charm. "And it uses devices such as inversion and retrograde."

The journalist scribbles into his notepad. Within moments, more people swarm around us, jostling to get close, shouting questions.

We're pinned with our backs to the bar. I have a strong urge to escape. I gulp my glass of champagne and order a second.

A stunning dark-haired woman in purple moiré wedges her way in beside Claude. Her perfume is intoxicating as jasmine. "My compliments to you, Monsieur Debussy," she says, handing him her playbill and a pearlized fountain pen.

Claude eyes the bodice of her gown and gives her a wry smile. "To whom should I sign?"

"Chloe," she says and titters.

He writes a few lines, but hands the program to me while lingering in her sultry stare. I sign the playbill and return it and the pen.

Two young Conservatoire students press in on us. "Maître Debussy," says one. "I'd like to ask about the mood and tonality. The first seemed darker with more complex rhythmic movement than the second."

"Simple modal melodies really, with successions of seventh and ninth chords that provide colorful underpinning to ease its dissonance," Claude says. Then he turns to look at me. "Wouldn't you say, Satie?"

"They are one piece," I say. "Repeated, but with the most subtle variations in phrasing, harmonic coloring, and balance." Hadn't Claude just said the same thing? Merde! I'm nothing more than Claude's echo. No one seems interested in what I have to say. My gut tightens, and I feel the blood rise in my throat. So much for meeting my public. After a few more thwarted attempts to assert my ideas, I finally give up. It wasn't supposed to happen like this. Everyone is so enthralled with Claude, I'm invisible.

When the chimes sound for the second half of the concert, we start for our seats.

"I knew this would stir controversy," says Claude, "and bring us lots of attention."

Us, I say to myself. You're the one getting the attention, Claude. I force a smile.

Doret retakes the podium and the Société orchestra performs a symphony by Vincent d'Indy. But I can barely listen. I could have taken rejection. But this is altogether shocking. Who would have guessed my music would add to Claude's celebrity? I'm sure it wasn't intentional. Was it? He's just as surprised as I am. He wouldn't use me. It doesn't matter, anyway. The main thing is my music is a success.

After the concert, I rendezvous with my family at the entrance. We walk to the street and climb into a cab together. With a huge grin, Father puts his arm around my shoulder, pulling me close to his side.

"I always knew you had talent," Father says. "Tonight, the rest of Paris knows it, too. You're on your way now, son."

He has no idea how disillusioned and cheated I feel. What matters more right now is that Father saw the music's glowing reception. His words are a sweet dessert to the full plate of audience approval.

Conrad draws one of Irene's hands through his bent arm. He peers at me with a skeptical brow. "Debussy's arrangement was not what I expected," Conrad says. "Are you satisfied with it, brother?"

Until now, I'd been so caught up in the excitement of getting my work performed, I hadn't looked at things more critically. "I'm the one who wanted the harps and cymbals. Didn't you like it?"

"It was beautiful," Conrad replies. "But the qualities that make your style unique were lost in a cascade of Impressionist shimmer. Just my opinion. Congratulations, brother."

Leave it to Conrad. He is always so observant and astute. Unfortunately, he is usually right. Claude carried off the laurels, and his orchestration overshadowed my original work. My hoped-for triumph was eclipsed by his persona. I allowed it, without question or doubt. Claude was genuinely trying to help me. But I will never make that mistake again. The cold air spreads over me, finding its way to my core. An unsettling ache in my chest weighs me down. I stare at the playbill still clutched in my hand, and my name printed beside his.

April 1897- Paris, 9th Arrondissement

Rodolphe Salis, the 45-year-old owner of the Chat Noir, had once staged his own funeral. He even published an obituary in the newspaper. That was before I arrived in Montmartre. But I'd heard the story of my employer's outrageous antics from Alphonse Allais. Dozens of poets, musicians, and performers participated in a staged procession. So, when news spread that Salis was dead, everyone suspected another publicity stunt.

Rumors abound. Some allege he'd been shot in his hotel suite in a dispute over unpaid wages while touring with a Chat Noir roadshow. Others claim he'd been caught in a compromising position with someone's wife, or more likely, husband. One newspaper reported he had become violently ill after eating tainted oysters. None of us ever suspected that he actually had tuberculosis. But the way he'd always isolate himself in the back room now makes sense. Salis is really dead this time.

The employees of the cabaret gathered in the back-room *Institut,* to plan how we might keep the operation going. But our efforts and intentions haven't been very fruitful. Now, four weeks later, the icon of Montmartre bohemia, Le Chat Noir is closing its doors for the last time.

"My heart is shattered." I mutter to Alphonse Allais as we stand staring up at the façade from the curb outside the cabaret. Huge beams have been affixed to the door, sealing it until the estate is settled.

"This truly marks the end of an era," he replies. "I've been asked to write the eulogy to the man. Imagine someone like me struggling to find the words."

"But who better?" I ask, clasping him by the shoulder.

"I know." He pats my hand. "He was one of a kind." He folds his arms and we stand in silence a few moments. Then he looks over. "I'll write you a reference if you need one. Guess we'll both be looking for work." He heaves a sigh and turns to go. The closing of this symbol of Montmartre also brings an end to the meager but essential source of income that has kept me alive in my utility closet. Once again, I'm about to become a beggar.

May 1897, Montmartre

Since the Société Nationale concert, I worked through the winter on a collection I call The Cold Pieces. Now I have more time available, I try my hand at orchestrating them. I'd learned only the most rudimentary elements of the skill. For the first time, I sincerely regret not remaining in school. As a student, I didn't understand how complex the process was. I complete nine bars of the first part, Airs au Faire Fuir and send a note to Gustave Doret requesting to meet for lunch. I'd like him to have a look at it.

We sit together at a café on a misty day. "Just tell me if I'm on the right path here," I say.

Gustave looks it over, his head shifting back and forth, his fingers following the various stanzas for a variety of instruments. Then he takes a deep breath and looks up.

"Well, I'm sorry mon vieux, I can tell you right now, this will not sound right. The problem is, you've lost the melody. It needs to stand out by strongly accentuating the dynamic shades and by contrasting timbres and strengthening resonance. You've got it eclipsed in the middle of the orchestral range, which only becomes prominent with doubling or tripling."

I don't fully understand what I must do. "Can you guide me?"

"It's not really my forte. I can show you what is suitable for which instrument, but I'm sure you already know this. You must have a sense of the sound you're after."

"Inventing something haunting and delicious."

"Yes, yes. The thing is, grouping them together and blending their sound is complicated. It's an art. The best resource I know is written by Hector Berlioz, his Treatise on Instrumentation. Work with that and I'll be happy to look at it again."

I throw the score away and start over. At national library and pour over Berlioz's reference book. But I already know a lot about the various instruments and their capacity and use. My study gives me an even greater reverence for Claude's talent and skill. Alas, I don't know enough to figure it out on my own. The Cold Pieces are still beautiful just as they are, for solo piano. But unless I can find a way to increase my level of skill so I can orchestrate my compositions, my work cannot move forward.

Chapter 23

March 1898- Paris, 10th Arrondissement

For the past year, Paris has been in an uproar, the likes of which I've never seen. The turmoil is all over the fate of this Jewish army officer Alfred Dreyfus. But the upheaval really reached a fevered pitch at the end of January, after Emile Zola's letter was printed on the front page of the newspaper, L'Aurore. Zola asserts the government colluded with the army to frame an innocent man as a spy, and hide the truth. It has split the country in half and filtered down to every part of society. Now, something as simple as crossing Paris on foot has gotten dicey. Dangerous, in fact. Twice I've encountered huge demonstrations against Alfred Dreyfus that blocked thoroughfares and tied up traffic. Brawls break out in cafés and bars between pro-and-anti-Dreyfus rivals. People I know from Nouvelle Athènes have been accosted, just for visiting the café Zola frequented.

My much-loved Montmartre is no longer a haven, either. Vigilantes come onto the butte at night, sit in wait, and attack innocent writers and artists in the dark. A young artist friend of mine was found beaten to death outside the Maison Rose this week. They presume all who live here are pro-Dreyfus. Claude's move to Wagram was probably a wise decision.

With a handful of change I've collected from neighbors and passersby, I have enough for a ticket on the train to gather with family for Sunday supper. Rosny sous Bois is the suburb where Conrad lives. At a brisk pace, it should only take an hour to reach Gare de Lyon by departure time. I stare down at my corduroy jacket and tug at the hem. Who would have guessed the style would become so popular? But now it marks me as a Montmartois. It's all I have to wear. I can't go out in formal attire, which is the only other thing I own.

I pick up the small claw hammer I borrowed from the concierge. Along with my umbrella, this could provide a defense if I need one. I tuck the hammer head first into my coat pocket. That way, I can grab it quickly to defend myself. I adjust my hat and set out. Today I'll leave plenty early, since there is no way to predict what I'll encounter.

I dodge between people traversing the streets and sidewalks. At the intersection of Rochechouart and Magenta, I veer southwest. This is where we once lived and Father had his stationery store. Now it hosts a drapery shop and a hair salon. For ten years, I've been living the bohemian life, tucked away like a hermit on the butte. But Le Chat Noir is gone. Everything around me is changing. I don't know if this changed Paris still holds a place for me. Father's comment after the Société Nationale concert last year still sustains me. "You're on your way now, son." But on my way where?

A short distance from Place de la Republique, I hear a tumult of chanting and shouts above the usual hum of traffic. I slow my pace and approach with caution. The center of the plaza near the monument honoring the Third Republic teems with people. "Death to the Jews" and "Long Live the Army" they chant. Maybe I should go around, rather than try to cut across. But doing so means entering the Jewish neighborhood, an even greater risk.

From the periphery, I watch them hoist an effigy, and set it aflame. Frocked clergy in black or red cassocks cheer them on. Royalist and anti-Dreyfusard extremists throw apples and shatter shop windows. Several topple a newsstand, and half a dozen men join forces trying to overturn a produce wagon. The gendarmes on foot and horseback watch at the perimeter, but do nothing. That would trespass on their Liberté of speech, they say.

"Hey, you, crotch lice!" shouts a man, pointing at me.

I freeze. Two ruffians head in my direction. Run. I reverse course, sprinting to evade the hooligans down a back street. The two men tailing me carry clubs. I duck between buildings, crawl over a fence, cross a courtyard, and head down another alley. Several blocks beyond the mêlée, I look back. I lost them.

I pause in front of a shop window to catch my breath. Peering into the glass, I straighten my tie and adjust my corduroy waistcoat. I've had enough of this madness. Nowhere is safe anymore. All of Paris is disintegrating into chaos. I must find a way to relocate, before something terrible happens to me. But where? How?

Once on the train, the twenty-minute journey allows me to relax. This is a pleasant trip to Rosny sous Bois, a quaint village east of Paris. When I disembark, I easily locate my brother's two-storey brick townhome. It sits on a cobbled street lined with budding trees. My sister-in-law Irene answers the door. Her belly bulges and her cheeks are aglow. She leads me into the salon, wallpapered in maroon. A comfortable rosewood settee and overstuffed armchairs encircle the artisan tiled hearth. The aroma of pipe tobacco, wood smoke, and aperitifs fill the air. I hang up my jacket and hat, and join my father and brother.

Father's hair seems snowier every time I see him. His skin has an ashen tone. It reminds me of Grand-père, shortly before he passed away. I know the day will come when I'll lose my father. But that time may be sooner than I expect. A wave of dread rolls through my middle. Time is passing too quickly.

Irene interrupts my dark reverie to offer a glass of Pastis and a shrimp canapé.

"How was the trip out?" Conrad asks.

"The train ride was just fine," I say. "But a demonstration at Place de le Republique turned into a riot. It was nearly disastrous for me."

"Heavens," says Irene.

"I'm glad you're still in one piece," Conrad says.

"Parisians are quick to make assumptions when they see someone dressed like a subversive," Father says.

I stiffen. What's made him so ornery? "Only a musical one."

"Anyone who plasters inflammatory and fallacious slander across the front page of L'Aurore is subversive," father says.

My heart sinks. I'd come all this way to spend a pleasant afternoon with the family and share a meal. The last thing I want is a quarrel. "Actually, Émile Zola is a very nice man."

Father glares. "You associate with this liar? You're putting your career in jeopardy."

I sit across from my father and brother on the settee. "I used to run into him occasionally at the Nouvelle Athènes. It's home to all kinds of artists, writers, and intellectuals. Nothing wrong with being friendly." I savor a sip of the apéritif and wolf down the shrimp canapé. A lacquered humidor sits on the central occasional table. I pry it open. "May I?"

"Help yourself," Conrad says.

I pack my clay pipe with the aromatic blend. "And anyway, how can you be so sure it IS slander?" I strike a match and take a few puffs.

"I like his novels," Conrad chimes in. "However, he's probably shortened his career by having the balls to uncover this disgrace."

"Exactly. Zola is just a journalist and merely brought to light what the army and the government have done."

My father hisses. "You actually believe the man?"

I heave a deep sigh. "If you must know, I think this is serious business." I enumerate the reasons with my fingers. "First, forging documents; second, burying evidence; third, coercing juries; not to mention complicity with the actual traitor who committed the crime... tell me, where's the justice?"

My father gets red in the face. "Don't you see? If you censure the army, you endanger the nation. Especially since the assassination of

President Carnot. Anarchist bombs are going off in restaurants and on the damned floor of the National Assembly." He grips the arm of his chair. "Do you really want to demoralize our armed forces at a time like this?"

"De-moral-ize?" I speak softly but resolute. "They're not above the law. I believe corruption among top-ranking officers and politicians endangers the nation far more."

"You're starting to sound like a monarchist, Papa," says Conrad. "Preserve the traditions at any cost; all of that royalist, Catholic, and ancien régime shit. Erik's right. The government can't turn a blind eye. I think the man deserves a retrial."

"No. Absolutely not!" My father pounds the armrest. "You don't attack the bastion of the nation's honor. I'm a veteran. It's a personal affront."

"I served my country, too," I say.

"We all served," says Conrad.

The arteries in my father's neck pulse. "Dreyfus is a convicted spy and a traitor."

"Fabricated evidence," I say. "It's morally wrong to send a man to Devil's Island on ginned up charges. Mon Dieu. Let the truth come out in open court."

Father blusters, crossing his arms. "Neither of you grasp the magnitude of the matter."

I shake my head as I relight my pipe. "Where are the descendants of the Enlightenment?"

Father bolts out of his seat. "Enough. I refuse to listen to another word. Your sympathies with these secret societies and foreigners will destroy our nation." He storms out of the room, eyes blazing.

"Papa, come back," I say. "No reason to get so upset."

"Can't we have a friendly debate?" asks Conrad.

The slamming door is his reply.

With a groan, I drop my head. "I was afraid this would happen. We should have avoided the subject."

Conrad retrieves the bottle of Pastis, pouring another round. "It's not your fault. He becomes overwrought more easily these days. He isn't well, Erik."

"I can see that. His color's not good," I say.

"Doctor says he needs to take life at a slower pace. That's why I moved him here."

"I didn't realize he'd become so frail."

"Maybe you should visit more often," says Conrad. "He worries about you."

"Me? I just seem to upset him."

"Oh, he'll simmer down. He always does. But seriously, maybe it's time you consider moving out of the city, closer to us."

"I'd need some assistance."

Conrad strokes his chin, studying me. "Let me think about that."

❧

July 1898- Montmartre

"I plan to leave at the end of the quarter," I tell Monsieur Jacques, even though I haven't found a new place yet. It's impossible to work in public spaces anymore with the mayhem of demonstrations and attacks. My musical creativity is being stifled. Montmartre has become a seedy, derelict place for prostitutes, drug dens, and thieves. Why should I have to carry a hammer around in my pocket? Between the noise, the thugs, and the sleazy inhabitants, none of the things I loved remain. Do I put up with this just to sleep in a utility closet? No more.

I take my brother's suggestion and look first at Rosny sous Bois. However, I discover the hamlet has no rentals, only privately owned homes. Rent is too expensive in the neighborhood where Claude lives. Some artists and writers have migrated across the Seine, to Montparnasse and the Latin Quarter. But according to my young acquaintance Henry Pacory, I can rent a flat in the suburbs large enough to fit my piano, all my belongings, and still have space to move around. It will cost less than my closet. Henry grew up in a rural village south of Paris called Arcueil, a working-class community strongly rooted in socialist ideals. He wants to give me a tour.

After coffee and pastries, the two of us set off on a trek across Paris. We're joined by another young friend, painter Augustin Grass-Mick. We take a route angling south past stately apartments on Malesherbes to the Roman pillared church at Place de la Madeleine. After we cross the Seine, we traverse three arrondissements by way of Boulevard Saint Germaine. This road feeds into the Boulevard d'Enfer. I can't resist joking about a street named the Road to Hell, and the omen it predicts. After a two-and-a-half-hour ramble, we finally approach the hamlet of Arcueil.

Gentle undulating green fields with wildflowers spread out under a brilliant sky. Long ribbons of cobblestone cut across the greenway beneath arches of an ancient Roman aqueduct. Open pasture flanks long houses of mason block with families and livestock. A gothic chapel, Église Saint Denys, stands in the center of town, next to the new town hall. It's an ornate Victorian building of yellow granite trimmed in terracotta. An equal variety of odors lace the air; fresh alfalfa, cow manure, smoke from the brick factory, and run off from the distillery draining into Bievre creek.

The apartment building crowns the summit of a grade at the convergence of two cobbled streets. The wedge shaped five story limestone facade appears out of place surrounded by farmland and the brickyard. Four sets of chimneys rise from the roof. On the ground floor, a cheery brasserie welcomes us. The Parisian eatery sports green and brown striped awnings, sidewalk tables, and woven cane chairs. Further up Rue Cauchy, the huge cooling tower of the brickworks kiln streams a column of smoke.

The building superintendent escorts us to the second door on the west side. She leads us up a short flight of stairs to a narrow corridor which opens into a spacious studio with a high ceiling. A layer of grime cakes the wood floor.

"This studio is huge," says Augi.

"Larger than any place I've lived in over ten years," I say. I can finally have Grand-mère's piano again! I immediately begin to picture where I might put it. How will I arrange the furniture to make it comfortable and inviting when Claude comes to visit? He will be so envious of the space.

"The one disadvantage," says the Concierge "is there is no running water. The pump is over at the school yard, up the rise there." She points to the window overlooking the street from which we'd entered. "There is an outhouse in the back field, and Chez Tulard, the café across from city hall, has those nice flush toilets.

"There's no stove or fireplace," I say.

"The walls are quite thick, and as you can see, it gets a lot of sun. It's plenty warm in the winter."

I'm not sure I believe that. But after spending winter in the closet, anything has to be an improvement. I gather with my two friends at the solitary window. Tall narrow panes look west. The sun will set through that window every day. If I position the piano just right, it will catch the afternoon light on the music and keyboard. The property on the other side of the street has a masonry retaining wall. An iron fence surrounds a garden cottage with dormer windows. Anyone standing there can see into my window. But for all its shortcomings, this apartment is the largest, newest place I've lived since leaving my father's home.

"What do you make of that?" Grass-Mick chuckles.

I turn back to the window. My eyes catch graffiti scribbled on the wall, faded, but still readable. The Devil lives here.

"Final destination of the Boulevard d'Enfer," I say, laughing.

"Maybe it's the fire and brimstone brick factory next door," says Grass-Mick.

Henry peers out at the wall. "No, I think it's really old. You know, the Marquis de Sade once lived down the way." He points southeast.

"Is that so?" I peer out the window in that direction

"Can we go see the place?" asks Grass-Mick.

The concierge interrupts. "Will Monsieur be taking the apartment? 20 francs a quarter."

That is what I pay for a closet. The only inconvenience is the distance to Paris, where Claude and all my other friends live. It's where the music venues are located, and where I most likely will find work. But the price and the space; how can I pass this up? "I'll move in next quarter."

I pay a 10-franc deposit Conrad provided, and sign the lease. Before departing Arcueil, Henry leads us down Rue Cauchy, where the 18th century aristocratic author of wild eroticism once lived. The Marquis' home is a dilapidated two-storey cottage with a dovecote tile roof and dormer windows. I find the idea droll, even a little inspiring, to live near such a nonconformist.

But can peace be found, here at the end of the Road to Hell?

Chapter 24

November 1898, Arcueil

I'm GRATEFUL TO Conrad for sending me half a dozen perfectly good shirts and suits he no longer wears. I'm less of a target in them and will cut a more professional profile on stage when the opportunity crosses my path. But as I fasten the buttons on my shirt, my hands tremble. It's not the first time. The quavering started gradually, a random thing. But lately I wake most mornings with it. I'm too young to have the palsy at 32. Maybe I'm just uneasy about having no work. Whatever the cause; shaky hands are a bad thing for a pianist.

Despite moving to the suburbs for peace and quiet, I'm plagued by restlessness. I have trouble falling asleep and then wake with the jitters. I hike into Paris every day before noon. The brawls and riots have waned over the past six months. The streets are a little safer to make my rounds and drop by my old haunts. So far, I haven't run into anyone with a lead on where to find work. But acquaintances seem more than willing to buy me a drink, the only thing that settles my nerves.

After several fruitless café stops, I arrive at the Auberge de Clou. I haven't visited here for a long time. The proprietors no longer offer live music; only drinks and light meals. When I open the door, the familiar

Norman décor fills me with nostalgia. But even better is the person seated at one of the café tables slicing up an omelet, Vincent Hyspa.

Vincent is not just a trifling acquaintance. Rather, he is a clever and talented friend from my days at Le Chat Noir. Like me, he'd fled Rudolph Salis' exploitation. I hadn't seen him much over the past five years. Hyspa's hairline has receded, much like my own. But he still wears a pointy little goatee and waxed moustache, which gives him a puckish charm. Like Aristide Bruant, Hyspa likes to wear a broad-brimmed hat, which lies beside him on the banquette.

"Bonjour, my good friend!" I say, rushing to the table, grinning.

"How are you, mon vieux?" Vincent sets his knife and fork down, stands, and embraces me. "Of all the people to walk in just now. What timing. Sit down, sit down! Let me buy you a beer," Vincent beams, and waves to the waiter. "Deux demi," he says.

I sit down at the table across from Vincent. "Last I'd heard; you'd opened at the Trianon. Was it… Song Masters of the Butte?"

"And lucrative it was; 1200 francs a month."

"Whew! That's a long way from the dinner and two francs Salis used to pay," I say.

The bartender sets two foamy glasses of lager on the table. I take a long draught.

"But I left the cast," says Vincent. "The sang-froid producers added La Belle Hongroise to the bill, a lion tamer, and a blindfolded marksman, all performing at once, like a circus. The audience couldn't pay attention to the music, let alone the parody."

I had heard Vincent's wonderful baritone voice many times. He'd come on immediately after the headliner balladeer and parody the chansonnier who had just performed. He'd become renowned for a marvelous flair, matching the song line by line and even imitating the crooning style of the balladeer with a deadpan expression that left people rolling in the aisles.

"Sorry it didn't work out," I say.

"The nature of the business," Vincent says, flicking his wrist as if waving off flies. "But it's so fortuitous you happened to show up just now. You see, I have a new run at Tréteau de Tabarin and I need a pianist and arranger. I don't suppose you'd consider it."

"Is that right?" I lean forward, stroking my beard.

"Steady work and it pays very well; 300 francs a month for the duration of the run. We'd perform Wednesday through Saturday; two shows a night and a Sunday matinee. And you'd transpose and arrange new material. You know this work. It's your forte. Probably you even know my repertoire."

"Probably." I tug at my moustache, recalling Vincent's funny scatological puns.

Vincent leans forward. "What do you say?"

As I reach for my beer, my hand trembles.

Vincent sees it and draws back, his eager face clouding with doubt. "I need someone I can count on. I had to fire the last guy because he kept showing up at the music hall drunk. You will not let me down, will you? You've got things under control, right?"

"Of course." I focused hard to steady myself. "I have a beer now and then like everyone else, but you can count on me, absolutely."

"Good. We start next week."

"Sounds like good fortune shines on us both, mon ami."

After we part, I'm ecstatic about our new collaboration. All my foraging has paid off and my fortune has changed. I have a job with steady pay, a predictable living doing something I do well. That is blessing enough. But now I'll perform in an upscale venue, the Music Hall. Granted, it's not a concert auditorium or theatre. Claude would probably say I was wasting my talent. But Claude has a rich benefactor, Georges Hartmann, who pays him 6000 francs a year. He can't fault me for wanting a roof over my head. The Music Hall guarantees a steady income. As to my drinking; this will not be a problem. I've always been able to control it when I wanted to. I can limit myself to only beer or wine and stay away from hard liquor.

December 1898

This place is a serious fire hazard, no doubt. The basement cellar at Treteau de Tabarin is a combination dressing room, rehearsal studio, and costume closet. I'm never sure the place won't ignite into flames when I turn up the gas lamps. Stiff net tutus with sequined bodices pack the clothes racks. Long satin coats with glittering braid hang next to Louis the XIV ruffled shirts. Two make-up tables are crammed against the far wall and a third one is in the corner. A crystal vase with dark brine and drooping spent blossoms stands prominently on the dressing table.

I sidle my way around the overflowing steamer trunk with a peculiar collection of props. It contains a fox horn, a wooden sword and shield, juggling pins, hoops, and various sized colored balls. Permeating every inch is a sickening mélange of talcum powder, grease paint, mildew and moth balls. Late afternoon sunlight filters into the subterranean space from the narrow horizontal windows near the ceiling, which is sidewalk level. I can see the feet and legs of passersby traversing Rue Pigalle.

My black paisley embossed cahier de musique is on the piano rest. I pull the bench out from the dusty wood grained baby grand to a comfortable playing distance. My hat finds a place on top of the piano. After a month working together, I've decided this is just a job; an easy, likeable one. People laugh at our social and political commentary. It keeps me from starving, provides an occasional cigar and brandy.

I sit at the keyboard and start my warm up with the first tune in Vincent's repertoire. He has a trademark song he always opens his performances with. It's a parody of the well-known Delmet song The Woman Who Doesn't Pass. Vincent comes out onto a darkened stage with a single spotlight, dressed in a wide brim hat and cloak with a red flowing scarf. He sings with deadpan seriousness. With a beautiful baritone voice, he croons the lyrics, recounting his worries about accidentally swallowing a prune pit, embellished with scatological puns. But Vincent's newer material has turned to more sophisticated political humor.

I copied my predecessor's arrangement for Vincent's song, Encounter at Noisy-le-Sec. The sleepy eastern Paris suburb was the whistle-stop meeting place between President Felix Fauré and Queen Victoria. She was on her way to holiday in Nice. Vincent penned the lyrics after seeing an uncomplimentary political cartoon, showing the elderly queen as a half comatose blob, with the President kissing her hand. The writer quoted the queen as saying Fauré was a gentleman and not at all an upstart. Vincent made this his refrain, while making allusions to the long-standing dispute over control of Africa. Rumors suggest our countries inch toward war.

Halfway through the first verse, I hear Vincent's deep voice bellowing the lyrics from the corridor to the basement. The door swings open and Vincent continues his serenade, making his way through the labyrinth of paraphernalia. He carries a white delicatessen package and a baguette, which he sets on the corner dressing table. Still singing, he worms a path back through the jumble to the piano and we finish the song with my added "ta-da" finale.

"Oh, I like that. A nice touch. Let's keep it."

"Of course," I reply, taking my pen from my pocket and scribbling in the notebook to end with a G major chord.

"Listen, mon vieux, have you seen this?" Vincent draws a copy of Le Petit Journal from under his arm and displays the latest cover art. The illustration features the Marchand Mission. It shows a group of bare-chested Africans squaring off with Frenchmen in pith helmets.

"No, I haven't gotten to it yet."

Vincent shakes his head. "The Marchand Mission is all a ruse, a pretense to hide the government's actual intentions to control the Sahel."

"Isn't that always the way they operate?" I ask.

"And President Fauré just issued a statement that France has no intention of becoming an occupying army. The mission is purely commercial and scientific. Just studying zebras, he says."

"He's lying," I say. France has pursued her interests in controlling the trade routes across the Sahel from Senegal for decades.

"According to this article, France has been mobilizing troops," Vincent adds.

"He's going to get us in another damned war! Merde!"

"And so, I won't stand by and be silent about it. I've penned a new song called Felix Fauré's Zebra. I'd like you to arrange the music."

"With pleasure," I reply.

Vincent slips a sheet of paper out from between the pages of the journal and I open the notebook to a fresh page. Vincent starts singing the words, while I jot down the melody line. It's a simple enough tune in 2/4 time. Once I transcribe the whole song, I'll improvise an arrangement. It is fairly effortless to play the melody and add his formula of alternating bass octave chords in oom-pah style. This adds a flippant mocking element.

"I love it," says Vincent. "It's perfect. Now, just get this all written down and maybe add a short fanfare at the beginning. I don't suppose we could premier it tonight?"

"I'll need a few hours, and we should rehearse it first."

"Fine. I brought you some supper so you can work on it. I'll be back in a few hours and we can decide if it's ready, then. What do you say?"

"I'll get started."

"Bon!" Vincent winds a course back out through the crowded studio, clasps hold of the door and closes it tight. I hear the rasping sound of the exterior latch being slid into place.

"Vincent, what are you doing?" I stand up from the piano.

"Be back in a little while," he calls.

I wobble around the jam-packed room to the door and grasp the door knob. "Vincent, open the door. Don't lock me in here."

"Have to, mon vieux. So sorry. You must be sober for the show."

"I won't drink. I promise."

"That's what you said last time. I can't risk it. I've got too much riding on it."

"Vincent. Let me out." I hammer my fist against the door. "Open the door!" But all I hear from the other side is silence. Then, through the window at the street, I hear Vincent's voice.

"I'll buy you whatever you want to drink after the show." Then, Vincent disappears.

I've been trying to cut back. Arriving late for a show was unintentional. Vincent's patience is wearing thin. I don't mean to tax our friendship. Perhaps having money is bad for me. It's easy to buy too many drinks, and it's made me sloppy. The walls close in around me. My face is hot and tingles and I can't breathe. I jar the window open, and stare out at the fast-paced shoes passing at eye level. Merde. I have to get a handle on this before it ruins everything.

Chapter 25

April 1899, Paris, 17th Arrondissement

"IT'LL BE HARDER than ever to get our work accepted," says Claude, rubbing his forehead. He leans against the velvety arm of his overstuffed chair.

"Everyone has an opinion, and a strong one," I say and bring a cigar to my lips and puff. The wood-spice aroma spreads across my palate. "They're all taking sides."

"Still, it's shocking," Claude says. "Saint-Sans shouldn't have refused to set someone's song to music just because he's a Dreyfus supporter."

I stroke my beard, shaking my head. "Who would have thought this conflict over the Dreyfus case would still be with us, and infecting the music world? I hate to imagine what we're in for, my friend."

"We thought we had a battle before." Claude turns his head staring off into the distance. "These extremists are now assigning political meaning to musical style. So, unless you prove you're anti-Dreyfus and your music is free of any foreign influence, you're not truly French."

I blow out a stream of smoke. "And if you're not truly French by their definition, you're barred from performing." I notice Claude's shoulders heave with a sigh. "Well, I didn't sign Zola's Manifesto," I say, "even though I believe the man is innocent. But I don't think that's any protection. They'll classify us regardless."

"That's my fear." His brows draw together and he bounces one foot. "The entire Paris music world will be torn apart."

I lower my gaze, stroking my beard, wishing I could think of something witty to say. But there's nothing funny about this. My gut feels leaden.

"There's a group of us who don't want to be forced to take sides. We've formed a committee in favor of reconciliation. Leave music and musicians out of it. I've signed the letter, along with Rene Peter, Charpentier and others. Will you join us?"

"You can't actually believe there is neutral ground?"

"One would hope." He looks down and grows silent for a moment.

"I'm lucky, in a way. The thing about chansons parodique is they're highly political," I say. "In the Music Hall, we can make fun of everyone and everything. I suppose that puts me on some list, brands me for surveillance as a sympathizer by those paranoids, Action Française. Truthfully, it's all a bunch of horseshit. Horseshit!"

"I agree," Claude says, waving his cigar. "I admire your tenacity."

"So how will you meet the challenge?"

"The nationalist demagogues may have thrown down the gauntlet. But I've taken it up."

"Is that so?"

He nods. "I've started a composition using the poetry of Charles d'Orleans."

"One of the greatest courtly poets of France. That should skirt any objections."

"Yes, and with my signature sound, too. Would you like to hear it?"

I gesture toward his grand piano. "Continuez, Monsieur."

Claude knocks the ember off his cigar and leaves it in the glass ashtray. He goes to the piano and opens the cover. I sit forward to absorb the stirring sounds from the keys, as my friend plays his newest creation.

The first few measures sound like a Renaissance madrigal. Reverent chords and worshipful progressions elevate the spirit. Then the tune surges into a frolic of modern harmony, opening a landscape painted with dappled brushstrokes. Soft treble notes and colorful bass rhythm promenade like a woman with a parasol strolling sun-drenched poppy fields on a windswept hillside. I attune my ear, analyzing, admiring.

My eyes drift from the Japanese Hokusai prints adorning Claude's walls to the immaculate teak and porcelain bric-à-brac displayed on every shelf and table. Alternating notes in the melody sway and flutter like branches in a zephyr; casting a glittering array of sunlight across the earth. Then the piece ends by repeating the first stanza in a stately, dignified coda. What a remarkable new opus Claude has crafted.

He takes his hands from the keys and turns around. "Now imagine; instead of piano, a choir is singing it a cappella."

"That would be stunning," I say. "You've continued the ethereal style you invented with Afternoon of a Faun. The Renaissance quality is striking."

"Bon. I thought you'd appreciate it," says Claude.

I smile. "They can't say it's not French enough."

"No. They can't question my nationalism." Claude leaves the piano bench. He goes to the credenza and pours a glass of whiskey. "It's the first in a set of three. I've started the second. With any luck, I can have them ready for next season." Claude takes a sip from his glass and sets it on the dining table. "Show me what you've been up to."

I glance at my cahier de Musique. "Between moving to Arcueil, work with Hyspa, and slogging six miles into Paris every day, I've been distracted. But maybe it's time to drag out a work I crafted two years ago and hear what you have to say." I snub out the smoldering tip of my cigar, stand and take my music notebook to the piano. "I'll just play the first two movements. I've inserted a traditional folk tune in the middle. See if you can recognize it."

Claude sits crosswise on a dining chair, leaning on the table.

I begin the first movement of Cold Pieces, the adagio. My fingers dance over the keyboard like satin laced shoes of ballerinas traversing the wooden floor of a dance studio. Elegant poised bodies and slender arms enfold and reach, fluid and graceful. Relevé, plié, repeating again and again. The tempo escalates to allegro. Rows of legs swing in unison with brisk precision. Then, they gallop away across the room in a chassé.

I proceed to the second movement, containing the reformulated folk tune. Claude leans forward and tilts his head to listen more closely. When I finish, he offers a one-sided smile, shaking his head.

"This sort of reminds me of the English pub we used to go to," Claude says. "I love the folk elements." He takes a deep breath and looks at the carpet. "It's too bad the collection is not exactly Français."

"No, not completely." I lower my head and rub the back of my neck.

"But you've taken a whole new rhythmic direction here. The melody is unpretentious and full of all manner of surprises. No one in the entire music world has such a free style. It's modern and unique."

Claude bends over, fussing with the nap of the carpet where a chair left an impression. He rights himself and looks at me, stroking his beard. "There is one other thing they would get you on, mon vieux. The work doesn't have form."

I stiffen. "Of course it does. It's a perfect ternary form."

"You know what I mean; concerto or sonata, etcetera. In this climate, getting something like this on the playbill for Société Nationale is doubtful."

He is right. The work doesn't conform to the expected traditions. But he's developed something that will meet all their rigid standards. I have nothing comparable. Nor am I inspired to cobble something together just to pander to them. Claude studies my face a moment.

"Just tuck it away for now, mon vieux. Its time will come."

My chest becomes heavy. I leave my music notebook on the piano, go to the credenza, pour a double, and sit at the dining table across from him. The room grows painfully quiet.

Finally, he breaks the silence. "On a different note; I see that Massenet's opera Cendrillon will premiere in May at the Opera Comique."

"I've read the score is so perfectly proportioned it's worthy of Lully's Armide."

"Lully?" Claude scoffs, shaking his head. "You see what I mean about the nationalist climate? The journalist drew that comparison."

He's right, but I hate hearing it. There is no way for any non-traditional work to find an audience. I relight my cigar.

"I was thinking about getting discount tickets for a dress rehearsal," Claude says, and finishes his whiskey, "to celebrate your birthday. Would you like to go?"

I try to balance the futility and disappointment I feel against Claude's sincere attempt to soften the blow. I take another sip of whiskey and a puff of my cigar.

The clink of a key in the door turns both our heads toward the entry. The door swings open and a stunning young woman enters the salon. "Bonjour," she says with a voice unexpectedly deep for a woman. She removes her straw hat and sets her purse on the table.

"Bonjour," Claude says. "This is my Lily." Claude has wasted no time replacing Gaby after the debacle with Therese Roger. Strange, he never mentioned Lily. He comes alongside her, toying with a tendril of hair that had escaped her coiffure. She shrugs a shoulder, titillated by his fingers on her neck.

"Lily, this is my dear friend, Erik Satie."

"Enchanté, Lily," I say, with a suggestion of a bow.

She offers her hand, staring back at me with large green catlike eyes. Her dyed hair is the color of caramel. Tall and willowy, her lithe movements add to the feline quality. Claude wraps an arm around her waist and nestles her against his side. "Lily is a fashion model at the House of Worth on Rue de la Paix."

"Are you still planning to take me out for dinner?" she asks and then tilts her head. "And will you be joining us, Monsieur Satie?"

I suddenly feel completely out of place, like a tag-along on someone's honeymoon. "Thank you, no," I say. "I was just heading out." I empty my glass.

Claude contorts his face. "Don't be ridiculous. Of course you'll dine with us."

"No, mon vieux. I'd be a complete bore. Really. What do I have to talk about besides Hyspa's latest lampoon?"

Claude's mouth drops open.

I cross the room to the hat stand. "Now, I think I shall get out of your way and let you enjoy the rest of your evening." I strain a smile, grab my umbrella, put my hat on, and leave the apartment.

Several blocks away, I realize I'm clenching my jaw. I'm not sure why I needed to leave so abruptly, maybe even rudely. Claude was complementary about the Cold Pieces, even if the nationalist assholes would disqualify them from any performance venue. His fine whisky is softening whatever burr was in my britches. But it makes me wonder. Is it just my unique way of looking at things, or is Claude pandering to the traditionalists? I refuse to sell out.

May 1899, Arcueil

The season at the Treteau de Tabarin is drawing to a close. Vincent has lined up several summer engagements for us, a wedding and two dinner parties. But the earnings will not be enough. The next quarter's rent is due for my apartment. I refuse to face another period of starvation. I hate scrounging meals, collecting others' leftovers, and exhausting the generosity of acquaintances. It's humiliating. As much as I dislike the prospect, this means taking any sort of work I can find. No one has to know.

I study the classified advertisements in the newspapers and journals, and scan the posters on the Colonne Morris at the omnibus terminals. One particular ad describes an outdoor bal publique that will remain open through the summer. I imagine it is like the Moulin de Galette. Several days after seeing the ad, I decide to drop by to see if they might have a pianist job.

The Port Royal train station sits at the boundary between the Latin Quarter and Montparnasse on Avenue de l'Observatoire. The place I'm seeking is the Bal Bulier. It stands opposite the La Closerie des Lilas restaurant, and resembles pictures of the Alhambra in Spain, with its horseshoe arches. But the main entrance has a ceramic relief featuring a nationalist placating Gallic rooster on the crest.

In the past, auditioning for a menial key tapper job would have been embarrassing. But after starving during winter, I've gotten over it. I swing the door open and peer inside. The place looks like a former equestrian arena or livestock auction now converted into a dance hall. Workmen on hands and knees sand the wooden floor. At the far end of the hall, the doors stand open and they're constructing a deck extending into the fenced yard. Two men are installing those remarkable new electric light fixtures. Someone has invested more than a small sum to make this place habitable. Perhaps that means he pays his musicians well.

The workers direct me to an open door to what was probably once a tack room. An older man in a white shirt and with matching linen waistcoat, wearing spectacles comes out. He has a halo of white frizz and thick muttonchops like Père Nöel.

"Oui, Monsieur. I am the owner, Arnauld Rouchard."

"Bonjour, Monsieur Rouchard. I wish to inquire if you might need a pianist. I'd like to offer my services."

The man looks over his spectacles. "We will need someone starting in June. What are your qualifications?"

"At present I'm performing with Vincent Hyspa at the Treteau de Tabarin. The season is wrapping up and I'm looking for summer work."

"This differs from Music Hall, Monsieur. We need someone who can play dance music, waltzes, polka and the like."

"Certainly. May I give a little demonstration?"

"If you please." He gestures to the nice upright grand on the bandstand.

I scale the few wooden steps, pull out the piano bench, and sidle into place. I open my music notebook where I'd jotted down several waltz strains. My fingers skip over the keyboard, letting the simple strains meld with a bass cleft rhythm. The workers pause their sanding and rise to listen. The fluttering notes echo through the barn. When I finish the few bars; the owner nods with a hint of a smile.

"You've got fine ability. But its variety they want, not the same thing over and over."

"I have an extensive repertoire, I assure you," I say, knowing full well I do not.

The engagement is four days a week, Thursday through Sunday for 20 francs, plus two drinks on the house. I'm satisfied it would pay the rent and get me through. He takes down my information. We shake hands and I leave the establishment relieved and enthusiastic. I could do this in my sleep. The only problem is, I can't improvise for six hours. I need dance music, plenty of it. There is only one place I'm sure to find it, my favorite music store.

The first thing to catch my eye as I enter Gabriel Astruc's shop is a finely dressed lady in a fitted bolero jacket and blouse with a voluminous lacy jabot. I admire this new fashion silhouette, like an inverted tulip or lily. And though she still has a wasp-waist, she probably doesn't miss the bustle and crinoline. She glances toward me for just a moment, alerted by the jingle of the bell above the door. Then she turns back to the rack displaying new sheet music.

Gabriel stands behind the counter and we exchange greetings. While I browse, I notice the woman selects several popular songs. She pays at the counter and saunters out of the door.

"Is that what everyone is buying these days?" I ask. "Those little solos?"

"Yes. I can barely keep them in stock."

"Which are the most popular?"

Gabriel walks around to the display rack, plucks several bi-folds and fans them across the counter. "Silly little things, but selling as fast as I get them in. But you know what? I have something you might be more interested in. You are ahead of everyone else introducing new music."

I grin. "Bon."

Astruc pulls open a cabinet door under the counter and takes out a packing box with postage from America. He removes a stationery box containing sheet music. "I just got this from my friend in New York about a week ago. I haven't even had time to go through it much. Would you like to have a look?"

A frisson of excitement spreads through me. "Fantastic."

"There's a similar place in New York to our music publishing district around Rue Magenta. They call it Tin Pan Alley."

"Tin Pan Alley." I stare with great interest at a cover sheet. In brown and orange ink, a cartoon illustration shows Negro couples dressed in fine clothes dancing. I sound out the title "At a Georgia Camp Meeting". "Do you know what that means?"

Gabriel shakes his head. "Not really."

I recognize the word march and polka next to the words cake walk. "What do you suppose cake walk means?"

"I believe it is the name of a very popular dance over there. Why don't you play it? Let's see how it sounds."

"Let's do." I take several pieces of the sheet music and go to the piano. I study the melody for a moment. "Look at that," I point to the staff, "such strange syncopations." I pick my way through the music, fumbling at first. But the sound is so thrilling I keep at it until I figure out the peppy little tune.

"They call this music Ragtime," says Astruc.

"Ragtime. I love it." After another play through, I try a couple of other pieces whose titles make no sense to either of us, "Smoky Mokes" and "Hunky Dory". They are equally lively.

"This is going to set the city on fire, Gabe."

Along with twelve waltzes, I take home five Ragtime pieces; the two cakewalks, and three Tin Pan Alley songs. I discover they are really slow waltzes, not unlike the Valse Chantée many Paris divas sing. These titles I can almost figure out, since some words are similar enough to French. "After the Ball"; "Hello Ma Baby", and "The Band Played On". But it doesn't matter whether I understand the words. I feel as if I'm walking a foot above the ground. Gabriel Astruc has just given me an edge. He's handed me a treasure few others in Paris possess, let alone compose. This has turned out to be a glorious day.

Chapter 26

April 28, 1902, Paris, 8th Arrondissement

THREE CONTINUOUS YEARS of stability in my life has yielded dividends for me. What started out as writing accompaniments for Vincent has grown into something much bigger. I'm now writing and publishing my own popular songs, which Hyspa adds to his repertoire. The best part is my lampoons allow me creative license to satirize every corner of society, while dabbling with Ragtime syncopations and sentimental waltzes. The audience eats it up and the sheet music is flying off the shelves. I love that part.

I'm prospering. New pince-nez, new shoes, new bowler hat, and of course, new umbrellas. But I've had enough reversals in my life to believe this is only a passing season, especially after watching everything I'd envied about Claude's life turn out to be transitory. Our fortunes seem to take turns, up and down like a child's seesaw.

First, Lily developed complications during pregnancy, winding up in the hospital, and finally having a miscarriage. Her moody disarray put such a strain on their relationship, Claude could barely work. Then, his patron Georges Hartmann suddenly died. Overnight, his stipend dried up. So, Claude was obliged to actually take a job. He's been writing articles for Revue Blanche; an anti-Dreyfusard arts journal.

Despite all this bad luck, his infiltrate and subvert strategy has put him far out ahead, leaving me in the dust.

"Now you're in an even better position to influence things," I tell him. But I'm still shaking my head at the irony.

Tonight, marks another milestone for my friend. Finally, his opera Pelleas et Melisande premiers. I'd nurtured a fantasy of one day doing something with Maeterlinck's play myself, but never did. I can't begrudge Claude, after all this time.

As we exit an upscale café together, Debussy reflects on his hard work.

"Fifteen weeks and 69 rehearsals; finally, this is it," he says, adjusting his top hat.

"The way I count, it's been nine years, my good Claude," I say, "since we saw Maeterlinck's play. I do so admire your persistence."

"This is all your fault, you know," says Claude.

"My fault?"

"You are the one who pointed me toward Maeterlinck. You're the one who planted the thought in my mind of creating an atmosphere like a Puvis de Chavannes painting, not to mention conceding your interest in the thing."

"It's nice to hear you acknowledge that." I raise my hand to hail a passing cab.

"It's true. You were the inspiration for all this innovation. Between you and me, you've influenced my ideas more than any other composer."

"More than Wagner or Mussorgsky? Merde. Don't get sappy on me, mon vieux."

"But it's true."

I give a gentle smile, feeling warm and satisfied. I played a role in this epic event, even if it remains a secret between the two of us.

The carriage driver slows to a halt curbside and hops down. He opens the door for Claude to board with me right behind him.

"It's a miracle this day ever arrived," says Debussy.

"And that you survived to see it."

Claude groans, shaking his head. "Mon Dieu, don't remind me. It's been dreadful." Debussy leans forward toward the driver. "The Opera-Comique, s'il vous plaît."

"Yes sir." The cab driver pulls away from the curb.

There had been many nightmarish obstacles, mainly because of Maeterlinck himself. Who would have guessed the Symbolist writer would be so maniacal? He'd become hostile when Claude hired Scottish soprano Mary Garten to sing the part of Melisande, instead of Maeterlinck's lover Georgette Le Blanc. The author tried to get a restraining order to shut the production down. But the judge denied his petition, because Maeterlinck had signed the contract.

Next, he published a letter in Le Figaro describing the production as "a work that is strange and hostile to me". After that failed, he threatened Claude with a duel.

The carriage slows in front of the theatre, where a throng of attendees wait in line. Critics and music academics are obvious in their lackluster suits and fedoras. Opera subscribers flash their jewels and furs, and eager university students surge against the velvet ropes.

Claude takes in the spectacle and sighs. "Look at them. It's amazing."

I return a grin of support, wrestling inside to hold back an unexpected flood of envy, despite the nightmare Claude has just endured. We enter through the far door, roped off and away from the crowd. Inside, several elegantly dressed men hand out brochures to attendees. I snatch one just before we ascend the stairs to the box seating.

"What's that?" Claude asks, leaning over as we arrive at the first landing.

"The program."

Claude rolls his eyes. "That's not the Programme du Spectacle I approved."

"Another snag?"

Only after we traverse the carpeted corridor to our box seats do I open the bi-fold, and skim the cast profiles.

Mary Garten is an exceptional actress, pretending to be a talented singer. She possesses the vocal range of a water buffalo. Her debut in Paris first occurred when she replaced, obviously without rehearsal, the star of Charpentier's Louise in exchange for sexual favors she proffered to the orchestra conductor. Now in the title role of Melisande, she is guaranteed to ruin what might have otherwise been the opera of the century.

"What a hateful prank," I say, pointing to the text. Every member of the cast, the composer, the conductor, and featured performers in the orchestra he similarly maligned.

"We've got to have these gathered up right now. Someone's trying to spoil the opening."

Claude bolts out of his seat and races to the nearest usher. I rush down the stairs to stop any further distribution. The ushers hurry through the aisles and are able to recover many of the scandalous programs. But the damage has already been done, as evidenced by jeers and cruel chatter spreading through the audience. I can only guess Maeterlinck had planted the programs in the theatre. But there seems no way to prove it. The production will simply have to speak for itself.

When the curtain finally opens, it reveals a set with breathtaking richness and detail, like walking into a painting by Millais or Rossetti. I'd heard portions of the opera over the many weeks, but this was the first time seeing it in full. Like no opera before it, there are no leitmotifs for each character, no arias or choruses. Somewhere between a chant and a recitative, Claude has composed it to sound like natural speech. He captures the elusive quality of character emotions.

The music blurs the temporal boundaries, drawing me into another world. I escape the limits of the flesh and transmute into another being, sensing the soul of the other person, hearing their language as if it comes from my own throat. With every crescendo and diminuendo; the character's euphoria and agony well inside me. In the moments of silence between measures, I can tell I'm not alone in this experience.

Emanating from the rows of patrons below, I hear sobbing and sniffling through the audience. Opera always had the power to move people emotionally. But this is on a whole different scale. This music possesses me, penetrates into me. The world fades away and I become the music.

Chapter 27

March 1903, Paris, 17th Arrondissement

IT ALL SOUNDS too good to be true. Monsieur Jean Bellon and his associates Cie and Ponscarme were just shareholders in Emile Baudoux's music publishing company. But when poor health forced Monsieur Baudoux to retire, they bought his entire catalog. Not only do they want to reissue my music, but Jean Bellon wants to promote it personally. His letter today invites me to meet with a rising diva, Paulette Darty, to discuss a business proposition. Fantastic!

I arrive at Bellon's well-appointed office on boulevard Haussmann. To my surprise, we're not meeting Madame Darty here, but traveling to her home. Bellon leads me to his high-priced Peugeot two-seater quadricycle. It convinces me he's quite the business tycoon. It sports a black canvas bonnet and tufted leather seats. The wheels resemble the spokes of an umbrella. How do those thin tires support the weight on this behemoth velocipede?

Monsieur Bellon gets behind the steering wheel and starts the engine. The incessant rattle is fearfully loud, and the constant shudder is quite unnerving at first. After a few moments, however, I decide it's quite a thrill. Many still associate these motorized vehicles and horseless carriages with being Nationalist, anti-Dreyfusard, and royalist. Has anything escaped being politicized? I'll have to write a song about it.

Jean speaks loudly over the rumble. "Madame Darty is between shows. Her operetta at Bouffes-Parisiens just finished a week ago. It's an ideal time to meet with her.

"That she's even agreed to meet with us is exciting. I was once introduced to her a few years ago. She performed at the Treteau de Tabarin at the same time Hyspa and I did. I doubt she'll remember me. But what a coincidence?"

"I tell you mon vieux, she's about to break out onto the Paris music scene in a big way; as big as Therese or Yvette Guilbert. I just know she'll love Je te Veux. And if she agrees to make it part of her repertoire, we'll all make a fortune."

The Peugeot turns off boulevard Haussmann onto Malesherbes, continuing toward Claude's neighborhood. I think back to the summer before I moved to Arcueil, when I set Henry Pacory's lyrics to music, just for fun. Perhaps my generosity it's paying off today.

Madame Darty lives in the upscale quiet neighborhood. There are fewer carriages and more automobiles in piano black and gleaming gem-tones. Trees alive with pink and white blossoms line the spotless street. Louvered shutters look freshly painted with lush pastels. Window boxes filled with spring tulips and daffodils enliven the wrought iron grills of balconies. Jean guides the Peugeot to the curb and stops the engine. When we enter, the concierge rings upstairs. A voice comes over the speaking tube and grants permission to come up. I'm suddenly twitchy and a wave of fluttery nausea passes over me.

A young woman in a black, high-collar dress introduces herself as the personal secretary for Madame Darty. She invites us into a small vestibule. I remove my hat, and set it on the mahogany hallstand, which bears a huge porcelain vase with a spray of yellow and vermillion gladiolas. The oval gilded mirror on the opposite wall doubles the entire scene.

"You may wait here, if you like," she says. She gestures to a chic sitting room with an elegant fireplace mantel and a camel back divan upholstered with green velveteen and strewn with embroidered silk pillows. As I walk across the Persian area rug, I notice a windowed alcove overlooking the street. In it stands a grand piano, with sunlight reflecting off the lacquer.

"I shall inquire if Madame is available yet." She excuses herself and turns to enter another set of tall doors.

Bellon tugs at the legs of his trousers and sits on a Queen Anne chair. "I hope this is worth our while. You know how unpredictable these divas can be."

We wait for a dozen or more minutes before the secretary returns. "Madame is nearly ready to meet with you. Please make yourselves comfortable. Would you care for some tea, or something stronger?"

"Yes, most certainly," I reply. "Would it be alright if I warm up at the piano?"

"No harm in it. Please, go right ahead."

I scoot onto the bench and open the music notebook. To loosen my fingers, I play a few scales, and end with several bars of a Hyspa song. The secretary brings the drinks, offers the first to Bellon, and then sets a coaster on the piano and my drink within reach.

"Thank you," I say and take a sip. It's fine cognac. This will certainly calm my jangled insides. I place my hands back at the keyboard and play the introduction to the tender waltz I wrote for Henry Pacory. For vividness, I add delicate hesitations and flirty twists.

Jean rises from his chair and comes behind me. He hums the melody. Softly Jean interrupts. "Start again, mon vieux. I'd like to sing it, if you would."

"My pleasure," I say, so used to such restarts in rehearsal with Hyspa.

Jean sings the lyrics. Instantly, I'm terribly impressed with the velvet quality of his tenor voice. My slow waltz tempo is like a lullaby, mixed with stirring entreaty and the touch of a music box. Jean endows the song with such passion and sentiment. When I finish the last note, I turn to look back at Jean Bellon. Beyond him in the alcove's arch stands Madame Darty. Her amber hair is coiled atop her crown and fastened with a comb. She wears a pale pink peignoir of crinkled taffeta and lavish rows of ecru lace. I try to overlook the fact she has nothing underneath. The fabric clings to her skin, outlining the shape of her breasts and hips.

"Messieurs, please forgive my appearance. I was in the bath. This lovely song impressed me, and you have such a fine voice. I had to hurry out to meet you. Sorry to keep you waiting. So many callers are offering their songs."

"Merci, beaucoup, Madame," I say, standing up from the piano and bowing.

"I am Jean Bellon, the publisher. And this is the composer."

"Erik Satie." I offer my hand.

Paulette comes toward me. The crisp rustle of her peignoir and the fragrance of sweet pea flood my senses. She narrows her eyes, inspecting me. "Your face is terribly familiar."

"We met at the Treteau de Tabarin some time ago."

"I knew I'd seen you before."

Her hand feels delicate as flower petals in mine. "The lyrics are by a dear friend of mine, Monsieur Henry Pacory. The title is I Want You."

Bellon slides a crisp new copy of the music from his folio and lays it on top of the piano.

"Perfect. Play it for me, Monsieur Satie. I'd like to sing it." She takes the music, opens it to the inside and eyes the lyrics.

I sit back down, draw a deeply gratified breath, and play the last stanza as an introduction. Her operatic trill gives me goose flesh. I have never heard a woman sing the piece before.

I understand your distress, dear lover

I surrender to your wishes

Make me your mistress

We'll be in ecstasy

I want you

Images begin to pass through my mind like the fleeting landscape from a streetcar. Yearning wells for all the women I've loved, tender hearts I could never possess. Paulette seems to express the very core of unrequited longing. A visceral flutter makes me misty-eyed. My own music! I glance up at her for a few moments. She's animated with a hint of sensuality in the way she lifts her chin, baring her throat to achieve optimal vocal range. She meets my eyes as I follow her inclinations and pace. The energy passing between us is magic, and the air becomes electric.

Bellon stands to the side swaying and Paulette's personal secretary rocks from side to side. When she finishes the last line, and I play the final chords, there is a momentary lull.

Paulette turns to Jean. "Monsieur, I can tell you right now. This will become one of my signature songs."

Jean Bellon's face blooms with a grin. "Madame, we'd like to issue a new special edition with your name and photo on the cover."

"I'm quite keen on your proposal. You understand, of course, I can't give it proper attention until I finish my obligations. I have a summer tour of Italy, and right now I'm rehearsing Floradora. But after that, I expect to return to the music hall again."

"Oui, Madame. If you're amenable, we'll send a contract to your advocate."

"Please do." She turns to me. "Monsieur Satie, do busy yourself creating more lovely work like this one. This is one collaboration I genuinely look forward to. I can't wait to see what you'll bring me next."

"I'd be delighted," I say.

"Now, if you'll excuse me. I really must dress." She leaves the room.

Bellon and I stare at each other wide-eyed. "This means big things, great opportunities," says Jean. "A whole new horizon is opening for you now. If a performer of her caliber and fame promotes your music, it will sell a lot and establish you as a top tier popular composer."

I have stars in my eyes. As we drive back to Bellon, Cie and Ponscarme, I grant myself the luxury of thinking about Paulette, the woman.

"She's married, I presume," I say.

Jean Bellon gives a wry smile. "Actually, she's a widow."

I sit back against the tufted seat, smiling to myself and look forward to seeing her again.

⁂

May 1903- Paris, 17th Arrondissement

I stare at the Legion of Honor medal fitted snuggly into its velvet-lined box atop the lace tablecloth. "I'll have to call you Sir Claude from now on. Isn't it just marvelous? To think you're a real chevalier, an actual knight," I say.

Claude slouches on the arm of the chair. "As impressive as that sounds; it feels more like a burden than an honor."

"Getting weighed down by all that precious metal?" I asked. "Prix de Rome and now Knight."

"It comes with expectations; that's all. Far from opening doors, it just gives them more reason to be critical; all the shoulds and ought-tos. It's actually very limiting."

"I can understand why you might feel that way. But Pelleas et Melisande was an unparalleled accomplishment and you deserve the honor."

"I'll tell you what a shining moment was. When I surprised my father with it." Claude takes a long draw on his cigarette. "I pinned it on." He taps his vest over the heart. "And covered it with an overcoat. I took a cab to the house. Papa was standing in the garden at the workbench. He didn't see me at first. So, I coughed." Claude's voice clouds with emotion. "He looks up as I'm walking toward him. I open the lapel." Claude shows with his jacket. "He doesn't say a word, but his jaw drops."

My throat swells.

"He couldn't believe it at first. After 20 years of disappointing him, he thought it was a fake. But when he realized I wasn't fooling, he threw his arms around me. You don't know how it felt to see him weep with pride. I was finally good for something."

"To have your father weep with pride," I say, with a hitch in my throat. My gut twists into a knot. Will I ever become the composer of fine music my father had hoped? I may have found a living in popular music. But in Claude's shadow, I'm still an amateur.

"Congratulations, my dear friend. You are so very deserving."

Claude grabs the newspaper from the sofa and returns to the dining table. He slides the paper in front of me. "I saw an article in here about an American Negro group. They're doing a show at the Dead Rat Café.

"Les Minstrels," I reply, "authentic Cakewalk and Ragtime. I didn't think you'd be interested."

"Of course, I'm interested. I might rub elbows with stuffed shirts, but I'm still a bohemian inside. How long has it been since we saw a café-concert show on the butte?"

"Years. But Le Rat Mort? You'd actually want to be seen in there, Sir Claude? I warn you, it's an étrange tavern."

"So what? I have nothing against étrange people. Allons-y."

Le Rat Mort is on the ground floor of a five-story building at 7 Place Pigalle, across the street from Nouvelle Athènes, the café of intellectuals. But Le Rat Mort Café is known for its libertine standards and for the unique clientele they cater to. That guarantees the shows they book will push the boundaries, as well.

From the outside, it looks like any other café-concert, with marigold and tan striped awnings, street side Thonet chairs and petit tables. But once inside, that's where the similarity ends. Huddled around the bar are women dressed in suits, trousers, and fedora hats. Men wearing flamboyant colors have their arms around other men. One even has on a black satin corset instead of a waistcoat.

"I suppose we should act like a couple," says Claude.

"If we don't want unsolicited company," I say, noticing how two men in lipstick and rouge are ogling us. I lace my arm through Claude's as we pass through the crowd. The host shows us to a table near the stage. We order drinks and wait for the show to begin.

"What do you know about this Cakewalk dance?" Claude asks.

"Gabriel Astruc says it originated when African slaves made a parody of their owner's minuet. Oblivious to the insults, the owners made a contest of it, awarding a prize. A cake."

"Every newspaper in Paris is writing about l'art negre. Guess it's huge in New York. Have you heard any of it?"

I chuckle. "Heard it? I've been playing it for years now. In fact, Astruc gave me a head start with some sheet music, Cakewalk, Ragtime, and Tin Pan Alley."

"Whoa! Just when were you going to share it with me?" Claude gives me a gentle shove.

"Like I said; I didn't think you'd be interested." I take a swallow of brandy.

"We're in such different spheres these days, mon vieux," he says. "I miss those times."

"I've always had a fascination with dance, as you know. But, this music breaks the rules. It sounds like a strange polka-march with syncopations, spiced up with unexpected trills."

"I just hope this is the real thing, not some commercialized re-creation. Not like Cirque Nouvelle, where they're foisting white men in face paint."

"It's supposed to be the real thing."

There's a row of chairs in a large semi-circle on the stage, beside which a cluster of band instruments awaits. Suddenly, a Negro man appears, dressed in a tuxedo with white gloves and a top hat. He leads a whole troupe of Negroes dressed in tan cutaway jackets, ruffled shirts, and spats.

They march around the stage, singing and throwing their gloved hands in the air in time to a peppy chorus, accompanied by the banjo player.

I can't understand the English lyrics, but it doesn't matter. I'm here for the music. After repeating the little tune; the tuxedoed man directs the troupe to sit. A comedy sketch begins between the leader and the men on each end of the semicircle. One holds a set of castanets, who he calls Mister Bones. The other jingles a tambourine, Mister Tambo. I know they reach the joke's punch-line by the rattle of the tambourine and a drum flourish. The troupe reacts with exaggerated laughter, echoed by a handful of English speakers in the audience. It's too bad I don't know English.

As the comedy routine continues, it's interspersed with dance and songs in synchronized movement. I pull out my notepad and jot down a few rifts.

"What are you doing? You're taking notation again?" asks Claude.

I nod, "Why not?"

"You're going to give me a copy, right?"

I tear a leaf from my cahier de Musique and hand it to Claude. "Take down what you like. You know how." I turn my attention to the music and fill my notebook with ideas.

At intermission, Claude folds the empty piece of notepaper and tucks it in his pocket. "What are you planning to do with all that?" he asks.

"I had a wild fantasy. I was considering some kind of marriage between this Ragtime music and grand Musique, and maybe throw in a little folk tune. What do you think?"

Claude feigns a cross between a cough and a laugh. "Only you would come up with an idea like that. Melding popular genre with grand art- it's hard to imagine."

"Why? Why is that so hard to imagine?"

"Burlesquing Berlioz? They're different genres, different worlds."

"So? You're sounding like a traditionalist. Who made the rule they can't be combined? Why not create a whole new genre?"

Claude eyes me with a smirk, shaking his head. "Decide which kind of music you want to compose and then get after it with a vengeance."

"Claude, that's exactly what I'm doing."

Chapter 28

December 1903, Paris, 13th Arrondissement

SOMEWHERE IN THE back of my mind, I knew this day would come. I'm aboard the ten-o'clock to Gare de Orsay. It's the fastest way to the Hôpital Lariboisière. The sooner I get there, the sooner I'll know Father's condition. From the station, I can cross over the Alexander Bridge and catch an omnibus. Conrad's telegram gave no details. My brother is enroute back to Paris from Grasse and will arrive this evening. I'd stepped right over his telegram in the dark, when I arrived home last night. Hyspa and I just opened at the new Boit de Fursy in the same building as the former Chat Noir. Such memories and meaning the place carries. I gaze out the window. Can't this train go any faster? I wag my foot crossed over my knee.

Raindrops run sideways against the window of the train, blurring the passing scenery. I take off my pince-nez to wipe them with a fresh handkerchief. Father went downhill the past few years, even though he's only 57. Still, I'm unprepared for this news. He seems too young to die. Grand-père lived to 70. There is so much left unsaid between us. He once was my wisest adviser. His opinion always makes me stop and take notice, even when we disagree. Why have we become so estranged? Surely, we can set politics aside. Is there still time to bridge the gap between us?

I've seldom expressed my gratitude enough for all the things Father has done for me. He gave me the money to establish myself independently, even though I faltered and got into trouble with alcohol. But Father never stopped believing in my talent. In the beginning, he supported me by publishing my music, my waltzes, and my melodies with Patrice's lyrics. My father's validation sometimes eased the painful process, the rejection and criticism of my innovations. It's been life-giving to know he believed in me. Yet, I still sense Father holds an intractable disappointment since my dismissal from the Conservatoire. He clings to the hope that one day I'll go back and finish. Allusions to it emerge from time to time. Probably he is right about that, too. My dearth of technical skill is what's holding me back.

It's a short walk from the omnibus stop to the plaza in front of the hospital, where statues of faith, hope, and charity keep watch. I enter through the columns beneath the clock tower. Nurses in long white dresses carry trays and basins through the corridors. Large light filled wards host a dozen beds on each side. I approach the nurses' station in the center.

"Please Sister, I'm here to see my father, Alfred Satie."

She looks at a registry of names. "Oui, Monsieur, your father is right over here." She guides me down the row of beds, separated by privacy curtains. My heart starts to race. Father lies semi-conscious, propped up on two pillows. His eyes are open, but he has a vacant look. I pull over a stool, sit beside the bed, and take father's hand. His eyelid droops on one side and drool runs from the corner of his mouth. My chest feels leaden.

Father's lips twitch on one side as if trying to form words, but he can only make soft sounds. "Khhh Khh."

Is he trying to say my childhood nickname, Crincrin? My gut wrenches as the severity of Father's condition registers. The most important person I need and love is slipping away. "I'm here, Papa.

I'm here." I can't hold back my tears despite squinting and contorting my face. Father's hand jogs slightly and his eyes well with tears. He still has some of his faculties, trapped by a body he can no longer operate.

Life is so fragile and transitory. We can hold on to nothing. Panic seizes the little boy inside me. I want to run and cry for help; the way I did the day I found my mother unresponsive on the bed. It's the sensation of falling, endless falling. I stand up and call to the nurse. "Sister. Pardon me. May I inquire about his condition and treatment?"

The nurse picks up the clipboard at the foot railing of the bed. "Monsieur may speak with his doctor. He has already made rounds and can give you a better understanding. Follow me."

"I'll be right back," I say, and follow the nurse through the ward to a small side office. I notice the doctor's engraved name plate over the door jamb, Dr. Georges Luys. Another consultation is underway. I wait across from the door, rocking as the nurses and attendants scurry back and forth, bring water and items for dressing wounds. When my turn finally comes, Dr. Luys invites me in. I sit down and Luys closes the door.

"I must be frank with you, Monsieur. Your father has suffered an attack of apoplexy. The damage has been fairly widespread. Did you see him?"

"Yes."

"Then you must have noticed he has lost the use of one side of his body and lost the ability to speak."

"What causes apoplexy?"

"A hemorrhage in the brain. A tear in the arteries makes blood leak."

"Will he recover?"

"The prognosis varies. In some cases, fatality results in a few minutes. In others, the patient sinks gradually. It is impossible to predict an exact outcome," he says. "Truthfully, Monsieur, if he recovers, he will probably have future attacks that will eventually take him."

"Is there no way to treat the condition?"

"We can make him as comfortable as possible. But it's best if you get his affairs in order and make the necessary arrangements. I'm so sorry."

❧

Ice clings to every leafless tree flanking the snow-covered promenade beside the water's edge. Like inverted crystal chandeliers, the branches catch the first sunshine in days, glittering against the pale sky, while ballet pink storm clouds bid farewell. I stand beside Conrad on the deserted banks of the Seine. My brother holds a perfume vial holding some of our father's ashes. We interred the rest beside our grandparents in Honfleur. We both stare into the water flowing beneath the arches of the Pont au Change, with the steeples of the Conciergerie above it. I sample the fragrance of five white roses in my gloved hand. Scattered patches of ice drift by on the dark mirror surface.

"It just seems like there should have been some kind of memorial service," I say.

"He didn't want that. You know how he was," says Conrad. "No funeral, and certainly not in a church."

I sigh, shaking my head. "So, we're just going to pour his ashes into the Seine?"

"He loved this city and the river threading through it," says Conrad. "It seems natural some part of him should remain here. Just make sure no one's watching. We could get arrested."

I pull my coat lapels tighter. "It's so cold and so early. I think we're safe."

Conrad glances in both directions, and I do the same. Then my brother removes the stopper, leans over the balustrade, and sprinkles the mealy grey powder into the water. It quickly disappears. I toss the roses into the flow, one at a time. Then we both watch in solemn silence as they're carried downstream. It is done. Father is gone; quietly slipped away. I gaze up at the frozen city. I'm numb, not sad, but just cold inside and out.

My brother pats the lapel of my overcoat. "Let's get coffee," he says.

We turn and ascend the slippery stairs next to the large civic theater, the Chatelet, on an avenue just beginning to stir with traffic. On the adjacent corner, the owner of Le Mistral Café is clearing ice and snow from the sidewalk and entryway. The warm glow beckons us inside. We find a table near the radiator and order coffee and pastry.

I cup the warm demitasse in both hands. "Do you think Father was happy with his life and accomplishments?"

"I'm sure he had plenty of regrets," Conrad says, and takes of sip.

"No doubt I'm the cause of that," I say.

Conrad's brow pinches into a knot. "Does everything have to be a reflection of you?"

My brother's sudden shift of tone catches me off guard. "No, but I failed him so many times. I just never seemed to get it right."

"You? Father always felt like he failed us. Do you not know that? He thought he was unsuitable to be a father. Our grandparents certainly gave him that message."

I lean forward. "Who told you that?"

"He did," Conrad says. "He felt responsible for mother's death and hated what we had to go through. He thought it was best to put us in better hands, which is why we went to live with Grand-mère and Grand-père."

I squeeze my eyes shut, and then gape at my brother again. "I never knew that. And here I used to think he just didn't want me."

Conrad shakes his head with a sneer. "And I suppose it never occurred to you that after Grand-mère died, he tried to make it up to us by marrying, to give us a mother. He chose Eugenie because of you, because she was a music teacher."

"You can't be serious," I say, rubbing my forehead.

"How could he know she'd turn out to be such a shrew?" His words are tinged with vitriol.

"Having Eugenie in the picture just magnified what a disappointment I was."

"Don't you get it? You were never a disappointment. He loved you, ached for you, agonized over you. So much so, it sometimes made me resentful."

I blink several times. "Your version of this story differs greatly from mine," I say.

"Obviously. Maybe it's because I'm a father now. I understand. He could have lived le vie Boheme or finished his studies at the Sorbonne. But instead, he curtailed his career and creative aspirations to provide for us. He did everything he knew to make us happy, you especially, giving into every whim. How do you not see that?"

My jaw tightens. "I know he supported my music. But why wouldn't he stand up to her?"

"What makes you think he didn't? You weren't there. You didn't hear them."

"If that's so, why did he let her throw me out?"

"That's not the way he thought about it, Erik. He saw it as you running away; refusing to face things. Your sense of yourself was so fragile. You could never accept your mistakes and face your problems. A prodigal son."

I huff. "If I was such a lost sheep, why didn't he ever visit me when I got hospitalized with hypothermia in the army, when I needed him most?"

Conrad releases an exasperated sigh. "Because he thought you hated him; figured you didn't want to see him. He didn't want to upset you more. It also happened the same time his music publishing business failed. He was going bankrupt. That is when he begged me to look after you."

"He went bankrupt? I always thought he tired of it, and you were just being generous."

Conrad narrows his eyes. "That's because you think the solar system revolves around you and can't see things from anyone else's point of view. You, you, you. Frankly, I'm tiring of your entitlement; like everyone owes you something."

My mouth falls open. "Why are you talking to me like this?"

Conrad's lips curl. "Because I'm sick of it. You're 37 years old. Grow up and stop being a parasite."

"Parasite?" I rear back. "That was completely unnecessary." I do not know what has gotten into my brother. But I can't just set it aside. I get up from my seat, throw several francs on the table, and leave the café without another word. I make my way through the slush, back toward the train station. My heart feels as though it is shrinking. What prompted my brother to turn on me? Maybe he is just despondent over the loss. Whatever it is, it doesn't excuse such vicious language. We are both hurting. I gaze out at the barren icy winter landscape. The cold takes hold of my gut. Have I really been as selfish as Conrad says?

Chapter 29

May 1904, Paris, 2nd Arrondissement

"Where's your good lady this evening?" I ask. "Isn't she joining us?"

"No," Claude says. "She's gone to her parents." Claude stands in shirtsleeves, craning his neck as he knots his bowtie in front of the mantel mirror. We have tickets to attend the spring concert of Société Nationale de Musique at the Salle Érard, where my orchestrated version of the Gymnopédies debuted seven years ago. I have on my father's tuxedo. It doesn't fit quite right, but I wear it with pride, recalling my father's joy on the occasion.

Claude makes a sour sneer. "Ever since she lost the baby, and the doctors said she's unable to have another; she's been unbearable to live with. Nothing I do makes her happy."

"Sounds like melancholia," I say, leaning against the arm of the chair and taking a puff from my pipe. "Perhaps time away will do her good."

Claude picks up a cufflink and fits it through his cuff. "Actually, mon vieux, I think the relationship is over."

I gape, blinking several times. "I'm sorry to hear that."

"We were incompatible, really. She couldn't have an intelligent conversation. She's just an empty-headed mannequin."

All these poor women, I want to say, but purse my lips in restraint. Claude was never faithful to any of them for even a day. Then he treats them like a change of underwear. I adjust my pince-nez. "I always thought she was a lovely person."

"On the surface, yes, but she despised all my friends and acquaintances. What you don't know is that of all the people to visit our home, you are the one she disliked most."

I sit upright as if jabbed in the back. "Me? Why?"

Claude drops his head and then looks at me for a moment, as if measuring his words. "She thought you were a sycophant, who drank too much and ate like a glutton."

Sycophant? What an unkind thing to say. My stomach sinks. "She always gave the impression of being gracious."

"Yes, the impression." Claude wraps his cummerbund around his waist, securing it in the back. "You didn't have to listen to her afterward."

It saddens me to think I could be the cause of their discord. But I'm horrified to learn anyone would think of me that way. "I apologize."

"It's nothing, mon vieux. Frankly, I'm glad she's gone. I think I've finally found the right person."

Claude is already on to the next one? Incroyable. I let out a groan, but check myself, turning my head to mask my smirk with my hand.

"I know what you must be thinking," says Claude. "Off he goes, after another pretty face. But this time is different. She is everything I've been looking for. She's smart, classy, and quite attractive."

Claude sounds like he is shopping for a pair of shoes. Women's only purpose is to supply his self-centered desires. Then I stop myself. My brother accused me of the very same self-centeredness. Maybe we are both too selfish to ever be successful in relationships. But a sycophant? It's not so easy to dismiss.

"Anyone I know?" I ask.

"Probably. Emma Bardac."

"Ah yes," I say, "I seem to recall that name. I thought she was Gabriel Fauré's mistress."

"Was." Claude dons his cutaway jacket. "But enough about that. Tell me what you're working on. Anything new?"

I shake my head. "Not yet." I raised my hand, gesturing as if chalking points on a scoreboard. "However, Paulette wrote to me saying my popular music received standing ovations and encores from Brussels to Geneva."

Claude flashes a one-sided smile. "Good news is always great to hear."

"I expect we'll make an even bigger impact when Paulette returns to Paris to headline with Mayol at the Ambassadeurs in June." I place one of my hands at my back and the other at my waist, bobbing as if taking a bow. "Ta-da."

Claude raises his brows. "The Ambassadeurs? You've really climbed the pinnacle of popular entertainment." He brushes specs off his top hat with the side of his hand. "Bravo."

I'm not sure how to take Claude's remark. It is as if I've been pinched with one hand and stroked with the other.

"I've got good news, too," he says.. "The piano manufacturer Pleyel approached me this week. They are introducing a new harp and want me to compose a piece to showcase it."

As soon as Claude says this, it's like a punch to the solar plexus. How ecstatic he must feel to have such an exclusive opportunity. I would love to be in Claude's position.

"Congratulations." I smile, but ache inside. My efforts to compose grand musique remains stalled. The kind of work I now envision surpasses my skills.

Together, we descend to the street to wait for a passing motorized cab. When we arrive at the theatre, I look up at the glittering Salle Érard. If only I could have my music performed here again. We ascend the stairs and show our tickets to the doorman. As we cross the lobby, young attendees recognize Debussy. In short work, they surround him. They pepper him with questions about his various compositions.

"I'll be happy to chat with you after the performance," Claude says.

"If you'll excuse me, I'd like to welcome and congratulate the Société's featured composers."

We make our way across the lobby toward another small huddle. At its center stands a man around my age, with thinning hair in a well-tailored charcoal gray suit. His beard is close-trimmed, and he used a little wax to curl the points of his moustache.

Claude needs no introduction. The circle opens.

"Monsieur Albert Roussel," Claude says. "I'm very much looking forward to hearing your work this evening. You are quite the rising star among this year's featured artists. Albert, this is Erik Satie."

The composer's eyes widen, his brows rise like little check marks. "Monsieur Satie. I'm very pleased to make your acquaintance. Your reputation precedes you."

"Is that right?" I grin. "Well, I hope it's a good one."

A crowd gathers, encircling Claude again, asking him to sign playbill after playbill, even though his music is not featured in tonight's concert. Within moments, I find myself on the fringe with Roussel.

"Your bio in the program says you came late to music," I say.

"That's right," says Roussel. "I'm still a student at the Schola Cantorum with d'Indy."

"I didn't realize they took older students. Is it more restrictive than the Conservatoire?"

"The opposite. They ground you in the classical traditions, but once mastered, you're encouraged to innovate and create whatever you might imagine. D'Indy is great to work with."

"I'm surprised to hear that. An orchestration course is costly, I suppose."

"Not with a scholarship program and opportunities to teach, like I do," says Roussel.

"You teach there?"

"Yes, the beginning courses."

The newly installed electric lights flicker, signaling time to take our seats.

"A pleasure to make your acquaintance Monsieur Satie," he says, taking my hand and giving it a pat. "Come by the academy. We can talk at length."

"I'll do that." Roussel's revelation plays a pizzicato with my heartstrings. Maybe I could get a scholarship. I'm certainly capable of teaching the basics. What I thought was an irreversible mistake of my youth might actually be rectifiable. Completing my education might actually be possible.

Claude and I find our places. Still fresh in my mind, I mention my discovery.

"You're not seriously considering enrolling, are you?" asks Claude. "Studying at the Schola would be a mistake. I've struggled my whole career with the shackles such training places on creativity. Don't do it, Erik. It will ruin your art."

But as the program gets underway, I can't stop thinking about how Roussel came to music and is in fact a student. I mistakenly believed it would be ridiculous to go back to school at my age. But Roussel's story has changed my mind. Enrolling at the Schola Cantorum could bring wonderful changes to my career and my life. I need to learn the skills if I want to orchestrate my work. I'm ready.

⁂

November 4, 1904, Opera District

The name Théâtre des Bouffes-Parisiens is traced out in little blinking lights, making it sparkle. Huge illuminated posters flank the entry doors: Paulette Darty with Erik Satie, tonight! I shake my head with a grin. Who would have thought my humble accompanist job would land me here as a headliner? I enter through the red carpeted foyer. Uniformed ushers with flat billed hats and gold braid on their red jackets collect coats and hand out programs. A small orchestra is tuning up on the stage, dominated by a grand piano. The seating is a third full, while lines of other patrons shuffle inside.

I make my way backstage to wait and watch from the wings. Paulette looks stunning in black sequined Chantilly over gold taffeta. She opens the show with solo material first. The set includes a mixture of old favorites, Boudeuse and Facination, interspersed with several pieces of operetta.

After the intermission, it is my turn to open the second set. When I come out on stage, the audience gives a hardy round of applause. I nod my gratitude and slide into place at the grand piano. The audience falls silent. I take a deep breath and launch into a piano slide and the happy, jaunty bass rhythm of Le Piccadilly. My right hand dances the lively syncopated jig; first picking out the notes and then repeating with octave doubling. I glance up for just a moment and can see the audience can't resist the beats. Heads bob and shoulders sway. By the time I get to the last lively chords, the audience has risen to their feet, cheering for more. I stand and bow. But the clapping doesn't stop. Voices call for an encore. I look wide-eyed at Paulette, standing in the wings.

"Well, go on, they want more," Paulette grins. The audience cheers even louder when I sit back down. I didn't anticipate this. My heart thunders at my throat and I rack my brain for what to play that will satisfy. I turn through the pages of my music notebook to the "California Legend". Though it is all new, un-polished and really a fragment of an unfinished bigger work, I decide to play it.

I loosen my shoulders, position my hands, and take a breath. My hands crash onto the keyboard and let loose with a bombastic timbre. The rhythm is a cross between ragtime and cancan. The sassy tune trots across the keyboard, capturing the zest of a Wild West show, the daring antics of rope tricks and stunts on horseback. The audience hoots and hollers with delight.

Now, I'll have some fun. I vary the loudness of the bass rhythm to suggest a three-dimensional flavor of a chase, adding in the galloping octave doubling of the cavalry. It makes for a wild ride through the imagined rainbow hills. Someone in the back row makes the war cry, and the percussionist in the orchestra thumps the bass drum. I grin, my fingers flying like the wind. Faster and faster I go, finally coming to the abrupt whoa Nellie finale. The audience explodes. I stand up and face the crowd, bowing several times.

Paulette appears from the side of the stage, applauding with raised arms. She makes a grand sweep with one hand, projecting loudly "Ladies and gentlemen, I give you Maestro Erik Satie!" Chills shoot down my spine. Paulette comes over and grasps my hand. She draws me center stage and into a bow with her. As I come upright, she kisses me on both cheeks, turns and holds out her hand, gesturing to me. The applause is unbroken.

"Let's do La Diva together," she says.

"Of course!"

I hurry to the orchestra conductor, informing him of our departure from the program. Then I move back to the piano. Paulette remains center stage. The audience quiets quickly as I commence the piano introduction and the orchestra strikes right on cue. Paulette's liquid voice trills as she sashays to the tempo. I have no idea what the music critics will print in tomorrow's paper, but it doesn't matter. I'm on top. The people in the audience are all going to run out to the music store to buy copies of my music. This may not be the Concerts Lamoureux, Chevillard, or Société Nationale, but my popular music is loved and in high demand.

Chapter 30

October 1905, Paris, Latin Quarter

Naïve and amateurish, that's how they've looked at me in serious music circles. It's taken the better part of a year to get myself organized. But my fantasy will now become a reality. My first course in counterpoint at the Schola Cantorum begins today. A diploma earned by disciplined study will give me the skills I need, and could take my music and my reputation to a new level. My father always believed in my talent. "Make me proud," Papa had said that day in 1888 when he handed me the inheritance as capital for my music studio. By returning to school, it will fulfill Father's hope for me and honor his memory.

I push open the two arching metal doors through the cloister wall to what was once a Benedictine monastery. A frisson of excitement courses through me. I enter a small tree-lined square flanked by Louis XIV buildings of oyster color stone. Tall Palladian windows gather the morning sunlight. I grasp the black filigree railing on the spiral staircase as I wind my way to the third floor. Several pianos and the strains of a string quartet echo through the stairwell. I locate the classroom, open the door a crack, and peer inside.

"Welcome, Monsieur Satie. Please, join us," Roussel says. I smile at my instructor and the curious faces of the students turn to inspect the mature class member. As I sit listening to Roussel's lecture, my entire body pulses with vitality. Now that I'm doing what I sincerely want, it consumes me. In my youth, lectures seemed pedantic or tedious. But now, I take meticulous notes. Every assignment will be my best effort. I grasp everything Roussel is saying in ways I never appreciated as a young man. Maturity and experience have blessed me with greater depth of understanding.

As the first month progresses, I have to admit, my earlier work would have benefitted from this knowledge. Each morning, I sit at my favorite café table near the Schola and work on my assignments. I can hear the compositions in my head and jot them down. I begin with a simple tune, the fixed melody known as the cantus firmus. Then I add a second melody, offsetting the notes against each other. Avoid parallels, begin and end in unison. There are more rules about suspending or sustaining notes, while others move against them, creating dissonance, consonance. Finally, I put the pieces together in varying combinations in each bar. I had a vague sense of this structure in my past compositions. But I'd used it awkwardly. Now, it is like I've grown wings and I'm learning to fly.

On Fridays, Albert Roussel sits at the piano reviewing students' work, one by one. I listen to the work of fellow students with a better-trained ear. I can almost anticipate Roussel's comments before he even utters a word. I prefer to go last. My classmates look forward to this finale of each week's instruction. I set my music on the piano. In a cluster of students, I look over our teacher's shoulder as Roussel plays my exercises. When he finishes, everyone waits in expectant silence.

"This is a fluid bass line and solid independent melodies. I like the way you write out the cantus firmus in red ink and the additions in black."

"Thank you."

"Your work gives us an opportunity to observe some things everyone should remember. The listener can't ignore either the harmonic or linear qualities of the music. Problems in either will grate on the ear. So, the task is to write parts that move independently in contour and rhythm, but are interdependent harmonically. Your work, Erik, suggests you are thinking too vertically, rather than horizontally. Your approach favors the harmonic, and it is the linear you need to develop more, especially as we move into greater complexity."

"Alright, thank you. That is very helpful," I say.

"However, you'll be ready to move on to three-part counterpoint very soon."

"Wonderful. I'm excited," I say.

After the other students depart, Roussel looks over his shoulder at me and smiles. "I have a confession, Erik. Having you hover there was more than a little disconcerting when you first joined the course. You certainly came with a reputation, strange and skeptical. But I'm impressed. You've never shown the slightest cynicism. You keep bringing in impeccable work with the most serious dedication."

"Albert, I've needed a firm base of knowledge for a long time. My progress as a composer would be impossible otherwise. I'm in your debt." I gather my music and shake Roussel's hand.

"You've made exceptional progress," Roussel says.

When I come out into the courtyard, I feel especially joyful. I look at the fallen leaves strewn across the bricks, which seem for a moment like they are made of gold. The Benedictine monks called this the Court of Miracles. At one time, they believed it was a place of miraculous healing, a rendezvous, and refuge. And this is exactly what I've found here.

~

November 1905- Paris, 17th Arrondissement

"We combined our names, Claude-Emma, like melding our essence into a tiny person," says Claude." He cradles his month-old daughter. They draped the baby in a long cotton gown with small embroidered flowers at the neckline. I marvel at the tiniest fingernails I've ever seen. A mottled pink hand clutches my finger.

"She's really got a hold of me, mon vieux."

"She just does that naturally. I guess all babies do it; a kind of instinct," says Claude. "Isn't she just a precious little thing?"

I can't believe Claude is a father. The baby stares up with dark gray eyes. I sit beside my friend. Emma beams a Cheshire cat grin at the two of us fawning over the baby so awkwardly.

"She certainly seems content and good-natured," I say.

"That's because I just fed her," replies Emma. "She can definitely fret when she's unhappy."

"Who do you think she most resembles?" Claude asks.

"Well, the dark shock of hair she surely got from you. But right through here," I gesture to the cheekbones across the nose, "she has her mother's fine profile, but definitely your mouth, I think."

"Would you like to hold her?" Emma asks.

"Oh my, well, are you sure?"

"Of course," says Claude.

"Let me just wash my hands." At the washbasin, I soap twice before drying with the towel. I sit next to Claude again, and stare up at Emma.

"The neck is very weak, you see. You must support the little head," she says, as she takes the baby from Claude.

"Oui, Madame."

"Make a cradle with your arms. I'll lay her right there."

I feel my stomach flutter as she nestles little Claude-Emma in my arms. How light and fragile the baby feels.

"You might need this," adds Claude, draping a napkin over the front of my suit. "She can leave a nasty decoration at the most unexpected moment."

As I stare into the tiny face, sensing the fragile life I hold, I realize this is probably as close as I will get to fatherhood. But there is something so captivating about this infant girl. She's captured my heart. A lilting cradle song waltzes through my mind.

Chapter 31

Spring 1906, Paris, 14th Arrondissement

FOR THE FIRST time, I'm turning elsewhere to preview my new compositions. While I still receive the occasional invitation for luncheon from Emma Debussy; Claude is far less available these days. He's been traveling abroad, filling his coffers by conducting his works in Brussels and Geneva. And he's become downright reclusive since the baby was born. I've turned to Albert Roussel on occasion. But I'm curious how a younger generation with a different aesthetic will receive my new compositions. Is my work still relevant, forward looking, and on the edge? So, when Les Apaches invited me to join their Saturday get-together, I gladly accepted. The only problem is, Claude would be appalled and offended if he knew.

Les Apaches are hooligans of the Parisian underworld who mug bourgeoisie for a living. It's also a name hurled at Maurice Ravel and his friends after they accidentally bumped into a newspaper vendor while exiting a café. They've adopted the moniker for their faction of young rebel artists, and hold regular gatherings for mutual support and creative exploration. Sounds familiar. But this younger generation seems rudderless. As Socrates once wrote, "I don't expect I can teach them anything; only make them think".

My destination is Montparnasse, for the home of the nine Muses of Greek Mythology. I pass through this neighborhood regularly, on my way to and from Arcueil. Baudelaire once lived here; which gives the community a kind of artistic authenticity. I reach the horseshoe shaped lane at the eastern edge of Parc Montsouris as evening paints the sky a dusty amethyst. Rustic stone fences, topped by wrought iron filigree, enclose private garden villas. Lush flowering vines cascade over the walls.

A striking young man greets me at the door of the villa, wearing a pale green painter's smock. He has a long Russian style beard, and a moustache waxed out in the most dramatic and unnatural way. He introduces himself as Léon Leclère.

"Ravel speaks so highly of you, Monsieur Satie," the young painter says. He makes a sweeping welcome gesture. "Do come in."

As I surrender my derby and umbrella, I hear a piano playing an unfamiliar melody in a very modern style. We enter a large drawing room turned art studio. It takes up half the ground floor. A wall of windows looks out onto the sunset hued garden of lengthening shadows. Easels bear paintings covered over with muslin. Other canvases lean on edge, askew in one corner. My thoughts turn to memories of Ramon and Santiago. In the opposite direction stands a baby grand piano. I recognize a familiar clean-shaven face with the most outrageous handlebar moustache. Spanish pianist Ricardo Viñes is Claude's frequent guest and preferred interpreter of his piano works.

"I did not know you were part of this little coterie," I say.

Viñes pauses his playing, looks wide-eyed, and stands to exchange a peck on the cheek and an embrace.

"Let's not tell Debussy, shall we? He might not appreciate our alliance with his rival."

The room gradually fills with a host of colorful people. Each time a new member arrives, Viñes plays a clever little fanfare.

"What is that?" I ask.

It's Borodin's 2nd Symphony, a kind of musical code," Viñes says.

I laugh, finding it amusing that Les Apaches have their own leitmotif.

Leclère offers a glass of Kir Royale, which I'm quick to accept. Then I make my way to an overstuffed chair. Positioned beside a large sofa in the center of the room, it has a view of the lush garden. I light a cigar and introduce myself to a young poet seated there. He's bedecked in a multicolored brocade waistcoat and ascot. He resembles a Persian prince with long eyelashes and a pencil-thin moustache. But I'm fairly sure he has rouge on his olive cheeks and lips. I also deduce that a distinctive moustache is a prerequisite for membership.

A writer joins us, Leon-Paul Fargue, who sports a dense but neatly combed moustache, and waves around several gaudy rings as he speaks. Another friend from my corduroy suit days, Florent Schmitt, arrives. The young composer sits with his legs crossed. He twists the waxed end of his neat S-curve, while discussing his Edgar Allan Poe inspired ètude, The Haunted Palace.

As I survey the gathering, it dawns on me that besides moustaches and being in their twenties, Les Apaches are probably all étrange. Had I somehow given the impression I am étrange, too? My bachelor status at forty, perhaps? The hair stands up on the back of my neck.

"Greetings everyone." Maurice Ravel has just arrived. Heads turn toward the entrance and Viñes plays the Borodin tune once more. Ravel wears an overcoat, noticeably out of place for a spring night.

"I have a little surprise for you this evening," he says. Ravel peals back his overcoat, flinging it aside, and exposes a pink tutu, with falsies, hose, and ballet slippers. Eyes pop and jaws drop, with a chorus of hoots and whistles. Clearly pre-planned, Viñes launches into a lively version of Tchaikovsky's Waltz of the Sugar Plum Fairy. With his short stature and slender physique, Maurice looks the part, except for his moustache. He flits around the room like a dainty ballerina. All Ravel's friends go into convulsions.

I sit there stunned, a cigar between my fingers. What on earth have I gotten myself into? Part of me wants to sneak out of the room. But another part finds the brazen high jinks too zany to look away. I haven't completely lost the reckless abandon and nothing-is-sacred ethics of my Chat Noir days. I surrender to stomach spasms and break a grin.

The Persian prince bounds to Ravel's side, joining in a pas de deux through the end of the short piece. Then Viñes starts over.

"Don't just sit there," calls Ravel, "Come on."

The contagion spreads. One by one, Les Apaches rise to their feet in tipsy pirouettes and arabesques. I'm no prudish wallflower. I snub out my cigar, stand, and feign a pas de bourée, flailing my arms over my head with a giddy laugh. When the young men notice my enthusiasm, it has the effect of throwing kerosene on embers. A frenzy of leaps and turns explodes. In a few bars, a dozen grown men are bouncing in riotous silliness. At the very moment when the dancing reaches a fevered pitch, the music ends. Maurice curtsies to vigorous applause, and disappears momentarily to shed his costume.

I don't know what to expect next. The open exchange of affection between a few of the men makes me restless. I have nothing against homosexuals. I worked among them for years, starting with Rudolph Salis. But I'm unsure what to do if someone makes an overture.

Relief comes in the form of food. Leclère sets out platters of hors d'ouvres, and I join the swarm of attendees circling the table. As I gather a few shrimps and some pâté onto a small dish, a hand gently touches me on the back. I stiffen.

"Good old Satie. I wasn't sure you'd really come." Maurice has re-emerged, now dressed in a fine linen three-piece suit.

"Are you Apaches always this irreverent?" I ask.

"I guarantee we're never dull," says Maurice. He takes a plate and selects several canapés and crudités. "You seem to fit right in."

I laugh at the irony of his remark and spear a stuffed egg, adding it to my plate. "I've launched more than a few wild pranks of my own," I say.

We load our plates. Ravel gestures to an uninhabited spot near the windows and leads me away from the noisy flock. "Most of my friends here are unfamiliar with your work," he says. "I've been trying to enlighten them. You were so influential to me. I was hoping I could persuade you to favor us tonight."

"How kind of you to say so." I'm warmed by the compliment, but now wonder if I'm to be the entertainment. Florent Schmitt wanders over to join us, along with a young pupil, Ravel introduces as cellist Maurice Delage.

"It may be selfish of me," says Ravel, "but I'd also like your opinion on a new work I've composed. It got a good reception in Lyon, but I'm not sure Paris is ready for it."

"That's probably the best time to premier a recent work," I reply.

"My one hesitation is my string quartet got such mixed reviews," says Ravel. "Some journalists dismissed the work wholesale and others declared me the successor to Debussy."

"Yes, I read that," I say. "But I wouldn't consider it a compliment."

Ravel tipped his head. "No?"

All three young musicians stop nibbling delicacies and incline an ear with an earnest crease in their brows.

"Don't misunderstand me," I say. "I have absolutely no criticism of Debussy's music. But when Mauclair calls debussyism a disease, the last thing you need is to try to fill his shoes. You need to make new shoes."

"Too many are modeling their work after Debussy's example," says Florent Schmitt, "as if he's some kind of god,"

I make a pontifical gesture. "Dieu-bussy shalt thou worship. Him only shalt thou follow."

The younger men break into guffaws.

"But don't you believe Debussy is the father of the modern aesthetic?" the young pupil Delage asks. "His 'Afternoon for a Faun' shattered a barrier."

"Actually, no," says Ravel. "Monsieur Satie was making inroads when Debussy was still playing Wagner. He's the forerunner of Debussy and us all."

Schmitt nods his head, and Delage offers his hand. "How fortunate to meet you," he says.

My face blooms with a satisfied smile and warmth floods my upper body. Not only has someone recognized the truth, but I'm getting credit publicly. "But I want you to know there will never be a school of Satie," I say. "I wouldn't hear of it. Every artist must find their own unique sound. And you must always keep growing and changing."

"Speaking of change," says Schmitt. "I was beyond words to hear you'd gone over to d'Indy and the Schola. He's the political opposite of the Satie I knew in Montmartre. I was wondering if you sold out."

"My affiliation is purely utilitarian, I assure you," I say. "I've brought a new piece to play for you bonhommes, if you're interested. It's my answer to the worn-out sonata form."

Ravel's eyes light up. "What a coincidence. The piece I wanted to play for you is my replacement for the sonata, too."

I grin. "Perfect. Why don't you start us off and I'll follow?"

Ravel removes his jacket and warms up at the keyboard. Schmitt and Delage arrange the chairs for this impromptu recital. Ravel offers a brief introduction as Les Apaches each finds a perch. I settle into the overstuffed chair. My training now allows me to appreciate not only the music's aesthetic merits but also to analyze the piece's compositional richness.

Ravel has a signature technique of tight flurries of notes, alternating with contemplative passages. His Sonatine is no exception. The first movement is in strict sonata form, but there is nothing old and stale about it. The harmonies sound sunny and vibrant, with dramatic variation and shading. Ravel's modern eye has browsed a curio shop filled with eighteenth century objets d'art. There are bursts of excitement hunting for treasure, turning every which way in the menagerie of relics. Then the music slows, as if to admire the rich colors of a cloisonné enamel vase or the detail on a carved ivory pipe.

In the second movement, Ravel's theme transforms into a minuet. He adds passionate crescendos and interludes of introspection. It acknowledges the era of bicorn hats and powdered wigs with a very modern yet sentimental feeling. The last movement bursts out like the jets of a fountain, surging and spraying with wild arpeggios, finally climaxing in a dramatic cascade of chords.

Les Apaches come to their feet with a resounding endorsement. Ravel stands up, with his hands steepled in front of him. He bows his head in appreciation. Then he hurries over to me, standing with Schmitt, Viñes, and Delage.

"Well, you certainly gave a nod to Couperin and Rameau," I say. "The nationalists can't grumble. But no one has heard a minuet or toccata quite like these."

"You know where I got the idea, don't you?" asks Ravel. "Your Sarabandes."

I smile. "Maybe so, but Sonatine bears your own unique autograph; a virtuosic tour de force. There may be some in Paris who are not ready for this kind of innovation, but its time has come. Bravo."

Ravel grins and gives me a stout pat on the shoulder. "Thanks for your vote of confidence, mon vieux."

We decide to have a brief intermission and another round of drinks. I elicit the skills of Ricardo Viñes, a phenomenal sight reader, to play secondo for my duet, The Pear-Shaped Pieces. I chose this work because Claude had disparaged it, saying I shouldn't mix popular and fine music. Now is my chance to test the validity of his assessment.

After looking over the music, Viñes sits together with me at the piano. From the very first notes of the introduction, the Trois Morceau en Forme de Poire engages the audience as a unique musical narrative. I've spliced mysticism with an added zing of Ragtime, punctuated by a jarring plink-plunk taunt of cabaret humor.

Viñes plays the final ostinato with a plodding cadence and comes to a stop. We both sit back from the keyboard. I turn toward a young audience with spellbound faces.

"Bravo," Florent Schmitt shouts.

Ravel jumps up, raising his hands, clapping vigorously as the other Apaches break into cheers and applause. "You see?" Ravel says. "What have I been telling you? Erik Satie is the inventor of modern music." He comes over to the piano as I and Viñes vacate the bench.

"It enthralled me," Ravel says. "You've done something unprecedented."

Schmitt approaches, offering his hand. "I'm utterly mad about the way you blended popular genre together with the classic sonata. Nobody has ever done anything like this before. Just amazing."

I grin, shaking hands with anyone who wants to. Vindication. What a breath of fresh air. It's a good thing I'd trusted my gut instinct with this work. Dieu-bussy's opinion is not the only one that matters. These up-and-coming, young composers represent the future. Why have I waited so long? This night exceeds all expectations and the future is both thrilling and daunting. This new alliance could cost me a 16-year friendship with Claude. Will he see me as a traitor?

Chapter 32

May 1908, Paris, Quartier Latin

TECHNICALLY, I DIDN'T have to be here. My attendance isn't required. But after three years of work and a realignment of everything in my life to reach this finale, I'm receiving my diploma today. I even wear a white tie for the occasion. Like a dignified gentleman, with my umbrella tucked beneath my arm, I amble toward the Schola Cantorum. Carriages and automobiles line the Rue Saint-Jacques for blocks. With a rattling engine and noxious fumes, a dark red taxi stops at the curb, shuddering while passengers disembark in fine coats and top hats. As I pass beneath the keystone in the arching entrance to the Court of Miracles, the huge sycamore waves its hailing arms in the breeze.

Students welcome parents and grandparents. They huddle together in small family groupings around the cobbled square. I nod or tip my bowler to classmates who make eye contact. But I walk a solitary path through the clusters of attendees with their backs turned. Amidst a mélange of colognes and tobacco smoke, I can't escape noticing the gleam in many a father's eye. Proud hands rest on shoulders, and mothers grin with admiration. A lump swells in my throat.

I'm not some 21-year-old beginning my life, but past the middle of my life at 42. Who would have come, anyway? Not Claude. He didn't think I should do this. My Music Hall associates? Perhaps Paulette might have come. I haven't talked to Conrad in five years, since the quarrel after our father's death. My teacher and now friend Albert Roussel will be here. He'll hand me the official license for my marriage to the Muse.

I cross the square to the entrance. Sunlight glitters through the canopy of leaves, throwing patterns onto the pale ochre stone walls and white mullioned windows. I scale the circular stairs stacked like a wedding cake, leading to the open double doors.

Inside the large salon, rows of seats face a lectern and piano, framed by royal blue carpet runners. A dozen high-backed armchairs with blue velvet cushions wait for the dean and professors to take their places. I find my seat in the front row, where half the graduating class is already seated and waiting. One of the second-year piano students plays Couperin.

At half past ten, the side doors open and the pianist launches into a march, as the faculty enters. They wear mortarboards and long black robes with jonquil stripes on the sleeves. The founders walk behind them wearing white lace jabots with their robes. Guilmant, Bordes and the dean, Vincent D'Indy, all sport a tam in place of the mortarboard.

The whisper of taffeta brings my grandmother to mind. She preferred black taffeta and wore a high collar dress with a row of tiny covered buttons. The thought of her makes my eyes glaze and I wince. Is she watching me right now? Could her spirit be smiling here with the other grandmothers? I've done it, Grand-mère. Despite everything.

Albert Roussel rises to the podium to give the first address. "The culture of spiritual values is the basis of any society that claims to be civilized. Music among the arts is the most sensitive and highest expression of those values." He continues, putting into words the philosophy of the Schola. It emphasizes instrumental music for its own sake. But it also embraces the traditions that inform being "French". I roll my eyes at the mention of tradition, classicism, the military, church, and royal heritage. All the ultra-right-wing sentiment. Oh well.

A performance of a string quartet and another address follow

Albert. This time, the chosen student is the most promising from this year's class, a violinist. When the time comes to issue the diplomas, they announce names alphabetically. We stride down the aisle and accept our scrolls.

I survey the audience row by row for an empty seat. My eyes settle on a vacant spot. Father didn't believe in God or the immortality of the soul. But I do. I'd like to believe my father is present for the one thing he most wanted for me, to finish my diploma. He's sitting right there, watching me go forward as my name is called. The pianist is playing the March by Lully as I approach the head of the line. As D'Indy calls each name, the teacher presents each certificate, giving a ceremonial kiss on each cheek.

I approach the podium with my head held high. This is my personal triumph. The skills I gained through Albert Roussel's tutelage has changed everything. I reach Roussel, and look him in the eyes with a huge grin.

"Congratulations," Albert whispers and gives me a peck on the cheek. I take my scroll and continue with the others, returning to our seats. My chest fills with a rondeau allegro more joyous than anything Vivaldi or Mozart could pen. No one can dismiss my work now, or call me amateur. I know enough about form to re-interpret them all or invent my own, if I so choose. This gives me credibility to do things my own way. Instead of being discounted, I'll have clout. Teaching positions and a livable salary are possible, going forward. Editors might give my journal articles more credence and offer publication. A Diploma in Counterpoint, Magna cum Laude has my name on it.

❧

August 1908, Paris, 17th Arrondissement

I jot down a few notes on my lesson plan before leaving for the train. The Sunday solfège class I teach at the Patronage in Arcueil is the highlight of my week. Teaching choir music and piano to the local children gives me great satisfaction. I've just finished a draft of a modern fugue for four hands. Lovers of Bach and Mozart will be shocked right out of their shoes. I carefully tuck the copy of my new creation into my notebook and head off to share it with Claude. But now I weigh his perspective alongside others.

Claude and Emma now live in a mansion near the Arc de Triomphe, where the traffic is always frenzied. But their street, the Avenue Bois de Boulogne, leads away from the chaos to palatial broad lanes, divided by a green beltway. It must be financially demanding to provide Emma and their daughter with this sort of lifestyle. The era when Claude would pack his small apartment for weekly gatherings is long past. He alienated many people when he abandoned Lily, some of whom even raised money to help her. Nonetheless, he premiered a second set of in winter with Ricardo Viñes performing, with great reviews.

This is the first summer Claude didn't leave Paris for the countryside. A housekeeper meets me at the front door. There's an air of formality now. "Madame and Monsieur are waiting for you in the garden, Sir," she says, taking my hat and umbrella. She leads me across the gleaming wood floor and oriental carpets. I place my music on the piano as we cross the salon toward the bank of paned glass doors and the formal garden beyond.

My footsteps crunch into the fine pebble pathway, transecting the garden. I meander beneath stately shade trees and Italian cypress. There's a private dreamland hidden inside this tall, manicured hedge. Emma stands beside the rosebushes. Her silk dress matches the color of the long-stemmed coral buds she is clipping.

"Oh Erik, I'm so glad you're here," she says, laying several roses in a basket on her forearm. "Claude's been so morose today." She gives me a peck on my cheek. "Your presence should brighten his mood. We'll bring luncheon out shortly."

I peer toward the far end of the garden, where Claude sits with his legs crossed. He wears a white, collarless shirt, and linen trousers. His daughter, nicknamed Chouchou pushes a miniature baby carriage nearby. I wave and continue across the green. Claude says something to his daughter and points in my direction. The little girl gleefully abandons her pram and scampers toward me, squealing, "Kiki! Kiki". This was her earliest attempt at saying Erik when she could barely talk. But it just seemed to stick. The pudgy-cheeked three-year-old has a mass of dark ringlets and yellow ruffles like a buttercup. Her father saunters along behind her.

I bow. "Bonjour, Mademoiselle Chouchou."

"How are you, mon vieux?" Claude asks. "Come sit in the shade."

"I have a new baby," Chouchou says, looking up at me.

I squat to her level. "You do? Congratulations."

"Want to see?"

"Of course. Allons-y."

Chouchou takes my finger and leads me back toward the baby carriage. I turn to Claude.

"You must enjoy this wonderland and your little Alice."

"Oh yes, a nice consolation for having to stay in town. Chouchou can play here all day."

I reflect on my grandparent's garden in Normandy and the hours I spent there.

Claude gestures for me to sit beside him on the white wicker bench. "I've been so occupied trying to finish several pieces, I couldn't justify going away. I took an advance on promised works, and now I'm obligated to deliver, while still drumming up new material."

What a nice problem to have. But Claude's comment confirms the burden he labors under to maintain this paradise. On top of his lavish lifestyle, Claude is probably paying alimony to Lily. For all the glamour and luxury, it seems no different from my hand to mouth existence, only on a grander scale. I don't envy him. Leaning back in the cool shadow of the chestnut tree, I light a cigarette. "What are you working on?"

"I've started a new orchestral suite with a Spanish theme."

"And how is it going?"

"Terrible," Claude growls, and gestures brusquely. "Nothing is working. I've been using that strategy of taking inspiration from the visual arts, but my imagination still gets stymied by conventional methods. Or maybe it is the deluge of work. I'm just treading water. Seems crippling at times."

A flutter of guilt brushes over me, like I should do something to help. Claude has often paraded his superior skill and knowledge. Yet he points to that same reason for his dearth of inspiration. I experience no such thing. My Schola training merely gives me tools to channel my innovations. Gone too are the days when we'd banter about whether insider or outsider strategies work better, since my detour into the Music Hall.

Chouchou brings a doll wearing a brocade dress. "See Kiki? She's from Dresden."

"How lovely; a doll from the land of Monsieur Wagner. And what is her name?"

In the distance, the housekeeper and Emma cross the lawn, bringing trays to a linen-covered table inside the pergola.

"It's Musette," says Chouchou, holding out the doll.

"Musette? A French name; clever." I glance at Claude, who wears a devilish smirk.

"Hold her," Chouchou says, thrusting the doll into my lap. "Don't drop her."

"Oh, I'll be very careful." I cradle the doll against my body with one hand, and take another puff from my cigarette in the other.

Glasses and porcelain clink, as Emma and the maid arrange the midday meal. Chouchou returns to her carriage and brings a white velvet elephant over, plunking it onto my thigh. "And this is my Jimbo, from the zoo at Jardin de Plantes."

I tuck it beside Musette.

"And here is Golliwog. And this is my Lambie." She crowds my legs with a black-faced patchwork doll with yarn hair; and a sleeping lamb with a nappy coat and felt eyelashes.

I wedge my cigarette in the corner of my mouth to free my hands, keeping the entourage carefully assembled. I squint one eye against the stinging smoke as I juggle the collection of toys.

Emma walks toward us. She takes in the scene with a grin. "Now, this is quite a picture. Luncheon is ready, gentlemen. Chouchou, come inside."

"But I want to play," she says, reluctantly slogging toward the house.

"After your nap."

Claude stands and turns, looking at me with a grin. "Where's my camera?"

We deposit the collection of toys in the miniature pram and stroll across the yard to the gazebo. Claude slides a wrought-iron chair out from under the table. I sit across from him.

"While I've been tinkering with several other works," Claude says. "Opera seems the most lucrative." He stares off, too pre-occupied to enjoy the surrounding beauty. "The most recent performance of Pelleas sold out."

"Sold out? The press called it a general massacre," I say.

"It was. The performers butchered it. Despite that, it's a success here and abroad, and keeps the wolf away from the door. The question is, can I do it again?"

I note again the allusion to financial problems, underscored by the fact I'm the only guest. Luncheon includes modest finger sandwiches and sliced fruit, where oysters and veal were fare in the past. "I've brought a new experiment I'd like to try out," I say.

"Great. I always enjoy your experiments. I have something new, too."

We dine to the hum of bees and a serenade of sparrows. I talk about my work with the children and my desire to build a full music program for the working-class youth of Arcueil. Claude mentions he's been collaborating with Andre Caplet, who is scoring some of his orchestrations to save Claude time. He isn't treading water, he's drowning. I can tell by his half-present stare.

When we finish the meal, we move inside to the music room. I settle into my favorite leather chair and lean with my elbow on the armrest.

Claude slides onto the piano bench. “I’ve started a suite of child themed pieces,” he says. “Give me your best guess. What inspired this one?”

The music begins with a sonorous bass tune, arrhythmic at first, the movement hesitating, expectant. Then, with a middle register reply, the music nudges forward, slowly shifting into a lullaby cadence. The whole-tone scale gives the melody a dreamy flavor, like an Asian caravan. The bass pulse reminds me of the lumbering gait of an elephant. An image comes to mind of a certain white velvet pachyderm traveling over the hills and valleys made by a tummy and knees under the covers. A tucking-in ritual between father and daughter could be its inspiration. I smile tenderly.

Conspicuously missing is the usual effusion of glittering notes, which I call Debussy’s sauce. Is Claude experimenting? The pared-down and straightforward technique has been my hallmark. The piece finishes with a fading sonorous sway; rocking like a cradle. Claude looks over at me.

I adjust my pince-nez. “That’s a rather different style for you; stripped down and bare. Seems familiar.” I flash an incredulous smirk.

“Rather.” Claude smiles. “But, could you guess?”

“The inspiration? Why, Monsieur Jimbo.”

Claude grins. “Precisely. Sweet little thing. I only hope my audience won’t find the collection trite.”

“It’s not trite. I like the way you quoted the children’s sing-song; the way they taunt one another. And the way you brought in the interval of the major second was well done.”

“You caught that. Good.”

Now it is my turn. “My intention here is to adhere to compositional rules, but create a modern fugue that will confound all naysayers.” I spread out the pages, sit on the left, having Claude take the primo role.

Claude begins the first phrase and I join in. As hoped, Claude smiles and snickers as he reads the funny performance directions. We work our way through the piece playfully in the beginning and then more earnest. But, when we finish, Claude leaves the piano bench saying nothing. He brings out the cigars and pours two whiskeys, handing one to me. At least that hasn't changed.

Claude sits down on his sofa, and I sink into the leather chair again.

"I have mixed feelings about this composition," Claude says, leaning his face into his hand. "It certainly has some strengths. It's densely chromatic." He takes a sip of whiskey. "You've done quite a magic trick here, with the spirit of wicked humor; a kind of fugal dialogue." He takes a few puffs on his cigar, letting the smoke filter out through his nostrils.

"That's my intention." I swirl the amber liquid in my glass.

"Here is the concern, mon vieux. I told you this when you enrolled at the Schola." Claude's tone grows cold-blooded. He waves his hand, his cigar leaving a wispy trail. "I fear the rigors and structure of the Schola have done damage to the free and original expression you once had."

"How so? Can't freedom and originality evolve?" I take a gulp from the glass.

Claude strokes his beard. "Conceptually, I'm enthusiastic about the notion of creating a modern fugue. And, technically, it's impeccable. But, if you want my honest appraisal; the rhythm is restricted to the point of monotony. You've used all even note values."

"By design." I shift in my seat.

"And that gives it a truly modern sound, like some industrial machine. But it loses any sense of musical direction."

"Who says it must have direction?"

"But it makes one cross-eyed."

"Cross-eyed?" I jerk back, my gut tightening. I've never taken criticism very well. This time Claude really cut to the quick.

"Better to hear it from me than read it on the front page of Comedia."

That doesn't soften the insult very much. My mouth goes dry. "Fine. I'll digest that a bit." I draw on my cigar and take another swallow of whiskey. Maybe it's better to take my leave. I don't think I can continue to veil my resentment much longer.

Claude condescends. "You're the one who asked me for help."

"Did I?" A flash of heat spreads down my face and neck.

Claude doesn't reply. He just stares at the carpet.

The housekeeper brings out footed glasses with raspberry sorbet. But it tastes bitter to me. Rather than finish it, I toss back what remains of my whiskey. I make an excuse for myself, ask for my hat and umbrella, gather my music, and make for the door. As I'm about to leave the Debussy mansion, Emma enters the room. She stares wide-eyed.

"Thank you, Madame Debussy for the lovely refreshing meal." I tip my hat and depart.

My pulse pounds in my ears and my breath snorts from my nostrils like a charging bull. I can't remember a time when Claude's critique was so insulting. To walk off my frustration, I march back in the direction of the Arc de Triomphe. My stroll crosses over to the Champs-Élysées, continuing to the Obélisque. I didn't waste three years at the Schola, only to compose yawn producing tedium. Claude is simply uncomfortable with my innovation and the new esthetic. He even ascribed his own creative stymie to me. But I'm not stuck. I will not change my work to suit him. He's wrong. I'll bring this piece to the next gathering of Les Apaches just for spite. We'll see who's really stymied.

Chapter 33

Autumn 1908, Paris, 9th Arrondissement

SHOWERS PATTER AGAINST my umbrella as I approach the new American-style bar where I'm meeting Paulette. Even in the rain, Le Manhattan spelled out in gold lettering makes a classy emblem against the fringed black awning. As I'm about to step inside, an automobile pulls up to the curb. Glancing back, I realize Paulette is riding in the back seat. The cab driver unfurls an umbrella and comes around to open the door for her. I hurry over.

"I thought I was going to get washed away," she says. "Perfect timing, Ricky."

I smile at her pet-name for me. "Let's get inside," I say, taking her hand.

I hold the door open for her and follow her inside. After stowing our wraps, the Maître'd shows us to a table. As always, Paulette looks like she walked off the cover of a fashion journal. The newest style makes women look like they are wearing lampshades of embroidered silk with long fringe. Her sapphire dress matches the lining of her platter sized hat, which compliments her cognac hair. Once seated, she takes out a slender ivory cigarette holder, inserts a cigarette, and I offer her a light.

"I've heard they have an American drink, called the Manhattan," Paulette says. "I've never tried one. Have you?"

"Bourbon, sweet vermouth, and aromatic bitters. Shall we order two?"

She agrees and I signal the server who takes the order.

"How was your run in Pourville?" I ask, taking a puff on my cigarette.

"Utterly marvelous, Ricky. Deauville and Trouville had such balmy, tranquil days and dazzling nights. Do you ever get back to Normandy?"

I flick the ash from my cigarette. "There is no one to go back to. Family is all gone."

"Pity. Go for the mussels and scallops then. Eduard is quite the seafood lover and an angler, too. We went yachting. Can you imagine?"

"Now, you're back to business in Paris."

The server brings the vermillion cocktails in V-shaped glasses garnished with a cherry. I take a sip, concluding it is more to a woman's taste, but pleasant enough.

Paulette stares off in the distance and grows quiet for a few moments. Then she removes her glove and brandishes an engagement ring. I inspect the glittering diamond on her finger with a mixture of resignation and relief.

"Congratulations, my dear. When is the blessed event?"

Next June, after the Spring Revue."

"This calls for a toast." I raise my glass and we clink rims.

Paulette takes a sip and sets her glass down. "You realize this will be my last season. I'm running out of time if I want to start a family."

I tug at my beard. "I expected as much. I'm happy for you."

She studies my face. "Are you?"

"Of course."

Paulette tips her head. "I must confess, Ricky, I still wonder what might have happened if you and I had taken a different turn."

I slowly shake my head. "I've often wondered that, too. But it wouldn't have worked, ma chèrie. A drinker like me wouldn't make a good husband or father. However, be assured, your marriage won't keep me from remaining your devoted friend, and Eduard's."

"Maybe so. But I want you to be happy, too."

I squeeze her hand with a bittersweet smile.

"Listen, I thought we might celebrate my last season, what with Eduard in Belgium on business. I noticed Harold Bauer was premiering Debussy's newest composition tonight, The Children's Corner, so I bought two tickets."

"Did you?" I fold my arms, smirking.

"Presumptuous, I know. Did you have important plans?" she asks.

"Nothing I can't postpone," I say.

We finish our drinks and I hail a motorized cab. The Cercle Musicale is an old mansion, renovated into a thousand-seat concert hall. We arrive in time to check our coats and find our seats. I quickly scan the room, but don't see Claude anywhere. We settle in, and the house lights dim.

Clean shaven and wearing tails, pianist Harold Bauer walks confidently center stage and bows to welcoming applause. He tosses back his rooster's comb hair and takes his place at the gleaming piano. He has an interesting posture at the keyboard, sitting back farther than I would find comfortable, and he's very stiff and straight.

The first movement bears the title of a piano primer long used for children's instruction. I learned to read music with Gustave Vinot using this Gradus ad Parnassum. The music begins with an arpeggio, swirling with delight, in Claude's hazy, impressionistic style. Then the melody shifts to a portrait of a child practicing her scales with a twist of whimsy. I can picture Claude with Chouchou at the piano, beginning her finger dance on the black and white keys. Harold Bauer teeters side to side, playing a quotation from a well-known lullaby. Knowing the child who inspired the piece, I find it an endearing portrait.

Bauer pauses between movements, takes out a handkerchief and wipes his hands and brow. I glance at the program, and notice he named the second piece for Chouchou's velvet stuffed elephant Jimbo. It's the piece Claude played for me back in summer. Each succeeding piece adds additional brushstrokes to the tender portrait of a father's love. When I read the name of the last movement, it brings a smile to my lips, recalling the garden and Chouchou's blackface rag-doll, Golliwog.

The introduction is a complete change in mood, with a bouncy pace. Then, the melody struts out in high stepping Ragtime syncopation. My jaw drops. The oom-pah bass is absent, but it's my own ragtime tune, Le Piccadilly, with minor inversions. I'm stunned. Unbelievable. A chill grips me and my head swims. Claude wouldn't do that, would he? But, when the first strain repeats, I grow queasy. Claude has more than quoted the song. He's stolen my music. I've performed this countless times on stage and for Claude's friends and family. Chouchou would even gyrate on the salon rug to it.

How convenient Claude never played this particular movement for me. Would Claude Debussy actually steal from his best friend and claim my music as his own? This Prix de Rome. This man they knighted. He has no shortage of spectacular works. Has he run so short of ideas he's resorting to plagiarizing mine? And my popular work, at that. I pinch my eyes shut.

However, as the tune continues, it shifts to a strange slow leitmotif, which seems familiar too. And when the phrase reiterates, I'm even more shocked. It's Wagner! The Prelude to Tristan and Isolde. Wagner meets Ragtime. I cover my gaping mouth. Clearly, it's Claude's attempt at parody, an insider's joke, perhaps. But he'd never given me the slightest clue. The irony is; Claude criticized me for attempting to meld together the popular idiom with Grande Musique. Now he is doing it.

The audience thunders with applause. Claude has capitalized on my idea and my music. He's getting the credit and the praise. How on earth can I ever address this?

As we ride together in a cab to take Paulette home, she effervesces with the thrill of the concert. I, however, seethe. Turmoil boils toward an explosive blast of profanity, alternating with waves of self-pity. But Paulette doesn't need to receive all that. I hold all my hurt and resentment behind a tender smile for her.

"I noticed something about that last movement," Paulette says. "It sounded strangely similar to one of your tunes."

As if to hold back a rupturing dam, I drop my head and fold my arms. Finally, I meet Paulette's alarmed stare and speak. "It should. It was Le Piccadilly."

"Oh! It was indeed." She searches my face. "I take it the two of you didn't collaborate on the piece?"

I bite my lip and shake my head.

Paulette brings her hand to her chin. "Oh my." She reaches over and clasps my hand.

Somehow, just the shared recognition of what has happened drains some of my fury. I blow out a resigned breath.

"Why would he do such a thing?" she asks.

"He's always had this drive to be the best, prove his superiority. And he is superior in certain ways; his talent is immense. He condescends to me, and I just brush it off with humor. But the ugly side of Debussy is entitled and exploitive. I've watched for years how he uses people, drawing them in with seeming generosity, bringing them into his circle. But with a closer read, there is a sub-text."

"He certainly has that reputation with women," Paulette says.

"Yes, but I think he's finally met his match with Emma. In all the time I've known him, whoever is au currant, in the public eye, Claude has to capture a piece of their glory. How could I delude myself into thinking I was immune?"

"Because you're so trusting, and he's done a good job seducing you."

"He either acts pitifully tragic, and you feel compelled to help him, or he turns things around so you feel you owe him. Back in 93, I was coming out of a terrible love affair. As consolation, Claude bought tickets to Maeterlinck's play, Pelleas et Melisande. I had intended to develop it. But when he was in a slump of despair, Claude talked me out of it because he wanted it. It's a masterpiece. But I was the one who pointed him toward the Symbolists."

"So you gave him direction. What did he give you?"

"He orchestrated the Gymnopédies and got them performed at a prestigious concert with Société Nationale," I continue. "Now, I wonder if it was really for me at all. I was so thrilled to have my music performed, and so destitute, I couldn't see. Maybe he was using me, even then."

Paulette squeezes my hand. "Poverty and desperation make you dependent on others. And your shame keeps you from finding fault in them."

"He disparages my ideas, but up until recently, in a gentle and kind way. As a result, I abandoned projects like the Dreamy Fish with my old-time friend Patrice. Last spring, I could swear I heard my composition reworked in his. While he altered the meter and phrasing, and smothered the work in shimmering Debussy sauce, the similarity was uncanny."

"Working with powerful producers has taught me one thing," Paulette says. "Some people have no scruples. They manipulate you any way they can. They take liberties and make assumptions, doing all manner of things to keep you under their control."

"He disparaged my Three Pear-shaped Pieces, saying popular or grand don't mix well. And now, he's doing just that. But most disturbing, this time he used my actual music, Paulette. He stole my music and claimed it as his own in front of all Paris."

"If the one person you thought was your ally robs you; what then? I'm so very sorry." She loops her arm through mine and pulls me close.

"Almost 20 years I called him friend."

"But you're not desperate, not empty. You're successful. You have things in your life to fill your cup. That's what allows you to see."

"He even tried to dissuade me from getting my diploma, and has disparaged everything I've written since."

"You'd almost get the impression he's trying to keep you from any genuine success."

"But why?"

"Oh, my dear, dear Ricky. Don't you know? Truly, don't you see? You're a genius. He wants to keep you as his own private diamond reserve."

Chapter 34

March 1909, Paris, 17th Arrondissement

No IMMEDIATE OPPORTUNITY presented itself to address Claude's betrayal of trust. He left for a tour of Great Britain right after the holidays. I busied myself with the Patronage and my studies at the Schola, auditing d'Indy's orchestration course. It gave me time to think and dissipate the magnitude of fury raised by my discovery. Finally, I receive an invitation from Emma for luncheon at the Debussy mansion. But how do I broach the subject of plagiarism?

Instead of the music salon, the housekeeper leads me into the library. Claude sits at his desk in his pajamas, and a burgundy velvet robe with quilted lapels wrapped neatly over them.

"Not up to my usual mayhem, I'm afraid." Claude says, straining a smile. He doesn't get up or offer the usual exchange of kisses.

"Je suis désolé. No one told me you were ill." I scout around for a chair.

"My doctor ordered me to bed. But the Muse comes when she wants."

I push a tufted ottoman to the side of the desk, sinking onto it and gripping my knees. "What's the matter?"

"Not sure. I have a persistent pinching ache here." Claude opens his robe to reveal a hot water bottle tucked under his ribs. "It brings a little relief."

"Not your appendix, I hope."

"No. Other side. I've been having some kind of hemorrhage."

I cringe. "You're bleeding?"

Claude nods slowly. "Something's very wrong."

"What could cause such a thing?"

Claude looks past me, unfocused and bemused. "They don't exactly know, yet. I think it's an acute case of neurasthenia. I've been working too hard." He has a slight pallor in his complexion.

"In London, I had to cancel visits to Edinburgh and Manchester. I was so ill."

"This is obviously not a good time for a visit. I should go." I stand up.

"No, please stay. You're no bother. Really. I could use a little company to cheer me up."

"If you're sure. I don't want to impose," I say.

"Emma made a big pot of chicken soup. It's a bland diet and bed rest. What a bore."

I'm torn. Would it be insensitive to bring up the issue? I'm in knots. I don't want to start an argument, but I deserve an answer. Perhaps I can just test the water. "You left town before I had a chance to tell you. I attended Bauer's performance."

Claude's eyes widen. "You were there? Why didn't you come backstage? Although I must admit, I was so unnerved, it doubled me over. I couldn't stay in the concert hall."

"Really?"

"I was certain the press would crucify me. Or worse, I'd get booed. Couldn't bear it. After it was all over, Bauer said they loved it. What did you think of my little surprise?"

I run my hand back over my scalp. "You mean the cakewalk?"

"Did you split your sides?"

I'm stunned. Claude seems oblivious to how his actions affected me. "About that…"

Claude is giddy. "More than anyone, you'd understand and find it hilarious."

I sigh and speak dryly. "I was surprised, alright."

Claude furrows his brow. "You're not cross, are you? My quoting your little Ragtime piece. Don't you see? The entire suite battered down a wall. I rubbed their noses in it."

"I have to admit, Wagner and Ragtime together are pretty outrageous. But you didn't even ask me to use my work."

"Oh. I assumed…"

We stare at each other for an excruciating few moments.

"Maybe we need a drink." Claude rings a small hand bell on his desk to summon the housekeeper. "I couldn't get the image out of my head, Chouchou piling her Dresden doll and her Negro ragamuffin in your lap."

I stroke my beard, feigning a smile. "Blending of the new with the old; making it modern. You've finally come around to my way of thinking." I know my words drip with umbrage.

"You always end up being right, Erik. I've been too timid."

And that makes it okay? The maid returns to Claude's studio, and he instructs her to bring me a glass of fine whiskey. Silence prevails until the servant offers the squat tumbler of tawny liquor to appease my rancor. My gut twinges and I want to cry. I stare into the glass. What could I say? Claude has subtly but effectively disarmed any protest.

Claude takes a tense, audible breath. "We can rejoice in knowing it opens a whole new direction. And speaking of new directions… my other good news. You're the first to know. Fauré has offered an olive branch and has asked me to join the governing body of the Conservatoire."

I look up. "The Conseil Supériuer?" I shake my head.

"Infiltrating and subverting. Finally, we have an official voice in the French music establishment."

The doors open again and the housekeeper wheels in a cart with dinnerware. She sets up luncheon at a small table near the window. I toss back my whiskey and move with Claude to the dining space, looking out over the garden.

"I never thought I'd see the day," says Claude. "But this coup won't be without detractors. They're already calling Fauré a Robespierre, because so many faculty members have resigned since he took over as director."

"A veritable storming of the Bastille of music. Change is in the wind." I sprinkle salt and pepper into my soup, and stir the steaming broth. "What are your thoughts about Ravel's latest revolt?"

Claude stops slathering butter on his hunk of bread and looks up. "Ravel? I'm not sure what you mean." He squints.

I smirk. "The Société Nationale refused to feature any of his students in this year's season again. So, Ravel, along with other former students of Fauré submitted their resignation to D'Indy in protest. He's starting his own organization."

Claude's mouth falls open. "Is that right? You've been keeping company with Les Apaches, have you?" He lowers a disapproving brow.

"Yes. These young composers are the future, Claude."

Claude strokes his beard with a lopsided smirk. The cogs are turning behind his eyes, the same way he studies the chess board, calculating his next move. I also study the interpersonal chess board. What moves remain? "They're calling it Société Musicale Independante. They plan a critical journal, too." Although it now seems miniscule in scale, I decide to mention my own triumph. "And that little community choir I started… the governing committee has approached me to become the superintendent of the entire Patronage- and better still, they're giving me full reign and artistic freedom to do whatever I like. It will become like my own little private arts academy."

"Impressive." But Claude's tone is derisive.

I stare out the window. Though the afternoon sky has patches of blue peeking through the haze, the trees still are without shoots or leaves, and loom stark and barren against the horizon. There will be no taking turns at the piano today, no trying out new compositions. I didn't even bring new work. Claude seems to lose his vigor after the meal. When it is time to depart, Claude walks me to the studio door. "Thanks for the diversion, mon vieux."

That's what I am? A diversion from more important matters. Although I have a full stomach, my walk home feels empty. I'm unsure if there was malice in Claude's intentions. He'd made no secret about his borrowing. Perhaps it's like Paulette believes. Claude is so consumed with himself; everyone else becomes an extension of him. We used to be on the same side. But it doesn't entitle Claude to use my music without my consent. None of his excuses helped assuage my hurt and frustration. Nor did I have my say or get satisfaction. Why does Claude have to take from the little guy, the poor one? Yet, he thought enough of my tiny gemstones to use them to embellish his grand diadem. I'm not sure I can forgive him.

Chapter 35

November 1910, Paris, 17th Arrondissement

RAVEL SLAPS A folded newspaper on the café table. "Will this battle with Action Française nationalists ever end?" he asks. Maurice Ravel and I sit with writer Michel Calvocoressi sharing a bottle of Pinot Noir. The café sits on the ground floor of Ravel's new apartment building. He invited me to discuss the spring concert season and the new journal of the breakaway organization, the Société Musicale Indepéndante. Having shorn his wild hair and Bohemian beard, Maurice has a rather elfin appearance with his sizeable ears.

"The article claims Debussy's latest music is amorphous and effeminate.," Maurice says. Raphael Cor's incendiary missive has caused a flood of responses, inundating the journals and newspapers. "How do you think we should respond to the uproar?"

I blow out a stream of smoke. "It's just the standard partisan line. By saying only sissies and pansies like his music, the conservative right discredits anything new and different. You see, they have always attributed France's defeat during the Prussian war to a lack of masculinity. It's what's wrong with the country, no one has any balls, don't you know?"

The young men both laugh.

"It surprised me to see Willy counter in Debussy's favor," says Calvo. "He said his music remains faithful to the French musical tradition."

"That IS a surprise," I say. "Sar Péladan's response was the most outrageous."

"Sar Péladan? I haven't read it," says Calvo.

"You don't know the history," I say. "He said Debussy has no place among the musical gods, and it's the only music that has ever made him physically ill."

Guffaws burst out all around. It's wonderful these young Turks seek my opinion and it matters to them. I read everything, and they know it. "Anytime you do something that breaks with tradition, you're bound to catch a tomato or two. They've already started on you, Maurice, and your new independent music society," I say.

"Yes," Ravel huffs. "Calling it the Musical Society of Invertebrates."

I smirk and adjust my pince-nez. "Some of my best friends are mollusks."

"It doesn't bother you?"

"Of course, it does. And we must answer it. I usually find humor is the best approach."

Ravel leans forward. "What if we demonstrate just how stupid these guys are by showing whose aesthetic and methods predate us both? Yours. What if for the first concert of this season we feature your music only?"

"Mine?"

"Yes. I want to present it personally. Your Sarabandes and the like."

"Are you sure you want to use my old material? I have several recent pieces I have never performed publicly."

"We can feature them in a subsequent concert. But I'd like to bring out the Sarabandes and perhaps the Prelude to the Sons of the Stars for this first concert."

"How about a transitional piece, my Three Pear-shaped Pieces?"

"Yes. That's of great importance, too. SMI will pay for performance rights, of course; and we could publish the Sarabandes in our monthly journal. I want to prove just what blind ignoramuses the critics all are; draw a line in the sand."

"You know how I feel about critics." I narrow my eyes. "They should all be flayed and salted."

"I'm writing the program notes," says Calvo. "I intend to show you were the groundbreaker, the pioneer of the modern aesthetic, decades before it ever came into vogue."

"What an honor. I don't know what to say." I raise my glass. "To the best snails, clams, and squids I've ever met. I say, a votre santé!"

"Santé."

I never thought this day would come. I'd all but given up on having my serious music appreciated. At the moment, I'm too thrilled to question or ponder what I just agreed to. What a blessing these wonderful young men have become in my life. They dare to defy the established order and refuse to prostrate themselves to the traditionalists. I've stuck to my ideals; never sold out or pandered to the music snobs. My music has stood the test of time. The only thing I did to engineer this was befriend them. As I sip the Pinot Noir, the vintage tastes richer and mellower than any I've savored in a long time.

&

January 1911, Paris, 8th Arrondissement

A music war continues to rage on the pages of all the journals. The torrent of rivalry in the press surrounding Ravel and Debussy has only surged more since November. They have each produced dissimilar works. But the press seems to highlight and question the coincidences. If I didn't know better, I might have wondered too about Ravel's Mother Goose Suite after Claude's Children's Corner; Maurice's Rhapsodie Espanole and Claude's Iberia; Ravel's Mirrors and Claude's Images. But I also ponder why I am being brought into the conversation. Is there another motive besides overthrowing the establishment, and bringing the truth to light?

Maurice confirmed the details of the SMI concert by sending me a copy of his Mother Goose Suite. He'd written an affectionate homage, calling me the Grand-père of modern music and signing it "from your disciple".

It's a cold snowy evening and a Monday, when theatres are usually dark. But the Salle Gaveau has patrons lined up into the street when the cab delivers me. Léon Leclère waits for my arrival, watching from the arched window lined with harps in the Gaveau musical instrument store. Leclère swiftly ushers me through the line to the special reserved seating in front, taking my umbrella, hat, and coat to be checked. My seat is next to Florent Schmitt and Michel Calvocoressi. Other members of the Apaches sit nearby. Even with the buzz of the growing audience, I notice someone whistling the Borodin anthem of the Apaches. I look around, grin and nod to my friends.

"Here," says Calvo, and hands me a copy of the folded program. "I hope you approve."

I examine the titles of my music in an elegant Edwardian typeset on the right-hand side of the program and then read the profile inside an Art Nouveau box on the facing page.

> *Erik Satie occupies a truly exceptional place in the history of contemporary art. At 20, he composed several works that make him the precursor of genius. They surprise one with the prescience of modernist vocabulary 25 years before our time and in quasi-prophetic character he penned certain harmonic combinations only now being embraced. His early work had been so forward looking that his contemporaries failed to understand or appreciate how his compositions anticipated and predicted the idiom of a new century. By performing his music, Maurice Ravel will demonstrate the high esteem which only the most progressive composers hold for Satie.*

A lump grows in my throat. I clutch at my collarbone. Closing the program, I turn to Calvo. "I'm truly moved by your words. Thank you."

"You've certainly earned it. Long overdue," Calvo replies.

When the lights dim, Monsieur Gaveau comes out onto the stage in his tuxedo. As Master of Ceremonies, he welcomes the attendees to the second concert season. He talks about the purpose of SMI to provide an alternative voice in the arts, and to present remarkable music to a discerning audience. "Now prepare yourselves for a feast of the ears as Maurice Ravel performs the music of Erik Satie."

Maurice appears in the wings and crosses to center-stage to booming applause. He looks like a little blackbird with his chiseled profile and his tuxedo tails. Maurice bows and then sits on the piano bench as the spectators calm down. My insides flutter and I grip my thighs. Slowly, the complex parallel ninths of the Sarabandes reverberate on the gleaming black grand, cadenced like a dance by Rameau or Couperin. How very French of me. D'Indy couldn't complain, although I doubt my teacher is in the audience.

Maurice's playing style is like a Swiss watchmaker; a technique of absolute flawless perfection. It's strange to hear my own music and not be the one playing it. I wrote this when I was still in the army. But we'd chosen just the right piece to open. As I glance over my shoulder, I see ponderous gazes and forward leaning posture, an intrigued twist of the moustache or a gloved hand to the lips. It all seems to convey intrigue and amazement. I relax just a little.

When Ravel completes the piece, he pauses and then turns to the audience. Fevered applause accompanies cheers and bravos. I release the tense breath. Ravel stands, steps away from the piano and bows several times. Florent Schmitt pats me on the shoulder and nods with a congratulatory grin. As the viewers settle down for the second presentation, Ravel returns to the keyboard and massages his knuckles. He sits still, focusing for a few seconds.

The Prelude to The Sons of the Stars begins with its mysterious stacked fourths moving in parallel motion. I wrote it that way, to capture the unfathomable splendor of the starry canopy under which I so often walked. Maurice's interpretation is dramatic and moving. It leaves the audience spellbound. When he finally takes his hands from the keyboard, the audience explodes with excitement. Maurice takes another bow and exits the stage for intermission. The house lights come up. Within moments, Leclère comes rushing over.

"Ravel needs you backstage," he whispers. "Come with me."

I follow him to the back room where Ravel is pacing.

"We're probably going to get an encore," Ravel says. "I brought a couple of other pieces, just in case. I wanted you to advise me on which one you think best achieves our goals." We discuss several options, but in the end decide on Danses Gothiques.

When Maurice returns to the stage, he invites one of his students to join him to play Trois Morceau en Forme de Poire. The faces of the audience show shock and delight at the unusual blend of Ragtime and rhapsody. And Maurice was correct. The audience is so enthusiastic, they call an encore. I feel spongy in the knees when Ravel asks me to rise and be recognized. Maybe the outsider actually got a few things right. Too bad Claude is not here to see it.

Chapter 36

June 28, 1914- 1st Arrondissement

What is a normal life? I believe my life has been anything but normal. Rubbing elbows with painters, writers, and musicians is something I always enjoy. And I love young people. But my life has become an endless stream of gatherings, one soirée after another. Tonight, it is at Misia's. There will be no shortage of drinks. A non-stop stream of introductions and new acquaintances will follow. Living all the way out in Arcueil in seclusion, getting dressed up, and walking miles into Paris has become my routine. This is how collaborations start, how deals get made. How else can an artist survive? No, it isn't what normal people do, but it's my normal.

Then, there is Misia. I have two things in common with the daughter of sculptor Cyprian Godebski. Three, if you count the handful of friends we share in common. We both play the piano, but who doesn't? And we both seem to be a favorite subject of painters. Although why they are so fascinated with me remains a mystery. In Misia's case, it is obvious. She puts the roses to shame. Renoir, Vuillard, Toulouse-Lautrec all fell in love with Misia. I, on the other hand, find her cloying sweetness disingenuous. But I'm not averse to stealing an eyeful of her ripe peaches.

She has no taste for minnows. She only wants marlins. In the ten years I've known her, she's changed her name from Godebski to Nathanson, to Edwards, and soon to be Sert. Her husbands' connections and wealth crowned her as arbiter of Parisian good taste. Behind her Venus allure is a power broker as strategic as any chess master. You don't want to be Misia's enemy. It's impossible to tell if anyone is really her friend. Unfortunately, this is how performing arts and music get produced. I'm not sure the title "benefactor" is really the right term. One becomes more of a pet, I imagine, on a rather short leash.

Why does this evening matter so much to me? Misia, the Queen of all Paris, wants to introduce me to Sergei Diaghilev. Diaghilev only offers commissions to compose for the Ballets Russes to the most preeminent composers. So far, this includes Rimsky-Korsakov, Stravinsky, Debussy, and Ravel. And the commissions pay a staggering sum. I happen to know Claude received 10,000 francs for Jeux last year. But Stravinsky's Rite of Spring eclipsed that. Ever since Ravel anointed me the Precursor of them all; my compositions have caught on like an epidemic. I'm no longer the marginal hack critics once considered me to be. Meeting Diaghilev is huge.

Summer evening turns the sky a misty periwinkle blue. I cross through traffic over the Carousel Bridge toward the upscale apartment facing the river. Jade waters churn below. I gaze up at the ornamentation above the pediments, like an elegant brooch pinned to a lacy collar. This is a new pinnacle; a summit in my musical career. It's hard not to think so. I hand over my bowler and umbrella to the doorman. Guests in cutaway jackets and glittering beaded gowns sweep by me. Just for an instant, I survey my sorry-looking suit. Who gives a fig? I am who I am. They can take it or leave it.

Misia holds court on a sky-blue Louis XIV divan with her little Papillion dog. Her luminous silk gown clings to her curves like spooned on béchamel. She stands up, holding her pet in one arm. I reach out to take her hand. The dog yips and growls.

"Têtue, stop that," she scolds.

"Dogs usually like me," I say.

"I do apologize. She is cross today. Come, let me introduce you to the other guests."

Yes, all those formal introductions; names I'll never remember. Misia's tawny port coiffure and the spray of feathers on her turban make her look just like little Têtue. I can't help grinning. Misia introduces me to a droopy-eyed bloodhound of a matron with too much cologne.

"Enchanté, Madame." I grin at the old frump.

After half a dozen more meaningless exchanges, Misia leads me to an alcove attached to the main salon with a waiting rococo chair next to Diaghilev. "I was just saying to Serge how it's taken him far too long to make your acquaintance. I'm so happy to bring the two of you together, finally." She swiftly gestures to one of her servants to bring over a tray of cocktails. I take what I guess is a cognac, and Diaghilev takes a coupe of champagne.

The tuxedoed Diaghilev squints one eye at snarling Têtue. His plump lower lip forms a natural pout. Opening a silver cigarette case, he reaches over, offering one to me.

"I'm quite certain you will get along divinely." Misia gives a sultry lift of a brow and turns to continue her rounds.

"Ostrovia," says the portly Russian, raising his glass to me. I reciprocate.

By some accident of nature, a colorless swatch of hair shoots back from his hairline like a white-hot flame through an angry dark pelt. That feature combined with jowls and melancholy eyes gives his broad face the look of a bulldog.

Why am I thinking of people as dogs? I laugh to myself. Yes, a room full of dogs. I look across the salon at Misia's current lover in white tie, Catalan muralist Jose Maria Sert. His sinewy muscularity and shaved shiny head make me think of a pincer. I turn to Serge Diaghilev.

"Have you ever wondered why people choose the particular dogs they own, or notice how they often resemble their pets?"

Diaghilev's mouth turns up first on one side, then the other. He snickers.

"Now my dog," I say. "A complete mongrel; he chose me."

Diaghilev laughs. "Your reputation for opportune drollery is well-earned, Monsieur Satie," he says in perfect French, with a thick accent. "We have to laugh. There are enough things to be serious about, n'est-ce pas?

"Yes, I remind myself of that often." I sip the cognac. "So, what gives you pause, Monsieur Diaghilev? Your Ballet season just finished. Did it meet expectations?"

Diaghilev inhales through flared nostrils. "The tickets sold out. Everyone got paid."

Is he being overly modest? From Calvo's description; who'd interviewed the Russian in his luxurious hotel room; I'd pictured an entrepreneur swimming in cash. But as I listen to him talk about the challenges, a different image emerges. Raising capital to finance the ballet season, ensuring his dancers have everything they need is exhausting. The impresario crosses one leg over the other, and I notice the tattered hem of Diaghilev's trousers. Yes, he might wear a tux and spats; but the man is broke.

"We'd taken a different approach this year." Cigarette between two fingers, Diaghilev rolls his wrist. "We went with a more conventional series, after the furor stirred up by The Rite of Spring." He leans forward, flicking ash into a crystal dish, and looks at me with a raised brow.

I blow out a long stream of smoke and mirror Diaghilev's quizzical brow. "Paris wasn't ready for that kind of genius, was it?"

Diaghilev smirks and gives a brief glance over his shoulder at the nattering hive of attendees, cocktail glasses clinking. "They never are. That's the nature of innovation." Diaghilev takes a long drag, slowly releasing the smoke as he talks. "It was painful. But one day they will embrace it. So, this year we were safer, yes. You must compromise when you're responsible for the lives of others."

I tap my cigarette on the rim of the dish. "You sound disappointed."

"Safe is not what built Ballets Russes. We've earned a name through doing things differently, breaking the mold. We brought back the male dancer, solo stars, in their own right." He waves his hands with fire in his eyes. "And instead of focusing on the rigid execution of classical technique; we brought in choreographers who are far more expressive and emotional."

"It's paid off." I'd faced the same dialectic in music, between rigid tradition and innovation. I like the big Russian. We are of similar minds. "I especially like the way you've brought together design, music, storytelling, and dance; a perfect unity of arts."

"Yes, art. The things we sacrifice for it."

This man is devoted to his dance company, putting it above his own wellbeing; the way I am dedicated to my music. He must live in a hotel, because he owns nothing, has even less than I do. He takes his meals in fine restaurants, probably as a guest of others, for the same reasons, though maybe on a higher scale. "Slaves to the Muse. Yes, that is what art demands of us; total and unswerving devotion."

Diaghilev returns the weary smile of a kindred sojourner. "I like you, Satie."

I try not to smile too big, like the gleeful boy jumping up and down inside me. "So, you're looking for something out of the ordinary, something a little dangerous?"

"Misia mentioned your name as the one composer who might be willing and able to go beyond; more than Stravinsky, more the Debussy or Ravel."

"Well, I must say right away; the work of those gentlemen is sheer genius. But if different is what you're looking for, if there is one thing I've doggedly endeavored to do, it is to be singular."

"Doggedly?"

We both chuckle.

"There is no question. This is the type of thing I'm looking for.

I see definite possibilities in collaboration. We'll need a librettist and designer. I'll have to hire a new choreographer, I'm afraid."

"Oh? Your Monsieur Nijinsky?"

"Unfortunately, things have…" says Diaghilev.

Mid-sentence, the housemaid rushes across the room. "Madame, Madame. Something has happened." Everyone in the room grows quiet. "Pardon, but we have an unexpected caller, Madame. Monsieur Limoux. He says it's urgent."

"Show him in," says Misia, leaving her divan and walking to the center of the room.

I recognize the name, the editor of Le Matin, the newspaper Misia's former husband owned. The pudgy bearded man clamors into the room, still wearing his hat.

"I'm sorry to interrupt. I've got the most unfortunate news," he says. "The story just came across the wire. Someone has assassinated Austrian Archduke Ferdinand in Serbia."

Gasps and mutters grip the circle of guests.

Diaghilev stiffens. "Serbia?"

"I don't understand," Misia replies.

"There's a good chance Austria will interpret this as an act of war," Monsieur Limoux replies. "If so, Germany and Central Powers will invade."

"And if they do," says Diaghilev. "Russia is bound by treaty to defend its ally. And since an accord with Russia links France…"

My stomach churns. This is just the pretense the royalists and the military have been waiting for. The lot of them, Action Française, League of Patriots. Look at the nervous eyes of these young people. Will those assholes really get them all killed? This is madness. Mon Dieu.

⁂

Every post office and transit station, every grocery and newsstand is inundated with official notices. France announced mobilization for the first of August. The government orders every able-bodied recruit and reservist to report to their local town center for military processing. Needless to say, the two big plans I had poised to get underway have been indefinitely postponed. Publishers aren't issuing new sheet music under these circumstances. So, the presses never rolled on my Sports et Divertissements collection, despite paying me in full. The theaters are all closing. The ballet project with Diaghilev has to be delayed. He's taking the company to America or Switzerland to wait things out.

I stand in one of two lines swarming the doors at the old Arcueil Mayor's office. The line shuffles forward as each man receives his instructions. What unit will they assign me to? Where and when do I report? Whatever I thought I was doing, whatever activity or plans anyone had, everything is cancelled.

When I reach the front of the line, the uniformed administrators inspect my military papers and then look up.

"We appreciate your valiant past service, Corporal Satie. And there is no question we need every able-bodied man. But you are exempt from further service."

"Exempt? Why?"

"The cutoff age is 47, sir."

"Yes, but it's only been a few months. I've served as a reservist every year since leaving active duty. Take me."

"I'm sorry sir. Perhaps you can play a role in our local civilian militia. We'll need vigilant men to guard our homes while we're away."

"Do you realize I walk 6 to 12 miles every day?" I protest. The officer hands me back my papers. They're turning me away.

❧

August 1914, 8th Arrondissement

The prospect of war softens hearts toward family. It's time I set aside whatever resentment I'd harbored and extend the olive branch to mine. From a distance, the man standing between the topiary shrubs and pink geraniums in front of the restaurant Medici's looks hauntingly like my father. Conrad's hairline has receded a little, like mine. His once dark hair is clipped short and streaked with silver at the temples. He's clean shaven but for a moustache, almost entirely white. Since our argument after Father died, we'd seldom even written in eleven years. Conrad actually looks older than I do. But he certainly isn't dressed like Father, in a sage green sack suit of windowpane plaid. He peers up and down the streets, but looks right past me.

"I thought I was looking at Father standing here," I say.

Conrad's mouth drops. "Oh, you've changed so completely, I can't believe it."

We embrace. My chest is full, my eyes water, and all the tension leaves my body.

"I was expecting, I don't know what, a bohemian. You look like a lawyer." He shakes his head. "Obviously you haven't done too badly for yourself."

"I'm not sure looking like a lawyer is a compliment," I say. "Come, let's get a table."

We go inside and shed our hats. A hostess leads us across a royal blue carpet swirling with ocean waves. I sit in the banquette seat with my back against the walnut paneling, and Conrad takes the high back chair across from me.

"I dine here regularly," I tell Conrad. "If I may, there's a savory white bean soup and the veal is excellent."

When an older woman wearing an apron comes to the table, she explains the menu is now limited, so we order the bean soup.

"How is Irene?" I ask.

"She's well, although she complains I'm never home. As you might imagine, since the mobilization, the factory is retooling to aid the war effort. Unfortunately, I can't be more specific, for national security reasons."

"Oh my. Sounds grave. I've joined the local militia," I say. "And how are the boys?"

"Jules is in cours moyen, and Leslie just started at the lycee."

"Already?"

"He's 15."

"I guess he is."

The waiter brings a bottle of wine, opens it, and pours a sample for me to approve, and then fills our glasses.

"To reunions," says Conrad, raising his glass.

"So much has happened, it's hard to even know where to start," I say. "You knew I'd been working with Vincent Hyspa."

Conrad nods.

"As it turned out, several pieces I composed for Paulette Darty became highly successful and rather catapulted me into Music Hall celebrity. I made a royal living for several years."

"That doesn't surprise me, since we always enjoyed those kinds of shows when we were young. Remember that time Father took us to a tour de chant with that gommeuse in a short skirt and exposed neckline."

"Who could forget the little gumdrop in sheer pink ruffles and a song about tasting her cream filled bonbons." I feign a cough and grin.

Conrad slowly shakes his head. "But it's been lucrative for you?"

"Quite, but it never satisfied my yearning to compose serious modern music. So, I enrolled at the Schola Cantorum and finished a certificate."

"Is that right?"

"Yes, and that opened other doors, teaching and such. Until a month ago, I was running the Patronage of Arcueil."

"Imagine that."

"But the irony is; here I'm holding a certificate that's taken me three years to achieve, and suddenly it's my old work that's in demand. The music for which I'd been labeled a crackpot and hack is now being touted as prophetic by these young composers, like Maurice Ravel."

"You've always been ahead of your time."

"The truth is I've been so thrilled that anyone wanted to play my music at all, that a part of me didn't want to examine it critically."

Conrad adjusts his glasses. "I might be entirely wrong. Maybe it's the competitive businessman in me, but I wouldn't blindly trust Ravel and friends. They didn't pull your music out of obscurity for no reason. There's some benefit to them. Let's just hope you profit by it and that it doesn't do more harm than good."

"Actually, Claude told me the very same thing. It's been staring me in the face. Ravel wanted to orchestrate my Sons of the Stars, similar to Claude's orchestration of the Gymnopédies. But this time, it merely boosted my popularity and income."

"I think it's marvelous how things finally came together for you, brother. Father would be thrilled. You have much to be proud of."

The waiter brings our meal. While we enjoy our soup, Conrad talks about developing perfumes. I can't help but notice how the intervening years haven't been kind to him. His eyes have lost their luster. Nice clothes, finely made shirt, gold cufflinks, fine Swiss watch. But he's stodgy and slow. Conrad has been crushed under the weight of a factory and employees and the bottom line; a wife and children, and paying a mortgage. I don't envy any of that. But I'm glad we are together again, even if it took a war to reunite us. I've missed him.

In the ensuing weeks, I join with other members of the Arcueil Militia digging trenches around the city of Paris, sealing off all roads leading into the city with barricades and barbed wire. I take my turn at the gates, where everyone must prove their identity. Men pour into the city in steady droves from the provinces and parade down major thoroughfares now devoid of traffic. Every omnibus is out of service, now painted blue gray, and parked in front of the Ecole Militaire for transport of troops. All motor vehicles, motorcycles, even bicycles have been requested for military use. Ordinary Parisians will have to go on foot. This is of no great consequence for me, since I'm quite used to walking. But there will be no wagons or carriages either, since all horses have been commandeered. The Grand Palais is now a stable for hundreds of them. Beneath the watchful eye of gilded goddesses of the Opera, they cordoned off the entire intersection as a holding area to transport livestock to feed an immense army. These are things I never could have imagined.

With each passing day, more and more signs go up in shop windows. There are liquidations sales as businesses close and their proprietors go off to the front; the tabac, the stationer, the wine shop. The tailor and his son board up the windows and seal the doors. Milk is only available at the town center. But, the most unusual thing is the line of uniformed men and their girlfriends outside the register's office waiting to marry. "Rest assured." I hear one soldier say. "If something happens to me, you'll be taken care of with widow benefits." It all makes my heart leaden.

Chapter 37

September 1914, Paris, 17th Arrondissement

SUITCASES AND A green enamel trunk with brass corners stand in the foyer near the front door. The housekeeper leads me through the salon. They have covered all the furniture and even the piano with cotton sheets. Out in the garden, Claude, Emma and Chouchou sit around a table for luncheon.

"So sorry for my tardiness," I say. "Very few trains are still running."

"We're glad you're here," says Claude.

"Chouchou was afraid you weren't coming. She just had to see her Kiki before we leave Paris," says Emma.

I look at Chouchou with an exaggerated pout. "You're leaving? Who's going to play bows and arrows with me now?"

"I apologize for the poor offering," says Emma. "The bakery is only making simple baguettes, no rolls or cake. I hope you like Vichyssoise."

"And fresh peach clafoutis for dessert." Chouchou gives a silent handclap.

"You needn't apologize. Nothing is finer than a simple meal on a hot day."

"So, tell me," says Claude. "With all the concert venues boarded up, what will you do?"

"Compose. Plenty of time for that, but one wonders what kind of music to create at a time like this."

"It has rather stymied my work. I'm considering something nationalistic, patriotic."

"I've been thinking about love songs. Memories of wives and lovers back home to sustain men in battle and keep the home fires burning."

"The biggest challenge will be to write something that doesn't have the slightest foreign influence. Although, you've always been wise enough to stay clear of that," says Claude.

"What a sad irony, my dear Claude. Loving the German Romantic tradition now gets you labeled an enemy sympathizer. Good-bye Wagner."

"French arts seem to be taking revenge on Germany as much as the French army."

"I never figured you for a Revangist, I say.

"A musical one, anyway. I've always envied your stalwart independence, Erik. Wagner's Hun music hopelessly tainted the rest of us. I doubt we can ever change, deep down."

"Hun music?" I shake my head. "These new, young composers who are fighting as we speak; they'll compose quite differently, a new way that previous generations can't even imagine."

"If they survive," says Emma.

"Yes. How is your son, Emma?

Emma looks at her daughter and picks up the ice bucket. "Chouchou, go inside and have Louise send out some more ice, won't you, darling?"

The nine-year-old scowls. "But I want to listen."

"Do as Maman says. Off you go." Claude watches her stomp away.

Emma blots her forehead and temples. "Raoul wrote that casualties on the French side have been staggering."

"I want to believe what's printed in the newspapers," says Claude, "but it's just not true. The information ministry is downplaying the extent of the slaughter."

I nod. "They think we're blind. On my way over here, I passed La Belle Jardinière department store. They've converted it into a hospital overflowing with the wounded."

"Do you think they'd tell us if the Germans were advancing on Paris?" asks Emma.

Claude huffs. "The government has gone off to Bordeaux. What does that tell you?"

Emma bites her lip.

"You're well aware of how strongly I opposed this war," I say. "But since it's a reality, here on our doorstep, we must band together and defend ourselves and our city."

Chouchou returns with a bucket full of ice, setting it on the table. Claude pulls her to his side, cocooning her with both arms. "I was Chouchou's age when the Prussian War broke out. I recall clearly boarding a train with my mother to Cannes. How much I missed my father. I can't imagine putting her through a similar ordeal."

Gazing beyond the hedge toward the street, I lift my wine glass as if to toast. "Despite the dire conditions, Paris, you're radiant and serene." I take a sip. "There's almost something spiritual, a delicate and supremely tranquil mood over this city. Haven't you seen it, Claude, felt it walking these streets?"

Emma lowers her eyes and begins gathering the emptied dishes.

"I stood in line outside the damn bank yesterday for six hours," Claude says. "The only thing I saw were abandoned desolate streets."

"Actually, many cafés and shops have reopened. Only now, women and elders wait tables and stand behind the counter. There is such resolve to keep our way of life," I say.

"You must be joking. Everyone is hiding or has already fled. We're sitting ducks here. All that's left are women, children and old men."

"Yes, those most in need of protection. It's amazing how people are pulling together. Last week, I passed the Comedia Française. I couldn't believe it. They've turned the theatre into a day nursery. Mothers drop off their children so they can be fed and cared for while their mommies fill in for the men who are on the front lines. Old matrons, grandfathers. Everyone's pitching in."

"Are you pitching in, Kiki?" asks Chouchou.

"Yes, indeed," I reply. "I joined the Arcueil militia as a corporal. We've been building the security barricades around the city and going out on patrol at night to round up looters and saboteurs."

Chouchou grins, but Claude's brows knit with irritation. "You make it sound like you're having a merry old time."

"Merry, no. But there is a kind of comradeship. We must not lose hope."

"You, at least, have military training. I feel utterly useless in that regard."

"Everyone can contribute. I know you despise the man, but the army rejected Ravel, just like they did me. They told him he was too small and underweight; a pitiful little pansy. But my hat is off to him. He's been driving an ambulance, ferrying the wounded from the battlefield."

Claude stiffens. "I can't have my family in harm's way. We're catching a train tonight."

"I gathered. So, you're going to the Cote de Azur?"

"No. Angers."

"Angers? I see." I flash an insincere smile. "Under other circumstances, I might have said something funny about Rabelais, who hails from there; although it seems more fitting to reference Joan of Arc at a time like this. I read about a remarkable medieval tapestry in the Château in Angers. It shows the story of the Apocalypse, battles between hydras and angels. Be sure to write me about it."

Claude glares at me.

With the linen napkin, I blot my mouth and moustache, and then set it beside the dish.

"Thank you most sincerely for a fine meal, Emma. I won't keep you." I scoot my chair back. "No doubt you have last-minute details to see to before your train. Farewell to you, my little Sioux princess." I reach toward Chouchou.

The little girl gives me a peck on the cheek and I kiss her on the forehead. Then I stand, as does Claude. We stare with narrowed eyes and heavy breath.

"You needn't bother to show me out, Claude. I can find my way."

November 1, 1914- Montparnasse

All Saints Day is a solemn occasion when all over France people visit the cemeteries. I'd done so as a boy in Honfleur; though not as a man. Today, I stop at Denfert-Rochereau station in Montparnasse to have a drink at Le Lion. I'll spend the afternoon with yet another young artist friend, Valentine Hugo in her studio on Isle Saint Louis. As I come out of the station and make my way toward the café, a flood of people streams all around me. They are mostly older, dressed in black. Hundreds fill the sidewalks, trudge in the same direction slowly toward the gates of the Montparnasse Cemetery. Flowers fill their arms. Their faces are sullen.

I'm compelled to go with them to pay my respects. Though I don't know any of the fallen, I want to honor their sacrifice. My eyes grow moist and a lump catches in my throat. The vigil inside the burial ground is staggering. Rather than children or grandchildren placing bouquets on the resting place of Grand-mère or Grand-père; it is the reverse. Matrons and grey-haired gentlemen with ashen faces kneel beside mounds of flowers. The only young people are wounded soldiers, arms in slings, limping awkwardly. A soldier, probably younger than 20, has lost a leg below the knee and totters on a crutch. He still finds the where-with-all to carry a wreath of chrysanthemums with a banner that reads "Our brother".

I wander, bearing witness along the arteries of small square blue paving stones lacing between the rows of vaults, tombs and statuary. In every direction they gather, shrouded in black. I refuse to avert my eyes. There's almost no weeping. Voices speak in hushed tones. Some hold small prayer books. The rhythmic cadence of their metered words carries across the cold mist.

I realize the same thing must be happening at Pere Lachaise, at Montmartre, and cemeteries all over France; thousands and thousands, their arms full of flowers, their faces frozen and footsteps slow. Everywhere in black, the mothers, sisters, lovers display pale cheeks, telling of sleepless nights. Their eyes have dark circles from so many spent tears. Each family rises daily to its own Mount Moriah, where the strongest and most valiant have been offered as sacrifice. Daily, hearts thunder at the ring of a doorbell or the delivery of a telegram. Every mother is trying to be loyal, but learns the little boy she once held on her lap lies unburied on a field in Belgium. No house is left untouched.

Chapter 38

March 1916, 17th Arrondissement

"Maurice Ravel is blacklisted?" I shake my head. "Bastards."

One of my young protégés, Roland-Manuel tugs at his light blue uniform. "The National League for the Defense of French Music is outrageous. They've barred him from the first concert season since the war started." He bares his incisors like a growling guard dog. "What gives them the right to tell us what kind of music we can or can't perform– or listen to? Music is supposed to be universal."

I lean back against the café banquette and puff on my cigar. "You just got home on leave and you're already knee deep in the mire," I say. "It's the same as twenty years ago."

"You mean, during the Dreyfus Affair?" he asks, and takes a sip of his beer.

"Exactement. They're at it again, Saint-Saëns and D'Indy. Seems they've joined forces this time. During the Dreyfus debacle, it didn't matter if your music was the greatest on earth. They assigned political meaning to particular styles and forms. If your music didn't possess the features of the anti-Dreyfus camp, you were ostracized, boycotted, and ignored. Now it's anything German."

"So, just like that. Never play Strauss, Mahler or Schoenberg. All banned. And you better not sound like them."

"Not that we shall miss them, particularly. I never much cared for sauerkraut." I swirl the Calvados in my brandy snifter and then take a sip. "But, I'm more worried about the rigid definition of what constitutes "French" in their lexicon of jots and tittles. It'll strangle young composers like you."

He shakes his head. "I'm stunned they got so many to endorse their manifesto."

I huff. "They didn't bother to ask me to sign. It's unfortunate, because with this paper shortage, I could have used it to wipe my ass and then given it a good flush."

Roland-Manuel nearly spits out his mouthful, chokes it down, and then howls. "Obviously they already knew your reaction, Maître. Ravel refused to sign, too. But now he's paying for it."

"Right or wrong, you can't escape politics. You're forced to choose; ham or music."

Roland-Manuel tips his head to one side, bunching his brows. "Ham or music?"

"If these are the people who control the purse strings for the arts, you think about starvation," I say. "Lucky for me, that is something I'm used to. I stand by my principles."

"What can we do? SMI suspended activities since the war started."

I stroke my beard. "We'll find another way; organize a concert of our own, perhaps."

Roland-Manuel straightens. "For blacklisted artists?"

"Why not? I know a few people in Montparnasse who'd be sympathetic to the cause."

"What's the worst thing that can happen if we take a stand against them?" he asks.

"Their hand-puppets, the music critics will try to pound us into the dust."

"I expect so," he says. "And we'll get ourselves labeled kraut-sympathizers."

I reach across the table and flick the medal of valor pinned to Roland-Manuel's uniform. "Yes, a decorated war hero, kraut-sympathizer. We'll just give them the finger."

April 18, 1916, Montparnasse

We might get ourselves arrested or shut down tonight. From the moment we sparked the idea of a blacklisted concert, the momentum grew. Roland-Manuel stirred up a cadre of like-minded young people by correspondence from the front. Meanwhile, I fanned the flames with a collective of Montparnasse artists and poets, calling themselves the Société Lyre et Palette. They hold small recitals and exhibitions in a rundown studio near the Montparnasse Cemetery. The project has mushroomed into a pan-arts counter-offensive, a riposte with the best and newest the avant-garde has to offer.

As I approach the venue, I can see the bright yellow poster pasted to the stone wall from half a block away. It announces the Festival Erik Satie-Maurice Ravel. The young people plastered these advertisements all over Paris on the columns, placards, and newsstands. Except for the Opera reopening in December, few music halls or theaters have re-opened in two years. I hope our publicity will draw out a sizable war-weary and arts-starved audience.

Another protégé, seventeen-year-old Georges Auric greets me at the weathered blue entry doors of the Salle Huyghens. He's taking tickets beside the newest addition to my circle of eager young composers, Francis Poulenc. They cut a futurist profile with clean-shaven faces, slicked back hair and the trendy cuffed trousers, showing off those crazy patterned socks.

From the open beams, the place resembles a onetime barn or stable. The scuffed and paint-spattered wood floor betrays its use as an art school before the war. Now, with a collection of garden benches dragged in for seating, it's a makeshift concert hall and art gallery. There is no stage. But they positioned an old church lectern at one end, beside a passable grand piano. It's even in tune. The Spartan furnishings are irrelevant. What matters most is the defiant "we'll show them" message of this undertaking.

Blue tobacco smoke curls upward toward the stark metal light fixtures. Young ragged artists in sweaters and flat caps stand with uniformed soldiers on leave. They mingle with a contingent of left-leaning upper crust in diamonds and furs. The one striking feature they share in common is the red poppy pinned over the heart, in memory of someone they've lost. I have my own blood-red bloom on my lapel in memory of Roland-Manuel's younger brother, Jean.

There's no concession bar, so the young people huddle together, passing around a shiny hip flask. I ensured my hinges were well oiled before I arrived. I make a beeline for the staging area, where Roland-Manuel talks with poet Blaise Cendrars. My friend and former Apache Ricardo Viñes is warming up at the piano. Cendrars has one sleeve pinned up; having lost his right arm in the Battle for the Somme last Fall. He helped me organize the event and is on the playbill to read his work. Cendrars' rugged face and mashed nose make him look like he stepped out of a boxing ring.

Roland-Manuel sweeps his dark hair back from his forehead and grimaces. "Blaise is worried that some official from the censorship bureau will show up. What do you think, Maître?"

"They might try to shut us down," Cendrars says, a cigarette hanging off his lower lip.

"Or arrest us," I say, peering over my pince-nez. "Poetry should be subversive."

The two young men grin. I survey the previously bare walls, now ablaze with vibrant canvases. A stream of attendees converses with the artists and admires their work. My friend Georges Braque has several of his Cubist paintings on display. Braque was wounded in the head by shrapnel and declared ineligible for further service. So was younger painter Moïse Kisling. They stand with other exhibiting artists, Chilean painter Ortiz de Zarate, and a young pipe-smoking upstart from Barcelona named Pablo Picasso.

One of Moïse Kisling's paintings La Peur, has become a kind of lightning rod. It features two French infantrymen in combat tattered sky-blue uniforms who stare out from a bunker with haunted eyes and gaunt cheeks. Their ready rifles angle from hip to heart. Visitors approach the large canvas, lean sideways to exchange reverent whispers. Then, as if standing before a shrine or monument, some salute; some make the sign of the cross, while others just cover their gaping mouths in solemn reflection.

"Incredible, how moved people are," I say.

"It's hard to fathom what it means to us," Roland-Manuel replies. "Unless you've been there."

"He really captured the intensity," Blaise says.

A hand touches me on the shoulder. "They're here," says Georges.

I straighten, turning to see a portly man in a brown suit and Homburg pushing his way through the crowd. Sheepish and wide-eyed, Georges shrugs.

"I'm sorry, Maître, he flashed a badge. The inspecteur had to be allowed in."

I pat Georges on the shoulder. "Don't fret. We have nothing to hide. Maybe he'll learn something." I watch the official take out a small notepad and pen. He moves along the perimeter with the milling guests, and studies the paintings. Like everyone else, he stops at Kisling's painting La Peur and jots something down.

I direct Georges to return to the entrance as the benches continue to fill. The public response is greater than any of us had expected. I take my seat with my co-conspirators behind the podium. We keep an eye on the censorship monitor standing midway on the left side with his back to Ortiz de Zarate's still life oil paintings.

As master of ceremonies, Roland-Manuel rises, straightens his uniform and approaches the lectern. He welcomes the attendees and introduces Cendrars' opening reading. As Blaise steps center stage, Roland-Manuel and I brace ourselves, with eyes riveted to the censor.

"I'll be reading tonight from my first book of poetry written with my left hand," he says. "This piece is called, The War in Luxemburg." A hush blankets the crowd as the poet fumbles to open his book of verse. Blaise's coarse image is a stark contrast to the smooth and smoky voice with which he reads.

"Left, right, left, right, and all is well, they sang…"

I'm moved by his metered words, describing a game of war played by little boys in Paris' Luxembourg Garden. He contrasts their play with subtle elements of the real war; the smoke of the munitions factory, the soldier with his crutch, candy and bicycles, trenches dug into the sandbox. The audience reacts with a knowing stillness. Faces are somber and eyes reflective. But when Blaise mentions a howitzer shower, asphyxiating gas, and a medal delivered to a grieving mother; the monitor stiffens. He brings his fists to his hips, rocking back and forth on his heels.

"Merde," Roland-Manuel whispers.

"It's alright. That just woke him up," I reply.

There is nothing seditious in the poem; only a young man's reflections on the way his country indoctrinates its young, contrasted with the discordant truth. When he finishes, the audience responds warmly, with scattered comments of agreement as he returns to his seat. The censorship lackey folds his arms, tips his head back and stares down his nose through narrowed eyes.

I feel a prick of conscience, warmth spreading through my chest. The event has risen to something bigger than just a protest against the League for the Defense of French Music. Here are all these young people, wounded and maimed, fighting for their country. It's a country that will not afford them the honor or opportunity to present their work any other way. What we're doing here is terribly important. I won't let some bumbling bureaucrat scare us or interfere.

Roland-Manuel returns to the podium. "Unfortunately, Monsieur Ravel could not be with us this afternoon," he explains. "He is in a Châlons-sur-Marne hospital recovering from dysentery and exposure." Groans and gasps multiply through the crowd. "The supply truck he was driving broke down, stranding him in a remote area for over a week. It forced him to go Robinson Crusoe, as he says. He's going to be fine, and he sends his regards. At this time, please welcome pianist extraordinaire Ricardo Viñes, who is performing on his behalf."

Viñes opens with Maurice's brief Prelude, followed by a piece from his Mirrors suite, Sad Birds. The movement begins like the warble of a meadowlark in the open countryside. Gradually, a looming shadow glides menacingly toward the hamlet. The birdsong tries to raise a clarion of bravery and hope against the coming storm, only to be inundated; plunging and tumbling in a violent struggle. As I listen, I can't help reflecting on the nightmare at the battlefront, Roland-Manuel confided to me. Constant shelling tears craters into the clay, strewn with hundreds of unburied corpses and body parts that cannot be retrieved under the barrage of machine gun fire. The rain, clay, and blood combine into a slurry the color of tea. It fills the craters and overflows into the trenches, at times up to their knees. Roland-Manuel explained the noir humor they used to cope with the horror. The French soldiers and their British allies refer to trench warfare as a Mad Hatter's tea party.

Viñes finishes the Ravel piece with a musical flutter of wings, the sad birds scattering, wheeling, and jetting in every direction. They seek safety for a time in the air, with dismal echoes of the doom far below. Though Maurice had written the piece a decade before, in this present context, the haunting melody is more poignant than ever. The audience shows its approval, on the edge of their seats and eager for more.

The bureau lackey scans the room, shaking his head, mystified. I stroke my beard and look edge-wise at Roland-Manuel with a satisfied nod. With a sly smile, Roland-Manuel twists the end of his baby-fine moustache. Then I notice, for the first time, that the inspecteur has his own red poppy on his breast pocket. Everyone has lost someone.

We reach the intermission and haven't been ordered to cease and desist, so far. I take a deep breath and wander over to the censor to introduce myself.

"Are you enjoying the performance, Monsieur?" I ask.

"I'm not fooled by cloaked language and hidden meanings, Monsieur Satie. You socialist-types are known sympathizers and defeatists. I'm warning you. I could clear this theatre."

"You could, my good constable. And it would be your duty to do so if seditious or treasonable content is presented." I keep my eyes pinned to the red poppy. "But that won't be necessary." I gesture to the flower. "Uncle? Or brother?"

The man draws a halting breath as a wave of anguish flashes across his face. "My son," he says. Then he looks away and sobers himself. "I have to believe it was not in vain."

"As do we all. Listen, mon vieux. We're just trying to find meaning in all of this, make sense of it. There are no enemy sympathizers here."

"I'll be the judge of that, Monsieur." The constable pulls out his handkerchief and blots away the tiny beads of sweat on his face. "All this weird sounding music. The truth is– he would have enjoyed it… my son." His voice breaks and his face wrestles to hold back pain.

I grimace, pat him on the shoulder, and offer my hand. "He probably would have." I make my way back to the staging area and a nervous, waiting protégé.

Roland-Manuel's dark eyes search my face. "Is it over? Is he shutting us down?"

I shake my head. "No. With any luck, I may have won him over."

Relief blooms on Roland-Manuel's face, and I relax.

When it is time to resume, Roland-Manuel opens the second half by reading his own essay about my compositional career and unique contributions to Modernism. He intends to publish it if the presses ever start rolling again. "This afternoon we will have the rare opportunity to hear the newest tour de force performed for the first time in public by our esteemed Maître. Madames et Messieurs, I give you Erik Satie."

The applause borders on riotous as I take my place at the keyboard. There was no scheme when I wrote this suite, Next to Last Thoughts. They don't fit into any compositional mode I tried before. They're just the fully spontaneous promptings of the Muse poured out onto the page as I reflected on the last moments in the lives of far too many young soldiers. With the left hand, I play a four-note ostinato, perpetual motion like the cadence of a train. Against that rhythm, the higher register notes awaken. Pure and simple tones meander through a winter-barren landscape. Questions arise with a touch of melancholy, aching and dissonant. Low on the horizon, the sun splays gold between the branches, melting the crystalline frost. The ostinato shifts to the upper range, now in dance time, a ticking clock, a rattle of artillery. My fingers skip the rigadoon, turning and swinging through the lower octaves. The rhythm is a Provençal folk-dance, overshadowed by marching platoons. The last movement is an ode to the wind; fluttering trills raising gooseflesh. My hands hurtle up and down the keyboard. Flags rustle in the breeze, the treetops tremble as the wind carries off serenity and hope.

I lay down the last chain of chords, a full octave reach in midrange. Then play the next octave lower, and lastly in the bass. My right foot presses against the sustain pedal. As I silently count the beats of the whole note, my entire body is suspended for an instant, as if I'm some great heron, with wings unfurled, about to take flight. My eyes catch on the poetic lines I'd penned between the staves. *He smiles mischievously while his heart weeps like a willow.* Then I released the keys, sink back on the bench, all tension spent.

"Bravo," someone shouts in the audience, followed by a torrent of clapping and cheers. I stand and turn, bowing several times. It's nice to be so close to the audience in this small venue. Like the old days in the cabaret, I can see the zeal and enjoyment on their faces; all except the proctor, who glowers with arms folded.

When the applause dwindles, I call Ricardo Viñes back to the piano for the program finale, The Pear-Shaped Pieces. What irony.

I'd written this composition long ago, to play with Claude. But the young people see Claude as part of the old Garde, out of touch with the modern aesthetic. Yet, here I am, performing music Claude once dismissed; now more popular than ever. Meanwhile, Claude's music is increasingly ignored by the young.

From the first few bars of introduction, I sense an uptick in the room's energy. While I plunk and jingle the prima in the treble cleft, Ricardo plays the seconda in the bass. Our white cuffs peek out from the edges of black coat sleeves side-by-side. Nimble fingers skitter over the keys. In my peripheral vision, silhouettes of shoulders and heads bob to the familiar rhythm. A growing bond resonates between me and the audience. The entire room seems to sway with us, right down to the last note. Then, they shoot to their feet in a riot of appreciation. Ricardo and I abandon the piano and take our bows. Roland-Manuel comes forward, gesturing to me, rousing an even more fervent ovation. I smile, throwing a kiss of gratitude.

Once the swell fades and the patrons mill toward the exits, the censorship official pushes his way through the crowd. I glance at Roland-Manuel, who returns a dubious smirk. What could the man say or do now? It's over. But the suit clad constable scans me up and down and then fixes his scorching glare on me.

"Congratulations, Monsieur Satie, for making a mockery of all we hold dear. At a time like this, when our music and art should rally the spirit behind the war effort, you've managed to burlesque every music tradition that makes us proudly French."

A chorus of protests and profanity flares among those standing nearby. Smiles turn to snarls and grimaces.

The official shoots a look at the young people over his shoulder and hisses like a scolding parent. "And the outrageous revelry. You ought to be ashamed of yourselves."

I speak in a monotone with deadpan expression. "Thank you for coming."

Roland-Manuel runs his hand back through his thick, dark hair. "Let's show the nice constable the way out, shall we, boys?"

Francis and Georges close in on each side, and a surging group of irate young men crowds in for support. The man dons his homburg and throws one shoulder back, as if to repel a hand that has not yet taken hold of him. He snorts and turns, breaking through the huddle, moving toward the door. The hostile faction shuffles after to insure his departure. I take a deep breath and turn to Roland-Manuel.

He smiles. "We did it, Maître."

"Yes, we did." I embrace my protégé. Then he goes off with Georges and Francis to gather up the clutter before heading out to the cafés. Our pan-arts counter-offensive was received as a mobilization call of a different order. What's at stake for them now is the same cultural battle I have been waging for nearly 30 years, the freedom of expression. As artists, they have everything to lose. Along with my own artistic veracity, I want the same creative license for them, even if we risk arrest. These young people have strong opinions and divergent aesthetic tastes. Someone has to defend their rights.

Chapter 39

April 1916, Montparnasse

WHEN I ARRIVE at Le Dome Café, I spy Misia, threading her way through a flood of café goers. Her high-waisted gown in fuchsia silk stands out, as she usually does. With all the work that had gone into this event, I suddenly feel my energy flag. I just want to go have a drink and relax. Why is she bringing that irritating young man with her? Cocteau. His name alone conjures up images of some loathsome sounding bird, cockatoo, cockatiel, or vainglorious rooster. Then there is his bill-like nose and billowy crest of hair.

I reach out to take Misia's hand. "Are you pleased with how it turned out, Madame?"

Misia smiles, tipping her platter-shaped hat at an angle. "You were such a dear to bring this to the public. You must be so proud."

"It was my pleasure."

Misia flicks her wrist. "You remember Jean Cocteau, don't you, Monsieur Satie?"

"We met last autumn at Valentine's soirée." Jean's voice sounds like he's been sucking on a helium balloon.

I cringe. "How could I forget?"

"I hope you've had a chance to read my poetry collection," Jean says, weaving his head from side to side, oscillating his eyebrows with a goofy smile. "The Frivolous Prince? Hmm?"

What is the matter with this idiot? I want to slap him senseless.

"It's quite the talk of Paris." Misia says, brushing her hand over Jean's shoulder.

I twist the end of my moustache. "Is it?" God, could they just shut up and let me have a drink and a cigar?

Misia leans in. "You know, Monsieur Cocteau has already collaborated with Diaghilev on a project for Ballets Russes. The Blue God." She smiles and winks.

I nod. "Ah, yes. Krishna, the Hindu deity."

Jean rolls his eyes. "It's so unfortunate Reynaldo Hahn composed the score."

"Unfortunate, oui," I say.

Jean latches onto my arm with talon-like fingers, giving a little shake as he speaks. "My perfectly brilliant libretto, Bakst's glorious costumes, and Nijinsky's marvelous choreography, were all ruined by Hahn's dull hideous music."

"Pity." I recoil from Jean's grasp. At least we agree on one thing. Hahn's lack of imagination contributed to the ballet's failure.

"Diaghilev telephoned," she says "He's returning this summer; the perfect opportunity."

I know this already. But as a self-appointed social engineer, if Misia can't take credit in some way, she'll be insulted.

Jean glances at Misia and then at me. "Mr. Diaghilev has promised me another chance at a ballet, but it has to be a spectacle, another Scheherazade. 'Amaze me,' he said."

"I see," I reply.

"I've proposed several ideas," says Jean. "A project about the biblical David, set in a circus arena."

"That's different."

"I pitched it to Stravinsky. I thought I might help him make a comeback. You know, after The Rite of Spring."

"You help Stra…" I stop myself. I lick my lips to keep from laughing. "How noble." I force a tame smile.

"Unfortunately, he was busy with another project. Another time, perhaps."

"What luck," I say. Spoiled rich kid. Thought he'd bless the avant-garde with his presence, did he? Self-styled genius. Insufferable.

"But this is the first time I've actually heard any of your music, Monsieur Satie." Jean strokes my arm up and down. "I was just so thrilled by your Pear-Shaped Pieces. I knew right away it was just the ticket."

I stiffen. "The ticket?"

Jean flaps his hands as if he is about to take flight. "To amaze Diaghilev."

The weird pixie voice, the gyrations, it's all too much. And if Cocteau touches me one more time, I'll deck him.

Misia pats me on the wrist. "Serge was so impressed when I played The Pear-Shaped Pieces in my music room. Imagine what could happen if you and Cocteau put your heads together."

Jean folds his arms and puts one hand to his jaw, whispering. "It could be positively explosive."

"Explosive. Yes, quite." I can think of some interesting places to lodge a stick of dynamite right about now. And Misia, she is trying to Shanghai me into working with this wonder boy. I'd rather leap from the Pont au Change.

❧

Loathe may not be a strong enough word. Ordinarily I love young people, and I'm not one to dismiss the creative ideas of any artist, out of hand. This is the first time one so difficult to like has approached me. Surely Cocteau senses it. Otherwise, why would he ask my young artist friend Valentine to be his go-between? She's the only reason I've agreed to meet with him. I'll have a drink, make polite prattle, and be done with it.

Jean has a reputation for flops and non-starters. Although, I've had my share of those. I know all too well the desperation of knocking on doors to find work. Nevertheless, I'm quite certain a spoiled rich kid like Cocteau has never scrounged for a meal a day in his brief life. I don't dislike him on account of his wealth. Roland-Manuel, Georges, and Francis all come from well-to-do families. Cocteau's affectations irk me. Forced and pathetic. But most of all, I simply have no stomach for conceit. Such a know-it-all. And that piccolo voice.

I sit on the terrace of La Rotunde, finishing an apéritif, and smoking a stubby cigar, when Jean approaches from the train station. If I didn't know better, I might take Jean for a military officer in his finely tailored uniform. But I do know better. The Count Etienne de Beaumont privately funded an ambulance corps. Couture designer Paul Poiret crafted the uniforms for the volunteer drivers. Had the flashy attire enticed the Frivolous Prince to volunteer? Today, he slicked his wild hair back with pomade. Jean has the good manners to offer his hand and I invite him to sit down. We exchange pleasantries and order drinks.

"You need to understand something," I begin. "In order for me to enter a project with someone, our aesthetic has to be similar or at least compatible. What are you trying to accomplish in your work, Monsieur Cocteau?"

Jean takes a fountain pen from his breast pocket and rolls the polished onyx barrel between his fingers. "To my way of thinking, the aristocratic right and the artistic left are at odds. They've been distrustful and ignorant of one another for a very long time."

I raise a brow. "I like your frankness. At least we agree on a point of departure."

Jean removes the cap of his pen and starts sketching little stars on the cardboard coaster. "My aim is to bring the two sides together, to convert the social elite; move beyond the limits of traditional institutions, like the opera, etcetera, and create a middle ground for the Modern in French culture."

I sit back in my chair and stroke my beard. I've been a foot soldier in this culture battle my entire career. Who is this pipsqueak to think he can shake the monolith? Then again, I once launched my own assault on the Opera, Patrice and I. "Just how do you propose to do that?"

"In order for anything modern to be accepted with the war going on, it has to be seen as patriotic and very French. My notion is to choose something so ordinary and fundamental, it's like bread, melded with High Art."

Jean's words scintillate through me like static electricity. This kid actually has a brain. "Are you aware I started developing that aesthetic years ago?"

"Not until Valentine, Roland-Manuel and others gave me a quick history lesson. Now that I finally heard your music– well, that's why I've come. Your music is not stunted by limiting traditionalism. There's no foreign influence. It's pure French culture at its most essential."

Is he just patronizing me? "There's a petrified faction that would disagree with you."

"They don't matter. Anyone under 30 can see the truth. We're the future."

I know the young people like me and admire my work. Perhaps my decades of struggle to bring about a change in music is finally having an impact. But how wise is it to cast lots with this oddball poet? Ballets Russes is my big chance. I don't want to lose it.

Jean continues. "I'm aware you don't want to discuss adapting any of your older material. But what I appreciate most about The Pear-shaped Pieces, Monsieur Satie, is the way you blended together the music of the work-a-day Parisian, the Café Society, nursery tunes, folksongs, with High Art. That is the very aesthetic I'm going for. At the intersection of elitist taste and base vulgarity we find –Surprise."

"Surprise, indeed."

He leans forward. "What would you think about creating a Cubist Ballet?"

"Cubism? I associate that term with the visual arts. But simultaneity; appreciating a thing from multiple perspectives at once. That's an intriguing idea." It's hard to take his peculiar pixie voice seriously. But I'm impressed. The ideas are cogent. I underestimated Cocteau.

"The circus has always enamored me," Jean says. "I loved Commedia del Arte, especially Harlequin. These classic forms are a perfect subject."

"Who doesn't love the circus? It cuts across class barriers, from the wealthy aristocrats who rent loges to lower class laborers in the gallery. And the symbolism is so rich."

"I'm eager to get started. Unfortunately, I have to return to the front in a few days."

"So, spend a little time jotting down some of your ideas. When you have a sketch worked out, send it to me. I can work up some music. Here's my address." A surge of panic makes me hesitate for just a moment. I'm about to compromise my privacy. Jean hands me the fountain pen he's been doodling with, and I write my address on the back of the cardboard coaster. This better not be a Pandora's Box.

Two weeks pass after his departure. My concierge brings me a fat envelope from Cocteau, filled with pages of notes. I've been reflecting a lot about "the man of ideas". He is just so full of himself at 27, trying to challenge the arts world. Cocteau has his affectations and wild hair. But I projected my own weird persona once, wandering the streets of Paris. If I came face to face with my younger self today, I'd probably consider him just as irritating as Cocteau. Maybe that's why he bothers me so much. He reminds me of an embarrassing chapter in my previous life. Cocteau might actually have the potential to become the next leader of Modernism, if someone doesn't strangle him first.

❧

There's another obstacle I've overlooked. Misia. I squeeze my eyes tight and release a groan. My meeting with Diaghilev is just around the corner. Why can't we just sit down like gentlemen and forge an agreement? It's hard enough without adding another layer of vacuous snobbery? But she'll consider it an insult if we move forward on a production without her, especially since she introduced us. There is no going around her. She has Diaghilev's ear. She's like the Red Queen. Off with his head! The looming turmoil roils like rancid bacon grease in my gut. It reminds me of the awful time with Péladan, La Rochefoucauld, and the Rose+Croix Salon. Lawsuits, and shouting matches. However, money matters. I hate this sort of knuckle-kissing, but this seems to be the only way. I must massage the vanity of rich people.

Misia's housemaid takes my hat and umbrella, and leads me into the music room. I sit on one of the oval-back Louis XIV chairs as she goes to announce my arrival. Tea and pastry have been set out on fine china. The doubled doors burst open and Misia flutters into the salon wearing a three-tiered chiffon frock resembling melted orange and lime sherbet. I stand up. Her ivory face powder, unnaturally pink rouge, and plucked crescent brows remind me of a child's porcelain clown doll. Ah yes, high fashion. I grin at her for all the wrong reasons.

"Your proposal to create a ballet, Erik, has quite encouraged me." She scrutinizes me with the acuity of a predator.

"That's gratifying to hear." I say and study a flaky pastry with thin sliced apple on the tea tray. I have had nothing this delectable since the start of the war.

"Oh, do help yourself," she says waving toward the confection, with condescension in the angle of her brow.

I slide the apple pastry onto a plate with the silver tongs and then take a bite.

She sips from a gold rimmed teacup and then sets it aside. "I've taken the liberty of reviewing half a dozen pieces of your music. I recall discussing The Pear-Shaped Pieces."

I stop mid-bite. She isn't just going to make recommendations; she wants to take over. Merde! "Pardon, Madame. I've only started to compose something new."

Misia wags her fork. "Au contraire. I think we should capitalize on the popularity of The Pear-Shaped Pieces and expand, orchestrate them for the ballet.

My collar suddenly feels too tight as the veins in my neck pulsate. "I'm flattered you think so highly of the collection. But truly, I want something fresh and new."

"Don't be silly. Why walk away from a guaranteed success? And frankly, Diaghilev is not the least bit interested in your recent work."

What? The hair behind my ears prickles. I have to tread carefully here. Is she bluffing? Or has she talked to Diaghilev and changed his mind? "What makes you say that?"

Misia blinks hard. "See here, you said you wanted my advice, so I'm offering it."

I'm trapped. What can I say? I take a breath. "You haven't given me a chance to develop the work. I'm sure it will please you." When did I ever need someone else's approval for what I compose? Ridiculous.

Misia draws an incensed breath. "I'm firm in this decision. I insist on The Pear-Shaped Pieces."

"Or what?" As soon as I say it, I regret my strident tone.

"It might incline me to withdraw support for the project."

I set down my cup and saucer a little harder than intended. "You've already decided on the scenario, selected the music. Are you planning to dance the prima ballerina role, too?"

"How dare you?" Her eyes blaze and her lips tighten to a slash. She juts out her chin. "You forget your place."

"No, Madame. You forget your origins. I think it's time I leave."

"Fine, do that. See if you get a single commission in this city." Misia rings a little bell on the tea tray. "Babette, get Monsieur Satie's hat, will you? He's leaving."

Meddling socialite. What a tyrant. I've already established myself in the same echelon as the loftiest artistic domains in Paris: Matisse, Picasso, Gazette de Bon Temps, Gallerie Thomas. Neither Debussy nor Ravel has been invited into that rarefied air. I don't need her money or her endorsement. Screw that. Surely there has to be other less meddlesome patrons out there. No wonder people call her the abortionist. She's trying to kill my fledgling project before it's even started. But I won't be bullied. One way or another, I'll get a ballet produced. The only question is; will Diaghilev go back on his word? Does she have that much power? Have I just cut my own throat?

ꟹ

If for no other reason than to piss Misia off, I'm hunting down Cocteau. The train to Yvelines pulls away from the platform at the Gare Saint Lazare, heading northwest. This journey is the farthest I've ventured away from Paris since my military service 30 years ago. I woke up angry, depressed, and ruminating. But several shots of brandy before boarding the train are now comfortably smoothing over the sharp corners of my mind. We're going to turn his crazy pot-pourri of ideas into a radical masterpiece.

I stare out the window, flying past apartments packed side-by-side along broad tree-lined boulevards. Gradually the urban muddle falls away, opening to rambling hills dotted with cottages, barns, and churches. Unpaved lanes intersect green fields stretching toward the vanishing point. I listen to the gentle rhythm of the wheels clacking against the rails, the rocking motion in my body.

Cocteau is waiting for me on the platform. The young poet stands up from the bench and closes the book he's been reading. Gone is the uniform. He left the ambulance corps to be closer to Paris so we can work together. I gather my hat and umbrella and merge with the handful of travelers disembarking from the passenger car. Jean leads me to a white four-seater Barré with black fenders and with the tan canvas top down. I hold on to my hat as we speed away.

"My mother is looking forward to meeting you," Cocteau says, on the ride to the family estate on the outskirts of a little village, Maisons-Laffitte. "She saw you perform a long time ago at some charity event."

"Is that right?"

"She claims you're famous for your popular songs. I assured her you are a composer of fine music and she must be thinking of someone else."

"No, she is correct. There was a time, earlier in my career, when I played in the cabaret and Music Hall to keep from going hungry. I even composed a little Ragtime."

"I didn't know that about you. That makes you even more uniquely expert in the blend of the everyday with high art."

A tall brick wall with a decorative grill surrounds the Cocteau estate. Blue slate gables and a charming cylindrical turret with fish scale tiles peek above the high hedge. Cocteau turns onto a central driveway bordered by a manicured lawn and dark foliage plum trees. The white plaster façade bears half-timbers, and louvered shutters welcome the eye.

After introductions and a cool beverage, Jean and I roam the grounds. My mood brightens under the shade of the purple leaves of ornamental plum trees. We wander beside flowerbeds full of snapdragons, delphinium, and hollyhocks.

"It's going to take something altogether stunning to persuade Diaghilev, now that we've been, shall we say, discredited by Madame Edwards," I say.

"Oh, I wouldn't worry about her," Cocteau says. "Maman will bring her influence to bear; call in a few favors. She'll put things back in order." Cocteau plucks off the blossom head of a yellow snapdragon, pinches the sides to make the dragon head open, and uses his helium voice to roar.

Silly kid. My smile returns.

The levity fades from Cocteau's face. "Removing a hindrance is one thing. But if we can persuade another rising luminary to join the project, I figure we'd have an even better chance."

"Who'd you have in mind?"

"A little pretentious on my part, but I commissioned a portrait of myself from Picasso to get in front of him."

"Picasso? That's inventive."

"As I was sitting there, I just started telling him my ideas. He was dubious about a Cubist ballet. But, I think I made an impression," says Cocteau.

What kind of impression? "We know one another."

"I was hoping you did."

"Not well, but I can certainly talk with him. And I agree, having the set and costumes designed by Picasso would definitely strengthen our position."

"How could Diaghilev say no to that?"

Chapter 40

August 1916, Montrouge

THE FIRST TIME we met was probably around 1900. On a cool autumn evening I was sipping a beer at the Nouvelle Athènes, when a young man with intense dark eyes and hair like a crow's wing sauntered over.

"Are you Erik Satie?"

"That depends on who's asking." I studied him a moment, deciding by his shabby corduroys, he was neither a detective looking for anarchist sympathizers nor a debt collector. In the endless stream of aspiring artists coming and going from Montmartre, he was just one more.

"I bring greetings from friends at Els Quatre Gats in Barcelona," he said.

I straightened. "Els Quatre Gats? You know Santiago Rusiñol and Ramon Casas?"

"Yes, and they've told me a lot about you. I'm Pablo." That was 16 years ago.

Cocteau gave me an address on Rue Victor Hugo in Montrouge. I make a short trek by foot from my apartment in Arcueil. Picasso's studio is in a barn beneath a neglected 18th century country manor, now hemmed in by new urban expansion. I close my umbrella, the portable shadow in the August swelter. I cross the fenced courtyard shaded by broadleaf trees. Picasso stands shirtless with his back to the open double doors. With a fist full of brushes, he studies a huge canvas alive with swatches of phthalo green, cobalt, and black.

"I didn't realize we were neighbors," I say. "Been here long?"

Picasso turns and grins, greeting me with his gravelly voice. "Satie? How great to see you!" He feeds the brushes into a wide-mouth jar reeking with muddied turpentine. After wiping his hands on a paint-stained rag, he ushers me toward a pair of tattered cane chairs and a small table. I take off my bowler and set it on the tabletop with the folded newspaper I brought under one arm.

"I moved here a few months ago." Picasso grabs a wrinkled white shirt off the back of a chair and puts it on. "After losing Eva, the country was appealing and quiet, the way Montmartre used to be." He fastens the buttons, and tucks the tail into his tan linen trousers.

"I heard about her passing. So sorry, my friend," I say.

The painter offers me a cigarette and plugs one into his mouth. Striking a match, Picasso lights both and sits. With eyes unfocused, he surveys some inner still life or portrait. Then he seems to shake off the reverie.

"Ever since I got your note, I've been thinking about this ballet thing." He holds his cigarette like a paintbrush and takes a long drag. "I must confess, I'm not sure what to make of Cocteau." He relays with amusement how Cocteau arrived to sit for his portrait in a Harlequin costume. He'd effervesced about being the bridge between the upper classes and bohemia. Then he talked about making art out of everyday things. "It's hard to see myself working with such a flamboyant peacock."

I blow out a stream of smoke. "He makes everyone uncomfortable, at first."

"Well, his agenda tries to preserve a place of distinction for an aristocracy that no longer has a function in the world. I could never support that." He takes another puff of his cigarette and crosses his arms. "But when he mentioned you were involved, I couldn't imagine you selling out; not after the Lyre and Palette concert. So, what are you up to?"

"We have an opportunity here to create something very bold," I say. "You know I'm a great lover of art and pay special attention to visual images and the messages they convey." I slide the newspaper across the table. "Take a look at this."

Picasso glances at the photographs. "Casualties of war."

"Yes, but have you ever noticed, they only show the enemy dead, and even then, at a distance? There are few faces. More importantly, what do you never see?"

Picasso's eyes review a mental gallery and then meet my stare. "They never show French fatalities."

"If they're presented at all, it's as a wreath or a plaque. That's intentional, a careful manipulation, making enemy death real and French losses heroic."

Picasso strokes his chin. "A photographer friend of mine works for Le Mirror. He's taken plenty of photographs of the carnage; women, children. But you'll never see them. Once they're turned over to the Maison de la Presse, they disappear."

I nod. "Zola once said newspapers come in two sorts: those that print outright lies and those that print the truth on unimportant matters. That way, they can slip in a distortion, so you believe them."

"They're shaping people's impressions without them knowing it," says Pablo.

"Wartime truth doesn't permit another perspective, dialogue, or dissent."

"So, what does this have to do with Cocteau's ballet?" He takes a puff on his cigarette.

"We could use Cocteau's scenario as our point of departure, but move beyond the shallow message?" I say. "Let's create something about propaganda and deception."

A spark of a passion reignites in Picasso's dark eyes. "Somehow depict what they're showing us is an illusion." He throws himself against the chair back, running his hand through his hair. "They are getting us to believe a sleight of hand, like a carnival sideshow."

"Exactly," I say. "The carnival sideshow versus the real events behind the scene. This could be powerful."

"What would we tell Cocteau? This is over his head."

I lean toward him on his forearm. "Look, he might be a bourgeois pansy with delusions of grandeur, but he's not stupid. He gets it. We could work together, n'est-ce pas?"

"It would be a different venture for me. I've never designed a set or costumes."

"But you'd have complete freedom and license to do whatever you want."

The painter toggles his head from side to side.

I adjust my pince-nez. "What do you say?"

Picasso gives a gradual nod with a one-sided smile. "I'm in, if you are."

We agree to meet at Picasso's studio each week to share our progress. First, we review his latest watercolor and gouache illustrations. Then we head over to the Montrouge City Hall where I try out my musical creations on a beat-up piano in the basement. Finally, we wind up in some Montparnasse café, drink, and spark new ideas spurred on by each other's work. Picasso's boundless energy and a fiery intensity electrify me. By the middle of September, I finish the piano reduction of two major portions of the score. According to Cocteau, the reign of Misia is at an end, at least for now. She left for Spain and Italy, after the dressing-down she received by Madame Cocteau. We now hold in our hands a creation that will genuinely "amaze" Diaghilev. The decisive chance is upon us.

~

October 7, 1916, 17th Arrondissement

A new patron could loosen the monetary vice grip Misia holds on Diaghilev's balls. Picasso painted several portraits for a wealthy Chilean woman, Madame Eugenia Errazuriz. She graciously offered her townhouse for our Ballets Russes summit. Now, if only she will become enthusiastic enough about our project to offer sponsorship.

On the rear seat of Cocteau's motorcar, Picasso clutches his portfolio. He's wearing a black fedora and pinstripe suit. I climb in beside him, clad in my usual black three-piece. When Madame Errazuriz personally greets us at the entrance, I almost mistake her for a servant. But Picasso introduces us. Her dress looks like blue and white mattress ticking. A pair of gardening gloves and a hand spade peek out of her large pockets. She lays them on a green metal garden table and shows us into the downstairs entry hall. Diaghilev hasn't arrived yet. The foyer has a simple rustic feel, painted entirely in soft green. With minimal furnishings the space is arranged to lead the eye upward, in cool tranquility.

To meet this moment, I'm completely sober, but there's a slight tremor in my hand. My belly flutters. We've put so much into this venture already. This is the largest and most important project I've ever undertaken. Will Parade go forward or die a premature death.

Madame Errazuriz's salon hosts glass and ceramic urns and vases in the same soft green, filled with garden cuttings. Neutral colored walls are a proper backdrop for a stunning private collection of Fauvist and Cubist paintings. Cocteau crosses his legs and fusses with his cufflinks. Picasso's pensive eyes recheck the contents of his portfolio.

"I think I'll just warm-up, Madame; if you don't mind," I say, standing.

"But of course." She escorts me to the piano and opens the cover.

I scoot onto the piano bench and spread out the score. I rehearse a couple of segments requiring tricky finger work. After only a few repetitions, the door chimes ring. I look at Cocteau, who returns a sheepish smile. Picasso's shoulders visibly heave with a breath as he gives me a nod.

Sporting a cane, barrel-chested Diaghilev lumbers into the salon behind Madame Errazuriz. The ruby silk tie and handkerchief peeking out of his breast pocket are an elegant touch to his dowdy suit. He's in the company of a young Pinocchio of a man, with a pencil drawn smile, eyes like steely marbles, and lamb ears. Diaghilev introduces him as the new choreographer for Ballets Russes, Léonide Massine.

We gather around the dining table. Madame Errazuriz has hors d'oeuvres, chilled vodka, and apéritifs brought out. She sits over to the side, leaning on the armrest, observing with discerning narrowed eyes.

"Ballets Russes will only stage one production this year." Diaghilev says. "Before we can agree to such a costly and grueling undertaking; our patrons and I have to be assured of a dazzling success."

What starts like a casual game of cards over drinks quickly becomes as solemn and calculated as high stakes poker. Cocteau begins by moving both hands like he was wiping windows. "The marriage between musician and artist, poetry and dance, a vanguard of talent, has been brought together."

I clench my jaw. This is no time for Cocteau's inane drama. He'll ruin everything. I kick Cocteau under the table, adding a disapproving glare. Cocteau flinches, his eyes widening.

Diaghilev takes a deep breath and then speaks with overly deliberate diction. "The libretto, Jean. Focus, now. Tell me about the libretto." Jean brings his hands together in prayer style. I have never seen Cocteau and Diaghilev together, but the producer seems quite familiar with Cocteau's histrionics; perhaps even patient. Massine sits silent with his head tilted toward Diaghilev. His unbelieving eyes shift like a tennis match. Madame Errazuriz wears an amused half-smile.

"Well, alright." Cocteau folds his hands. "A traveling carnival with three side show performers and their managers try to entice the crowd to buy a ticket to the show. Each performer gives a tempting demonstration, but can't seem to persuade the audience. There."

Diaghilev raises a brow. "And?"

Cocteau squirms. "It's about the perception of the misunderstood artists and poets. They never quite get the response they deserve."

Diaghilev rubs his forehead, puckering his mouth like a sour taste. "That's all? No love triangle, betrayals, no heroes?" He turns his palms up, cocking his head to one side.

I interrupt. "If I may say, Parade is far more complex. It's not a traditional linear plot, by any means. But you said you wanted something different, something amazing."

Picasso leans in. "The entire work is as multi-faceted as a Cubist painting; very much in keeping with the concept of simultaneity."

Diaghilev raises a brow.

I continue. "The theme deals with appearance versus reality. How the control of information is used to manipulate people. Propaganda."

At the mention of that word, Diaghilev's eyes light up. Massine straightens like a marionette whose strings are pulled taut. Diaghilev strokes his chin. "An interesting choice of words, Satie. What an àpropos subject at a time like this. Tell me more."

We talk briefly about propaganda wars for the minds of ordinary people. Germany is using propaganda to undermine the war alliance between Russia, France and England. The Bolshevik party alleges the Czar launched the war against the people's best interest. To counter this, Britain and France are spreading their own propaganda.

"Here, let me show you a few of the costume designs." Picasso opens his portfolio and carefully pulls out one of his illustrations. Diaghilev and Massine gawk at an ink and watercolor drawing; patchy images of towering skyscrapers, traffic signals, a top hat and tails, a huge trumpet, and a marquee, combined with colorful geometrical shapes.

"This is a dance costume?" asks Massine.

"Yes, the propaganda machine." Picasso lays down a second

illustration, a frenzy of bright fragments, a clay pipe, walking stick, moustache, tree crowns and the Paris roofline.

Massine and Diaghilev jabber with excitement to each other in Russian.

"The music," asks Diaghilev. "How does the music sound?"

"What Picasso has done with design, I've done with the score, combining classic and popular sounds. Let me play the dance of the Chinese Conjuror for you."

Picasso slides the costume and make-up illustrations in front of the two Russians as I move to the piano.

"I'd like to get a feel for the movement and rhythm," says Massine, rising from his chair and removing his jacket. In the open area between the table and the piano, he takes first position.

I play the passage with ascending quarter notes. Then the music plunges into a minor key, like a Chinese orchestra, taunting, "come inside, come inside". The music weaves together a complex montage of oriental mystery. The piece was written to summon the essence of Chung Ling Soo, a well-known magician at the Alhambra. Through a veil of smoke, billowing from the mouths of two enormous jade dragons, Chung Ling Soo appears on stage in a red silk embroidered coat. He tosses metal rings through the air and curiously links them into a chain. Then, just as inexplicably, they separate again. For his final fete, he makes real flames roar from his mouth. Then he bows fading into the mist.

I turn from the keyboard to face them. "Voilà." I'm met with stunned gazes and gaping mouths. Picasso flashes a knowing smile.

Massine responds first. "The rhythm lends itself nicely to choreography and I really like the variety and quick changes in the melody."

"What a monumental shift away from the folklore spectacles of Firebird or Scheherazade." Diaghilev is becoming positively giddy.

Cocteau flicks his wrist. "Tsk! Because no one has ever done anything like this before."

"What do you think, Madame?" Picasso asks.

"It's about the farthest thing from Swan Lake I've ever seen. I'm thrilled at the very idea of a Cubist ballet. Monsieur Diaghilev, I have all the assurance I need to sponsor this project, and there are others who will agree."

Nodding his head, Diaghilev meets each person's gaze. "It will be an enormous risk, probably the biggest leap I've ever taken. Everyone's neck is on the block. But I think you've finally got something here, Cocteau. We'll have to work like serfs to make a spring opening. Gentlemen, let's make a ballet."

Chapter 41

December 1916, Paris, 17th Arrondissement

A VISITING NURSE in white pinafore lifts a slender yellow vial, inserts a hypodermic needle, and draws the medicine into a metal encased glass syringe. She turns to Claude and smiles. "Where do you want it today, Monsieur Debussy, shoulder or derriere?"

Claude grumbles. "It already hurts to sit. Shoulder, I guess." He lets out a halting breath as he unbuttons his collar, peels off one side of his shirt, and reveals a pale deltoid.

I avert my eyes as the injection is given, but catch a whiff of rubbing alcohol used to swab him.

"There, that should keep you comfortable for the rest of the day," she says.

Claude rearranges his clothing as the nurse gathers her things into a canvas bag, dons a short dark wool cape, and leaves the Debussy library. Claude had surgery, supposedly to cure the colon cancer that is eating away at his insides. But afterward, Claude and Emma avoided discussing the outcome. I never probed. But I've noticed his once lusty plump constitution is wasting away to a sallow sketch of himself. He's receiving daily injections of morphine. The family left Paris in August, and stayed at a coastal resort in the Bordeaux region for the past four months. Having just returned to Paris, Claude invited me for a game of backgammon.

"I find myself in a moment of enormous good fortune," I say, as I line up my blue stones on the harlequin-patterned board.

"Glad to hear it," Claude says, arranging his ivory stones in mirror fashion. "I found a stellar idea for the finale of my violin sonata while walking on the shore at Le Moulleau. Such lovely white dunes."

"Diaghilev has offered me a contract to score a ballet; the only one Ballets Russes will stage this year. We're calling it Parade."

Claude's brow knots. "The Precursor finally makes the big time."

The Precursor? Does Claude still hold on to those old resentments? I shake my dice cup and roll a three and a four. I study the board a moment and then move two pieces onto open points along the U-shaped trajectory toward the home quadrant.

"The piano concert series at the Grand Hotel was second rate," Claude says. "Provincial mediocrity at its best."

Claude drops his dice into the ivory cup, rattles it around several times before inverting it onto the inlaid board. He wins the toss and moves his pieces into place.

"Parade will be the first ever Cubist ballet. Picasso is designing the set and costumes."

Claude shakes his head. "That's hard to imagine."

On my turn, I move two stones to take over a new point. "This ballet will be so far ahead of its time; the critics' heads will explode."

Next, Claude throws double fives. He chuckles and shifts two stones around ten spaces to his own new point. "I'll be happy to help you with the orchestration." Debussy says.

I blink several times. Why would I need help? And even if I did, I'd consult Albert Roussel, or even Paul Dukas, before Claude. His music is so far from Parade, he may as well be Saint-Saëns. No, maybe that's too insulting. But after all this time, why doesn't Claude believe I'm up to the task? "I appreciate your offer. I'll let you know if I need your help."

Claude jostles his dice, while his eyes scrutinize the placement of the pieces. This time he rolls a six and a one, allowing him to lay claim to the seven point. Play progresses at a faster pace now, with the lull in the conversation. The friendly competition seems to descend into veiled hostility. Claude purses his lips like he sucked on a lemon.

He has always been better than me at backgammon. So, I'll focus on leaving no pieces vulnerable. I throw my own six and two. Studying the lay of things carefully, I realize I'm in a position to set up a nice Prime. Claude captures another new point, but then hesitates. He mutters something under his breath and changes the configuration, building a blockade.

On my next throw, I move to protect, and take over another point. "There's other good news, too. Princess de Polignac has commissioned me for a new work."

He looks at me with a pinched expression. "You're kidding." Again, Claude moves to take over a new point.

"No. It's entirely serious. She wants me to develop a work from Classical Greece. I've never found myself with such an embarrassment of riches."

He seems to recoil. A veil descends over his eyes. "It was such a peaceful lagoon, with all the migratory birds. And the oysters and lampreys were outstanding. I was finally able to draft the libretto for the Fall of the House of Usher."

A shudder sweeps over me. "You're still working on that dark thing?" He's been chipping away at it for ten years.

With my next move, I see the opportunity to hit one of Claude's pieces, placing it on the bar. Claude's next throw doesn't get him off the bar either, and I continue prime building.

"This damned morphine makes me lose touch with things around me. I wouldn't be surprised if I saw the sister of Roderick Usher walk through the room," says Claude.

I hold my tongue. But I want to ask Claude if there is a place for Poe's grisly tale during wartime. Perhaps a crumbling empire and a wasting disease make Claude identify with Roderick Usher and being buried alive. My poor friend. I begin bearing off my accumulated playing pieces. Claude still has two stones barricaded in starting position. With each turn of the dice, I continue to take my blue stones from the home quadrant until finally, I win.

❧

March 1917, Paris, 1st Arrondissement

I stormed out of the theatre yesterday in an outrage. The Ballets Russes returned from a tour of Rome and rehearsals for Parade are underway. I should have gone with them to Rome. Maybe the bitter tonic would have been easier to swallow in small doses. But they handed me back the piano reduction covered in red ink, noting all the changes they want. While they were away, I worked diligently on the orchestration. Now, they expect me to change both to suit their ideas. My stomach is in a knot and my eardrums are pounding. The only thing holding up the show now is me.

Cocteau must have alerted Valentine by telephone, because a blue pneumatic from her greeted me this morning. Sullen and fuming, I make the trip back into Paris. Now, I stare out through the tall casement windows of her apartment on Isle St. Louis. She is the grand-daughter of Victor Hugo, and a surrealist painter in her own right.

"I haven't been able to sleep. I can't stop thinking about it," I say.

"You've really taken it to heart. Come, sit down, have a bite to eat. You'll feel better."

"What a dear girl, to go to all this trouble. I'm not sure I can touch a thing."

"Do try." She uncorks a bottle of Chardonnay.

"I'm just so angry."

"I know. Something's really gotten under your skin this time," Valentine says.

She listens without judging and makes me free to talk. "The

damned choreographer is only thinking of himself. The ballerina is only concerned with how she can get the audience to applaud. And where's the composer? Nowhere."

"You feel like they erased you from the page," she says.

"Completely. My music has been chopped into bits."

She understands so perfectly. Her gentle compassion drains away some of the vitriol roiling in my stomach. "Well, maybe I could try just a bite."

I move toward the dining area in her charming loft and sit at the table. "The thing that really hurts is Picasso, the only one who understands the music, keeps his mouth shut."

"He's let you down."

I might have said betrayed or disloyal. But Valentine's words soften things into a more reasonable perspective.

"The thing is, Picasso is now sharing a bed with the ballerina."

"Ah, so he can't take sides," she says.

"I suppose." I break off a crust of bread and spread a mound of pâté with a knife and take a bite. The goose liver and onion melt on my tongue. Valentine pours chardonnay into my glass to wash it down.

"I wanted to throttle Cocteau."

She clicks her tongue. "Doesn't everyone?"

I snicker. "He wanted dialogue to be inserted, delivered by a megaphone."

She rears back with an incredulous gasp.

"The group voted that down." A slow sip unlocks a bouquet like honey and grapefruit.

"I think when one collaborates with other artists you must be flexible," she says.

"Ordinarily I might agree, but Cocteau's latest hair-brained idea is adding non-musical sounds to the score, sirens, fog horns, typewriters. He insists they're crucial for atmosphere."

"Oh my."

I toss back the wine in one gulp and Valentine pours more.

"My dear Satie, at the risk of sounding patronizing, you have always said none of us owns art. It comes through us. We can't hold on to it."

"A stranglehold, eh? And I was right when I said that."

She tips her head with a gentle smile. "You mustn't be cross with them. Art speaks to them, too."

"So, I just need to trust art to find her way and stop trying to control everything."

"Have you forgotten? You're always about the new, about change."

I take a deep breath. She's right. I'm thinking too much about myself. I just needed someone to remind me. Art is a wild force of nature and regardless of our intentions, she has her own agenda.

I surrender my pride and focus on re-writing the score, making some changes easily. Other instances require more patience. Picasso and Jean add a third propaganda machine, and a life sized two-man horse, á la Fratellini Bros. I have to develop a whole new theme. Meanwhile, rehearsals with the orchestra begin under the baton of Ernest Ansermet. He's a young colleague of Stravinsky who Diaghilev hired to conduct while in Switzerland. We share the same aesthetic and I'm confident Ansermet can translate what I have on the page.

I arrive at the theatre for the day of rehearsal. Members of the orchestra are tuning up in the orchestra pit. Ansermet is at the conductor's podium, baton in hand. Maurice Ravel has dropped by at my invitation. We sit together in the first row. Cocteau and Diaghilev sit behind us in the second row. I locate the place in the score they're working on with the dancers. They're practicing the entrance of the propaganda machines.

"Positions," calls Massine. The ten-foot-tall cardboard and paper mâché costumes obscure the dancers' bodies except for their legs. Picasso transformed his renderings into three-dimensional living paper mâché sculptures in the Rome studio.

Ansermet raises his baton, "And one, and two..." He brings the baton down, but not all the musicians play on cue. Ansermet draws a horizontal line, pinching off the note. "Stop, let's begin again."

Several players in the woodwind section are muttering to each other, one bobbing his head, urging another to speak up.

"What is it?" Ansermet asks. "Is there a problem?"

"The transition, Maestro," says the flautist. "It doesn't follow proper modes of resolution."

"It may be different, Monsieur, but there is nothing improper," I say loudly.

Ansermet turns around, looking at me with an anxious, one-sided frown. "They've been grumbling all morning," he says.

"Well then. Let's have it out in the open," says Diaghilev. "Everyone must be unified on this production team. What's the problem?"

The flautist stands "The whole score is the problem. It's not substantial. Too flimsy, not enough harmony."

"It doesn't make proper use of all the instruments," says another.

"It's written that way intentionally," I insist. "Just play it the way it's written."

"But something doesn't sound right."

"Monsieur Ravel, surely you agree with us," says the flautist.

Ravel looks at me and then speaks. "Listen friends, this score may be a radical departure from what you're used to, but compositionally, there is absolutely no flaw with it. It's perfectly acceptable."

I stand. "Gentlemen, it's purposely pared down, purified of every unnecessary embellishment. I know you musicians love lots of extra notes flowing in a predictable pattern."

Cocteau's helium voice pipes in. "But that would be boring. We're going for simple."

"The way you might whistle a tune on the sidewalk," I add.

"Whistle a tune?" the flautist says. "This two-note ostinato sounds like a Paris police siren."

"Exactly," I reply.

The flautist raises his voice. "You think I'm some kind of idiot? That I don't know anything about music?"

I take a deep breath. "No, not at all. I don't think you're an idiot. But I could be wrong."

Cocteau makes a high-pitched snigger behind me. Groans and hisses swell in the orchestra pit and several grumbling musicians leave their seats, carrying their instruments and cases with them. Others applaud their departure.

"Anyone else have misgivings?" I ask.

"Leave now or shut up," says Jean.

Eyes furtively shift from person to person. No one else gets up.

Diaghilev raises his voice. "Now, let's move on."

Ansermet turns back to the orchestra. "From the top, gentlemen," he says, raising the baton and this time the animated sculptures begin their course downstage. They cross paths midway, with Massine coaching and clapping out the rhythm. The music transitions into the theme of the French propagandist. The pipe smoking mustached structure kicks, leaps, and executes fancy step-ball-change movements. The music and dance meld together seamlessly. As the piece reaches its culmination, a loud catcall emanates from behind us, up to the left.

"Boo, get off the stage. You're too ugly."

"Heavens, the noise hurts my ears," says a woman's voice.

"That's not music, it's street noise."

Ansermet cuts off at the end of the bar. We turn toward the distraction of the intruders. There in one of the box seats, Claude and Misia heckle with mocking grimaces. Unforgiveable. I ball my fists.

"Don't stop," calls Claude. "I'm quite enjoying this comedy."

"Well, I've seen enough." Misia rises from her seat. "Glad my name is not associated with this travesty." She mutters other things, but disappears into the upper lobby.

"Please, continue." Claude rises. "Maybe it will improve with practice." He vanishes.

"Who the hell is that?" asks Cocteau.

Picasso, Diaghilev, Ravel, and I all stare wide-eyed at him. "That's Claude Debussy," I say. It strikes me as poetic justice that the young poet doesn't recognize him. Still, their comments are a punch to the gut.

"Ignore it, mon vieux," says Ravel. "He's just sour grapes." Ravel surveys me up and down with concern in his eyes. "Let's have a cigarette, shall we?"

Cocteau calls a brief recess. By the time we get outside the stage door, I'm shaking all over. Claude's comments weren't delivered for the musicians or conductor, or the Ballets Russes dancers, or even Diaghilev. He would never have acted this way had I not been seated in the front row. No, it was personal. What had I ever done to deserve it? I feel a sudden weakness in the limbs, almost numb all over. I can't believe he did this to me.

Ravel says nothing, but offers a cigarette. We take several drags in silence, watching the alley cats scramble after vermin pawing through the refuse bins. Vehicle after vehicle putters by on the boulevard. I'm still shaking my head. My throat swells. "Yes, sour grapes." I pull off my pince-nez and tuck them in my breast pocket. Taking out a clean handkerchief, I blot the tears spilling from my eyes.

Ravel offers a knowing smile. "Shall we knock off for today?"

"Absolutely not. We must keep going." I put my lenses back on, take a few more drags on the cigarette, toss it to the ground, and crush the butt underfoot. Turning back toward the stage door, we return to our seats. Once re-assembled, Diaghilev wears an expression of dissident determination. Cocteau strokes his chin, shaking his head.

"If we didn't have a reason to set aside petty squabbles before," I say, "we have one now. Let's pull together as a team, and prove them wrong." This will be a work beyond all categories, all limits. We will rewrite the rules. I'll rub Claude's nose in it.

Chapter 42

May 17, 1917, Théâtre du Châtelet

THE INTERIOR OF the Châtelet resembles a golden honeycomb lined with red velvet. Flags hang on each side of the stage, the French Tricolor on the right, the Russian flag on the left. I intentionally sit with several young protégés in the same box where Claude and Misia made asses of themselves during the rehearsal. Diaghilev's and Picasso's seats remain empty, as they are working backstage.

The Grasshopper and the Ants play the fiddle and dance the bourrée inside my stomach. Whatever happens in the next hour, I'm confident I've given my best effort. We all have. Parade has emerged as a work of no single author, rather an ensemble creation, edgy, ambiguous, and thoroughly confrontational.

A quarter of an hour passes and the theatre fills with tuxedoed and bejeweled patrons in the front and middle rows. Young students teem along the balustrades in the gallery seats. The bassoonist practices a scale. Through the chatter and drone of hundreds of conversations, I can pick out various rifts from the score as the musicians warm up. The brass struggled with the timing on that part there, and yes, the bone of contention for the flautists. They've got it now.

At the two-o'clock hour, the first violinist stands up, draws his bow across the strings, and brings the orchestra to attention. The other strings join him in attunement. Late arriving guests hurry to their seats, and the tempest of voices subsides. The side door bursts open and Ansermet appears in an elegant black tie and tails, holding his baton. The audience breaks into welcoming applause. He takes the podium, turns to the audience, and bows several times. The house lights dim.

"Here we go," I say. My chest flutters as if a dozen tiger moths are trying to get out. I give a quick smile to Cocteau. Valentine reaches over and pats my quavering hand.

Ansermet raises his baton, turns his head left and then right to meet the gaze of attentive musicians. He begins. The trumpets boom the first notes. The overture is stately and dignified. Written in the key of C major, it conforms perfectly to the rules for chorale and fugue. They'll think it is classic, orthodox, flawlessly balanced. But tradition is about to fly out the window with the tiger moths. As we plunge over a cliff, I grip my knees.

The stage curtain opens, revealing Picasso's colossal painted screen, which depicts yet another red curtain being pulled aside. Neo-classical images arrest the eye with brilliant color. Seated at a table, Harlequin, Italian sailors, a Spanish guitarist, a black Moor, Russian peasants, and a dog watch another performance. A winged horse balances atop the world at its feet. An angel bestows a laurel wreath on the head of a monkey, who scales a ladder painted like the French flag.

"Amazing, beautiful," Valentine says.

"Just brilliant," says Georges, seated behind me.

Instantly, a low register drone filters up, and not from the base violins or cello. A collective grumble emanates from the high-priced seats as the provocative symbols sink in. I can see the white cuffs and ladies' fans fretfully moving in the dark. Several patrons rise and wobble their way past other attendees to the aisles and leave.

Right on cue, the lilting fugue culminates. The painted screen rises into the flies, revealing the ballet set. This new world is all askew. Balustrades and pillars from classic Roman architecture are painted black and white like a photograph, but distorted like a funhouse mirror. My music somersaults into Cubistic four-bar themes. The towering propaganda machines make their entrance on intersecting trajectories. A cacophony of color splashes against the off-kilter scenery, to an explosion of wild and mechanical sounds.

I slide to the edge of my seat to observe the reaction. Laughter erupts in some parts of the audience. In other places, a polyphony of boos. In full body gesticulation, Ansermet and the orchestra redouble their fervor. The ten-foot-high sculptures continue their dance, unperturbed. Just as we'd all agreed before the show; nothing will stop us from delivering this performance. But a new wave of groans and boos mounts.

"This is outrageous," one man yells.

"Go back to Russia," another shouts. "Dirty boches!"

Ansermet and the orchestra never miss a beat. The Cubist machines exit with step-ball-change strides into the wings. With Cocteau's spinning lottery wheel, the music transitions to the next movement. Massine makes his solo entrance as the Chinese Conjurer. For most of Massine's dance-pantomime, the hypnotic ostinato and magic tricks seem to mollify the complainers. I take a deep breath and slump back in my seat.

But when his dance finishes and the braggadocio of the monstrous moving sculptures returns, a few patrons blow on the hollow ends of their apartment keys. It makes a shrill protest. From the gallery, the young people reply with dissenting jeers, wad their programs, and rain them down on the snooty upper crustaceans below. In the box next to ours, Maurice Ravel jumps out of his seat. He leans over the railing and shouts, "Shut up, you stupid bitches! Let them perform!"

Ballerina Maria Chabelska enters for The Little American Girl segment. A woman's scream from the audience cuts through the cyclone of sound. The house lights come on. A handful of men reel and lurch in a scuffle on the main floor. It spreads into the other rows. I knew Parade would be controversial, but I didn't expect people to come to fisticuffs over it. We set this thing in motion and now it's a runaway train.

Having lived through the fiasco at the opening performance of The Rite of Spring four years before; Diaghilev put the Gendarmerie on notice. They burst through two doors like the keystone cops, blowing their whistles. Ironically, the whistles are in the same key as the music. The officers arrest tuxedoes and sack suits alike, ushering them by the coat collar out of the theatre. Frantic wives and mistresses scurry behind, clutching their skirts and opera glasses. If I wasn't so worried, I might have laughed. The timing seems to make this debacle part of the performance.

Because of the marvelous talent of Mademoiselle Chabelska in a sailor dress, The Little American Girl segment plays out well. The snippet of Cakewalk and my parody of Tin Pan Alley bring Chabelska the ovation she wished for.

Star-spangled acrobats enter the stage. The life sized two-man horse with cowboy rider accompanies them. But the sculpture wavers, comes loose, and topples onto the stage in pieces. The two acrobats improvise a brilliant cover, dancing with the pieces. The audience laughs and applauds, thinking it's part of the show.

When the finale comes, all the dancers return for the curtain call to a thunder of cheers and applause. The spot light swings from the stage to the conductor, still waving his baton in a reprise of the finale theme. He smiles and nods over his shoulder to a crescendo of approval. Finally, the spotlight pans around to our box. Cocteau and I stand up and wave to a last volley of appreciation.

"A Success de Scandal, my friend," says Cocteau. "We've done it."

Valentine gives me a peck on each cheek. "Congratulations, Satie. It was splendid!"

Georges, Francis, and Roland-Manuel beam and shake my hand with giddy vigor. But I'm exhausted, relieved, and craving a strong shot of cognac.

We hurry downstairs, where an entourage of supporters still packs the lobby. Some beg for autographs. Journalists bark questions amidst photo flashes. "What's the meaning of the acrobat's dance, those blue costumes?" "Why did you parody Charlie Chaplin and Pearl White?"

Valentine and the young people hurry off to make final arrangements for the opening night soirée at Valentine's flat. Cocteau pauses to respond, basking in the attention. I push through the crowd and hurry to the orchestra pit. I want to thank the musicians and especially Ansermet for the superb job they had done. Despite all misgivings, they helped me do something with music no one has ever done. Using popular motifs was shocking, a transgression of the boundaries. I may never get another commission after this. Only time will tell. But I've finally smashed the idols and thrown down the altar. Now there's a new order for a new generation. French music is free from the past. Next, I'll have to gear up for the journalistic backlash that undoubtedly will fill the press for weeks. But for tonight, I can revel in this.

For a moment, Claude enters my thoughts and my gut pinches. How very sad it is that he not only missed the triumph, but would count himself among the naysayers. After all these years and struggles we've been through, he is now my adversary. So profoundly sad.

During the weeklong run of Parade, I sit with Roland-Manuel and Georges, monopolizing a corner table at The Terminus Café. The smoke-filled room bustles with servers, diners, and the clinking of cutlery on ceramics. We pour over the stacks of newspapers and journals published each day. Savoring a Croque-Madame and Belgian beer, we comb through the articles. With my fountain pen ready, and a stack of postcards, I write letters to the editor and thank-you notes to respond both to journalists praise and criticism. One by one, in careful calligraphy, I rejoin every review. We didn't underestimate the impact of this week of performances. Parade's legacy as counter-culture art was sealed after the first night. All the little journals and freelance articles in the Avant-Garde press rave about the ballet. I send these writers a heartfelt thank you.

To my surprise, I receive a special delivery copy of reviews by D'Indy and Serieux, my former professors at the Schola. I fully expect them to scorn the production. Instead, they both congratulate me on the flawless composition methods, even if "the content is a bit controversial". I pen two notes, thanking them for all the valuable things they taught me.

But one very important critique goes above and beyond, with a highly complementary perspective. Guillaume Apollinaire heralds me as an innovative composer of l'Espirit Nouveau. In one stroke of the pen, he anoints me as sole representative of the national musical heritage. I take extra care with my reply, inviting Apollinaire to meet for dinner so I can thank him personally. Any opportunity to chat about a new vision for the arts is welcome.

The mainstream press is hostile. One paper calls Parade another bad Satie joke. La Figaro accuses me of taking laborious pains to produce what fairground clowns could do with their eyes closed. I scribble a counter-measure, arguing point by point. But out of mounting frustration, I become progressively more vulgar with each new retort.

Then, I come across the review by Jean Poueigh, author of The Tickets of the Week column. He went out of his way to congratulate me on the ballet score after the show. It surprised me, because of statements Poueigh made in his book, published years earlier. He stated, *"I should attach little importance to Erik Satie, a clumsy technician engaged in a search for bizarre new sonorities".* I thought he was an idiot then. Now, his article describes me as technically incompetent. *"The score was lacking any musicality, and the entire production was a nullity."* The blubber ball is at it again. But this time, he's added insult to injury with his duplicity. The boxing gloves are coming off. I want to draw blood. My fountain pen explodes on the postcard with colorful scatological jibes.

Two weeks pass. A small green notice shows up in my mail. I have a registered letter waiting at the post office. With the flood of correspondence arriving daily, I'm not in any hurry to retrieve it. But when I finally drop by the mail hub and sign for it, the return address makes my insides turn to writhing worms; Office of the Prosecutor, Tribunal de Grand Instance. My heart leaps into my throat. I open the letter.

> *You are hereby ordered to appear at the Court of the First Instance of the Seine, courtroom No. 5, on Thursday, July 12, 1917 at 1:00 PM., in the matter of Jean Poueigh vs. Erik Satie and on the charge of Criminal Defamation.*

Chapter 43

12 July 1917, Paris, Isle de la Cite

I HAVE NEVER been in trouble with the law a day in my life. Who would have imagined at 51 I'd be in the crosshairs, standing inside a mahogany paneled courtroom with my knees knocking? The door to the judges' chambers open. I steel myself as they enter the courtroom, one after another. The President de la Cour and his two Assesseurs take their places on the elevated bench. They resemble medieval royalty, in their ermine-trimmed red robes. But the silly hats like soufflé pans ruin the effect. A spasm erupts in my belly and I cover my mouth to stifle a less than decorous snicker. This forces a leak from my tear ducts, fogging my pince-nez. My lawyer turns and glowers at me. I can't help it. It's so bizarre. Maybe I'm just all nerves. The whole affair is a travesty; comical and horrific at the same time. When the bailiff directs us to be seated, I can finally take a full breath.

What's definitely not funny is that if the court rules in favor of my nemesis, I face a hefty fine and jail time. And why? It's all because of Music. That capricious jinx, that cruel taskmistress - she has landed me here.

With the sharp rap of the gavel, a shiver rakes my spine. "I will hear opening statements in the matter of Poueigh vs. Satie," says the President.

Attorney for the plaintiff, Maître José Théry, takes the floor. His black taffeta robe whispers in the silence as he crosses the room. "Under the Libel Law of 1881, defamation is defined as any allegation or imputation of an act affecting the honor or reputation of a person." He carries a file toward the evidence table, opens it and lays out three postcards.

Shaking my head, I glance toward heaven. No one could have invented a more surreal scenario. I've been hauled into court over three postcards. Preposterous. Are they really stooping to such lows to stifle me?

Théry straightens his white lace jabot. "With this evidence and testimony, I shall prove beyond a doubt that my blameless client, Monsieur Jean Poueigh, was deliberately and maliciously slandered by Monsieur Erik Satie. We will ask the court to deliver the full penalty provided by law and a remedy commensurate with the intended injury." He smooths his moustache and returns to his seat.

My advocate, Maître Peytel, stands up. "Your Honors, an insulting statement does no actual harm, prima facie. Vituperative statements made in anger are never taken literally or believed. We intend to show that this evidence represents the free expression of personal opinion, not a statement of fact. And as such, opinion is by nature not falsifiable. No libel has occurred. We shall ask for the case to be dismissed." He sits back down and glances over at me with a dubious brow.

When we entered the building this morning, my lawyer mentioned this is the very same courtroom where Emile Zola was tried in 1898 for slandering the French government with his "I Accuse" article. Small comfort, but at least I'm in good company, so long as I don't end up asphyxiated like Zola did. This isn't the first time I've tangled with a journalist. I never withheld the full color of language against Willy or any of his minions. Claude once praised me for being the only one brave or foolish enough to take them on. But I never expected this.

"I call as my first witness, Monsieur Jean Poueigh," Maître Théry says.

Poueigh looks like a cross-eyed penguin waddling to the witness stand. After he gives the bailiff his oath, Maître Théry presents him with the three postcards.

"Monsieur Poueigh; do you recognize these items?"

"Oui, Maître."

"Would you tell the court exactly how you came by these items?"

"The postal service delivered them to my address and my concierge brought them to me on three successive days."

He holds them up, flipping them over, displaying both sides. "Just as we see them now, with no envelope?"

"Correct."

"So both the postal carrier and your concierge and many other individuals handling such mail might have glanced at them, read them perhaps?"

"That is correct."

"No further questions."

Poueigh steps down and his lawyer whirls around, fixing his eyes on me. "I call to the stand, Monsieur Erik Satie."

Every trace of moisture vanishes from my mouth, precipitously re-emerging on my forehead. It dribbles down my temples into my starched white collar. I take a clean, neatly folded handkerchief from my breast pocket and blot away the steamy angst. I've been on stage countless times as a performer. But nothing prepared me for this. My legs nearly fold beneath me. They swear me in and I step onto the platform.

"I have one question for the respondent, your Honors." Maître Théry spreads the postcards, displaying them for my review. "Is this your handwriting and signature, Monsieur Satie?"

Two giant kettle drums pound in my chest, stealing my voice. "It is," I choke.

"Could you speak up, please?"

I clear my throat. "It's my handwriting."

"Thank you. You may step down."

That was fairly innocuous. What's the point? This isn't about postcards. It's really about my score, my ballet Parade, which caused such an uproar. This self-appointed expert, so-called music critic is trying to get back at me. It's not just because of a stylistic departure; albeit a radical one. With a team including Diaghilev's Ballets Russes, Picasso's Cubist set and costumes, and my musical score; what did Poueigh expect? Obviously, the riot it caused in the Théâtre du Châtelet was the first sign we'd done something big. It was more than we expected. After the gendarmes had to be called to break up the fights, why would I think the controversy would stop there?

My eyes drift over to the public gallery on the right. A retinue of young people crowds the pews with worried, defiant faces. My collaborator, Jean Cocteau, sits side-by-side with poet Leon Paul Fargue. Jean's appearance makes him rather conspicuous with his unruly hair and unnatural salmon mousse make-up. He looks as if he had just stepped off the stage, but he hadn't. In the same row, a trio of young Cubist painters is assembled; Lhote, Severini, and Gris. My friend, pianist Ricardo Viñes, is in the second row beside my three protégés. They're mere kids, Louis Durey, Georges Auric, and Francis Poulenc. Dancers and actors pack the rows behind them. It seems the whole Avant-Garde of Paris has rallied in solidarity with me. I meet Georges' gaze, which burns resolute and loyal.

When we met for aperitifs at the Dome café a few days after Poueigh's review appeared, the young man remarked, "This tripe is just one more example of the mentality that has paralyzed music for 300 years."

Francis chimed in. "Parade is a manifesto, a revolt for the sake of expressive freedom."

I smiled at their exuberance. Isn't that my fault, too, by peppering them with radical ideas? They are young, but they're figuring things out. But Parade represents more than freedom of expression. The same corrupt imperialist values have stonewalled anything creative or new for decades, is also spilling their blood. They're killing them by the thousands in the trenches with no end in sight, and lying about it.

"The arts are the only voice of truth," I told them. "The government has only one official version of the news. Letters sent home are censored. There is no freedom of speech or the press. All we get is suppression and lies. I refuse to be silent."

Maître Théry argues Poueigh's case. "I would like to address the matter of character. My client, Monsieur Poueigh, writes music reviews for Les Carnet de la Semaine. He takes that role with great seriousness. He sees himself as one of the guardians of time-honored tradition, high culture, and standards of excellence that are authentically French. You likely will hear the defense argue that Monsieur Poueigh criticized this so-called ballet, Parade for its novelty. However, most reasonable Frenchmen recognize the assault on the patriotic values for which our soldiers at this very moment are sacrificing their lives. The ballet not only outrages French taste but borders on an act of treason. Monsieur Poueigh is a true patriot."

Like a Greek Chorus, the young people in the gallery jump out of their seats in a surge of protest. Cocteau makes a megaphone with his hands. "Who is really being slandered here?"

The judge slams the gavel down several times. Their continued grumbling leads to a threat to expel them from the courtroom.

"I do not make these statements lightly," Théry continues. "But I merely call attention to the subversive activities of the perpetrators. The court will note that the director of the ballet company, foreign national Serge Diaghilev, was brash enough to rejoice at the overthrow of one of France's allies, the Tsar Nicholas. He hoisted a red flag on stage. And the artistic designer, if you can call him that, is another foreigner. Monsieur Picasso has displayed his degenerate boche art in the Kahnweiler gallery."

Jean Cocteau explodes, waving his fist. "Boches. How dare you? You're equating us with the German enemies? Outrageous! We served in the war."

Two bailiffs wrestle him from the gallery and haul him out of the court room.

"As I was about to say, if that wasn't evidence enough, there is the composer. Monsieur Satie is a card-carrying member of the Socialist Party, and it is a well-known fact that they opposed the war and efforts to liberate Alsace-Lorraine. Monsieur Poueigh is well qualified to determine that the ballet was inferior."

What about Poueigh's vile diatribe on the pages of Les Carnet de la Semaine? Wasn't that defamatory? My one fatal flaw has always been my weary heart, out there on my sleeve. I never could take criticism well. Thirty years' worth. Now, Music has me branded a treasonous degenerate and subversive. I shake my head with a groan.

Maître Théry continues his case. "I would ask permission, in all fairness to both sides, to have the evidence read aloud to all assembled by your honor." Maître Théry holds out the postcards to the judges.

I squeeze my eyes tight, shaking my head. Mon Dieu, I'm done for.

"Very Well," says the President de la Cour. Scanning the first card, his eyes widen, then his brows knot. He shoots me a condemning glare as he clears his throat.

"To Jean Poueigh: One thing I know for certain is that you are an ass-hole and, if I dare say so, a non-musical ass-hole. Above all, never offer me your cum-laced hand again."

Titters and snickers break out in both the press corps and gallery.

Alright, so perhaps I was a little vulgar. But I didn't make that up. I was just referencing the most popular joke being repeated all over Paris; the melodious fart. Jean Poueigh is a stink bomb for writing such a scalding diatribe. After coming to my box at the Théâtre du Châtelet to congratulate me, he's a double-dealing blubber-ball.

The judged raps his gavel to quiet the reactions. "To Monsieur Jean Poueigh, Head Dunce, Chief Gourd, and President of Turkeys. You're dumber than you look." He chokes back a laugh and his eyes water. After a moment, he regains control and resumes. But a high-pitched hoot from the gallery interrupts the judge. He looks fiercely for the offender, but continues. "You look at things from a distance, which makes everything of greatness look shrunken and insignificant.

It must be your vacuous skull and myopia that cause the distortion. Poor thing."

This time a surge of laughter rocks the room. My young protégés are reeling with malicious guffaws. The judge hammers the gavel. "Silence! I will clear this courtroom entirely if there is one more outburst."

The judge picks up the last postcard. I shade my brow and grit my teeth, knowing what is about to cross the judge's lips.

"To Monsieur Fuckface Poueigh, Famous Muttonhead." Red-faced, his moustache twitches like a fly has crawled up his nose. The judge takes a sip of water. "King of Idiots, and Emperor of Assholes: I'm here in Fontainebleau, from where I shit on you with all my force."

The laughter is deafening. The judge immediately orders the bailiff and police to herd the press and the gallery observers out of the court room. I used to be polite, eloquent, and contrived many creative ways of getting even. The criticism got the better of me this time. But I'm not sorry I wrote those things. And the postcards were – well, funny.

After a few moments, an eerie silence is restored. They banish the young people to the outside corridor. Maître Théry addresses the court.

"It would be one thing if the respondent here, Monsieur Satie, complained or disagreed with the article or review, even offered a well written rejoinder. However, these represent a carefully worded attack on the person of Monsieur Poueigh and one which has been circulated for the eyes of others. Can there be any question about slander? Certainly, the reaction of all those assembled in this courtroom today indicates the humiliating and defamatory effect these missives had on my client. We ask for justice."

This is bad. I'll be ruined. Not only will this bankrupt me, but I'll be branded a criminal. I'll never be able to get a passport, never be able to cross a border, which means my dream of performing in America and England will never come to pass. I'll end up rotting in a squalid dungeon. My stomach swirls and I have an urge to vomit.

Chapter 44

Autumn, 1917, Paris

I'll completely lose my mind and wind up in the sanatorium if I remain in Paris one more day. I've gone through nightmarish gymnastics staging Parade. Then the libel trial and the venomous verdict eviscerated me. I'm exhausted.

On the advice of Ricardo Viñes, I board a train to the farthest corner of France, to Céret, Languedoc-Roussillon in the foothills of the Pyrenees. How easy it would be just to flee across the border. My friends Santiago and Ramon will surely offer me refuge. But a former classmate from the Schola Cantorum, Déodat de Séverac, is a welcoming host and encourages me to stay. Déo's laughter and lusty red wine soothe the knot in my chest. But it's the stillness I appreciate most, embellished in the mornings by the song of starlings.

The court scene keeps replaying in my mind again and again. My advocate Maître Peytel presented several character witnesses to vouch for my decency and integrity. But it made little difference. The three judges came back from deliberation in favor of Jean Poueigh. They issued me a hundred franc fine, a thousand in damages, and eight days in jail.

"We can appeal the ruling," Maître Peytel said. "We might overturn the jail time if you will write a formal apology."

Every little bit will help. But there are also the court costs and my attorney's fees. Because I lost, I'll have to pay Poueigh's attorney's fees as well. Essentially, every centime I have in the world will be forfeited. Ruined, again!

When I finally return to the city, I begin shuttling from office to office in bureaucratic redundancy to mount an appeal. I complete paperwork, sign legal filings, and interact with perfunctory civil servants. But it's better than going to jail. The time away restored my sense of humor.

Out of this rigmarole, I manage to generate another set of humoristic pieces. By "deranging" a sonata by Clementi, I compose Sonatine Bureaucratic. My publisher, Rouart-Lerolle, buys it enthusiastically. But Lerolle fears they might seize my assets in the litigation, which includes rights and future royalties. Lerolle has everything placed in receivership until we settle the case, leaving me with nothing. The war continues to grind on at great toll. There is no work to be found. So after nearly six years of financial stability, I'm once again broke.

The injustice incenses Georges, Francis, and Louis. They arrange two concerts at Salle Huyghens to raise money for my appeal. To pay rent, I finally follow up on a referral Conrad sent me, to tutor an industrialist, Albert Verley, who wants to learn to compose music.

Only now am I able to turn my attention to the one project I most want to undertake, Socrates. My friend Jane Bartori agrees to perform an extract of the work-in-progress for the Princess de Polignac. She is so thrilled with the sample piece; she pays me the promised advance of 2000 francs. This life preserver keeps me from sinking.

In this entire ordeal, one thing gnaws at me more than anything else is Claude's complete absence and silence. Not an inquiry, not a note. Claude surely read and heard about all that has happened. But I've heard nothing from him. We really are enemies.

❧

March 15, 1918, Paris, 1st Arrondissement

Eight months of uncertainty trudges by. By the time my appeal date arrives at the Cour d'appel de Paris, a mood of foreboding, thick as clay engulfs Paris. Though my case is scheduled to appear at 2:00 p.m., I sit with Maître Peytel for two and a half hours, wringing my hands as other cases on the docket are heard. Finally, at a quarter to five, my case is called. I stand beside my attorney, facing the panel of three judges. My galloping heart tramples my vocal cords and I need to find a pissoir.

"Monsieur Satie," says the chief judge. "After careful review of the facts of this case and the legal procedures, this court of appeal has come to an accord. We have decided to let the guilty charge of Criminal Defamation stand."

My nose tingles and I feel like I might pass out.

"However, because you have no previous offenses and have an otherwise blameless record as a citizen and served your country honorably, we approve probation in lieu of jail time. We condition this on your continued moral conduct for the next five years. The fine of a hundred francs still stands."

I close my eyes and take a deep breath. Alright, that isn't terrible.

"Finally, in the matter of Jean Poueigh vs. Erik Satie; since to date there has been no action on your part known to this court showing remorse or restitution; unless your attorney has new information for us to consider, we uphold the damage amount of 1000 francs."

The hair on the back of my neck prickles, but I grip the handle of my umbrella with defiance. They might order it, but that doesn't mean I'm going to pay the bastard.

The gavel comes down. "This court is adjourned."

I shake hands with Maître Peytel one last time and we part ways outside on the Cour de Mai. From there, I decide to take the tree-lined path along the banks of the Seine, listen to the tranquil flow of the water and clear my mind. I can find an out-of-the-way brasserie, have a drink and a meal in peace, before catching the blue line for Arcueil. I don't want to talk to anyone right now. So what if I'm a criminal? I'll have to choose my words more carefully from now on, but they will not silence me. Thank God I didn't have to go to jail. It's over.

As I approach the Place de la Concorde, the air-raid siren raises its terrifying whine. I must get to the metro station and go underground until the bombing stops. But as I head across the plaza, the buzzing drone of engines overhead and the jarring rattle of artillery fire make people scatter in panic. Then the bombs start to fall. The ground shakes so violently, I lose my footing and fall to the concrete. Paving stones shoot in every direction as a massive explosion blasts a crater a few feet away.

Dust and smoke choke out the light. The planes move off toward Les Halles. I get to my feet, stagger a few steps, tripping over the rubble. I stop short. Where blue square pavers had spread in a fan-shaped pattern, there is now a gaping black pit. Through the haze, I can barely make out the Obélisque at the center of the plaza. Sandbags have protected it. I scramble through the debris toward it. The wave of aircraft changes direction and ferries its destruction toward the south-west, toward people I care about, Paulette, Ravel, Roland-Manuel's' parents. God, I hope they have time to shelter. Moans and frantic cries for help come from every direction in the dark. I crouch there at the foot of the monument, hugging the sandbags. Maybe I should grapple my way toward the voices, try to help. But I'm gasping for air. There's a searing pain in my hip where I landed on the pavement. My shoulder now flares like a boil to even move my arm. I'm in no condition to help anyone right now. I just need to stay alive. I hunker down at the foot of the Obélisque.

The headlights of a motorcar send two cones of light across the ground, illuminating the yellow dust. The side of a masonry building had rained down on the vehicle. Its roof is caved in. Its engine still rattles and the horn blares from the poor soul crushed against the steering wheel. Half a dozen bodies sprawl on the pavement, none moving. A handful of people stagger toward safety.

The sirens blare again and the menacing hornets draw closer. They have doubled back. This is it. This could be my end. I make myself smaller, curl my knees up to my chest, duck my head toward them. Pain wracks my body. Bombs explode on all sides and the earth spasms beneath me. I cover my head with the lapels of my coat. I've lost my hat and umbrella out there in the destruction. I wait for what seems like eons of time until everything grows still again.

"Are you alright, Monsieur?"

Someone touches me on the arm. I look up to see a familiar face; Blaise Cendrars, the young poet who'd lost an arm. Here he is with a flashlight rescuing people.

"Mon Dieu, Satie. What are you doing here? Let's get you to safety."

He pulls me to my feet and we hobble together down into the Metro.

~

The bombing continues in a random barrage for weeks, sometimes at night, sometimes by day. It's no longer safe to go into Paris. Arcueil, sitting south of the city and of such little consequence, remains essentially untouched. I spend my mornings at the local café, Chez Tulard, drinking coffee and cognac and reading the newspaper before returning to my apartment to continue work on Socrates. As I peruse the socialist weekly, l'Humanité, an obituary grabs my attention.

Composer Claude Achille Debussy passed away on March 25, 1918, after a lengthy illness. In his illustrious career, they awarded him the prestigious Prix de Rome and later the Legion of Honneur for his opera Pelleas et Melisande. He was 56 and is survived by his wife Emma and daughter Claude-Emma. He was buried in a private ceremony at the Pere Lachaise Cemetery.

That was a week ago. I fall back against my chair, cover my mouth, and stare out the café window. My face crumbles and my eyes well over. We hadn't spoken in over a year. I knew Claude was dying, but this still comes as a terrible shock. The most disturbing thing is after thirty years of friendship, I wasn't even told. I might not have been able to attend the funeral with bombs falling around. But the thing that hurts the most is being cut off, made an enemy. A month ago, music journalist Louis Laloy, who'd penned Debussy's biography, sent me a postcard after they confined Claude to bed on a morphine drip. I sent a brief note wishing Debussy God's peace, but that was all. Now he's gone, without a final word. He died as inexplicably as everyone I've lost, my mother, my grandmother, father, and now Claude. They have left me behind to nurse my wounds and try to make sense of it. All energy drains from my body and my throat constricts. How sad it had to happen this way.

In mid-April Sybil Harris, editor of Vanity Fair contacts me. She'd already published several of my humorous essays; and the magazine had featured articles about me, Jean Cocteau, and Parade. We were introduced to America as the leaders of the Futurist movement. Now she was asking for a piece reflecting on the life and contributions of Debussy. I could write volumes. But I decide to narrow my focus to what the readers of Vanity Fair most need to know.

Remembering Claude Debussy- by Erik Satie

From the instant I first saw him; I was drawn to him and wanted to live always by his side. For thirty years I've had the blessing of being able to fulfill that wish. We understood one another implicitly, without convoluted explanations, for we had known each other – forever it seemed.

Born in St-Germain-en-Laye on 22 August 1862, he did all his musical studies at the Conservatoire National in Paris; a huge, very uncomfortable building, and a sort of penitentiary with no redeeming features on the outside, or the inside, for that matter. In 1884 the man who would later compose Prelude á l'Après-midi d'un Faune, won the Prix de Rome award. In my humble opinion, that experience was irreparably harmful for Debussy and damaged the best part of him like corrosive poison. Oui.

When I met him, he was completely impregnated by Mussorgsky and was desperately searching for a way forward, which was not easy to find. On that count, I had a long lead over him; not being weighed down with prizes of Rome or any other town, given that I do not carry such things on my person or on my back. I explained to Debussy the need for us to value our own music away from the Wagner and German Romantic adventure. We needed our own music. Why not use the means of representation exhibited to us by Claude Monet, Cézanne, Toulouse-Lautrec, etc? Why not transpose these images into music. This was the point of departure which became fertile ground and enormously fruitful. Who was it that showed him examples? Revealed finds to him? Who suggested which piece of ground to dig in? The answer will likely never be acknowledged.

His arrival in the musical arena was a rather disagreeable event for some and a thrilling one for others. These "others" formed a tiny minority, while the "some" made up a huge mass, and a sticky and slimy one at that. In the end, the opinion of the tiny minority triumphed over the huge mass, which itself became stuck in the mud of its own blindness. But the appearance of a Genius on this earth is always the occasion for turmoil; so much venom gets poured out. The poor Arrival is immediately seen as an Antichrist, or Raving Lunatic who hardly dares leave his house. Of course, in the days of our dear old ancestors in the Stone Age, newly arrived geniuses were welcomed with a good stab between the shoulder blades from a flint dagger. Debussy did not escape this special treatment. Life was very hard for him. It is a miracle that he was able to write and develop his work at all.

There was a great sureness about him, too great to my mind. It hampered any flexibility and variety in his points of view. I suffered to see him so. After 30 years, we no longer followed the same path, our horizons diverging by the hour.

Dying generations inexorably lose their importance in the eyes of the young. However, Debussy remains eternally among the greatest musicians of modern times; and one of the few whose work has had such a profound influence.

Chapter 45

February 14, 1920, Paris, 8th Arrondissement

I STAND ACROSS from the austere building, looking up at the façade. This is the very spot my sheet music landed that day I pitched it into the street. I had just failed my jury exam, and they had dismissed me from the Conservatoire. I haven't been back inside since that time period. Euterpe and Terpsichore, two of the nine muses, still perch atop the fluted columns framing the archway. As a young man, I thought their weathered stone faces stared down with condescension. But now, as I study their expressions, they seem to display more of a wry amusement as they watch the dreamers come and go through these doors.

I can see my breath and my nose tingles. Wandering snowflakes glitter in the glow of the streetlamps. Most melt on contact, but small drifts accumulate at the corners of windows and door frames. Like a lady's fan in faceted crystal, the Palladian window above the double doors glows with interior light. Here is the entrance at which I waited for Jeanne de Bret to emerge on that wintry night. She inspired the emotion behind The Trois Gymnopédies, our naked dances of youth. There seems in this moment a peculiar alignment of stars that brings me back to this place. I'm here to premiere another work of Greek content, a work like no other. I have come full circle, back to the beginning, as Odysseus returning home.

Like brush strokes of a painter on a canvas, the events of my life have been layered with color and texture. The emerging image isn't what I'd imagined or intended as a man of 20. However, the image that has taken shape, melded together just as it should have, miraculously. Over time, I have been on an evolving crusade. The process of becoming is an endless one, I believe. I will never really arrive. Arrivisme is stagnation, creative death. As Socrates once wrote; "Life contains but two tragedies. One is not getting your heart's desire; the other is to get it." For all my efforts, destiny seemed to smile on me in her own time, and for reasons quite inexplicable. The compositions that brought money or renown are not the works I consider my best. But they sustained me, so I could make Art.

Tonight, is the first public performance of Socrates; the capstone of my 30-year struggle to change the musical landscape. I've recast the work over the past year from fragments of Socrates' life. In the end, they ordered him to drink hemlock for corrupting the minds of the youth. Some may say I, too, am guilty as charged. But it's ironic that Société Nationale de Musique should sponsor this performance. The Société had once sponsored the performance of the Gymnopédies, which Claude had orchestrated for me. But the singular thing that seems most remarkable of all is where the performance will take place. My music will be performed here, in the concert salon of the Conservatoire, the very place that throughout my life has represented failure and rejection. It shattered my spirit. My Absinthe baptism at Le Chat Noir and my journey into the Music Hall saved my soul. Without them, I might never have made music at all. And those elements imported from the popular milieu blended with the classical has transformed music for a modern age.

Le Conservatoire has been the bête noire for most of my life. Now I'm being welcomed back as a conquering hero. As nice as that sounds, it worries me a little. Has the institution changed? Or have

I become conventional? And the audience? They are no more likely to comprehend or appreciate what I've created now, than they did the Rose+Croix. The critics' reviews will undoubtedly span the full range of opinion. There will always be small-minded, self-appointed authorities with poison in their hearts. Their bite will always sting. But at least I will give them a heap to write about.

But it doesn't matter. I've scheduled a private performance in March for the arts community I love. Their opinion is what I value. We will hold the gathering at Adrienne Monnier's bookstore, La Maison des Amis des Livres. Many friends have promised to attend, including Andre Gide, James Joyce, Gertrude Stein, Picasso, Braque, and Apollinaire. Cocteau would have liked to take over or take credit in some way. But Plato was my librettist this time. Such a beautiful timeless text doesn't need anyone's music. My goal is merely an act of piety, an artist's reverie, and a humble tribute.

Over the years, I have never compromised, even though it surely made me the most criticized composer who ever lived. I've been faithful to the Muse, despite a life very much like the Greek masks of comedy and tragedy above the door to this theatre. I've left my mark, my unique imprint. This is gratifying, for a moment anyway. As I've told the handful of young composers many times, an artist must never stop growing and changing. I have a dozen additional works in development and visions of more to come including the soundtrack to a moving picture.

I watch as a group of young people assembles outside the Conservatoire, shivering in the cold. Les Six, I call them. Georges Auric, Francis Poulenc, Louis Durey, Arthur Honegger, Darius Milhaud, and a daring young female composer Germaine Tailleferre. They smile and wave.

"Bonsoir, Maître," Georges calls.

Germaine comes toward me and gives me a peck on the cheek.

With my umbrella under my arm, I cross the street to join them. Grinning, I lead them up the steps to the beveled glass entrance, and open the door for them.

Epilogue

Wednesday, July 8, 1925- Arcueil

I FOUND THE entrance to the apartment at number 22 on Rue Cauchy boarded over when I got there. Even though I expected it, the coarse planks and nails showed a clumsy indifference, sealing the passage with hasty finality. Such an uninspiring address too; so out of character for the colorful man who'd once been the pianist at Le Chat Noir cabaret. My mentor had been laid to rest two days before and the shock of his loss still left me raw. Pivoting, I gazed back down the sloping cobbled street I just climbed, trying to picture him strolling through this gritty working-class suburb of Paris. The arches of the old Roman aqueduct, the hamlet's namesake, towered stark against the cerulean sky, dwarfing lackluster tenements and industrial depots in its shadow.

Satie left no will. So, the government was obliged to take control of his estate. The law provided a few days for family to remove personal correspondence and papers before the rest went up for auction to defray the cost of his burial. A group of us, his intimate friends, were asked by the composer's brother at the funeral to gather at our mentor's apartment and carefully sift through his effects. Those gathered include Darius Milhaud and his young wife Madeleine, jazz pianist Jean Wiéner, conductor Roger Désormière, and me.

I probably knew Satie the shortest amount of time. I'd met the ailing composer less than a year before. But in the last five months, as his vitality ebbed away in a St. Joseph's Hospital bed; I came to see him daily and hung on his every word.

My friends were already waiting curbside. Darius paced aimlessly on the dingy sidewalk. Jean rocked back on his heels, his arms folded, staring up at the façade.

Roger hailed me. "Robert Caby, you finally made it all the way out here."

Jean turned to Darius, pointing up at the building. "Any of you ever been inside?"

Darius looked over. "Me? Never. How about you, Roger?"

"No," he said.

I spoke-up. "Boy what a scorching I got when I mentioned I'd dropped by to see him one time. And how!" I ran my fingers back through my shock of thick hair. "He definitely made clear this was his hermitage. No one was allowed to enter his inner sanctum."

"No telling what we'll find, then," Darius added. He stopped short of saying what I guessed we all were hoping; that we'd discover a cache of unfinished manuscripts or never performed masterworks. Scavenging vultures, we were not; rather a faction of loyal disciples, eager to preserve the maestro's vision. As the minutes ticked by waiting for Satie's brother Conrad to appear, my chest started to swell like an accordion and my knees felt unsteady, akin to the awe one might experience when approaching the Holy of Holies.

Having just begun my college life; I'd been deliberating on whether to become a journalist or a composer myself. So I asked Satie how he decided to write music and why he chose to make it a career. A naughty gleam sparked in his eyes and his thin opalescent skin crumpled like parchment when he smiled.

"Because I could." He chuckled in resonant bass. "Someone had to do it." He said this as if relegated to a thankless task, like unclogging the toilet. "What a terrible idea; a truly terrible idea. In fact, I quickly developed an unpleasant habit of originality, very original; beyond all understanding." He cocked his head back with a satisfied smirk. "Anti-French and against nature... according to some."

Over near a parked car, Madeline Milhaud primped her bobbed hair in front of a reflecting window, adjusting the angle of her lavender cloche. "What a charming little café over there, for such a dreadful neighborhood. It looks like the kind of setting Maurice Utrillo might have painted, with the bistro on the corner below Satie's flat."

Jean leaned against the wall, puffing on a cigarette. "I can picture Satie, lounging there, sipping sherry and scribbling out his music. You know, how he used to do at the Gaya Bar?"

I pressed my round rimmed glasses higher onto the bridge of my nose. "Sherry? He preferred Calvados."

Darius chimed in. "I once watched him down ten black coffees with cognac. He lamented how at every bar people are happy to buy you a drink, but few would think of lining your stomach with a sandwich."

"Poor darling," interjected Madeleine.

Roger shook his head. "I suppose it was that very diet of eau-de-vie and beer that deprived us of him. A rotten shame, if you ask me."

The rattle of an engine announced the motorcar before it came into view. A maroon Peugeot Quadrilette with black fenders and a tan canvas top turned the corner. Satie's brother Conrad, a well-off perfume chemist, sat behind the wheel. The Peugeot pulled in front of the Maison des Quatre Cheminées and sputtered to a stop. A Renault truck followed close behind, presumably there to cart away any detritus. Silver-haired Conrad Satie stepped out of the vehicle, sporting a tan silk suit, bow tie and a Panama hat. The shape of his nose and cheekbones reminded me of my mentor.

"Well, here we are, at last," Darius said. "How are you, Monsieur?" He threw open his arms. Conrad stepped toward him and the two embraced and exchanged the customary kiss on the cheek.

"I simply can't get over it," Conrad said. "It took me so completely by surprise." The older man's face trembled into a fragile smile. "He said nothing about going in the hospital."

"We knew he'd been ill for some time," said Madeleine. "We simply didn't realize how frightfully close he was to passing." She offered her own embrace.

"I'd gone into seclusion, you see, after my wife died last year and I'd asked to be left alone. Erik honored my request."

Madeleine fussed with her organdy drop-waist frock. "I want you to know, your brother never lost the twinkle in his eye," she said. "Even toward the end. You know the way he would do, when some amusing thought would cross his mind; sometimes he'd share it, but often not. Just that little laugh of his." She covered her mouth the way Satie would do, hiding his yellowed grin, and imitated the low-pitched staccato chuckle, ascending in a pentatonic scale.

My throat tightened and my eyes grew moist. I appreciated Madeleine's dedication to the irascible virtuoso, even after the disease began to ravage his mind. His mood would change instantly, shifting to rage; like the time Madeleine retrieved his laundry. He exploded because there were only 98 handkerchiefs instead of 99.

Conrad drew a halting breath. "You captured him so well, my dear." He removed his Panama hat and tucked it under one arm. Pulling a handkerchief from inside his breast pocket, he blotted the sweat from his brow and a few escaping tears. Darius folded his arms tightly across his chest. Jean and Roger dropped their heads and stared at the pavement.

A handyman in stained coveralls lumbered up the walkway from the Renault and came alongside Conrad. We all fixed our eyes on the crowbar he carried in one hand.

"Ah, Monsieur Guerin. Good," said Conrad. "The probate office said they were unlikely to get anyone out here to unseal this room today. We're running out of time."

"What's the worse they can do to us if we break in?" Roger asked.

"We'll simply seal it up again when we're finished. I just want to make sure we go through everything before they offer it to the public," said Conrad. He put his Panama hat back on, straightened the front of his suit. "Let's get on with it, shall we?"

Darius and Jean stepped aside as Guerin wedged the crowbar between the frame and the nailed-on planks and began to pry. The wood creaked and snapped, but did not give way.

"Let me help," said Darius. Tall and well-built, he braced one leg against the wall and using his full weight, he yanked on the side of the barrier, while Guerin pried with the crowbar. With a loud crack it yielded on one side under the force. Darius stumbled backward, tottering to recover his balance. The handyman loosened the other hardware, freeing the doorframe of its wooden barricade. Sunlight fell into the shadowy vestibule revealing warped floorboards on the staircase. The others hesitantly peered into the opening.

My heart raced as we ascended the single flight of stairs to a narrow corridor with a hallstand, dingy wash basin and hazed over mirror. The passage continued to the door of the atelier, if one could call it that.

Madeleine groaned with a tinge of urgency, fanning her hand in front of her face. "Open a window, for God's sake." She retreated back to the corridor, repelled by the pervasive odor of mildew, urine, and stale cigars.

"It's a spider kingdom in here," said Jean.

More like a cabaret latrine, I thought. Darius and I groped our way in the dim light to the grime encrusted window, unfastened the latches, and pounded on the frame to free it from years of stasis. Sunshine poured through a yellow haze stirred up by our footsteps across the floor.

Darius gaped, taking in the spectacle. "How surreal, almost like a Dada collage," he said.

The daylight revealed a labyrinth of shoulder-high newspapers and journals, with shabby old hats and discards piled on top. These towers surrounded the most meager of furnishings, a crude chair and table, a wardrobe with one of its doors hanging askew on one hinge, a steamer trunk and a cot made of wood scrap, which reminded me of a marimba. As I sidled between the newspaper barricades, I noticed umbrellas leaning in clusters, some still bearing price tags and store wrapping. In the far corner stood two grand pianos, one having the legs removed and positioned directly on top of the other. A layer of dust and cobwebs enveloped it all.

"It's far worse than I ever imagined," Conrad mumbled. His shudder of disgust hinted to a veiled embarrassment at having exposed his brother's eccentricities. "What is most important now is to collect and protect my brother's music. My only interest is to make his work as widely known and appreciated as possible." Conrad's shoulders heaved with several consoling breaths. He pointed to the stacks of papers and journals. "Monsieur Guerin, start by clearing away all these piles, please."

The workman hoisted an armful onto one shoulder and plodded from the room.

"Do you think he really lived here?" I asked.

"It's hard to believe," Darius replied. "Always so meticulous in his appearance; perfectly groomed with a spotless white shirt. How did he do it?"

Jean and Roger began to wander, peeking around the stacks. "This seems more like a warehouse than a dwelling. No running water or electricity, only this old hurricane lamp."

"A few of us believe he really stayed with a laundress in Montparnasse," said Madeleine, poised in the doorway. "You know how he would do, whenever we'd give him a ride home after late nights at Le Boef sur le Toit; insisting on getting out at some random spot in Montrouge saying, 'It's good to have a walk before bed'."

"Poppycock," said Conrad. "Then again, he kept his illness secret, why should I think he'd tell me he had a mistress?" Conrad gestured to a portmanteau on the table with the gold initials E.S. embossed on the side. Free of the layer of dust smothering everything else in the room, I wondered if he'd acquired it more recently for travel plans cut short.

"Should you find anything of value, we can gather it here," Conrad added. "Madeleine, darling, why don't you help me sort through the wardrobe."

Darius and I wound through the maze to the dilapidated pianos, the bottom one's pedals bound with twine. Darius picked up a parcel resting on the upper keyboard cover and brushed off the dirt obscuring the postmark. It had been delivered several years before and never opened. I lifted the cover and placed my fingers on the keys where Satie's hands would have touched. I froze in that momentary link, a quiver in my spine, filled with tenderhearted appreciation. Then, I began to sound a few notes, but something dramatically muted the sound. Before I could even open the top and peek inside, stacks of books and papers needed to be moved.

"Let's go through all this and see if there is anything worth keeping," Darius said. We both began grabbing handfuls, leafing through it, dropping the discards into a new pile on the floor. Guerin returned for another sortie against the barricades of journals. Across the room Madeleine pawed through the upper part of the wardrobe, while Conrad took stock of the collars, handkerchiefs, and accoutrement in the lower drawers.

"How peculiar," she remarked. "From La Belle Jardinière." She held up a loose-fitting chestnut corduroy jacket. "What strange costumes!" She tittered. "There must be half a dozen more exactly like it."

"Ah, yes," said Conrad. "A painters' garb from the turn-of-the-century, Montmartre. The Velvet Gentleman. That's what people used to call him."

She wriggled one hand into the pockets. The only forgotten treasures included a box of matches and a cellophane candy wrapper.

"He always preferred the company of artists; mostly Spaniards. Rusiñol, Casas. It's how he became friends with Picasso. And…" Conrad stood upright, a photograph in an ornate frame in one hand and a stack of letters in the other. "It is probably how he met her…"

Madeleine gasped. "Is that Suzanne?"

"I can only presume. These are all addressed to her. He never sent them."

She leaned in, eyeing the picture and envelopes. "Look at that, will you? She was quite beautiful. Why keep these, after all these years? Wouldn't you just love to know what he wrote?"

I didn't need to see. Suzanne's image graced some of the most loved and well-known works of art by Renoir and Toulouse-Lautrec. I turned back to the piano, finally clearing the top. Darius raised the lid. More unopened mail covered the soundboard several inches deep. Letters never sent and mail unopened. What did it mean?

"Look at all the stuff fallen down back here," said Jean, peering behind the pianos. Roger dropped onto hands and knees and started retrieving pages in batches, handing them to Jean who added them to the mounting collection. Crawling back out, black filth covered his trousers and he had to repair to the wash stand, using a crusty towel to brush it off. Monsieur Guerin slogged past in another foray, carting away bundles of dust covered refuse.

I shifted my attention to gathering the umbrellas now lying where the stacks of newspapers once stood. In threes and fours, I planted them in a rusty water pail.

"How many do you think there are?" asked Jean.

"Hard to tell," I replied. "Thirty or forty, so far."

"I remember running into him on the street, drenched in a storm, clutching his unopened umbrella in one hand," Darius said "When I asked him why he didn't use it to keep dry, he said it was too expensive and too nice to ruin it by getting it wet."

I could make sense of the starched white collars and could understand the practicality of always having a clean handkerchief. But why would he keep so many umbrellas? I reflected on a painting I'd seen at an exhibition of Impressionist art; The Umbrellas by Renoir. Was it Suzanne who had modeled for it? With a bittersweet expression in a dark dress, the woman is framed by a sea of rain-washed umbrellas, glistening in brilliant cobalt. Was it just coincidence?

The morning ticked away in sweat and dirt. Large patches of floor began to appear and the portmanteau bulged with treasures. At one point Jean came over, tugging at my shirtsleeve and gesturing to something, a dubious expression on his face. Against the baseboards of one wall, several piles of excrement had hardened and turned black. Dog or cat? Lord, how pathetic. I glanced over at Conrad, who sorted through the steamer trunk. Jean snatched several newspapers and we gathered it inside to spare Satie's brother the indignity.

"Goodness me, will you have a look at this," said Darius. Everyone paused as Darius shook the dust from several leaves of sheet music. He clutched a deluxe edition of Claude Debussy's Cinq Poèmes de Baudelaire. A handwritten dedication in the margin seemed to evidence a cherished friendship. Darius read, "To Erik Satie, gentle mediaeval musician, who turned up in our century for the joy of his good friend, Claude A. Debussy." Underneath that, Debussy's Poèmes and the Images were similarly personalized. These Darius carefully nestled in the portmanteau and hurried back to the precious trove.

I listened to the others speculating, trying to piece together what they thought they knew about Satie. But, I had been the recipient of so many Satie confidences about Debussy, their thirty-year relationship, and their music. I felt like a priest at confession many times and bewildered at others when Satie wept openly. Why had he chosen me, a twenty-year-old virtual stranger, to reveal his joys and pains? I struggled to reconcile the artifacts we were finding with the picture I'd formed sitting beside him over so many months in lengthy conversation. What a skewed image, if his life were reduced to the impressions generated by the peculiar contents of this solitary room. How did he live in such poverty and filth? Were these belongings the ones he most prized or things he couldn't pawn? His music remained the most sterling reflection of who he was as a person. He once told me, "I've never written a single note that didn't mean something to me."

"Hey! Have you ever heard of this?" called Jean. He held out a small notebook scrawled with another one of Satie's enigmatic titles, Jack in the Box.

"Amazing," I grinned. Satie had mentioned several works he'd lost somewhere.

Darius shook his head. "What a miracle. Let's hear it."

Jean stepped to the piano and everything came to a stop. The keyboard came alive with the playful color of an afternoon stroll in the park. A jaunty melody danced with touches of syncopated cakewalk as Jean's fingers fluttered over the keys; the tune rife with Satie's own brand of humor and hyperbole. But I imagined it held some hidden indictment about government corruption or bourgeois excess, despite the piece's lighthearted style. Le bon Maître could say the most profound things with his musical satire. At that moment, it was as if the spirit of the master had been summoned from beyond for one more encore. The bouncy rhythm enticed a bit of hip swaying, bringing well needed smiles to tender hearts. That was Satie. Whenever things started to get a little too serious, he'd throw down a banana peel for some clown to slip on. Bravo, Maestro. Bravo.

THE END

Did you enjoy this book? You can make a big difference.

Reviews are the most powerful way to introduce new readers to my books. Much as I'd like to, I don't have the influence of the New York publishers and can't take out a full-page ad in the New York Times.

(Not yet, anyway)

But I do have something that those publishers would love to get their hands on: a loyal circle of readers who love my books.

Honest reviews help bring my work to the attention of others.

If you enjoyed this book, I would be very grateful if you could spend just five minutes leaving a review (it can be as short as you like) on the book's Amazon page.

You can be the first to know about new releases and giveaways. Sign up for my Newsletter here: *Contact - Michelle Fogle, Author (michellefogle-author.com)* As an avid reader, you may be invited to join my VIP list and receive future pre-release copies of my books absolutely FREE.

Thank you very much.

Glossary for non-French readers

arrondissement- district
allons-y- let's go
atelier- studio
bal publique- public ballroom
bête noire- black beast, nemesis
cahier de musique- music notebook
chasons parodique- parody songs
connard- asshole
continuez- proceed, go ahead
d'accord- okay
deux demi- two half-pints
enchanté- pleased to meet you, enchanted
étrange- (literally), strange, used to refer to being gay
flâner- loiterer or wanderer
fumisme- searing satire
incroyable- incredible
Je suis désolé- I'm sorry
lapin chaud- hot rabbit
ma cheri- my dear (to a female)
merde- shit
mon cher- my dear (to a male)

mon frère- my brother
mon vieux- (my) old boy, old man, equivalent to dude, or as we said in the 60's man
n'est-ce pas- isn't that right?
pince-nez- glasses without ear pieces
pince-sans-rire- tongue in cheek
sang-froid- cold blooded
sil vous plait- please
tapeur à gages- key tapper

Acknowledgements

I first heard the music of Erik Satie when I was a 17-year-old hippie. My boyfriend and I were hitchhiking from our small town in Southern California to the Northern California Folk-Rock Festival in 1969. We got picked-up by another hippie in a Dodge Charger on Interstate 101. He had an eight-track tape deck, on which he was playing Blood, Sweat, & Tears, *Variations on a Theme by Erik Satie.* This song captured the spirit of the Flower Child era, but also cemented my love and curiosity for the composer. Only decades later did I discover it originated in another bohemian time and place, not unlike Haight-Ashbury or Greenwich Village.

Early drafts of the novel began in 2010. Although, it got sidelined a couple of times by other developing novels. But what followed was a trip to Paris, Arcueil, and Honfleur, Normandy, where I personally walked the streets that Erik strolled, and located many of the important places during his lifetime. When I was in Paris, where the Librarie de l'Art Independent book store once stood, there is now an Apple store.

For research, I've made extensive use of scholarly works. Biographies, and Satie's own writing. These include: Satie the Bohemian, by Steven Moore Whiting; Erik Satie, by Pierre-Daniel Templier; Satie Seen Through His Letters, by Ornella Volta; Satie Remembered, by Robert Orledge; Art and the Everyday, Popular Entertainment and the

Circle of Erik Satie, by Nancy Perloff; Erik Satie, by Mary E. Davis; A Mammal's Notebook, by Erik Satie. The University of California Geisel Library was a vast resource for a variety of works about Paris history, Montmartre, Debussy, Ravel, along with countless websites and historical centers.

The actual date Satie met Debussy is a matter of debate, anywhere from 1887 to 1892. However, Edmond Bailly's Librarie de l'Art Independent opened in October 1889, and according to The Centre de Documentation Claude Debussy, it places their meeting in Autumn 1890. I've endeavored to be faithful to history and characterize the man as I've come to know and love him. In those passages where I present something Erik wrote, it is often an excerpt, edited to capture the essence, not provided in its entirety for brevity. Shocking as they may seem, Erik's homage to Debussy for Vanity Fair, and his post cards to Jean Poueigh are authentic.

Naturally, my music collection grew during the research and early drafts. There are many interpreters of Satie's work, but among my favorites are Aldo Ciccolini's Satie Piano Works; Jean-Yves Thibaudet's Satie The Complete Solo Piano Music; and Reinbert de Leeuw's Satie The Early Piano Works.

Many of my descriptions of people and places in the novel were inspired by studying the amazing artwork by the Catalan artists; Santiago Rusiñol's paintings of Erik and Suzanne, and even El Patio greenhouse; the portrait of Erik in front of the Moulin de Galette by Ramon Casas and their many paintings and drawings of each other and their surroundings.

I've seen far too many uninformed publications about Satie that cherry pick certain events or behaviors, with no understanding of the context, and spin a tale of him as an oddball. As a psychotherapist for over thirty years, I became keenly aware of how the repeated catastrophic losses Erik experienced in childhood would have traumatized him and impaired his capacity to form attachments, or have a normal relationship with anyone, but especially a woman. These include the deaths of his infant sister, then his mother died "unexpectedly", suggesting post-partum depression and possible suicide, then taken to live with paternal grandparents and abandoned by his diplomatic translator father. He was put in boarding school, and then his grandmother drowned. Today, we know unresolved trauma, catastrophic loss and grief can manifest in hoarding behavior, depression, and addiction. Combined with his alcoholism, it might explain not only his loyalty to Debussy, but his extreme possessive behavior with Suzanne and why after their relationship ended, he had no other known love relationship. He had long-term close friendships with Paulette Darty and Valentine Hugo, but never crossed the line. While there are rumors that he had a secret relationship with a laundress in Montparnasse, there is no evidence.

I am indebted to my first mentor, author Amy Wallen, and a handful of talented writers in my first read and critique group, who helped me craft early drafts of this work; Ruth Roberts, Therese Rossi, Donna Marganella, James Alpert, Nancy Nygard, Tudy Woolfe, and Mark Radford. However, the most valuable growth and longstanding support has come from San Diego Writers Ink and the band of writers, the Inkwells, who first came together in a Novel Certificate Program with literary novelist and teacher Tammy Greenwood. I offer my gratitude to David Hoffer, Sarah Beauchemin, Carol Pope, Valerie Power, Steve Nickell, Will Barnes, and Ramona Josephs-Horton for the enduring moral and writing support.

With all of his complexity and many foibles, I fell in love with Erik Satie, the flawed human being and the genius. I felt guided by his presence in Paris, and wept when I laid roses on his grave in Arceuil. This work is intended to honor his legacy.

About the Author

Michelle Fogle is a former psychotherapist turned novelist, living in the Inland Northwest. Her passion for writing led her to coursework at the University of California, and finally to a Certificate in Novel Writing at San Diego Writers' Ink in 2016. She makes her online home at Michelle Fogle, Author - Crafting the Odyssey of immersive Historical Fiction (michellefogle-author.com) Or on Facebook at www.facebook.com/MichelleFogle.Author.

Made in United States
Troutdale, OR
06/07/2024